CW00540581

THE BOOTLACE BOYS

For Stan

THE BOOTLACE BOYS

Eric Collinson

MENIN HOUSE

Menin House an imprint of
Tommies Guides Military Booksellers & Publishers

Menin House
13 Hunloke Avenue
Eastbourne
East Sussex
BN22 8UL

www.tommiesguides.co.uk

First published in Great Britain by Menin House Publishers 2011

© 2011 Eric Collinson

A catalogue record for this book is available from the British Library

All rights reserved. Apart from any use under UK copyright law no part of this
publication may be reproduced, stored in a retrieval system, or transmitted, in
any form or by any means, without prior written permission of the publisher,
nor be otherwise circulated in any form of binding or cover other than that in
which it is published and without a similar condition being imposed on the
subsequent publisher.

The Bootlace Boys is based on a personal account of life in the trenches.

The views expressed are those of Private Edward Smith 2505 of D Company,
8th Durham Light Infantry and do not necessarily represent the views of the
author or the publisher.

ISBN 978-0-9563426-7-6

Cover design by Tommies Guides

Typeset by Graham Hales

Map illustrations User design (Thomas Bohm)

Printed and bound by CPI Group (UK) Ltd, Croydon, CR0 4YY

Contents

The Battle for Boetleer's Farm
Part of the Second Battle of Ypres
25 and 26 April 1915

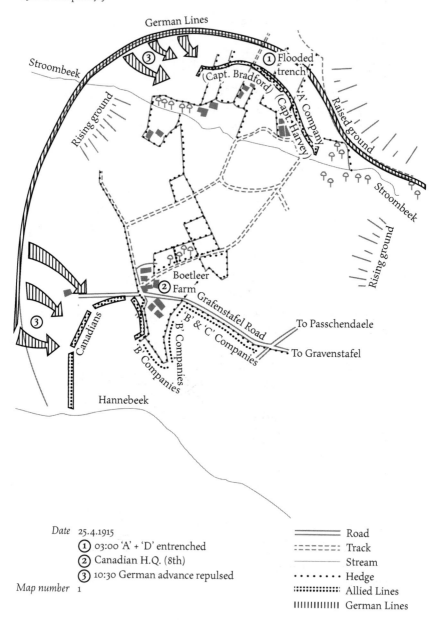

German Lines

Stroombeek

③

① Flooded trench

(Capt. Bradford)

(Capt. Harvey)

'A' Company

Raised ground

Stroombeek

Rising ground

Rising ground

Boetleer
② Farm

Grafenstafel Road

To Passchendaele

To Gravenstafel

③

Canadians

'B' & 'C' Companies

'B' Companies

'B' Companies

Hannebeek

Date   25.4.1915
① 03:00 'A' + 'D' entrenched
② Canadian H.Q. (8th)
③ 10:30 German advance repulsed
Map number   1

══════ Road
╌╌╌╌╌╌ Track
──────── Stream
• • • • • • Hedge
▮▮▮▮▮▮▮ Allied Lines
|||||||||||| German Lines

6

The Battle for Boetleer's Farm
Part of the Second Battle of Ypres
25 and 26 April 1915

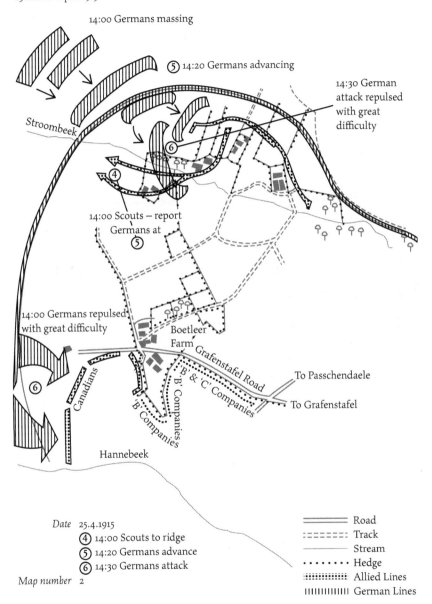

14:00 Germans massing

⑤ 14:20 Germans advancing

14:30 German
attack repulsed
with great
difficulty

Stroombeek

⑥

④

14:00 Scouts – report
Germans at
⑤

14:00 Germans repulsed
with great difficulty

Boetleer
Farm

Grafenstafel Road

To Passchendaele

To Grafenstafel

Canadians

⑥

'B' & 'C' Companies

'B' Companies

'B' Companies

Hannebeek

Date   25.4.1915
④ 14:00 Scouts to ridge
⑤ 14:20 Germans advance
⑥ 14:30 Germans attack

Map number   2

═══════ Road
═ ═ ═ ═ Track
─────── Stream
• • • • • • • Hedge
▦▦▦▦▦ Allied Lines
||||||||||||| German Lines

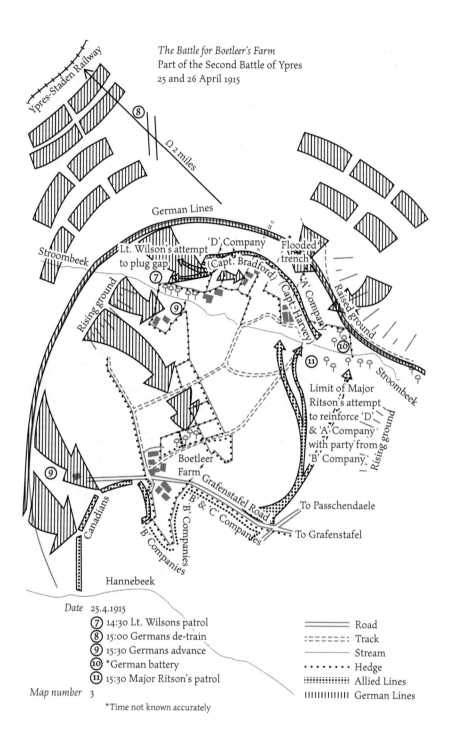

The Battle for Boetleer's Farm
Part of the Second Battle of Ypres
25 and 26 April 1915

Ypres-Staden Railway

⑧

Ω 2 miles

German Lines

Stroombeek

'Lt. Wilson's attempt
to plug gap'

'D' Company

(Capt. Bradford)

Flooded
trench

Rising ground

⑦

'A' Company
(Capt. Harvey)

Raised ground

⑨

Stroombeek

⑩

⑪

Limit of Major
Ritson's attempt
to reinforce 'D'
& 'A' Company
with party from
'B' Company

Rising ground

⑨

Boetleer
Farm

Grafenstafel Road

To Passchendaele

Canadians

'B' & 'C' Companies

'B' Companies

To Grafenstafel

'B' Companies

Hannebeek

Date   25.4.1915

⑦ 14:30 Lt. Wilsons patrol
⑧ 15:00 Germans de-train
⑨ 15:30 Germans advance
⑩ *German battery
⑪ 15:30 Major Ritson's patrol

Map number   3

*Time not known accurately

═══════ Road
─ ─ ─ ─ Track
─────── Stream
· · · · · · Hedge
▓▓▓▓▓▓ Allied Lines
||||||||||| German Lines

8

The Battle for Boetleer's Farm
Part of the Second Battle of Ypres
25 and 26 April 1915

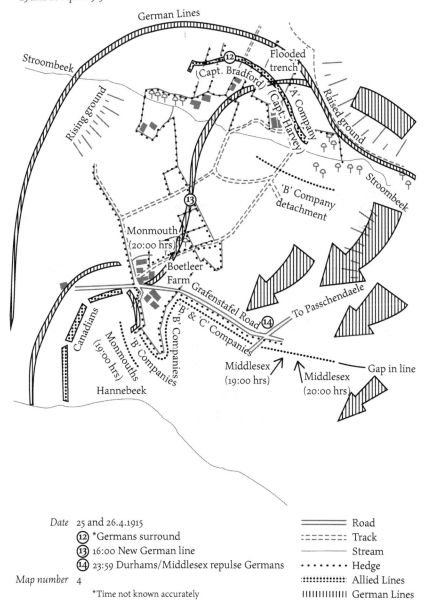

German Lines

Stroombeek

Rising ground

Flooded trench

(Capt. Bradford)

12

'A' Company
(Capt. Harvey)

Raised ground

Stroombeek

'B' Company
detachment

13

Monmouth
(20:00 hrs)

Boetleer
Farm

Grafenstafel Road

To Passchendaele

14

Canadians

Monmouths
(19:00 hrs)

'B' Companies

'B' & 'C' Companies

Middlesex
(19:00 hrs)

Middlesex
(20:00 hrs)

Gap in line

Hannebeek

Date 25 and 26.4.1915

⑫ *Germans surround
⑬ 16:00 New German line
⑭ 23:59 Durhams/Middlesex repulse Germans

Map number 4

*Time not known accurately

═══════ Road
╌╌╌╌╌╌ Track
───── Stream
• • • • • • Hedge
::::::::::::: Allied Lines
|||||||||||| German Lines

The Battle for Boetleer's Farm
Part of the Second Battle of Ypres
25 and 26 April 1915

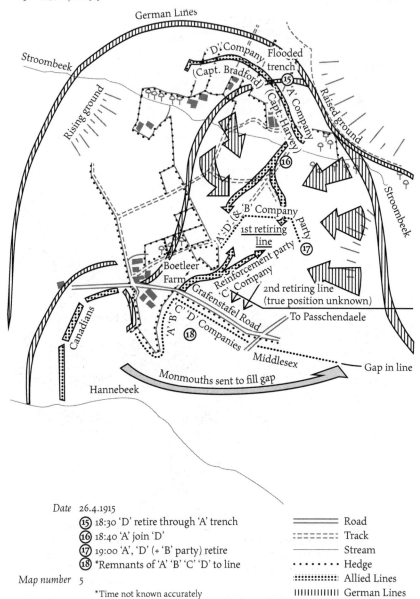

The Battle for Boetleer's Farm
Part of the Second Battle of Ypres
25 and 26 April 1915

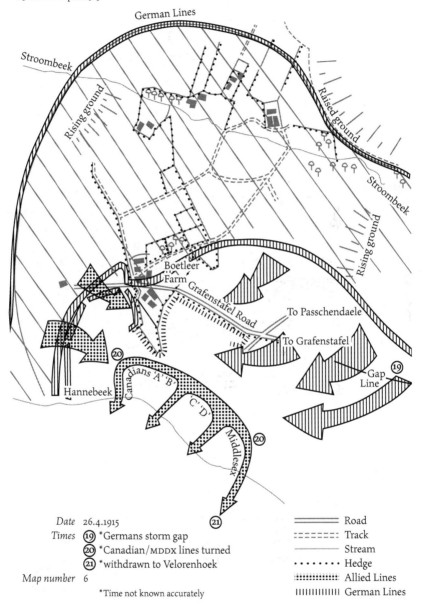

German Lines

Stroombeek

Rising ground

Raised ground

Stroombeek

Rising ground

Boetleer
Farm

Grafenstafel Road

To Passchendaele

To Grafenstafel

Canadians A B

C D

Middlesex

Hannebeek

Gap
Line

(20)

(20)

(21)

(19)

Date 26.4.1915
Times (19) *Germans storm gap
       (20) *Canadian/MDDX lines turned
       (21) *withdrawn to Velorenhoek
Map number 6
        *Time not known accurately

═══════ Road
╌╌╌╌╌╌ Track
──────── Stream
• • • • • • • • Hedge
▪▪▪▪▪▪▪▪ Allied Lines
|||||||||||||| German Lines

Boetleer's Farm, Ypres Salient, 1730 hours, Monday, 26th April, 1915

The Second Battle for Ypres

Jacky was well ahead, almost at the far end door when abruptly, inexplicably, four or five of the enemy appeared from nowhere in front of Ted. They were pointing their heavy rifles at him and all shouting at once. The buggers were pouring in through another doorway in the centre of the building as if they would never stop. One or two lifted their weapons and pointed them at the disappearing Jacky when Ted, taking a leaf from John Merrigan's book, screamed and threw his foreign rifle at them. They all looked round in complete surprise. He was fumbling in his breast pocket now, fishing out Bertha's silver locket, wrapped in the soggy mush that had once been the finest tissue wrapping paper.

'Leave him alone you bastards! Just you bloody well leave him alone! Jacky, catch, man.'

Ted slammed the locket in a perfect handball pitch over the heads of the Germans and watched it revolve, the silver chain unravelling as it alternately disappeared and reappeared in the motley light of the lamps. It was deftly caught by his friend the instant before he disappeared through the doorway and out into the darkness. A couple of the soldiers fired and made as if to follow but Ted was running towards them. He rapidly made up the distance until he was within the group. His fist downed one opponent and his elbow injured another who was trying to grab him from behind. He managed to get his hand up just in time to prevent a rifle butt from breaking his skull.

He was on his knees. Then he was flat on the floor, face down with half a dozen bayonets threatening to gut him from behind if he made another move.

Chapter 1

Fourteen years earlier. Sunniside Colliery Village, County Durham, July 1901

'Don't let me fall, man. Mam will kill us all!'

Young Teddy hung on to the disintegrating tussock on the steep bank. He glanced at the fast-flowing stream far below, then closed his eyes. At this point Stanley Beck was increasing in size to become more of a river. It wasn't that deep, but it was bloody fast.

His screams were rewarded with sniggers from the other boys, his brothers Robert, Harold, Walter and George. The 'Sunniside Smiths' calmly continued their search for the remains of monsters, digging into the shale with old kitchen knives or grubby fingernails. There was one non-member of the family, young Emmerson Beckwith, a quiet lad who tagged along more than he joined in. Emmy was in Teddy's class at school and was his particular friend.

Although the ancient slate was rich in fossils they were rarely rewarded with more than the broken stem of some long-dead tree or, if they were really lucky, a very recognisable fragment of a leaf. The monsters, however, remained elusive although each boy knew someone who knew someone who had sworn on the Holy Bible that they had dug up the tooth, claw or eyeball of the very beasts that had roamed Farmer Keenlyside's fields, millions of years before.

'Come on, man, somebody help us, will you?'

Robert, the eldest of the five, was first to recognise the real fright in Teddy's voice and, although he was furthest away, sighed and put down the piece of slate he was patiently splitting.

Teddy saw the tuft of grass in slow motion – pulled out of the ground, exposing shiny white roots to the fierce sunshine. Suddenly, everything happened very quickly as he began to slide on his stomach, hands outstretched and soil-laden fingernails broken back by frantic grabbing motions as he accelerated his descent to the shining water twenty feet below. A terrible panic thumped in his breast. He was seven years old, he couldn't swim and he was too young to die.

He had just had his birthday and was wearing his brand new second-hand boots and if he didn't die his Dad would kill him anyway. His feet hit the water, but the shocking cold was registered and forgotten in an instant when a shattering jar threatened to break his ankles. He had landed hard on a small table of slate a few inches beneath the surface. He instantly collapsed backwards, sat down on the polished stone with a thump and stared blankly at the tiny rivulets of blood flowing from his knees and mixing with the water.

When Robert saw that his little brother was in no immediate danger he slowed his own urgent scramble and arrived safely at the edge of the river. The remaining group of boys slowly edged their way down to join him while Teddy burst into tears.

'Well, are you going to just sit there or are you coming out?' asked Robert quietly. Teddy gulped a great sob and miserably heaved himself upright, standing forlornly watching the water cascade from his clothes. All the boys appeared to become aware at once of Teddy's incredible luck at landing on the slate table with such precision.

The water roared around the slab of submerged grey on which he stood. It was foaming, fast and dangerous to little boys. Teddy realised his possible fate and began to wail again.

'Stop that bloody racket and jump man, we'll catch you.'

Five boys lined up along the precarious edge and ten arms stretched out towards him. Teddy felt wounded, miserable and wet. His fingernails hurt, his knees hurt and his ankles hurt.

'Jump man, will you!'

He jumped, was deftly held by some of the outstretched arms, and pulled carefully a little way up the slope to safety. There was a hush for a few moments as the boys assessed the situation, partly in relation to the reception they would receive when they returned home to Mam, though rather more to whatever punishment would be visited upon them by Dad when he got home from the colliery.

Most of all they were in awe of the fact that their little brother had survived death by drowning through the miracle of landing on the Dare Stone, so called because of its use as a submerged stepping-stone. It allowed braver children to cross Stanley Beck by taking a run down the steep slope and launching themselves onto it, thus successfully crossing the water with the minor inconvenience of only one wet boot.

Teddy, however, had more than one wet boot and his brothers were well aware that their Dad treated them all with the same generosity whether he was giving them a treat or a beating. It was in all the boys' interests that Teddy arrived home, at the very least, no less dishevelled than the rest of them.

Within a few minutes his clothes were hanging on bushes at the top of the slope whilst the boy himself was wearing Walter's trousers, Robert's socks, George's vest and Emmy's ragged pullover, and so was content to bask in the sunshine and lose himself in the land of great and fearsome monsters waiting to be discovered within the damp layers of the small piece of slate he was dissecting.

'Sun's on the bushes,' shouted George and all the boys looked up at once like a group of jungle animals startled by a noise. Without a word they rose, exchanged clothes until they all looked more or less as they had when Mam had sent them out with strict orders not to return until teatime and come home clean or else.

The little rag-tag band crossed Grange Farm with great care, knowing only too well of Farmer Keenlyside's dislike for little boys who had no right to be on his property. They climbed walls, jumped fences and laughed as they forced their way through hedgerows and across mustard fields, revelling in the sharp, pungent aroma of the crop as it was crushed under their boots. Moving ever upwards until they were back to the little mining village on top of the windy hill where Mam would be waiting.

There was even time for a game of Netty Pirates.

As the boys approached Sunniside the short rows of grey stone terraces shone silver and gunmetal in the late afternoon sunlight. Across the road behind Garden Terrace, straddling an open water drain, were the little flat-roofed boxes that formed the outside lavatories, or 'netties'. There used to be a stream where the lavatories were built but with typical Victorian efficiency, it had been utilised as a natural sanitary disposal mechanism. Instead of constructing the usual sort of lavatories at the bottom of the backyard with an access door leading onto the street for the Ched-men, the privileged inhabitants of Garden Terrace had simply to cross the road to do their business, and nature, in the guise of the captured stream, would remove the ensuing spoil. It was a constant source of wonderment to the village children, who were often invited by their friends to visit the Family Netty and stare down through the bot-hole at the upstream soil as it flowed past two feet below their noses. Indeed such was the popularity of the Garden Terrace netties that the tenants were forced to the extreme measure of locking the doors to prevent wholesale use by any member of the community who thought they had a right.

Walter was the youngest of the family, but by far and away the most daring. With scarcely a word, but many a stifled giggle, the boys secreted themselves behind the upstream netty building and waited in gleeful impatience as Walter stole from door to door until he found one unsecured. Slipping silently in, he returned to the little gang with handfuls of newspaper that the thoughtful tenant had left lying beside the seat for use by his family.

It was to be used differently today. He handed the paper to Emmy, who was the best folder, and with purposeful movements the boy folded, creased and folded again until he had constructed a paper boat of sufficient sturdiness to sail from one end of the street of little box buildings to the other. All that was left was to wait patiently.

It wasn't long until a back door was heard to open, followed by a loud, hawking bark as an elderly miner coughed up the coal dust that had replaced his lungs. George poked his head out just far enough to see the man cross the road with a newspaper under his arm: evidence that proved the stay was to be a long one. George smiled and nodded to his accomplices. A key rattled on the inside of a door and then silence.

Harold, who somehow always had matches, mostly on account of the fact that he was the chief tab smoker, set fire to the boat. It was launched with great care and immediately disappeared into the gaping hole that forced the stream to run below the netties and the comfortably seated man. There was only room for one tousled head to look down the pipe and the privilege usually went to Walter, who after all had taken the risk of a beating in stealing the material for the fire ship. He watched with rising glee as the flame progressed through the darkness, flaring brightly as it sailed under a toilet seat and dimming as it journeyed through an enclosed portion of pipe to the next seat where it flared again. Soon they were rewarded by a roar of pain and surprise followed by a burst of profanity which surprised even Robert, who at thirteen was practically a man of the world.

Time to move.

The boys were up in a flash, scrambling and clawing upwards onto the roof of the netty end building behind which they had been hiding. They let out a huge whoop as they ran the short length of the roof and launched themselves into the air to land on the next netty. The little tribe of ragged boys yelled and shrieked their wild cries as they stampeded at roof height from one end of the street to the other, ignoring the opening doors and windows. The old miner who had emerged from his interrupted business was holding his trousers up with one hand and waving his fist.

'I'll have Copper Dobson on youse little buggers! I know who you are.'

Breathless, they reached the last roof and jumped to the ground, all red cheeks and panting and big smiles.

Now, home to Flag Row for tea. No monsters today, but a couple of fine leaf fragments as souvenirs and the tale of Teddy's adventure and his rescue from the jaws of death.

* * * * *

Mam hardly acknowledged the boys as they came in, so they were content to lie low, grateful to be back to the smell of faggots and gravy and a great pot of taties simmering easily over the fire in the spotlessly blacked range. They watched the faggots hungrily while they waited for the moan of the hooter to herald the end of the shift and the long line of miners to come home from the pit over the railway line.

It sounded clear as a bell down the length of Flag Row. For the workers at the Sunniside Colliery another backbreaking shift had ended. Dad was coming home.

'Mam, can I go and get Dad? Can I?' he wailed, followed immediately by little George, pleading, 'Me too, Mam, can I as well?'

Mam didn't even look up from the fire and her imperceptible nod was all that was required. The two boys collided in the back doorway, raced up the yard and out of the gate. Robert knew better than to ask – as the oldest lad, the responsibility fell to him to learn to play the violin. He only had one lesson a week from Miss McNair, the headmistress of the school, on a Saturday morning, but he had to practise enough to be spot on for the following Saturday or else.

He was a hard worker, though, and showed enough promise not to get too many scoldings. So while the Sunniside Smiths ran off to get Dad, Robert fiddled.

The colliery was a five-minute walk from Flag Row where the Smiths lived at Number Ten. In fact Flag Row and its adjoining streets of miners' cottages were built for the express purpose of serving the colliery, which was in turn built to serve the great Weardale Steel, Coal and Coke Company away up the road in Spennymoor.

There were many such villages all over County Durham. They were constructed to supply coal and coke to the company, and a network of single line railways, which transported the coal, connected them together. All across the county identical villages had sprung up to compete with the scattered farming hamlets, which were all that were necessary to support the few, scarce communities that dotted the region.

As the boys ran out into the cobbled back street children from many of the other houses joined them. They were all similarly dressed in hand-me-down clothing and boots that had seen more than one home repair. All were glowing with health, and full of energy despite a day spent in raucous play either in the street, or the surrounding countryside. As the growing knot of children reached the end of the street, the race slowed to a halt at the bottom step of the little footbridge that traversed the line of tracks linking Sunniside Colliery to all the other collieries and eventually to either Weardale Coal and Coke Company or the even mightier Consett Iron Company away to the north. The children never set foot on the bridge. Long ago Pit Deputy Coulthard had caught two boys on it dropping stones onto the track. He had given the boys a sound thrashing with his stick and reported the matter to the colliery manager who had informed the boys' respective fathers. The boys received another thrashing, but the damage was done. An edict was issued that children were no longer allowed on the bridge and that was that. The fact that those two boys were now grown up and worked down the pit, did not diminish the Rule. Nor had Time, and nor had Deputy Coulthard who appeared to live forever.

The little crowd pulsed gently at the foot of the steps as children swirled about, swapping stories and surreptitiously smoking roll-up cigarettes made from scavenged tobacco. Joe Batey from next door up and in George's class at school had cornered the market in roll-up tabs, reclaimed from dumpers found on the street and re-rolled in tab papers pinched from his Dad – outside the Sun Inn was usually a good harvest. Meetings were arranged for great adventures, or the following week's school was discussed. An apple was being passed about, bite for bite by a group of girls, and naturally the boys were not included.

'Didn't want a bite, anyway,' said the boys.

'Didn't want a smoke, neither,' replied the girls.

Eventually, the shifting crowd seemed to focus, like a flock of birds changing direction, and the object of their attention was the headstock gear at the pithead. The giant wheels had ceased their turning, which meant that the cage bearing the first load of miners had made the journey from the belly of the earth and would soon be disgorged into the dilute sunshine. Within minutes, the distant clanging of the cage gates could be heard and the long, black line of men trudged blinking in the light, along the track that led to the footbridge and the waiting children. Roll-up tabs were hastily extinguished under heels as the men descended the wooden stairs on the village side of the bridge – but their blackened faces were not split by the usual toothy grins. The children, heedless of the filthy coal dust, hugged the men or grasped their hands to lead them home to a bath in a small tin tub, a meal and a well-earned pipe in front of the fire. Those who had a few coppers would stroll down to the Sun or the Crown Inn and sup a pint and talk of their vegetable allotments, the forthcoming Leek Show, or just coal.

'Where's my bonny lass, then?' and 'What cheer, son?' vied, somehow flatly today, as the men located their children and vice versa. The children sang and skipped around the men, who trudged wearily, the bright-white cigarettes mysteriously glued to coal-black lips. The line wended its way down the streets of tiny terraced houses, to disappear one group at a time until the street was left once again to a handful of children playing stot-off-the-wall, or blockey, or knockey-nine-doors until it was teatime.

Walter and George, each proudly holding one of Dad's hands, stared hard at Teddy as they neared home – he was swinging on the wooden back gate. They waited for Dad to read the riot act but he didn't. As the trio approached, Teddy dismounted and held the gate open for Dad, who ruffled his hair on the way past. Mam, who was watching through the scullery window, sighed. More coal dust to shift! It'd be on the lads' hands, Teddy's hair and God knows where else as soon as Dad stepped over the back step.

'Pit's closing down,' he said as he bent to remove his boots.

* * * * *

Mam screwed her eyes shut until they hurt but the words rang and rang and wouldn't go away. Her guts were churning.

The bairns! The bairns!

Her dear sons, her dear, darling sons.

Men! Why the Hell do they always have to interfere, to argue with the pit owners?

The 'great lockout' came back to her in a shattering instant as clear and vivid as when it had happened nearly ten years ago. The men were already in an ongoing dispute with the owners about the eight-hour shift system when the falling price of coal had set the owners off on a wage reduction course of twenty-five per cent. She remembered Dad coming home that day grim faced and determined not to lose a penny of his hard-earned wages. She only had Robert and little George then but when the miners refused the pay cut and the owners locked the gates to the colliery it was the start of sixteen weeks of Hell, where families all over the coalfields were brought to the very edge of starvation during one of the most bitterly cold winters she could remember.

Irish police were drafted in because local coppers like the Dobsons were all from village families and, however much they had a duty to obey the magistrates, they also knew the miners and were known by them. It was hard to impose unfair and prejudiced rules of law on your own kin. Anyway, the Irish waded in with great enthusiasm for the letter of the law and settled a few old scores to boot. Sixteen weeks of deprivation, depression, starvation and sheer panic were all focussed into baby George's progressively weaker cries, and the stoic silence on the little pale face of Robert as he stared bleakly and uncomprehendingly into the cold empty grate, too weak even to complain. George had nearly died that awful winter and a rift opened between Mam and Dad that would never fully heal. Even when the owners capitulated, after the Prime Minister himself had stepped in, and the men went back to work on full wages, nothing could ever be the same. Though the newspapers reported singing and dancing in the streets, the women knew that this newly found power that was the Union of the Workers was a bitter, two-edged sword.

'Are you listening, pet?'

Mam shivered and inhaled deeply through her nose, her mouth a thin, bloodless line. She nodded and got on with dishing their meal in silence, waiting until her husband found the words, and the strength, to explain he was about to lose his livelihood and the roof over his family's heads. There was much talk of 'non-viability' and 'natural wastage' and anyway she knew all about the old National Union and the new Mining Federation of Great Britain and a new age for the miner and the ever-present Eight Hours Bill demands that upset the mine owners, and the minimum wage demands that upset them even more. And all this tomfoolery that cocked a snook at the Bosses ended up with what? Weren't they not long back at work after a strike action for this minimum wage that never happened?

'I won't be able to feed the bairns. How will I feed the bairns?' Dad stopped in mid-sentence, his mouth still open.

Mam could feel the hot tears coursing down her cheeks and the startled looks of her husband and children as her screaming outburst took them all by surprise. 'How? Will you tell us that you stupid bugger? You and all the other stupid buggers like you that don't know when you're well off. How will I feed my bairns?'

Mam's voice had risen to hysteria as she loosed all her fears on Dad. Then the sobs came, great, racking convulsions that completely overwhelmed her as she buried her face in her pinny and viciously fended off Dad's clumsy attempt to place a comforting hand on her shoulder.

He couldn't answer her question. They had shared the hardship and uncertainty of the strikes before and cleared their meagre allotment of food during the eternal weeks of no work and no money and every time Mam thought it would never happen again.

Now they'd closed the pit and Emmy was knocking on the door to see if Teddy could come out to play a game of handball on the back wall.

Chapter 2

The Black Prince Colliery, Tow Law, Co. Durham, November 1910

The hooter sounded, the cage gates clanged and the headstock gear far above the Black Prince Colliery at Tow Law whirred into life. The men quietly jostled to try to stand on their usual territory within the cage, but there was a disruption today. One of the pit ponies that hauled the tubs had gone lame and was joining the men on the trip back to the surface. It was frightened, though the little boy who held it did his best to keep it calm. The timid creature whinnied and shied; it was not used to the cage and the claustrophobic crush of the men. The ponies lived most of their lives in stalls deep underground and knew little of life on the surface, so this trip only added misery to the pain it felt.

'Keep that bloody thing still, will you!'

'What the Hell did you have to bring it up now for?'

Ted wanted to stroke the beast, to help try and calm it, but it would be a sign of weakness and Tow Law miners were not weak. He tried to stand stiffly to prevent the pony from barging him into the older men in the crush all around him. A man's place in the cage was sacrosanct; the etiquette deriving from tradition and bullying in equal parts.

The younger men like Ted and Emmy were first into the cage and squashed to the back while the older, more experienced miners entered last and stood by the gates ready to be first onto the surface. Robert and George were on the same shift as Ted, but they had started work a couple of years earlier and were therefore in the middle of the crush and that much nearer the gate. The bullying was not imposed through strength – indeed, the worst offender on Ted's ride was Old Jonty Shorten, a little walnut of a man and old at forty. His lungs had turned to slabs of coal after years of breathing the life-sapping dust through the meagre protection of a dirty cotton handkerchief that both diminished his health and increased his ill temper. Many a worker twice his size had fallen foul of Jonty's gaze, and had shuffled silently aside to allow the man his rightful place in the cage, or in the pub, or at the stinking slate urinal out the back.

'I can't help it man, Mr Shorten. She just keeps pushing, and she's scared, man.'

Ted's excuse fell on stony ground; the eye was fixed. All the miners in Tow Law and Sunniside lived either in houses from the original hamlets, which had been rented or bought by the colliery, or in the cramped, two up, two down terraced cottages that were purpose-built. 'No job, no house', it was that simple. The men were well aware that one day, if they were lucky, they would live to be as old and ill as Jonty and they hoped that they too would earn the incalculable respect owed to a man who had made such a sacrifice in order to feed his loved ones. Jonty would have scorned the idea of being a hero and cursed any who had the stupidity to commend him to his face, but he was a hero just the same.

The cage appeared to take longer than usual but eventually it reached the surface and the grumbling miners filed out into the November afternoon, freezing them to the bone after the warm, sultry conditions down below. The stable lad shambled out with his pony, both breathing clouds of hoarfrost, and headed off towards the blacksmith's shop. Ted smiled wryly as he contemplated today's pecking order for stepping out onto the surface: the lad, the pony, and finally himself; such is life! Robert and George were waiting for him with Joe Batey. He and Emmy crunched towards the little group on the black, coal-saturated ground, all the men rubbing their scarred hands for warmth and grinning broadly, all eyes and teeth in faces so black no other features were visible even at so short a distance. Without a word, they set off, hobbed boots cracking the freezing blackness. Already George and Joe had developed the slightly bow-legged, rolling gate that came from spending many hours crawling and half kneeling in claustrophobic tunnels as little as eighteen inches high. It got to be difficult to stand up straight, and sometimes it hurt to do so.

'Friday night, Ted,' said George. 'You'll be off to see Bertha again I reckon?'

'He'll have to get a move on then, there's always a big queue at the pay office and don't forget 'e's third in the bath an' all.' Robert grinned at his little brother and exchanged a conspiratorial glance with George.

Ever since Ted had started stepping out with this lass from Blackhill he was exhibiting all the signs of 'smit'.

And smit he was. He had met Frances Bertha Thompson in a chapel dance at Castleside. She was a year older than he was and worked as a delivery assistant to Croziers Steam Laundry at Consett. She was out and about on a brightly liveried horse drawn cart in all weathers collecting and delivering. Not just the private stuff off the gentry, neither. Mr Crozier had regular contracts with some very prestigious firms from Consett to as far away as Lanchester. She was no slouch wasn't Bertha! By their third meeting, the awkwardness and shyness were beginning to be replaced by an easy pleasure in each other's company. Even Mam had begun to enquire about why Ted was so late home on the dance evenings, even when he was on foreshift the next day.

'I had to walk her home, Mam, it wouldn't be right else', was met with raised eyebrows or snorted back giggles all round the tea table.

'What! Castleside to Blackhill and back home? That's nearly eight miles!' Mam's eyes narrowed as Ted shifted uncomfortably on the chair and said nothing. 'Well, I hope she's worth it. When do we get to meet her, then?'

* * * * *

George, Ted and Joe smoked roll-ups while Robert stoked his pipe and, as the group ambled from the pithead towards the pay office, Ted knew that Robert would collect his wages for him and that he would be in the bath before George even though it was traditionally Oldest First.

Ted left the lads at the pay office and set off for home. His trouser legs, wet from hours of crawling in black puddles deep underground, were beginning to freeze to his legs as he walked briskly into the biting wind, and he was looking forward to the warmth of the fire and the mug of tea that would be waiting for him back at Flag Row.

He was a lad of nearly eighteen, and such is youth that he had forgotten the enormous stroke of luck nine years ago when, after the pit at Sunniside had closed, his Dad had been fortunate enough to gain employment at the Black Prince Colliery at Tow Law, the next pit down the line. Dad was duly grateful and subservient to the manager, Mr Robinson, for the job and quite understood that it would have to be on a wage reduction and, yes, he was quite certain that he and his family would manage nicely, thank you. The rage Dad silently felt after closing the colliery manager's door as he fought to remind himself that his pride came a long way second to keeping a roof over his head and food in his belly, had hardly subsided as he arrived back at the tiny terrace to tell Mam that, thanks be to God, their lives were to be spared. Mam wept, but this time allowed her husband to hold her to him. She did not see that his eyes were also full of tears.

And so for the next few years the Sunniside Smiths survived on a reduced wage with Dad walking two miles to his new employment and back again in all weathers. Work was getting harder and the yield was less. Dad knew it and he knew the cause – beat-hand had got him and so had the dreaded shortness of breath that sounded the death knell for any man who spent his life breathing the black dust. But the lads were growing up fast. God knows how Mam fed them so well but she did. Dad wondered how soon he and Mam would be dependent on their childrens' income while he wheezed his life away sat in his chair like a dried-up husk, charitably handed a cut of Uncle Jeff Twist for his pipe or a few coppers for a pint.

Mam was content though. Of course she knew Dad was slowing down, they all did, but there were bits and pieces of money coming in and fewer mouths to feed (except at weekends) and the boys were also content with their lot, particularly now that there were only three of them sharing the bedroom.

Robert and George went down the pit as soon as they reached fifteen, along with Joe Batey next door up. A job had come up for Teddy as a trapper boy but Mam had put her foot down. Not while he was still going to school he wasn't, not bloody likely.

Harold had done them proud by getting a job at the Consett Iron Company as a pay clerk and went to work in a collar and tie. He had to stay in Consett for five nights out of the week, though, and shared a Company room with seven other lads. By the time his room and board were deducted from his wages there wasn't much to bring home to Mam but the room and board went with the job so that was that. Walter, the second youngest lad, had also got work away from the mine. He was apprenticed to a firm of glass-makers in Crook where he too stayed away for the week but this time in a nice boarding house run by an ex-schoolteacher, Mrs Potter, who clucked over her 'boys' like a mother hen. Walter was always singing her praises, and was even more forthcoming about her pretty daughter, Vera.

In fact, love seemed to be pretty much in the air in the Sunniside Smiths' household – Walter was stepping steady with Vera Potter and had been for several months now. She was far and away the village beauty, and such was the depth of their feelings for one another that they couldn't wait to get married, never mind engaged. Dad had acknowledged the relationship with his blessing of, 'Well you'd better get saving then!'

Robert was engaged to be married to Louise Blenkinsop but this was not a source of great joy to Louise's parents. Her Dad was Assistant Mechanical Engineer at the pit and therefore a cut above the common miner. He was also a Primitive Methodist.

But the pair were sticking stoically to their guns and anyway, there was always a welcome for Louise at Flag Row.

* * * * *

Ted had gone down the pit when he was fifteen and here he was, watching his greasy boots plant themselves one after the other on the so-familiar track back to the house. He looked up from his daydreaming to see that he was only five minutes from home. He always 'woke up' around the same spot, near the top of the hill where the abandoned pit was and where the wind hardly ever stopped, summer or winter. Daydreaming made the journey go quicker and he was able to forget the discomfort of his frozen clothes. Now, suddenly, his whole body was chilled. He fixed the motionless, derelict headstock tower firmly in his gaze, crushed his tab end under his heel and dug his hands deep into his pockets.

Home... Tea... Bertha.

As he approached the gate he noticed a knacked out old bicycle parked in the back yard. Frowning as he puzzled over who the visitor might be, and wondering if this was going to delay his bath, his tea and consequently his meeting with Bertha, he took the precaution of hawking loudly to clear his throat before he lifted the sneck to open the back door. The smell of taties and dumplings was wonderfully overpowering.

Dad was sat smoking his pipe and reading this week's *Advertiser* practically on top of the hearth. The fire, which like the Olympian Flame was never allowed to be extinguished, crackled loudly in an attempt to force the cold out of the draught-laden house. There was no sign of Mam.

'There's no dancing tonight, lad, so what you going to be doing?'

The bicycle was instantly forgotten, along with Mam's absence.

Here it comes.

Ted crouched on the scrubbed clippy mat and began to undo his boots, which, along with his kneepads and cloth cap were allowed no further inside the house than the scullery.

'Just going for a cup of tea, Dad, and mebbes a bit of cake.'

'She's from outside the village, son,' said Dad matter-of-factly, looking up from his paper for the first time.

Ted could feel himself going red around the neck and hated himself for it. *Bugger!* He was seventeen years old and still scared of his Dad.

'I know, Dad...'

He couldn't think of anything else to say, and his voice trailed off. Ted knew he loved Bertha but had to admit to himself in that second that he had never, ever thought beyond the pleasure of just being with her, either at the dance or in the smoky comfort of her parents' front room, despite her little sister, Olive, deputising as chaperone. In was also a source of wonder to Ted that a cottage so far from Sunniside could be so similar to Mam and Dad's.

'You cannot keep it up, lad. You know what'll happen if your work starts to suffer. You'll get the sack. No son of mine gets the sack, not if you want to live here you don't. Your Mam hasn't met the lass yet and you've been courting, how long?'

'I know, Dad...'

His voice trailed off again and Ted could feel the turmoil and humiliation build within him. The silence was overbearingly embarrassing.

'Well, are you going to shut the door or what?'

Dad was the world's worst diplomat, but his heart was good and he loved all his children with a fierce pride. He sorely wished he knew how better to conduct this interview.

'You know Bobby Stokoe's got the sack, do you?'

Ted swallowed silently. 'No Dad, what for?'

'Agitating.'

A slow, cold hammer tore a path through Ted's guts. Bobby Stokoe was up around fifty, like Dad, and had been a staunch supporter of miners' rights all his working life. The same life he had wasted away supporting his wife, their three daughters and the Consett Iron Company. He was in ill health, suffering from pneumoconiosis, nystagmus and arthritis, though he would describe his disabilities as miners' lung, pit-blind and beat-hand. As his years advanced, so his work grew harder, and so the more he tried to conceal the ailments that were the common lot of his livelihood. Three daughters meant no issue to follow him down the pit and no house for his family at his death or retirement. It also meant little in the way of income for there was scarce employment for girls in a mining village so there was no supplement to his falling wages.

Worse still, it meant three dowries.

Bobby Stokoe had used what energy he had left to try to improve the lot of the pit workers. He had been active during the last strike and was marked as a troublemaker for his efforts. The strike had been short and ineffectual but the colliery management had been made well aware of those who required a sharp eye.

The piecework system of mining was unfair, though on paper it appeared satisfactory. It was simple: the more coal you mine, the more money you earn. But the men who worked the coal knew differently. What if you were assigned a place with poor coal, or crushed coal, or a place where you couldn't get leverage to pull the coal from its resting place? What if you were given a narrow seam that took twice as long to work, or needed more shoring up; or even if you had a good spot, what if you were kept waiting with your bounty until the tubs turned up to take it away? What if? *What if?* God knows it was a miserable existence at the best of times, but the most crushing blow of all was to do three times the work of a comrade who was allotted an easier, more accessible face and come pay day, watch him head straight for the public house with a fat pay packet while you went home with barely enough to feed your family. It was no good. There had to be a minimum wage!

That was all that Stokoe was advocating at his Union meetings in the Station Inn and his impromptu soapbox lectures outside the Wesleyan Chapel every Sunday after the service. Everybody knew him to be right but everybody knew what happened when you rocked the boat as well. It was only a matter of time and it had finally happened.

Ted broke the awkward silence. 'But why did he do it, Dad? He only had a few years left.'

Dad shot Ted a look that spoke volumes, but qualified it anyway, leaning forward in his chair. 'Use your bloody head, son. Why do you think he did it?'

Ted's head was swimming, as emotions fought and tore at his soul. He wished he knew what to say. Why did he never know what to say?

'He did it for you, Teddy, and all the cocky little buggers like you that reckon you'll be young and fit forever, lads like you that cannot think past pay day and pubs and lasses. Anyway, he gets evicted tomorrow. Your Mam's round there now and she'll be back for your tea so you won't be late out to see your lass. Now sit down before you fall down.'

Dad went back to his paper and his pipe and the silence was excruciating. Desperate to say something, anything, Ted stammered,

'Er, whose is the bike in the yard, Dad?'

Dad didn't look up.

'It's yours son, it was Bobby Stokoe's. Mebbes now you'll get back from Blackhill in time to get a decent sleep before you go to work.'

It was all too much, completely tongue-tied and thoroughly embarrassed, Ted cleaned himself up a bit and pulled the cracket up to the fire to sit in blushing silence. Why didn't Mam come in, or Robert... or George or, or... somebody!

* * * * *

The front room in the terraced cottage of Mr and Mrs William Thompson at Number Eight Thomas Street, Blackhill, was spotless and welcoming. In truth, the front room, or just 'The Room' as it was universally known, was a source of pride to every colliery family. The working men of the north-east held a common love of quality furniture. Where every kitchen was sparse, so every Room was resplendent with mahogany presses, dressing tables, huge chests of drawers and the like. Every bit of wood was polished to a high sheen and the carefully brushed material of the couch and armchairs was immaculate. Mr and Mrs Thompson were obviously very fond of a large ebony elephant with real ivory tusks that had somehow fetched up in Blackhill from some distant shore. It stood proudly in the centre of a cotton doyley on a similar table to the one at home; but where the Smith's Room sported a none too healthy aspidistra, so the Thompson's exhibited their elephant.

The fireplace was identical to Mam's down to the last cast-iron fern and flower, as it was in every such Room in County Durham. It shone like a great, black mirror, reflecting every flame and spark of the fire. The mantel fringe was old and the colour had worn unevenly, but the peacocks and dragons embroidered upon it were as bold and alive as when they had first left the sweatshop long ago and far away in the Mysterious East.

Ted, who was playing draughts with little Olive, could scarcely suppress a smile as he stared at the fringe and the sharp little girl was quick to notice. She took the precaution, however, of finishing her move with the capture of two of Ted's pieces and a triumphant conversion to a crowner, before remarking upon it.

'What you laughing at?'

'Oh! I was just remembering when I was a bairn like you,' smiled Ted, deliberately not expanding any further and exchanging a mischievous look with Bertha. The pause was very short and it was Bertha, not her little sister who broke the silence with a clap of her small hands and an impatient grin.

'Eeh, man, Ted come on. Tell us, man!'

Ted looked at her and was tongue-tied once more. He could feel himself blushing but could not tear his gaze from her face. Olive also began to chatter but from a distance, or so it seemed. The sounds of her chattering and giggling faded rapidly as if she were falling down a mine shaft. Everything seemed to go out of focus and he felt giddy. All he could see was Bertha; there was nothing else in his universe. Her voice came to him from a very long way off indeed. He could just make out her words through the whistling in his ears.

'Yes, Ted, pet, what were you saying?'

His own voice sounded no nearer. The blood was pumping hard through his veins; it was like standing next to a cage engine.

'Bertha, pet. Would you, I mean will you... will you... '

His heart beat faster and he was vaguely aware of his hand suddenly being clasped tightly in both of hers, draughts skidding across the board, one slowly rolling like a wheel across the table.

Then he was very aware of a violent tugging at his other sleeve and Olive's voice increasing in volume.

'Come on man. Ted. What was it, what were you laughing at?'

He stared as if suddenly and rudely awakened from a deep sleep. He blinked at Olive, mystified.

'What was it Ted? You said it was when you were a bairn.'

What? Yes! When he was a bairn. Now it all came back in a rush.

'Yes, when I was little like you, my Mam had a mantel fringe as grand as yours. It wasn't green, though, it was a sort of blue and had flowers on it and a big, tasselly fringe. I thought it was grand.'

After a pause, Olive's strident voice sang out in irritation,

'Is that it?'

'Sorry, no pet. Erm... Dad had left his spills on the hearth and I set fire to it.'

How he wished he could tell a story like our Walter. He could have spun it out forever, calling on every nuance of suspense and action, drawing vivid pictures that shimmered with life and colour. No wonder he had won the heart of Vera Potter. Ted wished he could have made great literary capital of Mam sailing into the room, pinny flying and, tearing the flaming mantel fringe down, thrusting it into the fire. She had burned her hands and arms in the process, but not so badly that Dad had to know anything of the incident. She had then gone directly to Bessie Shorten's and borrowed a similar fringe so that when Dad came in from the pit all was as it should be. Ted never forgot that Mam had not told Dad, nor had she beaten him for such a stupid act. He never knew why and the time was long past for him ever to raise the subject again.

'Yes,' said Ted flatly. 'That's it, I suppose.'

He was rewarded for his storytelling efforts with a snort. Olive was not impressed, and exhibited her disgust by flouncing from The Room, taking great care to leave the door wide open as she had been instructed to do by her Mam and Dad.

'Better be going, I suppose. I'm on fore shift, you know.'

'Aye. I know.'

Bertha sat opposite her suitor, both elbows on the table and her chin cupped in her hands. She was smiling. He could still not believe she was smiling at him. He said his goodbyes to the Thompson family and Bertha walked up the yard with him. She kissed him easily and they chatted quietly for a while, gazing into each other's eyes by the light of a sharp, wintry half-moon: he, holding both her hands in his as their hoary breath mingled and faded in the moonlight. They said their farewells and Ted mounted Bobby Stokoe's bike to pedal the long, lonely road back to Sunniside and a cold bed.

'Yes, Ted.'

He stopped and turned, 'What, pet?'

She smiled, 'Yes... to whatever it was you were about to ask me in The Room when our Olive interrupted you. Yes.'

It wasn't such a long ride home, after all.

Chapter 3

The Durham Miners' Gala, The Race Course, Saturday 13th July 1912

'Gotcha you bugger!'

Ted's new cap flew upwards into the sunny sky and his hands punched the air as the coconut sailed off the stake and onto the sawdust-strewn grass of the stall. The chipped wooden ball, which he had pitched with such precision, was off on a separate journey to land at the back amongst the prizes. Little Olive clapped her hands and Bertha grinned as she admonished her escort.

'Ted, man, stop swearing, will you, or Olive'll tell Mam and we won't be allowed out again.'

'Oh, yes we will, pet, you watch.'

He picked Olive up in a great bear hug and swung her round until she squealed in delight and terror, momentarily drowning out the sound of steam-driven organs and fairground barkers.

'Are you going to tell your Mam?' he growled in his best threatening voice, and, before the grinning imp had time to reply she found herself being swung around again.

'Well, are you? Or will I spin you round until your head falls off?'

The shrieks and giggles rose by nearly an octave and even as a breathless Ted slowed to a halt, Olive continued laughing as if she would never stop. Suddenly quiet, Ted pulled the helpless girl to him and animatedly whispered something into her ear. The reaction was instant.

'I won't tell. Ted, I promise, promise, promise I'll never tell. Cross my heart and hope to die, please God. Amen.'

Bertha cast a suspicious look at the conspirators and folded her arms. 'What's going on?'

By way of a reply, Ted set Olive on the grass facing the wooden shelves full of prizes. Her eyes alighted on a little homemade cloth doll with mitten hands and pigtails.

'That one! That one! Can I please, Ted, man, can I have that one?'

'You pick what you like, flower.'

Although he was replying to Olive, Ted was grinning at his Bertha who was coyly smiling back.

'So that's it,' she said. 'Blackmail and bribery. Dad told me never to trust a Sunniside boy; looks like he was right an' all.'

Ted was instantly stumped. Mr Thompson never said that, did he? And even if he did he couldn't have meant Ted. Surely not!

Bertha burst into laughter as she spoke.

'Ted, man, you'll believe anything, you big daft gowk. Come here.'

She put her arms around his waist hugging him tightly to her. She buried her head into his chest, heedless of the crowds and the noise, and heedless of her carefully pinned hat being pushed back on her head. All she could smell was tobacco and the mothballs on his waistcoat and all she could hear was his heart beating. She felt his arms slowly and uncertainly begin to enfold her and she had never felt so safe, so secure, in her entire life.

She was aware of a hastily shaven, stubbly cheek which wasn't much more than fluffy down against her ear, and the words, 'marry me' spoken in a voice so quiet she was unsure whether she had imagined it. Had she? Then the words came again, just as quiet but clearer. Tears suddenly flooded her closed eyes as she pressed herself closer to him. She couldn't speak for the lump in her throat but she nodded, and he felt her response and hugged her all the closer to him.

'Will youse two stop cuddling? I have to go to the toilet, man.'

For the umpteenth time their private universe was interrupted by Olive, who was hopping up and down holding her newly acquired doll in one hand and Ted's retrieved flat cap in the other. Bertha was first to recover. Snatching the cap from Olive's grasp she thrust it towards his chest. It had been a present from her, last month, on his eighteenth birthday and although she wasn't best pleased that it had been treated in such a cavalier fashion her emotions were running far too high to comment upon it.

'I'll see you next to the shuggy-boats, the ones beside the river.'

With that, she seized Olive by the hand and dragged her off towards the straw-laden field, full of canvas cubicles, that was set aside as the Public Lavatory area. Ted grinned and noticed that Olive's necessity was sufficiently non-urgent to allow the pair to divert to an ice-cream stall for a penny lick.

He had done it! He had done it! He had finally asked Bertha to marry him and she had said yes: well, nodded anyway, but that counted didn't it? Suddenly everything around him shifted into crystal clarity. He could see for bloody miles. Looking down towards the river, across the crowded fields, he could make out every Lodge banner, stall, traction engine, roundabout ride, freak show and boxing booth that there was to be seen.

He could separate the sounds of the jostling merry makers from the thumping of dozens of steam engines, the oddly melodic cacophony of several brass bands, all playing at once over various parts of the racecourse. He could smell coconuts, tobacco, Bertha's perfume, sawdust, smoke and steam. Ted smiled to himself. This was a beautiful day.

* * * * *

A beautiful Big Meeting day: every mining family from every pit for miles around donned their best finery and watched their bands play.

All family differences and pit rivalries were forgotten as the great brotherhood of the mining community was united in victory over the pit owners. They had been lifted from poverty-stricken slave labour to working men with proper rights; in theory anyway. Village met village, Lodge intermingled with Lodge and at the end of a day of dizzy fairground rides, stolen kisses and a considerable intake of alcohol, every band from every Lodge would assemble at the entrance to the racecourse and march in a perfect column across the entire length of the City. The route was closed to all traffic and edged with throngs of revellers jostling for a better view of the procession.

Like a great multicoloured serpent, the bands wound their way up Providence Row, down Claypath and across the market square past the statue of that bastard, the Marquis of Londonderry, pit owner and exploiter of the honest mine worker. They marched down Silver Street, across Framwellgate Bridge and finally up North Road to be honourably dismissed with a well-earned pint in Wharton Park before finally taking their leave from formal musical duties and joining the rest of the merry makers for what was left of a truly wonderful day. By early evening there was never a uniformed bandsman that didn't have at least one fancy-free lass on his arm.

Ted had always fancied himself in a uniform but could never be bothered to
learn an instrument; Robert played a canny violin but apart from that, the Smiths remained a stalwartly non-musical family. Anyway, it didn't matter now, his Bertha had said yes.

Bertha! The amazing clarity that had invaded his senses departed as swiftly as it had come; it was like waking up with a start. A jumble of sights and sounds surrounded Ted and he struggled to make sense of his new world.

What do I do now?

He had to find Robert; he would know what to do. No! He would be with Louise and they could be anywhere. George and Harold! Still not courting, they would probably be in one of the beer tents; that was it!

He lit a cigarette and set off through the milling crowd, gently jostling his way to the nearest drinking hole, a crude open canvas shelter with a few wooden tables and chairs placed on the grass in front and the odd bale of hay for pissing on laid out not too discreetly at the back. God! All you could smell was beer and piss. It didn't take long to establish that his brothers weren't here so he turned to go to the bar nearer the river when a muffled commotion ran through the revellers like a breeze stirring up coal dust on the road.

Ted turned to see a dozen or more young men had appeared from nowhere and were swaggering in a tight group straight towards the bar. They were dressed like all young working men out for the day, in three-piece suits of varying quality and wearing the traditional flat cap. Some sported fobs and some did not, but all their waistcoats were done up except for the top two buttons and each man wore a piece of clover pinned to his cap. Ted could feel the chill that settled on the crowd at the appearance of the visitors – Toon Irish! Lads from Newcastle come down the road just to see if they could provoke trouble. They usually did.

Anybody daft enough to come twenty-odd miles in order to drink himself into a fight wasn't going to be stopped by a few conciliatory words, so nobody tried. The gang was served their ale in silent hostility and it was paid for in the same manner. Nobody actually attempted to start anything but nobody backed down either. Hard stare joined hard stare as eyes met, moved on and met again. One slight young Geordie took Ted's stare with a level gaze and it was as though they were instantly locked in a duel. Slowly and without taking his eyes off Ted, he took a pull from his pint. He had a wispy moustache that wasn't much more than bum fluff and as he lowered his glass the foam from his ale had soaked the straggly ends causing them to droop. Ted was reminded of the tassels on Mam's mantelpiece and he couldn't help smiling.

'What you laughing at, pit-yacker?'

The smile instantly left Ted's face and he felt himself going red, his neck burning. His concentration wavered as he heard all around him the sounds of the drinkers rising to their feet. Damn! Here were forty-odd people about to pitch in and do each other some fairly damage because of him.

'Stand down!'

A voice of enormous volume rolled like thunder over the tense crowd.

'I'm talking to you young 'un... yes, you.'

A shadow fell over Ted as a police constable of at least six feet in height and built like an ox brushed past him and slow-marched through the yielding mass to plant himself squarely in front of the crowd of Geordies, hands clasped behind his back. He was staring down, directly into the eyes of the young man with the drooping whiskers.

'My name, bonny lad, is Constable Albert Healy, and it is my job to ensure that a grand day like this is enjoyed by everybody. Now, by everybody I mean that young man over there... '

He fixed Ted with a look no less withering than Jonty Shorten, '... and all of his mates. And you, you little shite, and all of your mates. So, before all youse lads get off on the wrong foot I'll just point out that there's one of me and only about fourteen or so of you. Do I make myself clear?'

The constable's voice had dropped until it was hardly more than a whisper, but so palpable was the silence that it seemed it would carry for miles.

'So, bonny lads, what youse lot are going to do, is drink your ale in a peaceful and law-abiding manner and enjoy the Big Meeting without any fuss.'

Silence.

'Has anybody got any daft questions?'

Silence.

Constable Healy, absolutely in control of the situation, allowed his gaze to roam freely over the abashed crowd of Geordies, daring anyone to fix his eye. The atmosphere had transformed miraculously from simmering violence to quiet embarrassment.

Ted for one, was gobsmacked; he had never felt so threatened and so impressed all at the same time. A searing pain in his lower lip brought him suddenly and painfully back to earth as the glowing end of his tab reached his mouth to remind him of the penalty for forgetting he was smoking a cigarette.

'Bugger!' In his haste to remove it he burned his fingers and pulled a thread of stinging skin from his lip. All eyes were on him again. He gingerly touched his lip and cursed silently as he saw the blood. Bertha would never kiss him like that! Constable Healy allowed his eyes to roll skyward as stifled sniggers and giggles gave way to gentle laughter.

Ted couldn't leave now, even if he had wanted to, he would look even more stupid so he walked slowly and deliberately through the press towards Constable Healy and the crowd of subdued Geordies. He was nonplussed to find some of the lads were moving aside to allow him through. He reached the heavy trestle table that did for the bar and found himself standing in the shadow of Constable Healy, who was forming a quietly effective barrier between the young Geordie and himself.

He wanted to thank the big policeman though he wasn't sure what to say; then he heard himself, as if from a distance, offer the constable a pint. He was surprised to note that even though his heart was still thumping from being seconds away from a scrap, his voice was steady and his hand wasn't shaking as he gestured to the tapman to give him a pot of ale.

'Not for me, bonny lad. Not when I'm working for the King. But it is nice to have the offer, I thank you for that.'

Ted could not believe how calm the big man was, considering their close proximity to the mob of once belligerent Geordies; or how easily he had controlled and cowed them. There they were, not a yard away and all drinking as quietly as lambs, dirty looks aside. Some had supped up and instead of a refill they were starting to wander off in ones and twos or were waiting, ill-at-ease, for their mates to finish off their drinks so that they could try their luck elsewhere. Ted handed over a few pence in exchange for his ale.

It transpired that the constable was the village policeman for the mining community of Langley Park, up near Durham, and had Ted ever heard of it? Who hadn't! Langley Park was one of the newest, biggest mining villages in the area and was built exclusively to serve the Consett Iron Company. It had rich, accessible seams and was easily the biggest single contributor of coal and coke to Consett. It had a recreation ground with its own bandstand, swings and monkey bars for the bairns and, according to the now positively genial constable was just the place to be. Sunniside? Constable Dobson's patch? Stuck on top of a windy hill without even a pit to its name anymore? Not bloody likely!

Ted's mind was racing. He had to meet up with Bertha. He had to find his brothers. He had to tell Mam and Dad that Bertha had said yes. Damn! She would have to give up her job, she wouldn't like that much. There would have to be a wedding, Sunniside or Blackhill? They would have to live somewhere... Where? Langley Park?

'Sounds like a canny place, any jobs going down the pit? I'm just about to get married, see.'

Constable Healy's eyebrows arched and he nodded sagely. After first scanning the ever-decreasing flock of Geordies and judging them to be a spent threat, he beckoned to the tapman to refill Ted's glass. Ted noticed that he made no mention of paying for the pint and that after a quizzical glance the tapman made no attempt to argue.

'Married is it? Bonny lass, is she?'

'Why aye, man; she's the best looking lass for miles around. She's from Blackhill and she's got a job an' all...' It took Ted several sentences to realise his mouth was running away with him and reined himself in.

'So, er... any jobs going?'

He looked up to find he had spent most of the last few minutes talking to himself. Constable Healy's eyes and mind were elsewhere. Following his gaze Ted could not so much see, as somehow just be aware, of a jerky, jarring movement in the middle distance that was out of character with the relaxed, happy-go-lucky fluidity of this great sea of merry makers. There was a discordant note, a few faint voices raised in anger scraping erratically above the genial din, like fingernails down a blackboard.

'Pit manager's name's Mr Swallow. Say you were talking to me.'

Constable Healy was gone from his side, now a rapidly retreating figure making a beeline towards the disturbance. Ted's mind was now putting bits and pieces of information together.

Mr Swallow. Police Constable Healy. Mam and Dad. Langley Park. Bertha.

Bertha!

Too bloody much to do!

Chapter 4

St. Aidan's Church, Blackhill, Co. Durham, Saturday 12th April 1913

Unbelievable! Saturday morning finally came and they were all there outside the church, waiting for Bertha – everybody that was supposed to be. No panic though, she's supposed to be late. But how late? Had anybody thought to find out? Ted hadn't. Oh bugger, there was always something. He had to laugh at Mam and Dad though, especially Dad. When Dad was at home he was King Coal: best chair by the fire, sunniest spot in the allotment in the summer months when they all went up for a weekend tea, Mam doing everything for him at the raising of an eyebrow. Mind you, that didn't mean Mam was a slave; she had the measure of Dad all right. He didn't know it but he did more for Mam than he would ever believe. Best not to say.

Anyway, there they all were, Dad as smart as a carrot in his newly dry-cleaned suit (as were all the lads, courtesy of Bertha's laundry connections – and at a reduced rate as well). Scrubbed as Dad looked, Ted had to admit he had never seen him so uncomfortable: a proper fish out of water. Not to worry though, Mam was well in control.

With her arm firmly linked into his she kept Dad from shuffling about too much by sheer willpower and the odd hard squeeze. She proudly surveyed her sons. All fine boys, no, men and all standing up straight and tall in their Sunday Best and showing these Blackhill folk how men should carry themselves. Mind you, there were some right good-looking men amongst Bertha's lot as well, and all dressed up to the nines.

Mam amused herself by trying to spot family resemblances, and would probably have been surprised at her own accuracy. Then there was Ted. *Oh Teddy, my little son.* Second last into the world and first to be married, first to be a man amongst this, her brood of Sunniside Smiths. Fair enough, the other lads were all stepping steady now, but true love rarely runs smoothly and what with living away or snobby, objecting prospective in-laws, and finding homes and work in an industry that hardly seemed able to exist without in-fighting between owners and miners, and even the government sticking its nose in, it was a wonder the country managed to stay on its feet at all.

Indeed, the mining industry had just emerged from probably its biggest crisis to date. The bleak February of 1912 had seen the beginning of the most contentious national strike the mineworkers had ever experienced. The Miners Federation of Great Britain had proposed a fair wage policy that gave the more deprived members of the workforce a daily minimum wage. The owners, of course had objected and the usual war of attrition had begun. But this time the government had decided that enough was enough. Not so much because of the injustices to the working men but, simply, the country needed the coal. The country was dependent upon coal for its steam-driven industry, its steam locomotive transport, and its steam-driven ocean-going ships. Trade was dependent on steam, and steam was dependent on coal. It was as simple as that, and far too important to be left to the likes of profiteering mine owners and quibbling workers.

'You all right, Mam?'

She looked at Walter, tall, young and handsome, with his beautiful Vera on his arm and not a care in the world. Then her glance flitted to Robert, not yet twenty-five and his face already lined with work and worry. He was holding hands with Louise and there was something sad, almost despairing in the intensity of their companionship, brought about by the objections of her family to their union and Robert's failure to find a place for them to stay, which was so vital to any marriage. Her George was relaxed and chatting with his new lass, Betty. He had long been thought to marry Norma Stokoe, Bobby's youngest lass, but they had gone their separate ways and that was that. Only Harold had not got himself a lass but he had another love, his work at the Consett Iron Company where he was quietly determined to make something of himself. All her boys, all grown up, and today the first of them was to leave home a married man.

'Mam?'

She blinked, looked at Walter and blinked again. 'What, pet?'

'You sure you're all right, Mam?'

'Why, aye, pet. I'm fine. Where is that lass?'

The entire party was staring at the corner where St. Aidan's Street met Laburnum Avenue. A smartly dressed boy of about nine years old was on self-appointed sentry go, behind the bulbous based cast-iron lamp-post that sprouted from the corner slab of the pavement. Mam eyed the edifice critically; it was a magnificent piece of Victorian indulgence, resplendently clean, glossy and black, proudly sporting embossed hand painted ferns in red and gold. Sunniside had plain, green tubes to carry the coal gas to the mantles high above; but never mind, they worked just as well without all the fancy foolery. The boy was one of Bertha's lot and his immaculately pressed, if slightly too large, grey jacket and short trousers didn't exactly blend in with the colourful spectacle of the lamp-post but the lad obviously thought he was well camouflaged and alternately concentrated his gaze down the avenue or shook his head at the party waiting patiently outside the church.

For the hundredth time Dad looked at his pocket watch and returned it to his waistcoat, the action always accompanied by a loud, impatient sigh. Before Mam could perform the admonishing arm-squeeze a cultured voice came from the church door behind them.

'Would all parties concerned with the marriage of Edward and Bertha please enter the church?'

Looks were exchanged all round and with a quiet murmur the little crowd coalesced into an uneasy group and with many a nod and 'after you' and the like, they disappeared through the back doors to be swallowed up by the gentle music that wheezed alongside synchronised clouds of dust from the ancient pedal organ.

The surprisingly young verger ushered Ted and Best Man Robert to the front pew on the right and promptly abandoned them there to stare awkwardly at each other. He bustled quietly away to shepherd the guests to their seats. Not that there were many on the groom's side, Mam observed ruefully – but then, it was a train and tram journey to get here. Bessie Shorten and her family had made it, though, and so had the Stokoes, minus Bobby whose lungs wouldn't allow him to travel. Since Bobby's dismissal from the colliery and the eviction of the family from their home they had been living at his brother's house in Tow Law just up the road. God knows how they all managed but that's what you get if you upset the pit owners. Anyway, his wife had given Ted and Bertha a card that he had made himself. This gift had stunned Ted, who had known Bobby all his life and had no idea how beautifully he could draw. The front of the card was of a view down towards the valley and the allotments. The trees were heavy with blossom and the flowers were blooming. The wood behind the farm stretched into the distance and Ted wondered fleetingly why the old man had omitted the colliery. Inside, in a surprisingly firm hand, was a tender blessing that Ted would never have associated with Bobby Stokoe in a month of Sundays. But there you are, there's nowt as queer as folk!

The card was in Ted's jacket pocket and was his good luck talisman. He unconsciously patted it and Robert, seeing the motion, very consciously rubbed his waistcoat pocket and was reassured by the hard outline of the wedding ring.

Suddenly the organ wheezed to a different, louder tempo and was instantly accompanied by a flurry from the congregation. It was all Ted could do not to turn his head. Mam's threat to knock it off if he did, kept him staring resolutely at the carved cherubs on the over-decorated pulpit. He felt, rather than saw, his love arrive at his side and, with a few simple words, both their lives changed for ever.

* * * * *

The newly wed Mr and Mrs Smith walked together up the aisle with bridesmaid Olive, who could hardly contain her glee, bringing up the rear. They went past the tears and smiles, and knowing winks, out into the tiny vestibule of the church from which they could see the curious passers-by and the folk who always waited on the pavement to see the bride and give their best wishes to the happy couple. There were the local children, all smiles and mischief, preparing to throw handfuls of brightly coloured paper that were stored in old flour bags, and expecting to be thrown a few coppers in return.

The echoing ring of hooves on cobbles grew louder and Crozier's laundry cart hove into view. It looked wonderful in the watery sunlight. Mr Crozier had lent it for the morning, no charge, and his wife and daughter had decorated the already gaily-painted cart with bunting and bright ribbons. An old carpet had been laid out in the back and a leather two-seater settee facing forwards completed the conversion. It was more than Olive could stand. With a squeal of delight she pushed past Bertha and ran through the small crowd, petticoats flying, and speedily clambered onto the front board beside the driver who was Mr Crozier's only son, Gabriel. Olive was passionately in love with Gabriel, not just because he was a handsome fifteen years old to her seven, but also because he would occasionally let her hold the reins and steer Tappy Lappy, the little bay pony.

Tappy was a legend unto himself and quite as famous along the Consett roads as the brightly painted cart he pulled. He had contracted a disease in his right lung that prevented it from fully inflating and so rendered him completely unfit to pull the cart. The local veterinary was not capable of remedying the situation and suggested Tappy be 'sent away' but Mr Crozier, not normally known as a sensitive man, would hear none of it. He ended up paying a specialist handsomely to have a metal and glass tube fitted into the animal's throat to allow it to inhale properly. When Tappy breathed in it made the most awful gurgling sound and he was constantly spitting up bubbles, but this didn't seem to bother him one jot. He was a game little fellow and positively relished his new lease of life, hauling his cart around the streets of Consett with a new will and becoming quite the best-known pony for miles around.

Olive had never quite understood that in fact it was Bertha who was in charge of the cart and responsible for all laundry deliveries; after all, she hardly ever took the reins so she couldn't be. In reality, Bertha was entrusted by Mr Crozier not only with ensuring that the right laundry bags were picked up or delivered to customers at the right time but also with teaching his son everything there was to know about the delivery side of the business. On a Saturday they only worked mornings, so the work was local and the distances short. If it was a nice day Olive would often accompany her older sister and the gorgeous Gabriel on the round. To the amusement of Bertha she had taken an immediate shine to the shy, sober lad and soon had him nicely wrapped around her little finger. The colourful cart was a familiar sight around the streets of Consett as Tappy clattered and gurgled by and many a working man touched his hat with a grin to the lively little lass who, arm in arm with the lad on the reins, waved enthusiastically at all she knew and many she didn't, though their eyes always strayed to the quiet girl with the pretty face who accompanied them.

* * * * *

Today was going to be brilliant! Bertha would sit in the cart with Ted so that meant that Olive would have Gabriel all to herself for the whole ride home. The little tremor she had caused upon the calm of the proceedings was forgotten with a smile, as Ted and his new bride came out of the church and stood for a moment on the pavement. The couple stared awkwardly at one another as the communal cry of 'Shabby Wedding' erupted loudly and enthusiastically from all the children on the street and a positive storm of paper fragments rained down upon them as tiny hands disappeared again and again in quick succession into their bags and broadcast the shreds until all were spent and the pavement was a mosaic of riotous, ragged colour.

Discreet applause broke out from passers-by and the emerging congregation alike as the pair walked to the rear of the cart where the mounting steps were already swung down. Ted helped Bertha, who had a little difficulty with her dress, to successfully mount the cart and seat herself ready for the ride into the town to the market square prior to returning to her parents' home in Blackhill. Ted stood for a moment beside the settee and rummaged in his pocket for the handful of copper coins he had ready to throw onto the pavement for the children. The clatter of the pennies and ha'pennies were completely drowned by squeals of delight as they dived for the money. A cheer went up from the gathered crowd who waved merrily as Ted took his seat beside his wife.

Gabriel, assisted by Olive, flicked the reins and off went Tappy in the sunshine to show off the newly married couple to the people of Consett. The tour was also, of course, to allow the parents and guests time to get back to Bertha's Mam's in order to welcome the happy couple with a reception of tea and freshly baked cakes.

'It's all right for you, Mr Smith, nobody here knows you, I've seen tons of people that know me.'

* * * * *

Ted had read of people taking off for new lives in America and such, upping sticks with their families and sailing half way around the world to a new life, but it had taken all his courage to organise the adventure he and Bertha were going to embark upon. Only last week he had bought a new cap and sacrificed a precious day's pay to travel to Langley Park up near Durham and was impressed by the sheer scale of the colliery. The manager, Mr Swallow, had listened attentively to Ted and was also impressed by the quiet young man who laid out his plans for his simple life with his new wife in the village – provided he got a job as a hewer, like.

As Ted left the office his head was spinning. He was actually going to work at Langley Park Colliery, taking up his job on the foreshift of April 22nd and would he now go and see Mrs Sanders who would deal with the finer details and offer Mr Smith permanent rented accommodation in the village.

That afternoon, Edward Smith, hewer at Langley Park Colliery, walked out of Number Eight Logan Street, Langley Park, County Durham and carefully locked the back door to his empty new home. As he reached the wooden gate at the bottom of the yard he couldn't help but smile to himself as he turned and looked up at the tiny terraced house that was to be his future. It was neatly pebble-dashed in grey mortar and had nice sash windows both up and downstairs. Opposite, across the narrow back lane was George Street and Ted was struck by the mirror images they presented. Look towards the top of the street and the pit was right there, a ten-minute walk to the cage. Turn your head and at the other end were the back gates of the pub, the Langley Park Hotel, though it was known locally as the Blue Star on account of the magnificent wood and metal star that hung above the door, the proud emblem of the owners, the Newcastle Breweries. He was quite impressed by the pub – it even had its own handball court built onto the back. Ted had played handball back in Sunniside but only off the walls of the end house in Flag Row. It would be good to play in a proper league and on a proper court. It wasn't quiet like Sunniside though. The noises of the pit were with you every minute here: the hiss of the coke ovens, the continuous glooping of the tar stack, the screaming jack engines by the heapstead and the clank-clank of shunting operations as the little steam locomotives fussed and bothered over where the trucks had to be.

Ted separated and identified all these noises quite subconsciously in his mind and it reminded him of when he was a child. Sunniside hadn't always been a little backwater hamlet. It used to be a lively pit village too, though nothing like on the scale of Langley Park.

'Are youse going to live there, Mister?'

Ted turned to see three children staring up at him.

'What's your name, like?'

He hesitated, he didn't know why, but Mr Smith didn't sound right somehow.

The biggest child, a girl with a mass of curly brown hair spoke.

'Victoria used to live there, she was my friend. They got chucked out after the last strike.'

'So were Norman and David. They lived up there,' said the smallest of the two boys sadly. He was all hair and snot and he gestured vaguely towards the pit end of the street. Ted noticed the remaining boy had his head shaved; best cure for head lice in the world, that.

'Have youse got any bairns to play with, Mister?'

'No.'

The children ambled off up the street without a further word.

He dropped the sneck on the gate and without looking back headed off down the street to the pub. There was just time for a pint and a tab before the short walk to Witton Station and the next train to Consett then the tram to Tow Law.

* * * * *

'Hey, Mr Smith, are you going to join us, man?'

Bertha was squeezing his arm and suddenly Ted was back on Mr Crozier's laundry cart.

'Sorry, pet.'

He was surprised to notice that they were almost at Blackhill and Bertha's Mam's house. The game little pony grunted and then, making the most obscene bubbling noises, strained its way up the steep hill and turned into Thomas Street. Bloody Hell, we're going to the front door. He was about to remark on this unheard of action when Tappy noisily broke wind. Olive collapsed into fits of giggles and the corners of Bertha's eyes and mouth wrinkled into a restrained grin.

'Well, I certainly won't be sorry to leave that behind that when I start my new life, will I, pet?'

'Not if Ted farts just as loud, you won't,' shrieked Olive, practically in hysterics. She turned around and kneeled on the board to look at them, her eyes brimming with tears of laughter, 'Bertha farts an' all y'know, Ted, you should hear her, honest, she...'

The sentence was terminated as Gabriel, oozing embarrassment, whipped Olive around and dumped her unceremoniously back into her seat.

'Shut up, man, will you? We're nearly there.'

With a huffy whimper Olive's shoulders sagged as she fell silent. Tappy rounded the last corner into the street and slowed to a walk as he tugged the cart up the steep slope to the faded, green front door of the Thompson's house. The guests were all there and colourful, ragged bunting interspersed with Union Flags decorated the front of the house. An enthusiastic cheer erupted as Tappy clopped to a halt. Casually, he extended his generous penis and urinated all over the sun-hot cobbles. It was the last straw for Bertha who rolled her eyes Heavenward and burst into hearty gales of laughter as the pungent smell filled the air. She was hanging onto Ted's arm fit to break it and her infectious laugh soon dispersed any embarrassment amongst the tiny crowd who, smiling and shaking their heads at the innocence of animals and 'only nature', formed a double line from the cart to the door. Disembarking from the cart, Ted offered his arm to his new wife and the happy couple, for so they truly were, walked into the front room to the smell of freshly baked bread and pastries and the sound of cooing women.

The reception was as pleasant as it was simple. The speeches were short, quiet and self-conscious. After the tea came the viewing of the wedding gifts which were neatly arranged in the back yard and were a wonder to behold: a testament to the popularity of his new wife and the surprising affluence of some of the donors. Bertha too, gasped in wonder at the kitchen table with a real cutlery drawer, second-hand but lovingly polished. A brand new poss tub, stick and scrubbing board to make short work of cleaning his dirty pit clothes. A dissembled brass bedstead with two little ribbons, both blue, tied to the headboard. Three empty tea chests stood in front of the coalhouse door, presumably for the purpose of packing away all the smaller, more affordable items that comprised the majority of the gifts. An old trestle table had been set up and was handsomely bedecked with colourful bric-a-brac. A basket made from the shell of an armadillo sported a bright purple silk lining. There were two bed bricks, a pair of large brass candlesticks, a mandolin and a Napoleon clock. Ted smiled to himself to see a Stephenson pit lamp, long upheld by Bertha's Dad to be better than the almost universally used Davy lamp; nice try Mr Thompson! A cobbler's last, complete with hammer and box of segs. There were also two large pale green plaster ornaments, one of a cherubic looking boy bearing a large basket of fruit on his shoulder and the other of an Alsatian dog, sitting upright and staring, alert, into the distance. The dog would look grand in the middle of the mantelpiece in The Room in Logan Street; and the candlesticks...

'Ted, pet, you have to say something, man.'

Bertha's whisper cut into his thoughts. He looked up from the array of gifts to see the guests crowding around the back door and looking at him in courteous expectation. He could feel the awful, familiar blush creep across his neck and ears as he put his hand into his inside pocket, reaching for the piece of lined notepaper with his short 'thank you' speech on it. Harold had written it for him and helped him rehearse as well. It was short, polite and easy to read without sounding the littlest bit snobby. He had his uses did Harold; every family should have an educated lad.

Chapter 5

Langley Park Colliery Village, County Durham, Thursday 19th June 1913

Witton Gilbert Railway Station nestling by the river in the beautiful woodland of the Browney Valley, was owned and maintained by The North Eastern Railway, Lanchester Valley Branch (Electric Telegraph) Ltd. It was, like all such stations, named after the nearest sizeable community, the hamlet of Witton Gilbert half a mile away down a made-up road. When Langley Park Colliery opened in 1875 it was only one quarter of a mile from the little station and a half-hearted lobby surfaced to try to change its name. It was to no avail, however, and the conundrum of why a village called Langley Park has an attendant station called Witton Gilbert remains to this day.

Mr Eggleshaw was the station master, formally attired in top hat, frock coat and Turkish beard. He held his pocket watch in his hand and, at precisely fourteen minutes past twelve o'clock, was the only person inhabiting the single platform. It was a cold afternoon for June, but he appeared oblivious to the intermittent, heavy showers that punctuated the overcast day. The first indication of approaching traffic was the high, tinny screech of the wires below the platform edge as the signalman up the line heaved on the lever to put the signal to 'off'. The metal arm dropped with a thud and Eggleshaw, looking at his watch, gave a grunt of satisfaction; the approaching coal train would be off the main line and on its way to the colliery sidings in just over a minute.

The feeble sunlight glinted off the old Panther locomotive as it glided around the bend, hauling its line of dirty wooden trucks. The train advanced on the station, swaying independently for a moment as it swept over the points taking it to the rear of the platform and away to the colliery shunting yard. The rush and clatter of the coal train seemed to awaken the station from a deep sleep. Out of various shelters, rooms and offices, staff and passengers emerged even before the signals were reset and the handbell rung to announce the approach of the Consett-bound train arriving from Durham. Clearly, the arrival of the coal train was sufficient warning and by the time the official preparations had been made the platform was already alive with passengers.

The 12:18 arrived precisely on time, freewheeling easily into the station and coming to a clanking halt. With a tremendous 'whoosh' the locomotive was surrounded with a bluish cloud as it let off steam and waited patiently until it was time to go again. One of the disembarking passengers was Doctor E.E. Chrisp MD who was returning from Durham where he had been to buy presents for his daughter Annabelle's imminent eighth birthday. He was short, genial and running to fat, and his practice was that of GP for the village and colliery of Langley Park. He was also a widower of four years.

He lived with his little daughter in Wall Nook House, a stone's throw from the station, and was very much looking forward to showing off his purchases to Mrs Hedley, his housekeeper, prior to enjoying his luncheon. Clutching his leather briefcase, he smiled inwardly as he thought of the incongruous contents: a 'Lotto' game in a bright, smart cardboard box and a wooden harlequin marionette. He joined the small crowd leaving the station and heading towards the village. As he turned the corner at the foot of the little slope, he saw no one to chat to so allowed himself to become lost in thoughts of the forthcoming party and the sound of children's laughter.

A minute's walk and the carriageway to his home was a welcome sight, though Dr Chrisp frowned at the spectacle of an agitated pony chafing against the harness of the grubby collier's cart as it stood by his front door. He recognised Deputy Goodenough's crooked frame as the old miner stood conversing with Mrs Hedley. The crunch of the doctor's heels on the gravel caught the attention of both parties and they turned their heads towards him in unison. It was Goodenough who spoke first; he looked troubled and his eyes stood out blinding white against his face, utterly black from the grime of his interrupted shift underground.

'Sorry to bother you, man, Doctor.' His deep, gravelly voice was firm and businesslike. 'There's been an accident down the pit.' He paused, unsure of the correct etiquette, 'Good afternoon, Doctor, sir.'

The coal-impregnated planking of the cart was empty; they had brought none of the injured to his house, then.

'We've had a prop break in the Busty seam and Tow Law Ted's trapped under the fall by his legs, like.'

Chrisp filled the awkward silence inquiring about further casualties. There were two, apparently neither serious and both awaiting treatment in the little surgery at the Lanchester Road end of the colliery.

'Lead on then, Mr Goodenough,' said Chrisp kindly and turned to Mrs Hedley to ask for his doctor's bag, only to note that she had been holding it ready for him the entire time. The pair smiled at each other as they exchanged bag full of things that would bring joy for the other, full of things that would, hopefully, relieve pain.

A tiny thrill of pride welled in him as he noticed the spotless grey army blanket that had been draped over the board seat to prevent his clothes from being soiled by the ubiquitous coal dust. A guttural 'walk on' from Goodenough and they were off, the deputy hawking and spitting a dottle of black filth as soon as he had cleared the gate.

It began to drizzle almost as soon as the pair set off and the deputy controlled the pony expertly through the cracked leather reins, his blue-scarred hands deftly tugging and slacking as necessary. Chrisp took in the larger than usual knuckles and the stiff way the deputy held his fingers: arthritis, no doubt about it. He guessed correctly that the old man would never admit to his disability until the pain became too great to bear. Beat-hand went with the job!

A sharp turn to the right almost flung him from the cart as it left the tarmacadam road of Front Street by the Blue Star and rattled up Railway Street to the foot of the catwalk steps that was the colliery entrance. Goodenough drew the cart to a halt by the steps and loosely tied the pony to a rail on the wooden hut that passed for the community washhouse. Chrisp had, by now, been apprised of the situation in some detail and was aware that a team of six men, including Ted Smith had been taking the last lift off a wooden pillar when it had holed and looked fair to cause a slippage. The men hurriedly set a plank to try to prevent further slipping when it became clear that a fall of coal was imminent. There was a soft thump, like a distant explosion as the seam split at the top and the wall of coal moved through the gloom towards the men as if in silent slow motion. In a split second, the whole of the face seemed to rotate a few degrees and the ground beneath their feet slid gently sideways. An almost inaudible rumble gathered in volume and, as one man, they turned and tried to escape the creeping wall of black. Suddenly the strain of the shift caused the roof to smash into a thousand pieces.

When the dust had finally settled it was clear that Smith, the nearest to the face, had been trapped by his legs under the last of the fall. No fatalities this time, thank God... yet. When a similar accident had occurred last year, Bobby Crake had been killed instantly.

They alighted from the cart and ascended the steps to the catwalk, an elevated walkway that crossed almost the entire colliery and terminated just this side of the Colliery Offices on the Lanchester Road. The deputy led the way to one of the many open ladders that descended to ground level at various stages along the catwalk. They were heading for the base of Number Three shaft, a towering timber pylon surmounted by two sets of cast-iron spoke wheels that formed the headgear. It had originally been a furnace shaft but as the pit had expanded, it had been modified for access and was used mainly to lower equipment such as shoring timber. The noise was infernal; the jack engine operating the lift cable hissed and clanked alongside the rumbling of the endless belt just over their heads. Nearby, and overtopping all with its grinding screams stood the building that housed what was surely the wonder of the age, the 'Carr's Disintegrator' which, amid indescribable noise and choking black dust, pulverised the hand-hewn coal to the size of a man's fist.

The long, low attendant sorting sheds, streaked with grime, disgorged timber gantries that transported the pulverised coal on endless belts to the 'Ottos', the coke ovens whose furnaces had been built by Krupps of Germany in two parallel lines hard by the north side of the railway. They were much longer than any street in the village and their purpose was to convert the coal into high-grade coke suitable for steel manufacture at the Consett Iron Company. Black dust was everywhere, forming a fine mist that took away the clarity of the damp daylight. Chrisp could feel it, sharp and gritty, as he rubbed his tongue across the roof of this mouth. The jack engine let off steam with a shriek which made him jump and the metal gate clanged shut on the lift cage as a ragged boy of about thirteen nimbly shot the securing bolt. Chrisp was alone with the boy now, Deputy Goodenough muttering that he must go and see to the abandoned pony and he would catch up later. Chrisp was plunged into gloom and finally utter blackness. His eyes gradually adjusted and he could make out the pale orange light of two Davey lamps bobbing gently at waist height a few feet away.

Squinting, he could just discern the outline of two miners waiting patiently and in silence. One was Joseph Simpson, a young man with a pockmarked face known to all as 'Cockney Joe'. He hailed from Twickenham and God knows how he had fetched up in Langley Park as a hewer; but here he was, married to Lettie, a local girl who had presented him with a daughter only a couple of weeks ago. Chrisp remembered with regret the ill-disguised expression of disappointment on the man's face at not receiving a son and heir. The other was William John Merrigan, who hailed from South Shields and had been lured to Langley Park by wages he could not hope to achieve if he remained a fisherman. They touched their caps respectfully.

'Will you come with us, please, Doctor?' Simpson's singsong London accent had taken on an oppressive resonance in the still, humid air of the gallery. The procession set off at a ragged walk – a natural pace was impossible because of having to negotiate the rails and sleepers beneath their feet. No one ran when underground, since it added to the chance of accident and therefore injury. Nobody could afford injury, which meant time off work and no money; and that meant no food.

Chrisp was familiar enough with this twilight world to be careful to duck below the wooden cross-beams that supported the fragile roof. They were in the 'Busty' seam, one of the dozen or so coal layers that Langley Park Colliery mined. It was, at just over four feet high, the thickest and most easily workable, for which the doctor was grateful as he could at least walk. However painful the stoop, it was better than shuffling on his hands and knees. He shivered as he remembered an incident two years previously in the Victoria seam, only eighteen inches high, (and that not the smallest) which sadly involved an amputation in order to save the hapless pit man involved.

The pain in his back pulled Doctor Chrisp sharply to the present moment as the half-stoop was really beginning to hurt. The others made no complaint, however, so neither would he. The only sound for the next ten minutes or so was the crunching of hobbed boots on fireclay and coal grit, and the rasping breath of those who inhaled the dust-saturated air. The unevenly hewn floor and the newly laid sleepers for the bogie rails were treacherous and more than once threatened to turn ankles.

Eventually, from up ahead, beyond the meagre range of light thrown by the lamps, came a low moan. It was followed by comforting words from Tom Dodds, the miner who had remained with Ted. Moving around a tight bend in the gallery another source of light appeared. A Stephenson lamp stood on the dank floor and illuminated the scene. Within the narrow confines of the dim halo was a miner, lying on his stomach, facing the approaching party. His head was lowered and he was resting on his elbows, his hands grasped tightly together, fingers interwoven. From his lower back downwards, his body disappeared in a fall of coal that was almost as high as the tunnel itself. Chrisp silently berated himself for not having removed his overcoat prior to the descent; he was by now perspiring freely and was forced to disrobe to his shirtsleeves before crawling over the chunks of coal in order to reach the stricken man. So much for the army blanket on the collier's cart! As he approached, scrabbling over the slack, the injured man raised his head to face him. The black face was streaked with thin lines of livid white where tears of pain had washed away the grime.

'Bit of a mess, eh, Smith,' he said through a forced smile. 'Let's have a look then.'

From his legs downwards, Ted was hidden under the fall, disappearing into a forbiddingly narrow gap between the side wall of the gallery and the shivered remains of the wooden pillar. A large splinter, over an inch across, was still attached to the pillar and was embedded down into the muscle of the left thigh. With the aid of a lamp, Chrisp inspected around where the legs were trapped. Not much blood in evidence. Hopefully then, the legs were just trapped and not mangled.

'I won't lose them, will I, Doctor? Y'know?'

Chrisp didn't know, nor did he reply. He opened a bottle from his bag and poured some chloroform onto a muslin square and offered it gently over Ted's nose and mouth, intoning that he must breathe deeply. The wide, frightened eyes staring up at him spoke far more eloquently than any plea. Eventually, they glazed and flickered, then they closed and the body went limp. With the help of Cockney Joe, Chrisp gently folded Ted's arms as comfortably as he could and rested his head on them.

'Has anyone a small saw for this splinter? We're going to try to free him.'

John Merrigan got up from where he was sitting on his jacket and began to rummage through a large, canvas bag containing a collection of crowbars, jemmies, bolster chisels and the like. The group of miners now knew exactly what to do. Had the doctor decided to amputate they would have patiently waited until the operation was over then attacked the fall vigorously and professionally. He had not, however, and they knew the alternative was to reinforce where they could, remove the rubble and slack and lever the shattered, splintering pillar away from the gallery wall as much as was necessary to try to release the injured man. This could take many hours of risky, patient work, which is why they always awaited the doctor's decision. No point in doing all that if the lad's going to lose his legs anyway; waste of effort, that. By now, Deputy Goodenough had returned and taken charge of the job.

Luck was with the little knot of men huddled far beneath the cool drizzle that now blanketed the surface world. Just over two hours of careful clearing and shoring were rewarded when two of the sweating men levered on the long cuddy bar and the shattered pillar inched away from the wall. The seconds ticked by in agonising slowness, but no sign of a further cave-in appeared. All was as still as the dead. Chrisp closed his eyes and shuddered with relief.

'Keep it there, lads,' said the deputy evenly.

Gently, gingerly, willing hands pulled the injured man clear of the wall. As soon as he was completely free, four lamps were automatically held up to assist the doctor's inspection.

Chrisp let out a sigh of relief. 'Crushed,' he said wiping the sweat from his brow with his shirtsleeve. 'Crushed and the left leg has a clean break at the lower thigh. But not mangled, thank God. He'll mend.'

An audible sigh of relief went up from the small band and he deftly splinted the fractured limb, taking care not to disturb the stub of sawn-off splinter that was still protruding from the thigh. Then he sat back onto the gallery floor with a gasp.

'Let's get him to the surgery.'

Less than an hour later Ted was cleaned and bathed, and lying on one of the drop-down bunks in the back room of the small, white-tiled surgery that nestled against the gable end of the main Colliery Office building. He had been given an injection of morphine to further ease the pain and his temperature had gone down a little. Of the other two men slightly injured in the fall, one had arrived at the surgery but then decided his injuries were not so serious as to be worthy of consideration, and so departed for home. The second man had his cuts and bruises dressed, and was instructed to rest for a day or two. Chrisp did not have to look through the window to know that the miner would hobble painfully back to work.

The doctor knew of old to keep a change of clothing for himself in the tiny annexe, and he began to strip wash at the sink. Cleansed of coal dust, at least on the outside, he began to dress and turned his attention to his patient who was slowly recovering his wits and staring confusedly at the mass of bandages that swathed the lower half of his body. The effects of the anaesthetic were beginning to wear off and Chrisp judged his patient fit to talk.

'Well done, Lad' he began quietly. 'Can you remember anything that happened?'

After a short pause the hoarse whisper came back. 'Why aye, Doctor, every bloody thing. Does Bertha know?'

A spear of guilt jabbed at Chrisp: you've saved his life; you can't think of everything, now get on with it.

'No, I'm sorry, I'll see to it now.' He moved to the telephone that was mounted on the wall, black and shiny against the white tiles. He removed the earpiece and turned the handle, which rang the bell in the Colliery Offices. Just as he did so, the hooter began to wail. Shift change.

'You needn't bother, Doctor, she'll know soon enough, now.'

The little message lad arrived at the door of Number Eight, with his important news for Mrs Smith, to find the house empty. He shuffled from foot to foot. You got a ha'penny for running messages off the pit site, and however close Logan Street was, it still counted – but only if the message was duly delivered! He wrung his cap thoughtfully for a few moments as he peered through the window looking for signs of life. The fire was on but it wasn't damped down. You always damped the fire down if you were going out for a while because coal was too precious to waste by letting a fire burn brightly for nothing. He listened at the netty door at the bottom of the yard and hearing no sound of habitation he knocked timidly, just in case. He wasn't sure if women made a noise when they went to the toilet, or not. Gingerly, he stuck his head around the door. Nobody there either. Bugger!

The lad was very impressed with the cleanliness of the little earth closet. The brickwork around the seat had only recently been painted white and the surrounding walls were a deep, glossy green. The wooden seat itself was one of the new sort that hinged at the back so you could lift it for cleaning underneath. Still smelled of shit though. A little pile of old newspapers was stacked to one side, and on the floor behind the door was the poss tub next to the axe for chopping sticks for the fire; much more sensible than keeping it in the adjacent coalhouse. He exhaled thoughtfully through pursed lips as he mulled over his situation. He would have to wait for Mrs Smith to return and receive her message if he was to get his ha'penny, and the run from the offices had loosened his bowels a good deal... Oh! What the Hell!

A few minutes later, there was a great commotion in the street. A strange, animated procession was heading down from the pit end through the cold drizzle towards Number Eight. Two filthy black miners, both shift enders, had volunteered to carry Ted on a stretcher back to his home. There were equally as many men available for the job amongst the cleaner men going the other way but nobody wanted to be late in just in case their pay was docked, no offence, like. Bertha, her face set grimly but with no tears in her eyes, walked alongside holding her man's hand in a firm grasp. It cut her to the heart to feel Ted's hand tighten in a spasm of pain at almost every step. His face was as set and expressionless as hers. There would be no flinching here.

A small band of curious, ragged children completed the group. Observed by the women of the street looking over their gates and wiping their hands on their pinnies, the sneck was lifted and the gate banged off the coalhouse wall as the men marched through and stopped by the back door.

Bertha hurriedly unlocked it and flung it open. She stopped dead, throwing off her shawl. The design of the little house was such that the scullery wall was hard onto the inside of the door and it would be impossible to get the stretcher indoors without tipping it almost vertically to get it around the corner into the living room. The stretcher-bearers blinked at each other for a moment.

Bertha was startled by the contrast between the bright, white eyes and the faces so jet-black as to be rendered almost expressionless. In all her young life it was something she had never become used to. Without exchanging a word, the miner who held the stretcher at Ted's feet began to lower it to the ground but Ted let out such a groan that Bertha thought her heart would stop.

'The window!' she blurted without taking her eyes off Ted. 'Hold on 'til I open the window.'

The men stared blankly as she ran inside and soon appeared through the glass, tearing at the catch with breaking fingernails and trying to pull the sash open. Tears now ran freely down her face as she mouthed oaths at the obstinate frame. The squealing of her nails on the glass made one of the men wince but the wood gave and the window slid grudgingly upwards. Bertha seized the kitchen table and, heedless of the baking dish crashing to the stone floor scattering flour and eggs and shards, dragged it bodily across the stone floor until it stood just inside the sill.

'Well, put him through, man!' she shouted.

Within moments, the three of them, Bertha in charge, had the stretcher inside. First resting one end on the table and finally, comfortably in front of the fire, on the hastily cleared floor. The morphine had almost worn off now and Ted was becoming more and more agitated but Bertha was satisfied that they had done all they could to get him into the house as humanely as possible. She thanked the men quietly and offered them a cup of tea for their services. Both declined politely but said their wives would be round a bit later on to see if she needed anything. They shuffled off without any further words.

She placed a hand on his chest and smiled.

'Hello, Tow Law Ted,' she whispered, and gently kissed his forehead. 'I'll be back in a minute, pet, don't go away, will you?'

He smiled back weakly as she left the house for a moment to see the men out of the back yard.

As she went to close the gate, her mind began to race. Bed! We need the bed bringing down. Best put it in The Room. And we need a chamber pot, oh God! Suddenly feeling the urge herself she turned and opened the netty door to see a small, frightened child staring wide-eyed at her. They both took an involuntary step back. He was kneading his cap hard with both hands and his mouth was opening and shutting like a sticklebacks.

They stared at each other for a few moments until Bertha said, 'Well?'

The broken silence opened the floodgates and the boy, inhaling hugely, disgorged his message in one great breath.

'Yer man's been in an accident down the pit and broke all his legs but he'll be all right and Mrs Sanders in the office says will you go up to the surgery and carry him home, like. Thank you, Mrs Smith.'

With which he ran round her like a whippet dog, darted through the gate and was gone up the street in a flash. All she could think about was that it was Ted's birthday next week.

Chapter 6

Langley Park Colliery Village, June to November 1913

The summer of 1913 was a long one for Ted. After the accident, Bertha was quick to organise everything so that he was comfortable. His birthday went uncelebrated apart from the small display of cards that vied for attention on The Room mantelpiece. She had also tried to find some sort of work to bring in a few coppers, but no luck so far. The Room at the front had been cleared and rearranged and the lovely brass bed that was a gift on their wedding day, brought downstairs and installed facing the front window. He saw precious few people through it, though, as the residents of Langley Park rarely used their front doors. The back door led through the tiny concrete yard to the dirt street where the children played. It was to the back street that the hawkers and cheapjacks came to sell their fruit, vegetables, fish or meat from horse-pulled carts or man-pushed barrows of every sort. In terms of entertainment, it was fair to say that the knife sharpener, with his great pedal-driven grindstone-cum-tricycle that sent out showers of sparks at the merest touch of a gully knife always drew a bigger crowd of children than the barrow-mounted pedal organ of the Reverend Doherty's 'Sunshine Corner'. Papers were delivered to back doors and so was the post.

During the following weeks, Ted and Bertha had the dubious privilege of getting to know one another probably far better than many young couples, who had just self-consciously celebrated their first wedding anniversary, had a right to do. For the first few days Ted slept alone in the bed with Bertha on the floor beside him using the stretcher – fortunately it was of the military variety with short metal legs that held the canvas off the floor and was surprisingly comfortable. Dr Chrisp visited regularly, but not gratuitously. His visits cost precious money and he was well aware of the fact that his new patient was earning nothing while he was bed-ridden. Eventually, the massive swelling subsided and the wound caused by the splinter was pronounced clear of infection. The stitches were removed, though the fracture would take longer to heal but at least there were no complications. Over the coming weeks, as his health improved, Bertha's role changed subtly from dedicated nurse to boon companion. He reckoned she was a hard taskmaster, though, making him wash every day even though he didn't get dirty. Still, he was fed and kept amused as best as she could manage. They played draughts a thousand times, and floater just as many. Before he was able to sit up she would read the *Durham Advertiser* to him from beginning to end and there was great fun to be had doing the crossword. Initially they both hated the episodes with the chamber pot, which had been discreetly donated, wrapped in a blanket, by Tommy Raper's Mam, Fat Ena, from down at East Cross Street.

Ena had lost her husband to miners' lung and kept a little sausage dog called Clementine that she conversed with continually as though it understood every word she said, as indeed, she swore it could. It followed her devotedly everywhere and its yapping announced her presence as they waddled together around the village.

She had come to Bertha's back door late one evening.

'I didn't want anybody to know so I've come quietly, on my own, like,' she whispered conspiratorially as she handed over the disguised bundle. 'I'll have it back when you're done but there's no hurry, and it's best to empty it every day, you know, don't you, pet?'

Bertha nodded, trying not to laugh at the wrinkled, dumpling of a woman who looked so concerned.

'And keep some paper by the bed at night to save you going down the yard to the netty for some, you know, don't you, pet? Come on, Clementine.'

The dog gave three yaps in reply for all the world as if it had understood perfectly. Bertha watched her go gravely on her way home, the dachshund yapping along to her conversation. Sometimes she felt sorry for Ena. The cheekier children would make fun of her and her little dog but she was happy enough. Since the death of her man she had steadfastly refused to leave the little house on the edge of the railway line so her son and his wife, who only lived two minutes walk away in Bridge Street, kept an eye on her and paid her rent.

The intimacy of bodily functions was something Ted got used to but Bertha never did, though he would never know that. Day by day his strength grew and so did his impatience and day by day some uncalled for, though unmeant, remark caused Bertha's lips to tighten into a hard line as she resolved to say nothing in return. He would soon be fit and well and off to work again, and she would have her old Tow Law Ted back and everything would be the way she had imagined it would be on their wedding day when he promised to have and to hold and chamber pots didn't come into it.

During his early convalescence, Ted could hear life going on in the back street but saw none of it. Even when he was able to sit up in bed, his view was the blue front door of Number Nine Railway Street, directly opposite across the narrow path between the two rows of houses.It wasn't particularly interesting but it was better than nothing to note that on a given day, at more or less the same time, the same people used to walk up or down the path, locally known as the 'Ball Alley'. The kids made the most noise as they ran laughing and screaming, throwing balls and insults as they raced to the bottom of the road next to the Blue Star so that they could play stot-off-the-wall or handball on the gable ends of the houses. Handball was a good game, man, and if you were to improve your skills and play in the handsome court that was built onto the back of the Blue Star you had to practise somewhere! Ted stared forlornly at the great cast that encased his leg. Not for a while yet though, bonny lad, not for a while yet.

One morning, while he was having a doze, Bertha had been sweeping the yard when Harry Fairbairn, the nosey, permanently miserable postman handed her a letter over the gate. He looked even more depressed than usual as he did so.

'It's from the pit, flower. From the manager. That's his secretary's writing'.

She took the letter and muttered her thanks, feeling her heart beat suddenly more quickly against her breast. She hated Harry Fairbairn. He thought he was a ladies' man and she thought he was a lecher. It was odious to watch as he implied certain things that she – and no doubt other ladies on his round – had to pretend to ignore. The cheek of the man, and him married with four bairns! She hoped he hadn't noticed her hand tremble as he passed the letter to her. It was in the brown envelope and hand-franked stamp of the colliery. Bertha's eye was immediately drawn to the beautifully crafted italic script in which the address was written.

Not an eviction notice, please God, not that!

Harry was still standing staring at her, obviously expecting her to open it there and then. He looked like a cow staring over a stone wall and she suddenly hated him more than ever.

'It's addressed to our Ted, I'll just take it in.'

Harry shrugged and moved on up the street without a word. Leaning her broom against the fence she walked indoors as casually as she could and closed the door quietly behind her.

Why don't I just open the bloody thing? Why can't I? But she didn't. It was addressed to her man, so she had to wake him to open it. That was that. She couldn't help breaking into a run as she headed for The Room where Ted was sleeping. She had no thought of leaving her man to his rest as she took him by the shoulder and gently shook him awake. Ted blearily stuck a broad thumb into the corner and sawed the flap open in great, jagged chunks, like sharks teeth, alternately looking at the contents of the letter and his young wife's worried expression. If he'd had the strength he would have laughed; as it was he smiled wearily and allowed his head to fall back onto the bolster. He offered the letter to Bertha, who snatched it from his hand and read quickly, silently mouthing the words as she did so. Warm tears formed in her eyes and she wiped them away with the back of her hand as she gave thanks to God in Heaven.

Far from being evicted, it was a letter of commiseration, and from no less a person than Mr Swallow, the pit manager, himself! It was a sign of the progressive times that although Ted was given no pay while he was away from his work, Mr Swallow sympathised with him on his injuries, assuring him his job was safe and wishing a speedy recovery. Further, as a charitable gesture, his weekly allotment of coal would continue to be delivered as normal.

Oh, Dear Father in Heaven, I thank you with all my heart, Amen.

It was the coal that had saved them, and the God-sent glorious weather that meant they had little need of it. You could always sell coal. Ted was healing well and, according to Dr Chrisp, would be back at work long before the weather broke, so by Christmas the whole unfortunate episode should be behind them, though there would be fewer coppers in the tin.

Ted's view may have been restricted but his visitors were regular enough. Jacky Tait, his particular friend, had kept him up-to-date with news of handball, pigeons and the gossip from the pit as well as supplying him with the good wishes of his comrades and the odd bottle of stout, purely for medicinal reasons. Cockney Joe brought him old newspapers and Jimmy Barker would call in for a yarn and a pipe and amuse Ted with tales of his life as a Territorial soldier. He and his mate, Harry Clarke called in early one morning in their uniforms on their way to Burnhope for a Saturday camp, all shining brass and boots polished such as Ted had never seen.

What a commotion they caused in the street; all the little boys marching and saluting and all the older girls hanging over the gate and practically swooning. Bertha liked the lads but voiced her opinion about objecting to the soldiery, what with the Germans being awkward with France about some colony or other in Africa of all places; there was nearly a war there! In fact, there were little wars breaking out all over Europe and Germany seemed to be behind most of them. It must surely just be a matter of time before Great Britain was dragged in somewhere or other, and Jimmy and Harry would be carted of to join in and get shot and they would be sorry then!

* * * * *

'We're just Territorials, pet. Jimmy'll tell you. We don't even leave the country, man. We let the Regulars do all that. We get a few weekend camps up at Burnhope and once a year we spend a few days in Scarborough. Everybody's doing it, man, honest. It'll do your leg a power of good Ted, will a bit o' marching.'

'We still get paid an' all,' chipped in Jimmy lighting another tab. 'And when we're done for the day sometimes they let us go off camp. Have you ever seen Scarborough, Bertha?'

'Of course I haven't, you daft gowk. How in the world would I ever get to Scarborough?' An awkward silence hung in the air for a second.

'Will you go and make the lads a cup of tea, pet?'

Ted's attempt at diplomacy was circumvented by a look that passed between his visitors.

'Er... thanks anyway, Ted, but we'd better crack on, like, it's still a canny walk to Burnhope,' said Jimmy a bit awkwardly.

'Aye, anyway, you get yourself back on your feet, man, all right?'

Bertha saw them to the back gate and waved them off cheerily, trying not to look as embarrassed as she felt, then slowly walked back into the house and sat heavily on the rocking chair in front of the fire.

'What was that all about, like?' Ted shouted through to her. She closed her eyes for a second and sighed. As if he had to ask! Fetching and carrying for your man all day was one thing, but when his mates come and show off their fancy uniforms and tell you about places you've never seen and aren't likely to see and they get paid for going, well! Of course she'd never been to Scarborough, and never bloody would, neither. Scarborough! It wasn't as if the lads were talking for her benefit, it was all for Ted. He could go to Scarborough with his mates and where would she be? Sat in the house without a man. She pressed her lips together and stared at the fire.

'Bertha? You all right?'

'Yes, pet, I'm just making a cup of tea.'

'Will you nip round to Jacky's and see if they've finished with the *Advertiser*?'

* * * * *

Long weeks passed and summer turned to autumn. Mam and Dad had made the trip from Sunniside as often as they could and always brought a little bite to eat with them. Mrs Thompson had visited as well and the two Mams had really begun to get on together, to the point that the Sunniside Smiths had been invited for Sunday tea to Blackhill! Bertha had still failed to find herself some temporary employment, which had meant a considerable drain on their already meagre resources but had busied herself around the house until it shone and sparkled in every nook and cranny. She had also taken to baking more bread than she needed because the oven was burning anyway. Word soon got round that some tasty Blackhill baps were available at a very reasonable price. One of her best customers was Cockney Joe's young wife, Lettie Simpson from four doors up, She was as sackless as it was possible to be and her new baby, Sarah, made her even more so, if that were possible. Although she would never have admitted it, Bertha had sort of adopted the lass and would often show her how she cooked meals. The fact that she had to be shown again and again was a bit disheartening but Bertha was tolerant and Lettie did improve... a bit. On very rare occasions, after the men had gone to work she would run round to Number Eight all smiles and inform Bertha that Joe had eaten all his food yesterday and had hardly complained at all!

One Saturday, Robert came down with Louise for the afternoon. He played cards with Ted while the lasses chatted over a cup of tea. Later on, Robert went down the Blue Star bottle-and-jug to fetch a couple of ales and while they were having a beer and a smoke Bertha took Louise for a walk to show her around the village.

Robert took his chance and asked Ted what opportunities there were for work. He confessed his depression about his protracted courtship and the effect it was having on his beloved Louise. She was finding it all such a strain what with her parents always being so distant and criticising her choice of man at every opportunity. If he could only get a job at Langley that would eventually mean a house and, most important of all, it would put a few miles between him and Louise's parents. The trouble was, although Louise had not said so in as many words he was positive something was going on between her and her folk. She was being told it would be disloyal to want to leave them or she was making a mistake marrying below her station or some other such bloody nonsense. Either way, it seemed to him that everything possible was being done to put pressure on her not to continue with their relationship. The only chance their married life would have would be to get away. If Robert had a good job and a nice house like Ted and Bertha it might help to tip the scales in his favour a bit.

Langley Park was one of the newest, most advanced pits in the north-east, surely there must be a few jobs going? Ted replied that they were always on the lookout for good hewers and Robert was certainly that. They were going to open up a new seam just after the Christmas holidays so now would be as good a time as any to apply.

'Get your name down before some bugger else does, you can always stop here until a house comes up'.

A bit later, they were quietly playing dominoes on a tray across the bed when the lasses came in. Louise was obviously delighted with her tour. Her favourite bit was the Silly Steps on the hill to the south of the village. She also enthused about how organised the Co-op was, having all its shops especially built together in one street. Langley Park was just so modern. Not long afterwards, they said their goodbyes and Bertha saw the couple to the back gate.

Pull yourself together you daft gowk! You're the luckiest lass in the world. Just look at Robert and Louise if you don't believe me.

Visitors tripped in and out of Number Eight, Logan Street with pleasant frequency and Bertha wondered if it were not for Ted's accident would they have got to know their neighbours half so well. By the end of September 'Tow Law Ted' had become just plain Ted, finally cementing his acceptance into this little community. The back end of autumn wore tediously away and Bertha watched her man progress with the aid of crutches and then a stick as he gradually regained his feet and with this newfound mobility he was able to shake off his frustration and impatience. She was grateful to the Lord for this mercy and whispered it often.

* * * * *

She was in the yard doing a little wash today, making the most of the weather before it finally gave way to winter, and she smiled at Ted as he set off to sit and yarn on the bench outside the Blue Star. It didn't matter who was there as long as it was company, and luckily the weather had stayed fine past the point where it had a right. Granted he didn't always have a pint, he knew the money situation as well as she did. It was just that he never seemed to notice there was no smile in her eyes any more. She looked down at her fingernails in the soapy water of the dish. Short and shiny just like Mam's; but Mam was old, past forty! She closed her eyes and bit her bottom lip. Plunge and scrub! Work the washboard! She looked across at the yards opposite with their lines of clothes hanging limp in the air.

If they can bloody well do it, so can I! But oh God, I miss Mam and Dad and Olive and Tappy.

All done! The washing hanging on the line, the washboard neatly stowed back in the netty next to the poss tub and the fire expertly damped to keep the water in the boiler right without pushing too much heat into the house. Time to peel the taties, sweeping the yard would keep, just for now. While the weather was nice, Bertha decided to take the bowl of potatoes out into the yard to peel and have a nice cup of tea at the same time. She was sitting on the back step with her bowl on her knee when she heard Ted lift the sneck on the back gate. She looked up and smiled as he walked in, letting the gate slam behind him. She ignored the fact that he stubbed his cigarette out by crushing it under the heel of his boot onto her well-groomed yard. His walk was much more assured now, she noticed, he was still limping but it hardly seemed to slow him up at all. He parked his backside on the windowsill and surveyed the yard with satisfaction as if it were the gardens of a great house. They kept each other company in silence for a while, both content that their lives were returning to normal after the accident, which had so unfairly threatened to de-rail their companionship. It was Ted who spoke first.

'I've been up the Colliery Offices. They say I can start back as soon as I can get a note from Doctor Chrisp. I'll go down to tonight's surgery, shall I?'

'Do you want me to come, pet?'

Can if you want, Shall we get chips on the way home?'

She rolled her eyes in mock exasperation. Here she was peeling taties for tonight and all he can think about is buying chips. Men!

It was a pretty walk to the evening surgery at Wall Nook House. Once under the railway bridge the narrow road wound alongside the river and if you didn't look back you could almost forget that the colliery existed. Ted and Bertha, arm in arm, nodded affably to other villagers using the road but apart from having to move to one side in order to allow a cart from Langley Brickworks to pass on its way to the station, there were no interruptions to their contentment.

The surgery queue was short and the consultancy pleasant. Dr Chrisp signed Ted off as fit to work, though with a cautionary note to begin with light duties and feel his way gently back to a full shift. He knew, of course such advice would be ignored. He liked the Smiths and he thought their new life in Langley Park had got off to an awful start; many a couple would not have withstood the tribulations of such ill-luck. But he felt that this quiet boy and his resourceful young wife were made of sterner stuff than most. Ted pocketed the letter to the colliery manager and thanked the doctor for all his help. As he and Bertha left, arm in arm, he silently wished them the very best of luck. Were all his patients getting younger?

On the way home, they called into Todd's Fish Shop on Front Street to share a bag of chips. Bertha could hardly help noticing that her man was trying not to stare at the army recruitment posters that had been newly pinned up behind the counter. The damned things were everywhere now, even in the Co-op, and all extolling the threat of Germany to world freedom and the need for young men to come forward to fight for their country when there wasn't even a war on! The usual one, where the picture of the private soldier holding his rifle and crooking his finger towards the onlooker appeared harmless enough at first sight, but Bertha didn't like the silhouettes of the scores of soldiers in the distance behind the heroic figure, they looked tired and unhappy and she didn't know where they were marching off to. Far more cosy was the second poster, which appeared brand new and consisted of another private soldier, this time pointing to an idyllic country scene of sunlit fields and little thatched cottages. It was accompanied by the caption: 'Isn't this worth fighting for?'

'That's a new one, that is. The soldiers just came in and put it up yesterday. D'youse want just chips?'

Little Lizzie Todd, who was eight years old and hardly tall enough to see over the counter took their order for a large chips and began expertly folding the newspaper that was to form the bag. Her Mam looked up and smiled wearily, brushing an oily rope of hair from her face as she used an enormous ladle to stir the great vat of boiling fat in which the fish and chips were cooked.

Ted and Bertha studied the new poster together.

'Looks bonny enough to be worth fighting for all right; if you live there,' observed Ted.

'Aye, wherever it is it hasn't got a pit near it, has it, pet?'

'It's just an example, Bertha, man. It's supposed to mean the whole country.'

Her sharp intake of breath forced Ted's attention from the poster.

'Eee! Ted Smith, don't you dare lecture me! Do you think I'm an ignoramus or something?'

For a second he was confused, he could feel his neck reddening, then he caught the little grin flickering at the sides of her mouth and felt the sharp jab of her finger in his ribs. Relieved, he grabbed her roughly around the waist and pulled her to him. Quickly she wrestled herself away.

'Ted, man, where do you think you are!' She busied herself straightening her shawl and trying not to look at the other grinning customers; they would all be bloody men!

'Obviously feeling a bit better then, Ted?' observed a chubby lad in his mid-twenties a bit further down the queue.

It was Bertha's turn to blush.

'What cheer, Dicky, we were just looking at the posters, like.'

'Aye, we can see that,' replied his friend with a mischievous grin. He continued, 'Hey, Bertha, you want to get him to join the Territorials, then mebbes you'll get a bit of peace, eh!'

There was a general chuckle and Bertha looked daggers at Dicky, who immediately stopped his banter and began inspecting his coat sleeve for frays.

'That'll be a penny, please.'

A neatly folded newspaper bag full to the brim with crisp, golden chips was held up from the other side of the counter where all that was visible of little Lizzie was her brown eyes and beautifully brushed hair. Relieved at the diversion, Ted handed over a copper and they left the shop. As they walked around the corner towards Logan Street, they could hear Dicky's voice followed by raucous laughter from the rest of the queue. Ted was holding the bag and offered it to his wife as an excuse to study her face and see how her mood lay; luckily, she was smiling at him.

'You know some funny buggers, you do. Who's he, when he's at home?'

'That's Dicky Howell. He's all right, man, just a bit brassy, that's all.'

'I know the name; don't think I've met him though.'

'Why, aye, you have, pet. You've just never met him clean, that's all.'

They both liked lots of salt and vinegar so the chips were liberally dosed and there was the usually good-natured fight over who would get the last few, the ones that were really soggy and encrusted in salt. When they had finished the packet, Ted ran his fingers over the cold fat and licked away the last remnants before crumpling the bag into a small, tight ball. He then tossed it a little way into the air and whacked it hard with the flat of his hand. It pitched accurately into the side of the letterbox on the corner.

'Think I fancy a pint now,' he said casually as they approached the Blue Star.

'D'you want to warm the bed up and I'll bring you a bottle of stout back?'

'Ted Smith, you've just been signed off half an hour ago and you're not even back at work yet. You can just come home with me and have a cup of tea. Plenty of time for supping when you've earned a few coppers.'

The remonstration was interrupted as Fat Ena hove into view around the corner, in the middle of a discussion with her dachshund. She appeared not to notice the young couple and sailed clean past them towards the bottle-and-jug door at the side of the Blue Star.

They stood listening and smiling for a moment then Bertha turned to look at him. He thought that somehow her eyes were huge and unusually bright. She tilted her head and puckered her lips so he instinctively bent to kiss her. Suddenly she broke into a teasing smile and pulled her head back.

'We could always take our tea to bed.'

*　*　*　*　*

The belated good weather may have been a Godsend during the day but the depths of the night betrayed the true time of year. The colliery never slept: the shift pattern dictating that coal production was as high during the hours of darkness as it was in the middle of the day. Nothing was allowed to interfere with the race to drag as much coal as possible from under the fields and meadows of the Browney Valley. Day and night, during the hottest of summers or the most treacherous of winters, columns of men trudged like worker ants to and from the pit in order to satisfy the appetite of the ever-hungry smelters of the Consett Iron Company up the line.

The village slept though, and during the small hours in the middle of a shift it was like a village of the dead. Not a movement, not a sound; hardly even a wisp of smoke from the expertly damped down fires would betray the fact that a single human being was alive in the entire community. All signs of life were hidden away under blankets, striving to regain the energy sacrificed the previous shift at the coalface or in the kitchen. Pickaxe or poss tub, crow bar or scrubbing brush; all took their toll. The village snatched its few precious hours of peace and warmth and slumber that it had earned at such cost the previous backbreaking day.

The dark red, cinder glow of the Ottos shone like a false dawn at the north end of the village. When observed from Esh Hilltop the distance softened and paled the luminescence to a feeble glow; but here in the village the red phosphorescence, though still dull, reflected from the low clouds and dominated the sky like a hint of Hell itself.

All was not quiet at Number Eight Logan Street, however. In his fitful half-slumber Ted was apt to thrash his legs around and Bertha was almost at the stage of wishing she had not returned the ex-army stretcher.

'Ted, man, will you keep your feet still, you've just about kicked me to death.'

The reply was just a drowsy, 'Sorry Pet, I was just thinking.' A long pause followed.

'You're going to enlist, aren't you?'

'Aw, come on, it's just a bit of daft carry-on, man. It's a few Saturdays a year plus one annual camp. The army takes care of the war in Europe, the Navy makes sure that nobody invades England, and if they do, we're the lads that stop them. We never even leave the country, man. Honest.'

'Aye, and you get to go to Scarborough with all your mates, and I stay in Langley and do just what, exactly? While you're gallivanting about playing soldiers and doing just what? Eh?'

'Well, I'm enlisting and that's that!'

Bertha said nothing, knowingly allowing the stony silence to make Ted feel uncomfortable about his decision. Neither made a further sound that night, though they both lay awake, eyes wide open in the black. Ted's thoughts dwelt over-long on the comments of his mates about how he was under the thumb of his pretty young wife. In truth it was only gentle teasing but he was young himself and took it all to heart so he had to be seen to be master in his own house. Joining the Territorial Army was both his heart's desire and a signal to the community that he was his own man and he was dead set on doing just that. There was no embrace, not even the fleeting touching of fingers that signalled mutual affection; they lay separated by a few inches that might as well have been miles and they slept in lonely sadness.

The next morning they awoke to a sharp frost. With only a few days to go until November the phenomenally mild weather had broken at last. No one could remember such a long spell of bonny days; and no one would forget the snow laden, freezing winter, which was about to follow.

Twice, leading up to Christmas, the Recruiting Men came to Langley Park for the day and twice there was an uneasy atmosphere at Number Eight, Logan Street. Ted and Bertha went about the house as if the floor was red-hot, not exactly ignoring each other but far from on the best of terms. Ted hadn't enlisted either time and neither of them mentioned it. Relieved as Bertha was, she still felt sorry for him; there was no victory for her here. When he came in from work he moped around the house or sat in the rocking chair, hands thrust deep into his pockets, and stared at the fire. He was not interested in playing draughts or dominoes or floater and in the end she packed him off to the Blue Star for her own sanity. After the first recruiting day his mood only lasted a couple of days, by the second it was nearly a week. Familiar faces in the uniforms of the Durham Light Infantry were becoming noticeably more numerous in the frozen back streets of the village and she knew she could not keep her man from becoming one of them for much longer. She wasn't being possessive about him, nor was she frightened for him. It was just that he treated the whole thing as if it was, well, trivial. But it wasn't, it really wasn't. He read the same hand-me-down newspapers as her, didn't he? The German threat was real; those buggers were up to no good and if they fancied taking a swipe at England they might just bloody well do it. The government was up to something an' all! You don't just start putting twice as many posters up in chip shops for no reason. All right, she took Ted's word for it that the Territorials were never to leave the shores of England and that we had the world's mightiest Navy between us and any enemy; but if everything was so safe why did we need the Territorials at all? Why was everybody from the government down being so bloody cagey?

It was all right for Ted, though, it was just a lark to him; a few Saturdays training at Burnhope and then the Annual Camp at Scarborough. Bloody Scarborough! She wished to God she had never heard of the place. But her heart was big enough to understand the pressures being brought to bear on her man. More of his mates were in the Terries now and some had even left the pits altogether and joined the Regulars. Well if her man was gone for a soldier it would be the temporary type! He would be amongst the men he worked with down the pit and however bad things got at least he wouldn't have to leave the country. Even if he did go to bloody Scarborough.

Chapter 7

Langley Park Colliery Village, December 1913

Christmas was coming to Langley Park. Certainly the weather was seasonal enough, with snow and ice having been a permanent fixture for some weeks now and the villagers going about their business doing their best to ignore the bitter cold. The trains ran on time, the shops filled with the same customers, the back streets were just as busy with cheapjacks, knife sharpeners and wild children as ever. Only a few of the more infirm inhabitants stayed at home by the fire, and all were taken care of by a relative or kindly neighbour who would look in on them on their way to work or the shops. Children who ought to have been at school were seen on the street tightly clutching a scribbled note and a handful of coppers as they ran messages to the paper shop or the greengrocers.

And of course the colliery ran like clockwork. The men trudging in straggling columns to and from the dirty wooden steps that ran over the line to the catwalk. Ted had been at work for some time now and was beginning to get back into the swing of it. At first it had been torture, all those weeks of recuperation had drained him of his youthful stamina. He had not even realised he had put on weight until he tried his work trousers the night before his first shift. To Bertha's amusement and his confusion he had to let the belt out two holes.

'At least nobody will say I don't feed you, pet,' she grinned impishly.

Back shift was a rotten time to start work. Going to the pit at ten o'clock at night was the least favourite choice of any miner and having to do so after a long convalescence was about as bad as it got. He came home so weary the next morning that it was all Bertha could do to get him to have the bath she had prepared for him before he collapsed into bed to sleep for ten hours solid. When she had gently awakened him and offered him a cup of tea he spoke of how dog-tired he was and that he ached everywhere. His leg was the worst. The unfamiliar exercises of crawling and kneeling at the coalface engendered great shooting pains, which arched through it causing him to bite his lip in order not to cry out. He was to suffer agonies of cramp for weeks to come until his fitness returned. But he had endured it all without a word of complaint, and he never saw the silent nods that passed between his workmates, nor even noticed the odd extra shovelful of coal that mysteriously found its way into his tubs during the course of his first few shifts.

The onset of the festive season caused a ripple in the otherwise monotonous existence of the villagers. The children still went to school, but came home with decorations carefully made out of old newspaper, and painted in jolly colours. Stars, ribbons, angels and table centre-pieces were lovingly created and taken home to be suspended from the ceiling or given pride of place on the mantelpiece, though the cards they made were brought home in secret and stashed carefully away to be presented to parents, brothers or sisters on the Great Day. Attendance increased at the railway station as men and women used their carefully saved coppers to make the trip to Durham, especially on market days, in order to purchase more exotic presents or foodstuffs that could not be had in the pit village stores. Not that those stores didn't make the effort either. In amongst the bread, cheese and vegetables, strange things began to appear. Marzipan, dried fruits, and nuts the size of pigeons' eggs that came from far away Brazil of all places were in hot competition with the little tin toys, the whirligigs and the acrobatic monkeys on sticks that had suddenly materialised in the newsagents. The Langley Park shops seemed to have taken on a new lease of life as they sported goods rarely seen this side of Durham itself.

Tick lists were started, too. Anyone not thrifty enough to have saved hard-earned cash could still enjoy the luxuries of the season by acquiring loans which they could pay off at a later date when they had the money – plus interest, of course. The fact that the very folk who had not been able to save in the first place were the least likely to be able to pay off an accumulated debt was irrelevant to the smartly dressed men who knocked at doors and promised worried families a Christmas to remember for ever. Constable Healy, the big village policeman, did his best to stamp out this practice. It was fair to say he knew practically everyone in the village and took his duties very seriously. He lived on Quebec Street up near the Post

Office and was a family man himself. One day, a few Christmases ago a tick man had the unfortunate opportunity of knocking on the Healy family's front door. The good constable was home at the time but it was his practice to allow his wife to answer to any caller.

After a few moments of listening carefully to the man's sales talk he rose from his chair, put on his uniform jacket and went to join his wife at the door. It was to the credit of the tick man that he did not retire immediately but tried to carry on his patter as if he were not intimidated by the authoritative presence of the constable. It was also to his credit that he had the sense to stop in mid-sentence when asked bluntly to do so. In fact, he co-operated so fully that within half an hour he had rounded up all of his comrades and assembled them in the bar of the Blue Star at the bottom of Logan Street at the express request of Constable Healy who, gently but firmly, and without raising his voice, asked them to leave Langley Park and never return upon pain of having their bollocks yanked off and served up for Sunday Dinner. Accordingly they left but of course they did return; year after year, but more covertly and still managed to snare the poorer, more desperate families and send them reeling into a downward spiral towards further poverty.

One sleety morning just such a man had knocked on the door of Number Eight, Logan Street while Ted was at work and, though the promise of immediate cash sounded Heaven-sent to Bertha, she had the good sense to see through this plausible-sounding man and resist his offer. He left with a pleasant goodbye and she was haunted for days by the sight of the wad of pound notes he had shown her. How could one person have so much money? She stood in the doorway watching him courteously sneck the gate when Harry the postman hove into view immediately after. The festive season had done nothing to brighten his pessimistic outlook and his long, basset face was as sad as ever. The freezing weather had accentuated his miserable appearance by adding more than a touch of red to his now permanently running nose. After catching her eye over the gate he made no attempt to enter the back yard but simply waved the letter he held. Bertha had neither the time nor the patience to enter into a duel of wills so she walked down the yard to receive her mail.

'What cheer, Mr Fairbairn, are you looking forward to Christmas then?'

'Naw, just makes more work, man. Couldn't half fancy a nice cup of tea to keep the cold out, though, and mebbes a bit warm by the fire.'

His innuendo was unmistakable and she hated him for it. She made up some excuse about just being on her way out that minute and he had the nerve to look her directly in the eye. Bloody cheek!

She watched him walk a few doors up the street, rummaging in his smelly leather shoulder bag for the next delivery. Miserable lecher.

The letter was from her Mam and in amongst the gossip about Olive and church and Christmas was an invitation to Christmas dinner and mebbes stay the night. Grand! She put it on the mantelpiece beside the one from Ted's Mam, which contained the very same offer.

Eventually the grand plan of who goes where and with whom, resolved itself, if not totally amicably then at least to the satisfaction of most parties concerned. Bertha was pragmatic enough to realise that marriage was never going to be a bed of roses, even before Ted's accident; but it dawned on her during the furious letter writing leading up to Christmas that this was her last battle for adulthood. One of the phrases that her Mam had used was 'the chicks always come to the mother hen' and that had irritated her even more than Ted's tab ash on the hearth. Chick indeed! She was nearly twenty and decided that she was not going to be spoken to like that; well, written to anyway. In reminding her Mam that she was a married woman herself and, by the way, lived in a pit house just as big and a lot newer, she was demanding the equal status she reckoned she was entitled to.

She also knew that despite the words she was putting down on paper, deep in her heart she wanted nothing more in the world than to sit with her Mam and Dad and little Olive and enjoy Christmas Day as they always had done ever since she could remember. As she put her signature to the letter, Bertha's lips tightened into a thin line. She remembered how she had felt so grown up on her wedding day, a woman at last, and now just a few short months later all she wanted was to be a little girl again with none of these complications. She sealed the letter into the envelope and turned it over and over in her hands wondering how such a fragile piece of paper could be responsible for such monumental repercussions. Another stamp, another couple of coppers spent. Harry Fairbairn was right, Christmas just makes more work!

Put it in the fire and it would be forgotten. Put it in the letterbox and it would change her world forever.

Taties! We've got no taties! Come on Bertha, man. Ted's due in and we've got no taties.

* * * * *

The Crown Inn at Sunniside stank of tobacco smoke and it was nigh-on impossible to see through it. It was not yet midday and the establishment had hardly been open an hour, but it was Saturday the 22nd of December 1913, the first day of the Miners' Holidays and the men were determined to make the most of it.

It was also a special day for the Sunniside Smiths as it was a family reunion. The horrendous complications that hound far-flung families at such times had been resolved and there was little else to do but relax, have a pint and wander back to Mam's for a big, hot dinner followed by a smoke and a yarn in front of the fire. The racket was enormous – the clatter of glasses and the attempts of the men trying to be heard over each other, mingled with raucous laughter and the barked orders of Harry Wilson to his staff to shift their arses as there were customers waiting.

Ted turned away from the bar with his fingers forming a protective web around the four pint glasses he held close to his chest. Buying a round was the easy bit as he now had to negotiate his way through the throng to the table by the blazing coal fire. This was done mostly through the diplomatically applied use of elbows and the odd cry of 'Ale coming through.' By some miracle Ted and the pints made it safely to their destination and after distributing the glasses he collapsed thankfully onto the wooden chair with his back to the room and lit a tab. He inhaled and closed his eyes, feeling the smoke go to the bottom of his lungs. It was good to relax – the last few days had proved bloody hectic but diplomacy was done with and it was soon to be Christmas.

All the Smiths were present except for Robert, who was coming to the house later with Louise. Dad was up at the bar with a couple of his cronies setting the world to rights and complaining about Christmas getting more expensive and Germany trying to take over the world. The conversation was more or less same all round and the Smith's table was no exception.

'The old Queen's cousin or not, what that Kaiser wants is a bloody good kick up the arse, teach him to keep his hands off countries that don't belong to him.' Harold was already beginning his third pint and discoursing enthusiastically on the main topic of the day. Walter however was still on his first and drinking cautiously as it was in his mind that not only would he have Mam to answer to when they got home but his beautiful Vera too. She was there along with Bertha giving Mam a bit of a hand to make the dinner and three disapproving women in one house was about as intimidating as it could get.

'Howay man, Harry. Who cares about Africa, man. It's either jungle or desert; there's nowt else there, is there?'

'Doesn't matter, man, it's not his to take, is it? That little bugger should be stopped before he gets carried away and tries it on closer to home.'

'He won't man, nobody lives in Africa and everywhere else has got armies.'

'Even Sunniside's got an army, Harry,' interrupted George who was looking past Ted to the door. 'Here it comes – look.'

Ted turned around in his chair and caught a fleeting glimpse of a couple of lads in uniform walking in. The entry caused little excitement. In fact, the sprinkling of uniforms was becoming more and more commonplace all over Durham.

'It's all right lads, we're safe now,' grinned Harry. 'The Durham Light Infantry's arrived!'

'Why aye, man, the Kaiser wouldn't touch Sunniside now, he wouldn't dare.'

'He might have a go at Langley Park though, mightn't he Teddy?'

'I doubt it,' Ted beamed back at his brothers, 'The Germans practically built the bloody place.'

'Never in the world!' said George, 'How's that like?'

Before Ted could answer he suddenly felt his cap being lifted from his head and slapped roughly back down, peak backwards. He had already begun to rise when he saw the smiles on the faces of his brothers as they stared over his head. Flustered, he turned to see the beaming face of Emmy Beckwith, teeth firmly clamped around a half-smoked fat cigar. He and his companion were resplendent in the khaki uniform of the Durham Light Infantry.

'What cheer, Teddy. How's married life treating you then?'

'Emmy, you little bugger, I was just about to clock you.' Ted's face split into a huge grin as he playfully punched his childhood friend in the shoulder before continuing. 'We're doing canny, just canny, y'know. And what about you, like? And what's all this?' Ted looked the uniform up and down with badly disguised envy while Emmy explained his new look.

* * * * *

The kitchen was so full of steam it looked like mist. The three women had sweated blood to set the dinner out, complaining light-heartedly all the time that it wouldn't be appreciated – men were like that!

The huge joint of roast pork was now on the hearth staying warm while the taties and vegetables were in covered tin pots on top of the boiler, ready to serve. Vera was pounding the block of gravy salt in a bowl with some warm milk. She had let it get soggy and now it wouldn't blend, so a rescue was in order. Bertha showed her how to break it up into smaller pieces so it would mix and it seemed to be working. Mam gave her an encouraging smile whilst thinking God help our Walter when they get hitched, Vera's a bonny lass but she couldn't boil an egg!

Mam eyed up the situation expertly and told Bertha, who was putting the dumplings on a serving dish, to ladle them onto an enamel plate and stick them back in the oven with the Yorkshire puddings to crisp up a bit. That would give the gravy time to catch up and everything should come together in time to be dished at one o'clock. Mam had told Dad to have the lads back from the pub by half past twelve, allowing for the twenty minutes or so they would be late. That would still leave enough time for them all to go to the toilet and wash their hands before they sat down. The table had been laid in The Room where the fire was blazing merrily – a rare treat – and chairs had been borrowed from neighbours to accommodate the extra bodies.

Mam, Bertha and Vera looked at each other – Vera smiled and nodded to Mam. The gravy was going to be all right. Silence hung heavy in the air like the quiet lull before a thunderstorm as Mam's eyes scanned and rescanned every last detail of the component parts of the feast.

'Right!' she declared finally, 'Everything's ready. Finish your stout and give me those cups to wash. Vera! Rinse them empty bottles and put them on the scullery floor with the rest. Howay now!'

The three women raised their cups in a smiling, silent salute and downed the contents to the last drop. The cups were washed and dried and the bottles stored on the pantry floor awaiting the trip back to the pub for the deposit. The windows were opened a critical couple of inches, wide enough to let the steam out but not so much as to let the cold in.

'Vera pet, will you run up the yard and see if they're coming? They should be by now.'

'Eeh! Mrs Smith can I not just wash my face and take my pinny off first? I don't want our Walter to see me like this.'

'It's all right Vera,' said Bertha with a smile, 'I'll go.' And wiping her hands on her pinny headed out of the back door and up to the gate. Bertha wasn't sackless; she would go to the netty now, before it was assaulted by a gang of half-cut men with poor aim.

The lads turned up more or less when Mam said they would and the dinner was served with all efficiency. There were no formal toasts and the women showed practiced surprise when they were each presented with a bottle of stout by Dad who then mumbled a quick Grace and carved the delicious smelling roast. The meal proceeded with quiet grunts of satisfaction, indeed, the only sound for the entire main course was the scraping of knives and forks on the rapidly emptying plates. Then came the pudding – spotted dick with a bit of milk drizzled over. Ted was the only diner who declined, opting instead for leftover Yorkshire pudding liberally spread with jam, his Sunday treat ever since he had been a little lad.

'I thought you might have cured him of this by now, Bertha, pet,' muttered Mam under her breath as she prepared the delicacy.

'Nah! Every Sunday,' came the reply as Bertha headed for The Room with two enormous helpings of spotted dick. Suddenly the meal was over and hours of preparation had dissolved away in minutes of feasting. The table had to be cleared so once again the women teamed up in perfect harmony and the debris was removed to the scullery where it was piled high awaiting the water that had been heating up in the boiler during dinner.

Little plates of nuts and raisins were dotted strategically around the place and the dominoes, draughts boards and cards were brought out of hiding in preparation for the afternoon's entertainment.

Robert and Louise were supposed to arrive about three o'clock after having been to the Primitive Methodist Chapel followed by dinner at her Mam and Dad's. Louise was such a nice lass, why did she have to have such bloody awful folk?

None of the men wanted to play forfeits or do a turn, stuffy buggers, so a draughts league was organised but since there was only one board, the non-participants competed at floater or dominoes until it was their turn to play. Meanwhile the washing up miraculously seemed to do itself with the women only disappearing fleetingly to the scullery now and again. Cigarette smoke mixed with pipe smoke and the low, gentle murmur was reminiscent of a quiet evening in the Crown. Three o'clock came and went and it was damn nearly four before the back door sneck clicked up and Robert walked in followed by Louise. They stamped their feet on the clippy mat to dislodge the rime from the rapidly forming frost and Mam and Vera, who were both knocked out of the draughts by now, rushed to relieve the couple of their overcoats.

'What cheer, pet,' said Mam cheerily as she reached up to peck Robert on the cheek. His skin was cold on her lips but he was beaming contentedly.

Good! No major disagreements with Louise's folk, then.

'Hello Louise, pet,' she continued, giving her a hug while Vera bustled away with the coats and scarves. 'How was dinner at your Mam and Dad's?'

'Aw! It was canny, Mrs Smith. The chapel was freezing though; it took us ages to warm up when we got home.'

'Are you sure youse two have had enough to eat?' chipped in Bertha 'We've saved a bit just in case.'

'Aye,' said Vera, grinning, 'We even managed to save some spotty dick from the lads.'

'Aw! No, I'm fine thanks. So is Robert; aren't you, pet?'

Robert was standing warming his backside in front of the kitchen fire and watching Walter and Ted playing dominoes. 'Er! Aye, I suppose so, pet. I wouldn't mind a bit of spotty dick though, Mam.'

Louise's eyes opened wide in astonishment. 'Robert Cecil Smith! Not half an hour ago you managed to put away two helpings of my Mam's Christmas pudding and custard. Are you telling me you're still hungry?'

Mam looked sideways at Louise: 'Get used to it, pet, that one's got hollow legs. Now, come in and have a cup of tea, eh?'

They all trooped through to The Room where Louise sat in the rocking chair next to the fire. Robert hung back in the kitchen ostensibly watching the dominoes but keeping a weather eye on Vera who, de-pinnied and with her hair newly brushed, was dishing up a helping of spotted dick.

It was hard not to notice that Louise couldn't sit still; even Dad looked up from his semi-final championship draughts match and nearly smiled.

'What's the matter pet, are you too hot? Do you want to sit away from the fire a bit?'

'Eeh no! I'm canny Mr Smith, I'm just waiting for Robert, that's all.'

Dad tipped his chair back and craned his neck so that he could see into the kitchen.

'He won't be long, he's nearly finished. Aren't you, Robert.'

A split second later a spoon and bowl were heard to clatter onto the table amid badly stifled sniggers and Robert appeared in the doorway. He looked at Louise and she at him. Her lips formed a thin, determined line and she stared unblinkingly at her man, almost willing him to speak.

Robert, in turn, appeared to concentrate on the draughts match in hand. It was Dad's move and he deftly captured two singles and a crowner before landing triumphantly on George's back line to pick up a crowner himself. He then stared up at his eldest son whose neck was visibly reddening in traditional Smith fashion. Just as George was about to take his turn, Dad shook his head to forbid the move and deliberately took his time over filling his pipe, carefully knocking the dottle into the ashtray and cutting a slice of twist tobacco.

'Right, young Robert.' He looked from his pipe to his son and back to his pipe. You could hear a pin drop. Nobody was sure whether the heat in the room came from the fire or Robert's neck. 'Son,' said Dad quietly, 'You've got until I light my pipe to tell me and your Mam what the Hell's going on.'

Silence.

After an agonising pause Louise spoke in a low hiss, 'Robert, pet, you've got something to tell your Mam and Dad... haven't you?' She nodded towards him once as if she were cracking a whip with her head and it was all that Bertha and Vera could do not to laugh aloud as his mouth just kept opening and shutting like a stickleback. Dad pointedly made as much noise as he could selecting a match from the Vestas box whilst loudly clearing his throat. 'Stop catching flies and spit it out, son. Put me and your Mam out of our misery, eh!' The sound of the match scraping down the side of the box was the loudest Robert had ever heard. Dad puffed his pipe into life.

'Time's up, bonny lad.'

'Oh for God's sake!' said Louise. The outburst drew gasps from the other women. Primitive Methodists never take the name of the Lord in vain. 'Our Robert, you're a big, silly... gowk! Mr and Mrs Smith, Robert had a big, long talk with my Dad today, who, if it's all right with youse, has consented to allow me to become Robert's wife.'

You could cut the silence with a knife as every head turned to Robert, awaiting some kind of reaction. Louise glared at him as if her eyes were about to pop out of her head and when it was apparent he was to add nothing to the news she continued, 'Of course there must be a suitable length of engagement.'

She paused and her voice dropped almost to a whisper. 'And we are to be married in the Methodist Chapel and nowhere else.'

She was standing now and staring half defiantly and half apologetically around the room, not sure whether to smile or burst into tears. Taking a deep, shuddering breath she continued, 'And that's what we practiced all the way from our house and that's what that big silly bugger over there should have said instead of me!'

Louise was sure now; she was going to burst into tears. Mam saw it coming and swept across the room to embrace the trembling girl in a great, matronly hug.

'Oh pet, that's wonderful news! We're all so happy for the both of you.'

Suddenly the silent room was alive with laughter and chatter. Dad sat and waited for all the daft carry-on to subside. When the chatter had died away a bit he stood up and dug his hand deep into his trouser pocket and fished out a couple of silver coins.

'Walter, you're doing nowt. Nip back down to the *Sun* and get a couple more bottles of ale and some stout for the lasses, will you? And take them empties back.' He then stood and raised his glass, 'Welcome to the family, bonny lass, our Robert's caught a good'un.'

A couple of hours later all the fuss had died down and the Grand Games were over. Dad was undisputed champion of the draughts board while Bertha had just pipped Walter as floater champion. Ted and George were half-heartedly playing dominoes and the women had clustered round the kitchen table with a big pot of tea and were chatting in muted tones about funny things that had happened at past weddings. The men in The Room were talking about coal, as they always did, content that they had eaten their fill and survived another year.

Then everyone was shushed by Mam who insisted Robert play his violin for them all. After the customary persuasion he was finally cajoled into picking up his instrument and delighting the family with a couple of merry reels. Hands clapped and feet tapped in cheery rhythm until he changed the mood with a graceful ballad, ending up with '*Danny Boy*'. Bertha thought it was the most beautiful thing she had ever heard. As the last note faded away into a reverential silence she held her hand in the air as if she was a little bairn back at school and in a quiet voice requested Robert to please play it once more. Not a word was spoken as he smiled at her and began again. This time as he ended everybody politely ignored the fact that Bertha's eyes were filled with tears.

Folk were getting restless, though. Soon the buses and trains would be filling up with revellers and any self-respecting couple would be on their way home before the bustle and bad language began. There was a flurry of activity that jarred everyone out of the comfortable torpor that had settled on the assembly and Ted was aware that Robert had asked him once again to put in a good word with the manager at Langley Park Pit as he was going to try for as a job as a hewer. Coats and scarves were sorted through and Ted and Bertha were first at the door. It was after the goodbyes that, to Ted's astonishment, Bertha announced the latest news – that he was joining the Durham Light Infantry at the next signing on parade at Langley Park in the New Year. It was registered and forgotten in the midst of all the cheerios but it hadn't passed Ted by. They were sat on the bus before he brought the matter up and even then he did so obliquely.

'It's just for larks y'know.'

'I know, pet'

'It's only a few days a year.'

'I know.'

'What changed your mind like?'

Bertha paused and sighed, feeling her shoulders tense. It had started to sleet and she watched it flow down the window in spasmodic lumps. It was dark now and the window shone like a mirror, she could see herself and her man in every detail and Ted's reflection looked puzzled.

'Early Christmas present, pet. You were going to do it anyway and God knows what tall stories you would have had to concoct when you did, so let's just say I've made it easy for all of us.'

There was a silence between them for a while then she felt his hand find hers and squeeze it gently. She relaxed and looked at him. He was grinning all over his face like a big kid. Silly bugger! She leaned forward as he put his arm around her then cuddled in, contentedly resting her head on his shoulder.

'Pet?' Ted's voice had that nervous edge to it.

'Yes, pet?'

'I told our Robert I would try to get him a job as a hewer at Langley. If I can, would you mind if he stopped with us for a bit, just until he got on his feet, like.'

Chapter Eight

Langley Park Colliery Village, March 1914

Christmas had come and gone, and so had most of the bad weather. Winter was trying to hang on but its grip was slowly being eroded by the courageous appearance of snowdrops and daffodils along the road to Wall Nook. The millstone that was Langley Park Colliery, ground on as remorselessly as ever, with complete disregard for wind or weather. But if the same men trod the same path to and from work, their heads were held all the higher as the days grew warmer. Within the clockwork confines of shift patterns and coalface timetables there was a stirring in the hearts of the miners who, during the long cold winter, had steeled themselves to set out over the frozen ground. It wasn't so much a lightness in their step, more a surge of spirit as thoughts turned from mere survival to the pleasure of actually living again.

Robert had been living at Logan Street since the middle of January. He was quiet enough not to be in the way and after the initial irritation at having her dreams of a normal married life with Ted shattered yet again, it didn't take long for Bertha to accept him. In fact, her worst fear of having her nose shoved out once the pair were living under the same roof was never realised. Robert was far too sensitive to allow that to happen.

The interview that led to employment at Langley had been successful. Mr Swallow had been just as impressed with Robert as he had been with his younger brother and was more than happy to give him a job as a hewer. The bicycle had come as well so that Robert had a means of travelling back and forth to Sunniside and his beloved Louise, and interestingly enough he had been christened 'Tow Law Bob' by his workmates. Wedding plans were well underway and the big day was to be August 15th 1914 at the

Primitive Methodist Chapel at Tow Law. Ted was going to enlist when the recruitment party came to the village this March and he hoped to have his uniform for the wedding. Wouldn't Mam be proud of him being Robert's Best Man, standing straight and proud as Private Edward Smith, Durham Light Infantry? At this rate, Ted grinned, Sunniside would run out of eligible Smiths by 1916 and Mam would have nothing to do. He also made the mistake of voicing his theory in front of his wife.

* * * * *

The notices were up all over the village: The Durham Light Infantry were enlisting in the Wesleyan Methodist Chapel on Tuesday, the 31st of March 1914, from half past eight in the morning until half past seven the same night. It would be a long day's recruiting but it would ensure that whatever shift the patriotic men of Langley Park were working, they would have ample time to make their way to the humourless grey building on Front Street and sign their pledge to the King, proving that they would be ready and willing to fight for their country should the need arise.

It was not long after six in the morning and Ted was due in any minute now from his shift down the pit. Bertha had been up just over an hour. She had put the little zinc tub in front of the fire and the water was heating quietly in the boiler. Robert was sound asleep in the back room upstairs and she had made herself a cup of tea. She was bone weary. Looking after one man was bad enough but with two in the house! Not that she had any complaints about Robert. He was a gentle soul who made himself as unobtrusive as possible and always appeared to be aware that he was intruding despite protestations from Ted and Bertha that he was doing nothing of the sort. Anyway, he was upstairs asleep so Bertha could at least pretend she had the house to herself for a bit. She had seen the notices as well and knew that it was no longer a subject to skirt around but if today was the day that Ted was going to enlist in the Durham Light Infantry then he would have to bloody well work for it. She swore to herself that when he came in she would resolutely avoid the subject and let him suffer having to bring it up himself; that'll teach him. Sure enough the gate creaked open and the sneck clicked loudly as Ted slammed it behind him. Why did he have to do that? His Mam said he had done it ever since he was a lad and she could never stop him so that was that. The clacking noise of the hobbed boots grew louder as he approached the door and there he was, standing on the clippy mat in the scullery and grinning from ear to ear, his teeth white as snow against the jet-black of his face and clothes.

He needed no telling to stay in the scullery until he had stripped down to his combinations. Boots, cap, kneepads and clothes were in neat piles on the floor and he padded in to perch on the cracket and drink the mug of tea his wife had handed to him. He watched as she busied herself filling his bath, and as the tea warmed him he grinned again as he realised that life was grand! Fancy being married to a bonny lass who gives you a cup of tea the minute you step through the door and draws a bath especially for you. No more being third or fourth in with half a ton of coal dust floating on the top any more. He had his own wife and his own house and his own bath. Yes, life was all right. He was eyeing up the frying pan on the hearth along with the thick rashers of bacon sat on the table still in the greaseproof paper. His eyes positively twinkled in his coal-black face.

'Don't suppose I could have one of those while I'm in the bath, eh, pet?'

'Ted Smith, you'll have your bath first and when you're respectable you can sit at the table like decent folk and have your breakfast there.'

He made no reply but put his mug on the hearth and rose up, arms outstretched, and bared his teeth in a mock snarl. Growling, he advanced towards her, his filthy, black fingers clenching and unclenching. Bertha backed away immediately.

'Ted Smith don't you dare touch me with those hands, just don't you bloody dare. I'll tell me Mam I will, so help me God... Ted!' she almost screamed the last word but stifled it immediately as she remembered their Robert was upstairs. She was the opposite side of the bath to him but it offered no protection against those rangy long arms and big hands. As she circled past the hearth she swiftly picked up the poker and waved it menacingly. She tried to look ferocious but only had to look at the comical black face grimacing at her and all resistance broke down. She was laughing so much there were tears in her eyes as she threatened him again.

'Just you watch it, I've got a poker here for you!'

'Fancy that pet, that's just what I was going to say.'

Bertha gasped loudly at the lewdness of her husband's remark. But whilst her sensibilities raged at him, yet she could feel her heart smashing ever faster against her ribs and knew that she was blushing furiously. She placed her free hand across her mouth, not daring to speak. For what seemed like ages neither moved, and the comic aspect of the last few moments evaporated into thin air. Bertha was quietly aware of two black hands reaching out towards her shoulders. There was nothing else in the entire universe but Ted's hands. They filled her vision. She could make out every individual speck of coal dust so clearly it was as if they had been carefully placed there, one by one. And there, just underneath, was the flesh of her husband.

She was aching so much it almost hurt and she knew she was visibly shaking when suddenly, out of nowhere, her upbringing snapped back into control and she reacted instantly.

'I've told you, don't touch me with them hands!'

Ted just seemed to crumple in front of her; it was as if a spark had gone out of him. She hadn't meant it like that! She hadn't meant to hurt him! Now there he stood, crestfallen and vulnerable with his hands hanging limply by his sides. Many a man would have lost his temper and got angry, but not her Ted. All she wanted to do now was hold him but the coal dust said no, and she still ached terribly.

'Not until you've had your bath. Make it quick, I'll be upstairs.' She moved to the door that led up to the bedroom. 'And mind you don't make a noise, remember our Robert.'

* * * * *

It was Tuesday 31st March and heading for the middle of the day but there was less of a crowd at the chapel than Ted expected. The skillfully rigged Union Flag hung above the door without so much as a single crease. Thin ropes shot from the corners and disappeared into the metal-framed stained glass windows to be secured God knows where inside the building. There was a low wall separating the tiny front yard of the chapel from the pavement on Front Street and standing at the entrance was a tall soldier with an ungodly huge chest and an equally huge moustache. He was ramrod straight in the at ease position and was talking quietly to a small group of onlookers. As Ted approached he recognised a few of his mates chatting to him. The notice board that usually sported service times and parish news had been commandeered and now proudly displayed two recruiting posters. The one that took Ted's eye was of a crowd of soldiers marching in a smart column into the distance with a few men joining them from the sides. The bold words 'Step into Your Place', shone above the picture.

'Which one o' them's you, Ted?'

It was Jacky Tait who had spoken and John Merrigan who replied. 'Why he's the one walking with the limp, man. Look.' The little group laughed quietly and the laughter faded into a self-conscious silence.

The corporal spoke next in a soft Scottish accent. 'Well you've come this far lads, walk through that door and you can call yourself a King's Man like me. I'm Corporal Tremaine, by the way. Anybody brave enough to go in?'

George Moody, a Witton Gilbert lad, spoke first. 'Well, we can stand here all day or we can sign up for a free trip to Scarborough. Who's for coming?'

Before anyone could reply, Billy Robson walked out of the front door. 'What cheer, bonny lads?' he said grinning. '2494 William Robson, Private, Eighth Battalion, New Durham Light Infantry at your service. Who do you want us to shoot first?'

'Never in this world!' exclaimed Jacky. 'You're the last bugger I thought would join.'

'Keeps us away from the wife for a few days, doesn't it? Go on, man. Get yourselves in, we'll have some canny crack between us.'

'Aw, why the Hell not, we've waited this long, Howay lads!'

The men shuffled into the front yard and entered the building under the approving eye of Corporal Tremaine, automatically forming a rough queue behind the three or four men already inside. They were in a fairly spacious corridor and off to the right was the minister's office, now commandeered as the Enlisting Officer's temporary HQ. Next door down was the verger's office, then the corridor ended at the Grand Entrance to the chapel itself. The double doors to it were permanently open but barring the way today was a burly sergeant sporting another enormous moustache. He was standing in the at ease position and his barrel chest was thrust out, proudly displaying a row of shining medals. He fixed them with an unblinking stare and in seconds there was total silence.

'Morning lads. I'm Sergeant Malone.' The voice was quiet, measured and comfortingly local. 'How very nice of you to turn up. We've come all the way from HQ in Birtley just to see you. Please stand in an orderly line along the left-hand side of the corridor – that way you won't be in the way as your fellow recruits go in and out of the offices. Anyone coming in after you, please direct them quietly to the back of the queue.' Then, almost as an afterthought: 'Thank you very much, lads.'

The silence of the next minute or so was torture. Ted, in the queue behind John Merrigan felt that he was breathing far too loudly. He turned to look at Tommy Raper behind him to find the man pulling such grotesque faces that he almost burst out laughing and in trying to stifle it he let out a loud snort that set everyone giggling.

'Gentlemen!' The corridor was quiet in an instant. 'No skylarking, if you please.'

In the silence somebody's stomach rumbled reminding everyone that it was about time for dinner. A few subdued giggles ensued but under the glare of the sergeant soon died away. At that moment the door to the minister's office opened and out loped the lanky frame of young Danny Collinson. The lad wasn't even fifteen and had only been working down the pit a few months. What the Hell was he doing signing up at his age? As he emerged he saw the men standing staring at him, his freckled face suffused into an embarrassed blush and he stopped, unsure of how to proceed.

It was the sergeant who broke the silence. 'Wait outside the medical officer's surgery, son,' he said kindly. 'Smartly now.' He jerked his head in the direction of the verger's office, which, for the day, housed the civilian doctor who accompanied the enlistment crew to ensure that all who signed on were healthy enough to perform their duties for the King. Danny stared timidly at his ragged boots and tried not to look conspicuous.

'Right, lads, first man in the line into the attestation room.' He fixed 'Fat' Harry Guildford with a stare. 'That would be you, off you go. And a word of advice, hold your stomach in.' The sergeant gave a conspiratorial wink. 'Try to impress the Recruiting Officer.'

Harry did as he was bid. He was already wearing his broadest belt to try to control his more than generous bulk, and he cut a comical figure as he swelled out his chest, trying to emulate the sergeant before rapping smartly on the door. 'Hold your breath, Harry,' grinned George.

Ted was confused; this was not how he had imagined it. First under-age lads and now Fat Harry! Not that Harry wasn't a canny lad – he was surprisingly agile considering his bulk and was a constant source of both amazement and amusement as he wriggled and crawled his way through the workings down the pit every bit as well as any of his leaner comrades. He was a good sort and defused the worst of the teasing by making fun of himself. For instance, when asked how he could negotiate crawling through the smaller tunnels he would laugh and say that he simply threw his belly in first and crawled in after it. Ted tried to imagine a line of uniformed soldiers including, side by side, Harry and young Danny. A frown wrinkled his forehead. It wasn't like this on any of the posters.

The medical officer's door opened, out walked Dicky Howell and in went Danny. As Dicky walked past the line he gave the thumbs up sign and a huge grin split his florid face.

'Sound as Bow Bells, lads! Just here me ring,' he said cheerfully and let out an enormous, rasping fart. 'Didn't want to do that in front of the doctor, did I?' And he cheerfully strode out of the door and was gone.

Almost at once howls and moans of disgust arose as the smell permeated the air. The sergeant was not best pleased. He remained immobile in the at ease position and fixed the remaining men with a threatening glare.

'Aw! Come on mate, it wasn't us.'

'That was bloody awful, man.'

'Dirty bugger, something must have crawled up his arse and died.'

'Gentlemen!' the sergeant barked and once again the silence was instant and complete. Some of the lads even tried to come to some sort of attention. 'You will please stand quietly and there will be no repeat of that sort of behaviour. Now stand still!'

They all looked at the floor and Tommy stopped pulling faces. Within a few minutes the routine had become clear. First you entered the attestation room, then the medical officer's surgery then finally you went to the Blue Star where another sergeant bought you a pint to welcome you to the DLI. After that, Ted supposed, you went home. Danny Collinson came out of the medical officer's and Fat Harry Guildford went in. As Harry had left the recruiting room John Merrigan disappeared inside. The queue shuffled down and a few more lads joined onto the end. John came out of the recruitment room and winked at Ted before knocking on the medical officer's door. Ted swallowed nervously and looked from John to the sergeant, who raised his eyebrows and inclined his head in the direction of the office. Taking a great breath Ted moved in a manner that he hoped looked nonchalant towards the door and rapped sharply upon it twice. 'Get your arse into that office you sackless bugger. Didn't you hear the officer say to go in?'

Sergeant Malone's voice ripped through Ted's brain like a jack engine. His heart leaped in his chest and he felt his neck go red. He swallowed and hurriedly opened the door. He'd never been in a minister's office before. It was bigger than he thought and really quite comfortably furnished with pictures on the walls and a worn leather sofa in one corner. Today, however it had been transformed by the addition of recruiting posters and a large Union Flag draped across the front of the big wooden desk. Behind the desk sat a surprisingly young officer with greased down hair and an immaculate parting, sporting a rather dashing pencil moustache. His hands were clasped and resting on a blank form which was placed with absolute precision in the centre of the big blotting pad. Either side of the pad were neat piles of forms and to the officer's left was a bible, and to his right an inkwell. All these items were absolutely square and parallel to each other. Ted was fascinated by this orderly presentation. Even Mrs Sanders at the Colliery Offices didn't have a desk half so neat. A wooden nameplate inscribed with the words, 'Brass, J.R. 2nd LT', completed the geometrical elegance of the desk.

* * * * *

To the right of the officer stood a tall, stout corporal as immaculately turned out as the one in the corridor and equally bedecked with medals. He also sported a walrus moustache and was standing in the at ease position. Ted, lacking both girth and facial hair wondered suddenly if either were a pre-requisite of enlistment. He then realised he was staring at the corporal, who was staring icily back. After a few agonising seconds it was the corporal who spoke first in a gentle Scottish burr.

'Why don't you shut the door, son, then come and stand behind the line on the floor.'

To his horror, Ted realised he was still holding on to the door handle. His knuckles were white and it was almost as if he was powerless to let go. His ears were burning like coke furnaces but he regained his composure and closed the door; quietly moving forward to the line of brown tape on the floor just over an arm's length from the desk. The officer looked at him for a moment then took up his pen. He smiled at Ted. 'My name is Brass. This is Corporal Lawrie. If you have any questions please keep them until before you take the oath when due time will be given to you. And of course you must call me, 'sir'. Do you understand?'

'Yes... sir,' Ted stammered.

'I notice you walk with a slight limp, a recent injury perhaps?'

'Yes, I broke my leg down the pit last year, it's fine now though... sir.'

'Good, let's get down to it shall we?' The pen was poised above a large form. 'What is your name?'

'Edward Smith.'

The pen scratched his name onto the form. 'In or near what Parish or Town were you born?'

'I was born in Sunniside near Crook in County Durham... sir.'

'Are you a British subject?'

'Yessir.' The 'sirs' were coming easier now.

'What is your age?'

'Er... Nineteen years and nine months old, sir.'

'What is your trade or calling?'

'I'm a miner, well a hewer actually, like, erm. I work on the face on the Top Five Quarter seam. I used to be on the Busty but after my accident... '

Lieutenant Brass cut him short abruptly 'I think 'miner' will suffice, don't you, Smith?'

Ted swallowed for what seemed like the thousandth time. He tried to say, yes sir, but only managed a squeak. God, he was making a right balls up of this! He cleared his throat and tried again.

'Yes, sir. Sorry sir.'

'Please try to restrict your answers. Now, in whose employ are you?'

'Langley Park Colliery. No! Er... sorry, Consett Iron Company... sir.' He wanted to shut his eyes to close out the stare Lieutenant Brass was giving him prior to carefully scoring out what he had written and putting down the correct answer then fastidiously initialling the error. Ted glanced towards the sergeant to see the man was rolling his eyes Heavenward. Why did that pen have to scratch so bloody loudly?

'Very well. Consett Iron Company. Where do you now reside?'

'Eight Logan Street, Langley Park, sir.'

'Are you an apprentice?'

'No, sir.'

'Are you married?'

'Yes, sir.' Wouldn't Bertha be having a right laugh if she was here. He couldn't even enlist properly, never mind march about and shoot a bloody gun! The questions continued and so did the form filling and so did the scratching.

The officer's voice settled into a practiced drone as he recited the many conditions on the attestation form. Ted replied 'yes' or 'no' accordingly and tried to concentrate as the barrage of information exploded around him. He was aware that he was joining for an initial four years and he would train for no less than eight days and no more than fifteen or, later in the drone, it transpired that if somebody or other said so, it could be increased to thirty days a year. On top of that, in a National Emergency his four years could be extended to five. And to his horror he heard that he could be fined five pounds if he missed a drill with no excuse. His mind was working full tilt to store this information as Bertha was sure to ask him all about it when he got home. It sounded like there was a Hell of a lot of conditions involved considering it was only a lark, though.

Suddenly Ted noticed that the droning had stopped and all was silent. He was instantly alert and wondering if he had made another gaff but luckily not. Lieutenant Brass had apparently come to the end of the talking bit. There was a moment of quiet, a definite pause; was he waiting to see if Ted had anything to say, or to ask?

Questions! What had he said earlier on about questions? Was this when he should ask them? He thought about young Danny Collinson, under-age by bloody miles. Should he ask about that or was that interfering in somebody else's business? What about the amount of gut on the two NCOs and the fact that Fat Harry was accepted apparently without question? Would a question about that be in order or would he be impugning the two soldiers and his workmate unfairly? How would the corporal standing beside the desk react if Ted brought up the subject in front of him? What if he was the sort to hold a grudge?

He remembered Dad's advice, 'When in doubt say bloody nowt!' and decided to follow it to the letter. He remained silent and Lieutenant Brass shifted in his chair and stood up. He turned the form around so it was the right way up for Ted to read and pushed it across the desk. Carefully charging the pen from the inkwell he offered it to Ted, who obediently signed in his best handwriting and handed back the pen. He couldn't help noticing that his writing was far neater than that of the young officer.

The top line of the form swam into sharp focus: No: 2505. Name: Edward Smith. Corps: Eighth Battalion, DLI.

The lieutenant then picked up the bible.

'I'm going to ask you to swear the oath of allegiance now, Smith. Would you please take this bible in your left hand and raise your right hand like so?'

He held his own hand up, palm outwards. Ted did likewise. So far so good. Abruptly, he was very scared. His cheekbones felt icy cold and for a second he actually thought he was going to faint. Suddenly this was important; this was bloody important!

Shit! The officer had actually started speaking and he had missed what he said.

It must be somewhere in your bloody brain. Find it!

The officer stopped and Ted hoped he had recalled correctly. He found he was actually listening to himself as he recited the first part of the oath, almost as if he were eavesdropping on his own voice. Was there an echo?

'I, Edward Smith, do make oath that I will bear true allegiance to His Majesty King George the Fifth, His Heirs and Successors.'

The lieutenant's voice had become a drone once again as he read from a well-thumbed piece of card he was holding. Ted repeated the words.

'And I swear that I will, as in duty bound, honestly and faithfully defend His Majesty, His Heirs and Successors.'

The drone continued and Ted repeated, 'In Person, Crown and Dignity against all enemies according to the conditions of my service.'

'So help me God.'

That wasn't a drone! Ted heard that with crystal clarity! He swallowed, no going back now. He cleared his throat and managed a hoarse whisper, 'So help me God.'

The officer retrieved the bible and inked a stamp which he thumped down on the bottom of Ted's attestation form. The noise seemed to split Ted's eardrums.

'Well done, Smith. You're officially a private soldier the Eighth New Durhams.'

Ted was vaguely aware of a hand being proffered across the desk and he automatically took it, finding the handshake warm and friendly and the smile genuine.

'You are to report along with your friends to the senior NCO at Burnhope Camp at 0800 hours on Saturday, April the 4th. Do you understand?'

'Yes, sir.'

'Off you go next door to Doctor Kirkland. I'm sure if there's anything wrong with you he'll be able find it.'

Almost in a daze, Ted turned about and left the room. Should he have saluted or something? Well, nobody stopped him so it must be all right. He didn't remember passing his mates in the corridor and somehow he was in with Dr Kirkland taking his shirt off. John Merrigan was pulling on his jacket and he winked at Ted as he adjusted his cap.

'See you in the Blue Star, mate.'

Dr Kirkland examined Ted dutifully and conscientiously. He was a bit taller, thin as a rake and all saggy as if he had lost a lot of weight suddenly and his skin hadn't shrunk to his new size yet. He might look a queer bugger but he was as polite as Lieutenant Brass had been and soon finished the examination.

If you could call it an examination! Height, weight, listen to his chest and back with that thing that Dr Chrisp had, then have a good look in both eyes and ears. Finally, it was drop your trousers and cough while he held your bollocks. He never examined or even mentioned the broken leg and that was that, really. The man scribbled something on a form a bit like the last one and told Ted to get dressed. Just then, a rap came on the door and

Ted wondered if the doctor and the officer rehearsed to get the timing of both operations the same. It certainly seemed to work like that.

In came Tommy Vickers and, breathing a long sigh of relief, out went Ted. He noticed the queue in the corridor had grown and he nodded affably at the apprehensive faces. Suddenly he felt relaxed and confident.

2505 Smith, Edward, Private. Eighth Battalion, New Durham Light Infantry. At your service.

Somehow Jacky Tait had lost his place in the queue and was a couple of places further back, talking quietly to Tommy Raper and Tom Dodds. He saw Ted and raised his eyebrows, a tacit query as to how things had gone.

Ted grinned generously, 'No bother, Jacky. See you in the Star, lads.'

As Ted pushed open the door, he nodded to the little stout figure of old Freddy Wardle who was seated on the bench outside. Freddy had come to Langley Park from Weardale when the pit first opened. He must have been old then and was now near to retiring. He was a veteran of the Boer War and often regaled the younger miners with his tales of derring-do at Eden's Kop and Hoortpoort. Truth to tell, they didn't believe half of what he said and with his penchant for exaggeration he would have made a fine fisherman. In the course of his three years' service with the DLI, the lads reckoned it was impossible for one man to have threaded so many exploits into the time. He was a grand talker, though, and immensely entertaining. On Big Meeting days and Lodge meetings he wore a string of medals a mile wide so there must be more than a grain of truth in it all somewhere.

'What Fettle, Ted. Get us a pint, young'un, will you?' He emptied a couple of coppers from his purse but before he could hand them over, burst into a racking spasm of coughing that seemed to go on forever. He spat great gobbets of coal-black phlegm onto the pavement beneath his feet and sat back wheezing. He wiped his mouth with a dirty cotton handkerchief and tried to control his breathing. He exhaled loudly, trying to clear his throat. 'Bollocks to this!' he managed to gasp and put the money into Ted's palm before another attack of coughing shook him apart. He feebly waved Ted away without looking and Ted obediently entered the pub, unable to do anything to help the old man and feeling all the more embarrassed because of it.

The bar seemed dark and indistinct after the sunshine. It took a couple of seconds for his eyes to get used to it just as the familiar voice of George Moody rang out. 'Get to attention lads, it's General Smith.'

A ripple of good-natured laughter ran around the room and Ted saw all his friends gathered together at the far corner of the bar near the bust of Queen Victoria. They were smoking and drinking happily and chatting to a sergeant. Oddly enough, this one wasn't fat, though he did sport the walrus moustache obviously favoured in the unit.

'Private Soldier Smith? Step forward, lad.'

Ted hesitated for a second. He had had enough of being caught dithering today and walked smartly up to the sergeant, though when he was standing in front of him he really didn't know what to do. Luckily, the soldier was well used to hesitant young men and thrust out his hand. 'Sergeant Hanson. Welcome to the New DLI, Private Smith. On behalf of the Eighth Battalion let me buy you a pint, lad.' He waved at John Brannon, the landlord, who nodded and began to pull a pint into a straight glass.

The next half hour was a happy one for all the young men who now swelled the ranks of the DLI. A few more lads came in – Tommy not far behind Ted and eventually Jacky Tait Tom Dodds and Cockney Joe. Sergeant Hanson happily answered many questions and, once their confidence in him was cemented, he allayed a lot of their fears. He was more than happy to relate tales of bravery both individual and per company and they were fascinated by stories of actions at Salamanca and Vittoria against Napoleon and at Sevastopol against the Russians. The 'Faithful Durhams' were in action against the Boers in South Africa (where, to the tune of a few intakes of breath, Sergeant Hanson mentioned the individual heroism of a certain Corporal Frederick Wardle) and were instrumental, at great cost in casualties, at The Relief of Ladysmith.

There was a lull in the banter, which was immediately filled by the deep barking of Caesar, the publican's dog, who lived in the handball court at the rear of the pub. When the yard was not used for sport, John stored his kegs and bottles out there and Caesar was a useful deterrent against those who might consider unlawfully appropriating the drink. The strident tones of Fat Ena were also heard in the bottle-and-jug, along with the yapping of her little sausage dog.

There was a momentary embarrassment as everyone looked at Private Soldier Tommy Raper, who happened to be her son, but he was used to his mother's eccentric behaviour and knew full well that there was no ill will in the fun poked at her and the little dog by the assembled company. He simply shrugged his shoulders, smiled self-consciously and listened along with the rest of the lads. She was arguing with Patrick, the landlord's son, over the amount of stout he had pulled into her pewter pot and while she bickered with him so the tethered Caesar squabbled with the dachshund and pandemonium resulted.

It was a habit of Ena's to try and give silver instead of the right money because that way the staff were obliged to go back into the main bar to get change from the drawer. When they returned to the bottle-and-jug they would find a couple of mouthfuls missing from the pot and Ena complaining that it had not been properly filled in the first place. John always put some change in his apron pocket when he went to serve her in order to prevent her and her dachshund from siphoning off the profits, but Patrick was only thirteen and was not yet wise to the unscrupulous ways of Fat Ena. Blushing under the tirade of complaints, which were punctuated at intervals by the yapping sausage dog and the deep bass barking of Caesar, he refilled the pot and reluctantly stood his ground until she had left the building.

The sniggering silence in the bar was maintained fairly well with lots of arm waving and fingers on lips, and, as the group heard Ena say, 'Come on Clementine,' everyone in the group yapped three times in perfect unison with the little dog before dissolving into laughter. This impromptu chorus again set off Caesar and John Brannon shook his head at the childishness of the clientele and left to placate his dog.

Ted was well into his second pint when Harry Clarke came in. 'Who's supposed to be buying old Freddy his pint, he's cursing somebody out there!'

Ted almost spluttered into his glass. 'Bugger! John, give us a pint for old Freddy will you or I'll get me bollocks chewed off.' He fished into his pocket for the coppers and put them on the bar whilst his mates all took an exaggerated intake of breath and tut-tutted before breaking into laughter once more. He dutifully took the glass of ale out to the old man who was seated on the bench with his eyes shut and his face turned up towards the sun. His cap was set right back on his head as if to expose as much of him to the sunlight as possible. The cotton handkerchief in his hand was black and sodden, and his wheezing was much more pronounced than when Ted had spoken to him on the way in. Was he asleep? One beady eye suddenly opened and inspected Ted for a moment. Then Freddy motioned for the proffered pint to be put down on the wooden bench beside him.

'How many pints you had?' gasped Fred through the wheezing.

'Only a couple. I'm sorry about your ale, Fred, I just got talking with the lads, like, and...'

'Don't have any more. Finish your drink and bugger off home.'

Ted opened his mouth to reply, but was cut short. 'That bloody sergeant is there to see who drinks too much and who doesn't. Just you make sure you're one of the ones who doesn't, right?' The old man jerked his head towards the door to the bar. 'Now bugger off.'

After a moments' hesitation during which he dismissed the idea of thanking Freddy for fear of a further tongue-lashing, he simply nodded and walked back into the bar, thanking God that the place was dim enough so that nobody would see he was blushing. He was slightly apart from the crowd of young men now, quietly finishing his drink and listening to the conversation rather than joining in. For the first time he noticed that Sergeant Hanson was hardly drinking at all. He was continually taking coins from a leather purse to buy the first pint for the lads who were dribbling into the pub from the chapel, but all the while his own pint, with a couple of inches missing from the top, never moved from its place on the bar. Crafty bugger. Well, thanks to old Freddy Wardle, Ted was just as crafty. He drained the last of his pint and refused another from Cockney Joe, who was sinking his fourth. With a polite nod to the sergeant, he left the pub and set off up Logan Street for his dinner. Luckily, Bertha didn't say much apart from asking him how he'd got on.

Then it was back down the pit.

Chapter 9

Burnhope Village TA Camp, County Durham, Saturday 4th April 1914

The lads had never felt so miserable, so cheated or so bloody wet. It was half past seven of a Saturday morning when sensible blokes on a day off were in a warm bed. It was cold, it was pissing down with rain and they'd been trudging sullenly up the road for the best part of an hour. The rain had started in the night and most of the recruits, who were sleeping fitfully anyway because eight o' clock the next morning was their first parade, were suddenly wide awake and groaning.

Nineteen souls from Langley Park, nearby Wallnook and Witton Gilbert had prepared themselves all they could to impress the officers and men at their Inaugural Parade on the grassy rectangle that served as a square-bashing ground for the Durham Light Infantry, Durham and Birtley area. Burnhope itself was small and inconsequential: a huddled cluster of cottages and one shop, no pub, no pit, not even a church. It was built on the very top of a hill for no apparent reason other than to expose its inhabitants to every extreme of weather and to make them miserable, which they were. At odd weekends, however, the village came alive with another purpose. It became the training camp for all new recruits within a twelve-mile radius, and it was here that on many a Saturday morning the future heroes of the British Army trained hard to master the skills of military life.

So the bunch of keen, smart lads they had all hoped to be were, instead, a bedraggled and sorry sight when they took the short cut over the pit catwalk that put them onto the Lanchester Road. By the time they were walking past the Old Castle ruins there wasn't a man who couldn't feel the cold rain running down his back. They walked in sullen silence but Cockney Joe was the most morose. Ted thought he had changed since Christmas, becoming more edgy and bad-tempered. George Moody, up at the front with John Merrigan was first to pipe up.

'Flag ahoy, lads, looks like we've reached land at last.'

All heads jerked up through the mizzling rain.

'He must have bloody good eyes,' murmured Jacky Tait who was walking with Ted near the middle of the group.

Ted had to blink away the rain that misted his vision before he could make out the top half of a dirty white flagpole rising over the brow of the hill. Suspended from it was what looked like a black, sodden rag. It had to be the Union Flag but it was an unrecognisable and sorry sight hanging limp and lifeless in the rain-soaked sky. Without a word the ragged gang formed itself into the semblance of a two-man column and, nearly in step, they marched until they reached the crest of the hill.

Ted looked up at the dilapidated flagpole and down to the two tents, one large and one small. A squad of uniformed men was drilling smartly with complete disregard for the driving rain. The white lines that someone had painted on the cropped grass to form a giant square were diluted and blurred, and over to their right a group of men like themselves was standing around a trestle table under an awning, drinking tea from enamel mugs. A couple of miserable looking women in headscarves and shawls were doling out the tea while another with a crying toddler hanging onto her pinny was cutting loaves of bread into chunks on the driest bit of the table.

'That looks a bit more like it, lads,' said George, rubbing his hands gleefully, and the ragged column swerved to aim itself directly at the tea urn.

They hadn't gone half a dozen steps when a voice roared with a volume none of them would have believed.

'YOU LOT! STAND STILL!'

The column faltered as every head turned in the direction of the voice, locating a tall, burly, khaki-clad figure standing rigidly to attention outside the smaller of the two tents.

'I said, stand still, you sorry-looking bunch... STAND STILL!'

Ted was too slow and bumped straight into the back of Fat Harry and a cursing Dicky Howell bumped into him. The column was now more or less stationary and the figure was heading directly towards them.

He was almost upon them when he stopped to allow the squad of marching men to pass smartly in front. Ted marvelled at their precision; it was like watching a machine, with every man in perfect step executing crisp movements in almost complete silence. No beat of heels cracking down on paved roads here, only the soft whispering squelch of hob-nailed boots sinking into grass that oozed mud at every step. As the last of the squad passed the lone figure, Ted could see the two white chevrons on the soldier's arm denoting his rank as corporal. It was the soldier who had been outside the recruiting office when Ted had enlisted. He was standing to attention facing the lads and only his eyes were moving as he looked at each man in turn. After what seemed an age he spoke, his Scottish lilt surprisingly gentle.

'Good morning, gentlemen. For those of you who don't know me I am Corporal Tremaine, and you mongers were about to shamble onto the parade ground, weren't you. So, let me give you your first lesson right here and now. Unless you are in a formed squad under the orders of an officer or NCO you will at all times walk around the parade ground paying very careful attention to the white lines. You never walk on the parade ground. You always march. Is that absolutely clear?'

'Hey mate, what if you're desperate for a shit and the netty's on the other side?'

Most of the lads closed their eyes in disbelief as Billy Robson chirped up. Nobody laughed and all eyes were on the corporal who was now staring at Billy. After a while, Ted wondered if he ever blinked. Billy, grinning broadly and totally oblivious to his folly, was content to try and outstare the soldier but the depth of his blunder gradually dawned even upon him and he began to wither under the furious gaze. The grin faded and suddenly Billy was staring at his boots and all that could be heard was the drumming of the rain.

'What is your name and number?'

It was said so quietly and politely that the threat behind the words was multiplied a thousand times.

'William Robson, 2494.'

The corporal's expression remained inscrutable. 'That's "William Robson 2494, Corporal". Would you like to repeat it please?'

'William Robson, 2494. Corporal.' It was almost a whisper.

'Right you lot! Mr Robson seems to think the army is a lark. Who else thinks the army is a lark?'

No one moved. No one spoke. 'Very well. I see you've had the good sense to carry your best boots rather than wear them. Very commendable. Hold them up.'

Hesitantly, inch by inch and with many a sidelong glance, the hushed group held out the sodden footwear for inspection. Ted was blushing with embarrassment. Although his boots shone and the rain ran off them, as it should with such a high polish, they were poking out of soaked and disintegrating newspaper that the rain had lashed into ribbons of grey.

'No! Hold them up over your heads so we can all see what a good job you've made of the shine. Don't be scared, boys. Hold them right up so we can all see.'

'Here it bloody comes,' whispered somebody behind him.

'Hold them UP!'

Nineteen pairs off hands instantly and obediently shot into the air.

'Now run, you useless buggers, run round the square that way and keep running until I tell you to stop. And if any man sets foot inside that white line I'll make you do it again... and again until you'll wish you'd never laid eyes on me. Now MOVE!'

They were, of course, a complete shambles. They were in neither ranks nor files or any kind of order. They were a sodden, motley group of men burning with humiliation because they knew what a comical sight they must present. As they rounded the second corner they ran, some in front and some behind the awning that sheltered the other group of newcomers drinking tea. They could hear laughter and jeering, which only added to their misery. They had completed a circuit of the square and were heading back towards the corporal who had, without relaxing from the attention position, rotated to observe their progress. Optimistically, the group slowed down a fraction, each man searching the soldier's face for any sign of an end to their degradation but there was no change in expression. They bunched together and ran on, boots held high. Already Fat Harry was beginning to wheeze and curses and threats were aimed at Billy. They approached the corporal again. They ran on. They approached him a third time and ran past again. They ran past the jeering and the tea, their arms slowly lowering as even the small weight of the boots became insufferably heavy. The group had just passed the motionless corporal for the fourth time when his voice rang out.

'Squa-a-ad... HALT!'

They did so immediately and gratefully, some leaning forward with their hands on their knees, gasping to get their breath back. Amazingly, no one, not even Fat Harry had dropped out. Ted caught the eye of Tommy Raper who smiled and winked but nobody uttered a word as the corporal came up to the group and they began to straighten up as he approached.

'Well done, boys. Did you enjoy your little run?'

Every pair of eyes in the group immediately shot a threatening look at Billy.

No one spoke.

'Go and get a mug of tea and a tab. Somebody will come and get you in ten minutes.'

The tea was lukewarm and so was the reception by the other bunch of recruits. It turned out they were mostly from around Stanley way with one or two from this side of Consett. This district presumably made up the rest of the area that used Burnhope for training. The crack with the lads was desultory to begin with, but they lit their tabs and drank their tea, and talked, as young men always will when together in adversity and the mood was beginning to warm when Dicky Howell spoke.

'Watch it lads, enemy in sight.'

The group followed his eyes to see the figures of a corporal, accompanied by a skinny lance corporal approaching the group from the direction of the two tents. It was the other Scottish corporal, who had been with the officer in the recruiting office.

'Fags out lads, mugs on the table and boots and any other loose articles underneath it... NOW!'

There was a slight hesitation as everyone was reluctant to abandon their valuable property so casually but since nobody was going to risk incurring the anger of the corporal by being the last to do so, an untidy pile of rain-soaked boots soon built up under the dubious shelter of the trestle table. Meanwhile the lance corporal had strategically placed himself under a part of the awning that didn't have rain dripping through it, before opening a shabby, leather-bound clipboard, telling the men that as soon as they heard their names they were to go and stand on the white line immediately to his left. He then reeled off sixteen names in alphabetical order. An almost inaudible sigh of disappointment circulated as the recruits realised that the names formed a list made up of both groups. Gone was the forlorn hope that mates would be allowed to stick together. Over to the line went George Moody, John Merrigan, Tom Dodds and Fat Harry, plus a few others Ted wasn't bothered about. But Ted stayed where he was and so did Billy Robson and Jacky Tait and Cockney Joe. Bloody great!

The lance corporal handed the clipboard to Corporal Lawrie and turned to the ragged line.

'Right you lot.' He spoke with an unfamiliar accent that nobody could quite place, though they later learned he hailed from somewhere in Yorkshire. Ted wasn't the only one to wonder if there was anybody in the Durham Light Infantry who was actually from Durham. 'From now on you are known as Number One Squad. I am Lance Corporal Carter. I understand you are already familiar with Corporal Lawrie because of his recruiting duties. It is our job to introduce you to army life. During the course of today I will teach you to march in step so that the next time you come to a parade you won't look like the God-forsaken bunch of mongers you look like now. Walk smartly around the edge of the parade ground until you come to the flagpole then stop. MOVE!'

With many a backward glance at their mates and at the sorry pile of personal effects under the table they set off towards their first taste of military life. Had they been allowed to speak they would have agreed to a man that this was not at all what they thought it would have been like.

And learn to march they did. The rain was beginning to ease off and weak sunshine emerged from behind the clouds. Two disparate bodies of men trying their hardest to march like the uniformed squad with whom they shared the parade ground, they were crude and clumsy and a professional soldier would have laughed at their attempts, but as they grew more confident and the rain finally ceased, they also became more proficient and got more into step with each other. Ted found it easier if you didn't try to think about it, just let your feet do the marching for you. Unfortunately, the spotty young lad next to him hadn't quite mastered this and was always bumping into Ted or catching his heels as they marched. He was constantly whispering 'sorry' and if it weren't for the fact he would be caught doing so Ted would have told him to forget it as long as he kept his bloody mouth shut. The lad couldn't have been more than about fourteen. so how the Hell had he got this far without anyone else seeing that?

Every so often Lance Corporal Carter would call the halt and rearrange the men in order to prevent those who couldn't walk in a straight line from ploughing into their fellows, or to put those with the longest stride at the front until they learned the art of marching with a step the same length as everybody else.

Surprisingly, even Lance Corporal Carter wasn't the monster everyone had expected. He was firm and gruff to be sure, but there were no insults hurled and he encouraged the men with brusque praise whenever the occasion demanded. However, although he never swore at them, he was never seen to smile either. They stopped at precisely twenty minutes to one, or twelve-forty hours as it was apparently known in the army and had a small but hearty helping of thick broth and a chunk of white bread served up in what looked like a big sardine tin.

The men ate with relish. The sun had come out properly now which cheered them up immensely and they were all proud of the progress they were making with their drill and discussed it enthusiastically. The corporal and lance corporal stood just outside the awning in the at ease position and talked quietly together while the men ate. At that moment a piercing whistle blew: one long blast and one short. Although the men had never heard the combination before, they immediately recognised it for what it was. It was done with the same timing as the orders they were given whilst drilling. Squa-a-ad Halt! or Le-e-eft Wheel! An order was an order and already instant obedience was instilled; everyone fell silent and looked at the two NCOs.

It was Corporal Lawrie who spoke. 'Right men, you now have five minutes to finish eating.' He pointed at a zinc bath few paces away. 'Wash your mess tins there and relieve yourselves behind that screen over there.' He was indicating a sorry-looking canvas windbreak that had been erected at the bottom of the parade ground slope near some trees. 'And don't mix them up.'

A desultory laugh broke out amongst the lads as they shuffled amiably towards the battered bath.

'When the next whistle blows you will all assemble on the edge of the parade ground in your squads... MOVE YOURSELVES!'

They accelerated accordingly, washed out their mess tins and placed them on the trestle table indicated before running to the latrine area. But it still took four or five minutes to form up into the two squads again, as the lads were watching, fascinated, while the uniformed soldiers were crawling in a well-formed line across the still soaking ground, holding their pick handles in the firing position. The squads did not move off immediately but were allowed to observe as the uniformed men rose and spread into skirmish order, moving silently, man covering man, towards the two squads. Sheepish grins broke out amongst the lads as they were approached but nobody uttered a sound for fear of reprisal from their NCOs.

Suddenly, the order to charge was barked and each man in uniform let out a blood-curdling howl and hurled himself at the horrified recruits, using the pick handles as though they were bayoneted rifles. The squads disintegrated like chaff and an instant before he broke Ted was stunned to recognise the maniac bearing down on him as none other than Jimmy Barker, his mate from the pit at Langley. It was all over in a few seconds. The uniformed men ground to a halt and relaxed, grinning like Cheshire cats at the confused and scattered recruits. A burst of laughter to his right made Ted look round in time to see Fat Harry climbing clumsily out of the zinc bath and swearing in the most awful way.

'YOU! Cut that language out, there are women and children present. Now form yourselves back into your squads... MOVE!'

Although they were all still shaken by the sudden and brutal attack, the lads formed up at least quickly enough for Lance Corporal Carter not to have to shout at them again. Once they were in line, Corporal Lawrie walked up, staring each man in the eye as he did so. He then planted himself smartly front centre and spoke.

'You have just experienced your first charge, gentlemen, and you behaved more like a bunch of schoolgirls than the soldiers you are supposed to be. That is how the enemy attack – suddenly and with great ferocity. And you, gentlemen, will learn to stand. You are no earthly use as soldiers to King George if you cannot stand. Remember that above all else. Now, let's learn to march some more, shall we?'

Now it was the turn of the uniformed soldiers to spectate as the raw recruits practiced their way around the parade ground. Tarpaulins had appeared and were spread on the ground for them to sit on. Some of the men had discarded their battledress tops, which hung like washing from the shelter's guy-ropes. They sat in the watery sun drinking tea and eating snacks they had brought with them in their bait-boxes and the whole thing had the easy air of a picnic. It was obvious from the comments and laughter that they were being thoroughly entertained.

Each overheard derisory comment served only to harden the resolve of the new recruits. It didn't take long to realise that marching together was nothing to do with magic or talent. It was simply application and hard work. Somewhere along the way the uniforms went missing but there was no time to dwell on where or why; the lads were marching! Nobody knew exactly when the mood changed but by the time they were into their last half hour before dismissal, the air of apprehension had gone, and so had the rain. In between the barked commands and the sarcastic insults, a mood of confident defiance had descended on the two marching bodies.

Finally, they were dismissed for a ten-minute break and a mug of tea. They began queuing and lighting tabs when they heard the distant clacking of iron-shod boots marching towards the camp from the direction of the Old Castle road. The uniforms were returning. The clacking grew louder and when they came into view, an officer was leading them on horseback. It was Lieutenant Brass from the recruiting day in the chapel. Where the Hell had he come from? Ted filed away the question with the others that would never be answered, like 'what's a monger?' and 'when do the NCOs eat?' He could not help but admire them just the same. You would never know they had spent a hard day drilling in what started off as bloody awful weather. The soldiers' heavy khaki uniforms were still wet, as was his own civilian clothing, but it was almost as if the soldiers took no notice. They marched up that road as if they were off to a great parade in Durham. There wasn't a recruit who didn't have a lump in his throat just watching them.

The squad came to a cracking halt on the road immediately behind the flagpole and did an 'into line' left turn. Their heels dug into the road with a snap like the report from a single rifle, and the sergeant in charge about turned and stood rigidly to attention. He said something quietly and a couple of men left the end of the formation and ran off to pick up a little wooden podium and set it up to the right of the flagpole. A refreshing breeze was getting up now and all the men were thankful for it. Uniformed or not, this amount of marching was bloody hard work, but even the Union Flag finally managed to unfurl itself and ripple out a bit into the weak sunshine.

'A and B Companies... wash your mugs out and get formed up... NOW!'

The lads did so swiftly and efficiently and were marched to the opposite end of the parade ground where they were halted facing the flagpole across the square. Lieutenant Brass and a sergeant none of them had seen before were standing on the podium and the two sergeants that were on duty on recruiting day were marching smartly towards the apprehensive squads. Their immaculately turned out uniforms contrasted sharply with the damp, mud-spattered ones on the main body of men.

'Now we're for it lads!' It was Billy Robson's whisper.

The whole squad saw the lance corporal twitch at the misdemeanour and collectively willed Billy to drop dead there and then before he got the bloody lot of them killed.

The stout sergeant from recruiting day marched up to Ted's squad and came to a halt beside Lance Corporal Carter. It was Carter who spoke first, snapping to attention.

'Number One Squad ready for inspection and parade, sergeant.'

'Thank you, Lance Corporal. Dismiss.'

Lance Corporal Carter executed a smart right turn and marched off leaving the lads to the sergeant. As he did, they heard exactly the same words being spoken away to their left as the corporal handed over the other squad.

Ted's guts were tying themselves in knots with apprehension. He had never forgotten being shouted at by the sergeant in the chapel on recruiting day and wanted no repeat of the incident.

'Now men, I'm Sergeant Malone. You might remember me from my recruiting duties. I'm one of the few senior NCOs in the Eighth Battalion Durham Light Infantry who is actually from Durham.'

That raised a smile from the lads and put them at their ease a bit. Even as he was smiling, Ted remembered the roasting he took in the recruiting office from this apparently affable man.

'Well, lads, you've had a wonderful day being taught to march as a body and now you're going to show Lieutenant Brass up there what you've learned. I'm not going to ask you to do anything you haven't already done so just keep your ears open and do everything sharpish when you're told.' He looked across to the other squad and got the nod from his opposite number, who happened to be Sergeant Hanson, the soldier who had bought all the lads a pint in the Blue Star the day they enlisted. 'Right, men, we're leading off. Look smart now.'

He took a breath so deep it looked like the buttons on his tunic would pop.

'Squa-a-ad, Atte-e-en-shun!'

Bloody Hell! Ted had done it. He was at attention and didn't remember how he had got there.

'Into line, right turn!'

And they were off. For the next quarter of an hour the two squads performed every manoeuvre they had spent the entire day practicing. It wasn't perfect but it was bloody good; even the spotty kid next to Ted was managing to keep in step most of the time. Ted's nose had started to itch abominably but there was bugger all he could do except keep his gaze hard in between the shoulder blades of the man in front and thank God he wasn't in the lead. All he had to do was listen and follow. He was even beginning to enjoy it. They were marching in column along the road side of the square towards the podium now. Out of the corner of his eye he could see a line of muddy uniforms standing rigidly to attention on the road and as the sergeant drew level with the podium a brisk, 'Eyes Right', made every head except the left marker's, snap round. Lieutenant Brass was saluting and staring right into the eyes of the men, who were staring right back. He caught Ted's eye and held his gaze for a moment, Ted could not resist smiling slightly with the sheer joy of it all. If this is what it's like to be a soldier, it's bloody great!

A few more manoeuvres and the men were halted in front of the podium.

Lieutenant Brass stood at ease and made a short speech about how well they had progressed in such a few short hours from raw recruits to soldiers who could be proud of their ability to take orders without question and march together as a seasoned unit. Quite a few of the lads thought he was laying it on a bit thick but he was likeable enough chap and they knew that there was nothing wrong with a bit of encouragement. Ted's nose had stopped itching but he was bursting for a piss. He had no idea what time it was. They were told to be proud of their achievements, what to look forward to in the coming weeks, and that their uniforms would be arriving in a month or so, when they would look like real soldiers. He then dismissed them and gave the order to strike camp.

Ted practically ran to the latrine. He wasn't the only one either, and after abundantly relieving himself he lit a tab and sauntered back. The camp was practically struck already. The uniformed men all knew exactly what to do and each man bent to his specific duty. Tarpaulins were rolled up and tents neatly stored on a flatbed wagon while the village children fussed around the horse and fed it chunks of bread. Most of the new recruits were milling around in groups, smoking and chatting. Some had retrieved their boots and belongings from under the trestle table and that's where Ted was headed when he noticed his squad was re-forming over by the flagpole.

His brow knotted and a fleeting moment of indecision overtook him. He glanced at the quickly dwindling pile of boots and was suddenly worried that his own might not be there when he went for them, but already the iron discipline of the army was too instilled to ignore. He changed direction towards the squad and broke into a trot to join them. Lance Corporal Carter was standing rigidly to attention, as were the men, when Ted fell in.

'Thank you for joining us, Smith. I suppose none of you have the slightest idea why, when the rest of you are off home for a bath, a meal and a pint of ale, you lot are stood to attention awaiting orders. Anybody?'

There was an eminently sensible silence from the squad.

'We are here, gentlemen, because we are the worst squad. It is my privilege and honour to be in charge of a squad that can't or won't obey orders. It's not that you can't drill or that you can't march. It's that you can't keep fucking quiet. YOU!'

The men watched in horror as spittle flecked from the lance corporal's mouth as he practically screamed the word at Billy Robson.

'2494 Robson.'

Christ, he even remembered his number!

'One pace forward march!'

Billy executed the step smartly, his bottom lip was trembling and his knuckles were white.

'Robson, gentlemen, is a little chatterbox, aren't you?'

Billy said nothing. His eyes seemed to be bulging from his head with the strain of standing so rigidly to attention. He stared straight ahead.

'What's the matter Robson? Now that I have given you the opportunity to chatter away, you don't seem to want to. Is it just that you prefer to chatter when you're not supposed to? Like when I'm just about to hand the squad over to Sergeant Malone for the Inaugural Parade?'

Billy was fighting to keep back the tears as he blurted out his protest, only to be cut short as Carter screamed at him again.

'He saw your lips move, you fucking monger! He saw you and I heard you!'

Billy began to wave his arms as he pleaded his innocence, only to be cut short again. 'Shut up! Stand still! Get to attention!'

There was a pause as Lance Corporal Carter stared pure hatred at Billy.

'Right gentlemen. Because Robson finds himself unable to obey the simplest order and keep his mouth shut it has fallen upon this squad to tidy the latrine area before final dismissal. I do not take kindly to this, and nor should you. You marched the arse off the other squad but you were let down by a comrade who thinks so little of us and so much of himself that he dropped every one of us in the shite. I do not take kindly to that at all. Robson, one pace to the rear, march! Squad, into line right turn! Quick march!'

And the squad marched smartly and ever so silently towards the latrine area, where someone had thoughtfully thrust eight or nine shit shovels into the still damp grass all ready to use. While Ted was cutting new turf he ran over the events of the day and came to a few conclusions about how to improve his lot for next time. Bring more bait and some toilet paper in a greaseproof bag were two things that sprang to mind, plus threaten Billy Robson with actual bodily harm. Not much else though.

When the onerous duty was at an end and the pits had been neatly turfed the men were dismissed for a final time and Ted was reassured to find his boots were still in the small pile that remained. It was John Merrigan's that had gone missing.

Chapter 10

Langley Park, Colliery Village, Sunday 5th April 1914

Sunday morning! Ted was awake bright and early and was relieved to see sunshine trying to force its way through the thin curtains covering the bedroom window. Beside him, Bertha was snoring softly and he decided to be the gentleman and go downstairs to break the fire open and, if the noise didn't wake her up, bring her a cup of tea in bed. He smiled to himself as he stared fondly at his wife. He had half a mind to run his hand gently through her hair, or to trace the little wrinkles at the corner of her eyes with the back of his fingers. Did she have more wrinkles? Or were they the same ones etched a bit deeper? In the end, he did none of these things and slid quietly out of bed.

He had hardly begun to move when he inhaled sharply with the pain in his leg. Yesterday's camp at Burnhope had taken its toll of his injury and neither the hot bath that had awaited him in front of the fire nor the early night afterwards had served to relieve the ache of the fracture. He was a young man, not yet twenty, and it seemed terribly unfair to him that he might have to carry the pain of his accident with him for the rest of his life. He managed a wry grin as he swung his feet carefully to the floor and philosophised that it was probably due just as much to the exercise he had taken in bed last night, as it was to the exercise at the camp. At the thought, a warm ache abruptly thrilled through his body. He looked again at his young wife who was blissfully unaware that she had suddenly become the object of his desire.

No! Sort the fire out and bring her a cup of tea, she'd be even more keen then! Ted pulled his jumper on over his combinations and padded downstairs grinning to himself. A bit more exercise and his leg should be nicely warmed up for the handball match later on at the Blue Star.

Once the fire was roaring merrily away he put the kettle on without the whistle and went back upstairs to collect the dirty cups from the bedrooms. Since it was the weekend, Robert had gone back to Sunniside on the bike to see Louise but he was by now famous at Number Eight Logan Street for having a collection of dirty cups under his bed which, were it not for Ted and Bertha, would never find their way downstairs again. Ted looked in on her. Good! Still snoring. He pushed open the door to Robert's room and, sure enough, there on the floor by the unmade bed, next to his violin, were two cups and a mug, which left to their own devices, would surely start growing things.

* * * * *

Bertha heard her name being quietly called; it was fuzzy and distant but as sleep retreated it became clearer.

'Hello pet, I've brought you a cup of tea.'

'Oh, aye? What's this, Christmas?'

'No,' he smiled gently, watching the redness begin to disappear from her nose and eyes. 'Just Sunday morning, pet, and I thought mebbes I would bring my wife a cup of tea in bed, that's all.'

He went to the foot of the bed and bent down to retrieve the two mugs he had set down on the floorboards. They were no longer boiling but were still hot enough to be welcome, especially when you didn't have to get up to a cold house and put the fire on first.

Bertha heaved herself up, pounded the bolster pillows into a comfier shape and took her tea. 'Thanks, pet.'

'I'm really good to you, you know that?' he said as he climbed back into bed beside her, being careful not to spill his tea. Her eyes widened in disbelief.

'Aye, well, just wait 'till I tell your Mam you bring your wife cups of tea in bed.'

She almost exploded into laughter as she saw the complacency driven from his face and instantly replaced with a look of serious concern as he stared at her open-mouthed.

'You wouldn't... would you?'

She couldn't help grinning. 'Well I might. If you didn't do as you were told from now on, like.'

Ted stared at her for a second then drank off his tea in one great draught. 'Anything you say, pet.' He grinned putting the mug on the floor. 'Where do I start?'

* * * * *

Ted's leg was hurting like Hell. They were losing the handball match three Aces to two and it wasn't fair. He was teamed up with Jacky Tait against a couple of lads from Wallnook. The last point against them was a complete fluke. Jacky volleyed the ball low and it had rebounded a fraction above the tell-board, the horizontal plank at the bottom of the wall. If the ball hit the plank, the opposing team was awarded an Ace and the referee, old Matty Jobling, hadn't seen it right, so called the Ace to the Wallnook lads. Bugger!

It looked complicated but really it was just like footy except played up against a wall. It was all properly marked out but sharp eyes were needed to keep up with the play. Langley Park, always biggest and best at everything, had its very own purpose-built court here in the Blue Star yard. The lads played on.

Lost ball! Mr Jobling waved an arm for play on. Caesar began a spate of gruff barking from where he was tethered beside the gates, presumably to chivvy the lads up not to lose on home ground.

The teams lined up ready for the next point. With only five Aces per match there was no leeway. Somebody Preston, the older of the Wallnook lads, slammed the ball with all his might low against the wall and ran back in front of Jacky. Ted was right behind him though, reading the move well, and when the ball shot back (Christ! these India rubber buggers couldn't half fly!) he was in a good position to return it. The ball sailed towards him. He opened his palm ready to clout it back when suddenly he felt a burst of pain in his ribs. That bastard Preston had elbowed him on the way past and the split second it took him to recover was all that was needed for the Wallnook lads to pick up the advantage and send the ball sailing towards the back wall again.

Miss! Serve the buggers right!

Still, three Aces to two to Wallnook; all to play for now and Jacky's serve. The antagonists positioned themselves quickly. They were all knackered and sweating but this had turned into a real grudge match and nobody was about to concede

Unstoppable serve... three Aces each.

The lads lined up again and in the few seconds of quiet, Ted snatched a glance around the small crowd. He registered two or three of his mates, pints in hands, nodding towards Freddy Wardle who sat on his old cracket. His cap was pushed back on his head to keep the sun on his face. He held a small book in one hand and a stubby pencil in the other. Some of the miners were crowding around him and putting their hands into their pockets for coppers. Good. The odds were going their way again. All that could be heard was the feral panting as the lads gasped, open-mouthed, for breath. Even Caesar had fallen silent.

It was Preston to serve and he was standing well inside the short line. Jacky was up near him while Ted and the other Wallnook boy, somebody Hoggard, hung back, marking each other with fierce concentration. Four–three to Wallnook. Damn!

Then something shifted in Ted's head and when the next serve hit the back wall he saw, he actually saw it connect with the stonework and gradually appear to compress before returning to its original shape and float off noiselessly upwards into an unmarked space. Suddenly Preston was there, waiting; he knew what was going on all right. Ted smiled to himself. *Too slow, way too bloody slow.*

As far as Ted was concerned, the play may have lasted for seconds or hours. Everything was flowing in graceful calmness. The noise of the crowd had receded and his leg had stopped hurting. There was nothing else in the whole world except that little black ball. It was the only thing in focus against a backdrop of blurred images that constantly moved and shifted unhurriedly as the opposing teams drifted around the court endeavouring to overcome one another. But again and again the ball refused to go out of play, and the languorous dance went on.

Then something jarred, Preston had caught the ball! That could cost you an Ace! Yet there he was, the bastard, with his back to the crowd and in Jacky's blind spot with his fingers firmly encircling the bloody ball. Hoggard knew what was going on, though, and was loping over to the corner, all arms and legs, to block Jacky.

The noise from the crowd was a low rumble, like snow sliding off a roof. Ted saw Preston open his hand and throw the ball a couple of inches vertically before sending it slamming past Jacky towards his mate. What in God's name was Jacky doing? He finally galvanised himself into action and crashed into Hoggard in the process. Hoggard yelped and began to collapse like a sack full of bones. The low rumbling of the crowd increased in volume and there was Caesar, barking in sympathy.

Don't Jacky, man, leave it!

Stone and rubber connected and the rebound left the ball a good six inches in play as Jacky, skidding along on his stomach managed to grasp it firmly in his fist. He slid to a stop with his chest over a big piece of dog shit that Caesar had deposited before the games began. Ted's shoulders dropped like two sacks of taties. He didn't need to be told that it was all over. Jacky's dive had caused a foul on the Hoggard lad, which meant an Ace would be awarded against them making it five–three. Abruptly, the bass rumble of the crowd burst back to hysterical familiarity. All sounds speeded up and raised an octave, blurring everything together again, and Ted felt the change like a blow to the head. He looked at Jacky sitting by the wall; his shirt was covered in dog shit and he was still holding the ball in his hand. Guilty as Hell! Mr Jobling's whistle sounded like it was miles away and his thin, reedy voice pronounced the score of five Aces to three and a win to the Wallnook lads... Bugger! Jacky stood up and looked just this side of bursting into tears. He came over to Ted and was all apologies, saying he didn't know what had come over him and all the rest. The truth was he had panicked and done something daft, and that was all there was to it. Ted thanked the Lord that it hadn't been him, and tried to forget the whole thing.

There would be other matches and up to now, touch wood, Ted and Jacky had won a sight more than they had lost. He collected his jacket and cap from the pile by the door leading into the bar, and picked up Jacky's at the same time. The crowd around Freddie flowed as winnings were collected then ebbed away again to be replaced by another mob betting coppers on the next game. The new contestants had already been called and were removing their caps and jackets in preparation for the match.

Young Patrick Brannon had emerged from the bar and was cleaning up the remaining shit. That was his job prior to every match day and indeed he had dutifully done so that morning, but either he had not been as attentive as he should or else Caesar managed a secret one after Patrick had finished just to confound the lad. Either way he was in trouble with his Dad, whose customers didn't like being covered in dog shit unnecessarily.

Normally, Ted would have stayed to watch a couple more games but he was no longer in the mood. It was one thing to bask in a bit of glory and backslapping and quite another to have the piss taken, however good-naturedly, by your mates. He would have a pint and go home. The ribbing would soon stop anyway, these men would only bet what they could afford and they could afford very little. The last games incidents would be forgotten as soon as the next one started. Pulling on his jacket, he fished in his trouser pocket for the coppers to buy Jacky and himself a pint and walked into the twilight, smoky atmosphere of the bar.

Jacky walked in a few moments later and the smell of dog shit wafted in with him, provoking all the appropriate comments, both serious and comical. John was just in the middle of pulling a pint when the odour hit his nostrils. He looked up sharply. He was a genial, rotund man of middling height and, unusually, he sported a short beard. He stared at Jacky over the top of his spectacles.

'Mr Tait, if you were me, do you think you would allow that smell to annoy your paying customers?'

'It was your dog that did it in the first place and your lad who's supposed to clean it up.'

This was true. Patrick Brannon was given the princely sum of a ha'penny worth of chips from Todd's Fish Shop for keeping the yard clean. Nobody quite figured out how Patrick came to be paid in chips but most reckoned something was going on between John and Mrs Todd. He was a real Langley Park lothario, was John.

Although the reply was defiant, Jacky stared at his feet like an errant schoolboy. 'Besides, I live at the other end of the village, man. I'm buggered if I'm going home before I've had some ale.'

John had finished pulling the pint and put it carefully onto the counter. All eyes were now focussed on what looked like a juicy argument and bearing in mind it was John's pub there was no doubt who would win it.

Ted stepped in, warily holding up Jacky's cap and jacket.

'It's all right, John. He's just collecting his gear, man.'

The landlord said nothing but tipped his head slightly to one side and stared at Ted... no words were required. Ted felt himself start to blush. Damn! He spoke in what he hoped was a casual manner.

'Jacky, just nip up to ours and tell Bertha to give you a clean shirt, will you? You can give us it back later, eh?'

There were a few sharp intakes of breath and whistles at that! Langley Park women were pretty good at doing as they were told but this was pushing the boundaries. Jacky never took his eyes off John as he put his cap on and took his jacket in his clean hand.

'Get us a pint in, Ted. I'll be back.' With all the dignity he could muster, which wasn't much when he was covered in dog shit, he turned on his heel and left the pub.

Ted dutifully ordered the pints for himself and Jacky and stood at the bar, rolling himself a tab. The banter had died down a bit by the time Jacky had returned, resplendent in Ted's best Sunday shirt, minus the collar. The wolf whistles soon started.

'Hey, Ted, your Bertha dresses Jacky better than she dresses you, man.'

'Aye! You'd better ask him what he's done to deserve that shirt, eh?'

'Why, aye! Considering he was only gone five minutes I'm surprised he isn't more in demand.'

The comments and the laughter rolled around the pub and a red-necked Ted wished it would settle somewhere else; and in a little while it did. By the third pint, it was getting well on towards midday and, it being a Sunday that meant the best meal of the week. A well-oiled Cockney Joe was offering to buy a fifth round but was also becoming more belligerent. Ted and a couple of others had refused as dinnertime was looming. It looked more and more like Joe would be late for his dinner again but with some of the men folk this was normal, as it was normal for their wives to sigh patiently and try to keep the meal fresh and warm until their husbands rolled in drunk, or in some cases throw it in the bin as a lesson they knew their men would never learn. Ted lit a last tab and prepared to leave, saying he might be back again later. He always said that but rarely turned up; it was just easier to depart that way. He was looking forward to a walk with Bertha that afternoon if the weather stayed fine and anyway, he wanted to know why in God's name she had given Jacky his best shirt, his best bloody shirt! What was the lass playing at?

* * * * *

The afternoon had been really pleasant and the world was a lovely place to live in. Dressed in their Sunday Best clothes, and arm in arm, Ted and Bertha set out for their after dinner walk. Nor were they alone; it was the custom all over the county for families to round off their Sunday dinners by dressing in their finest clothes and setting off into the countryside surrounding their villages. It was a rare chance for the entire family to be together.

So, every Sunday just for a couple of hours, the men and women of the north-east proved they could rise above their monotonous existence, proved they were more than work-weary miners with downtrodden wives and wayward children. Once a week, scrubbed clean and decked out in all their finery they would set off out of the dirty villages into the countryside beyond and show the world they were more than that!

It amused Ted no end to hear his wife say, 'That's the same hat as last week but with different feathers' or 'She's borrowed that coat from such-

and-such and put a different brooch in.' Apparently there was no end to the permutations women would try in order to look fresh and exciting.

As they headed back they could hear the strains of a brass band floating up towards them. From their high vantage point overlooking the village it didn't take Bertha long to locate the source.

'Salvation Army outside the Blue Star, pet. Come to save us all.'

Ted had never been deeply religious, though he had faith, but Bertha had been brought up in the bosom of a God-fearing community and it would remain with her all the days of her life. Anyway, it was a rare treat to hear any kind of music and as often as not when a band assembled on the little square in front of the Blue Star the couple would join others in wandering down just to sing a few of the hymns, as would Patrick Brannon, temporarily excused his public house duties and sent forth by his father. Unfortunately so would their dog Caesar, who could be heard from the handball court barking loudly and enthusiastically if not precisely in time.

They arrived at the little gathering holding hands and feeling wonderfully content. Little Lizzie Todd, the chip-shop girl with the beautiful hair, held out a hymn book in one hand and a little wooden offertory box in the other. They declined the hymn book with a smile and Ted took a couple of copper coins from his pocket and dropped them into the box. Captain Forsyth, thin as a rake, bespectacled and resplendent in full uniform gave his tiny congregation a benign smile. Ted's eyes swept over the band. They were all ages and sizes with the usual clean but ill-fitting uniforms and indifferently polished shoes. He felt a thrill of pride to be in the real army where such slackness would not be tolerated – until he remembered he didn't have his uniform yet.

The next hymn was *Abide with Me* and the first verse was sung as a solo by Mr Eggleshaw. He may have held the lofty position of stationmaster at Witton Station but here, on a calm Sunday afternoon, he was a mere private in the army serving the Good Lord. The second verse saw everyone lift their voices in praise, and if the singing was not perfect then the music from the band lent dignity to the efforts of the flock. As Ted sang quietly, he noticed that though the uniforms did not equal his expectations, the instruments belonging to the band members were so lovingly cared for that he felt a brief stab of shame for his sin of vanity. His gaze met Bertha's and he followed her eyes to little Jimmy Raper, Tommy's lad, who, at ten years old, couldn't lift the big bass drum he was beating and had to rest it on a bit of linoleum on the ground in front of him, holding the top with one hand while he struck it with the other. They exchanged a grin and sang on through *The King of Love my Shepherd is*, at which point big Walter Timms and his mate Tommy, who had just left the pub and were somewhat the worse for drink, joined them.

Now, it was the turn of Captain Forsyth to begin his customary short sermon.

'Welcome one and all,' he intoned in his high, reedy voice. 'Welcome to the Lord's gathering. My heart is filled with gladness at the sight of you all on this fine, spring evening. I am so happy that my faith in the Lord Jesus Christ has swollen tenfold at the sight of you all. Search your hearts, dear brothers and sisters. Search your hearts and souls and share with us all here the reason for your own joy and happiness in the sight of the Lord.'

As if on cue and to help any newcomers to the little congregation, one of the women in the band, a tambourine player who neither Ted nor Bertha could place, stepped forward and chanted,

'I'm so happy I could sing hymns in praise of the Lord for ever.'

She stepped back into her place with a little flourish on her tambourine and the scene was set. Immediately a member of the congregation, a middle-aged lady in a ragged shawl but wearing a stunning bonnet that appeared to contain an entire bird's nest, stepped forward and chirped, 'I'm so happy that being with the Lord makes the sun shine in my heart.'

A little ripple of applause ran around the group, and big Walter nodded his drunken head and beamed stupidly as the mood caught him. He clumsily fondled the head of the little bass drummer, nearly knocking his cap off. Polite clapping gently punctuated each subsequent affirmation of faith.

Fat Ena and her little sausage dog had just rounded the corner from one of her trips to the bottle-and-jug. Ted saw her first and rolled his eyes skyward at the same time as receiving a warning elbow in the ribs from his wife. Walter hawked loudly and cleared his throat, spitting a huge dottle of coal-sodden phlegm onto the ground behind him. He had just taken a shambling step forward when Fat Ena sang up in the shrillest voice Ted had ever heard.

'I'm so happy that when the Lord took away my man he left me the gift of Clementine here, to accompany me on my journey through life, like.' She winked at her grandson on the bass drum and little Jimmy blushed furiously. Sometimes it was a good idea not to have a Gran.

Walter, who was not in the least offended by this blatant queue-jumping felt his heart soar as he joyfully bellowed, 'And I'm so happy I could put my foot through that fucking drum!'

He stuck his thumbs in his waistcoat pockets and beamed around at the little group for approval, totally oblivious of the blanket of stunned silence that had settled over them. After what seemed like an eternity an embarrassed Tommy shuffled forward and put a couple of coppers in the offertory box before gently taking Walter by the arm and leading him away, still smiling, up George Street.

A signal from Captain Forsyth and the band hastily struck up *Dear Lord and Father of Mankind* and, by the dying strains of the last verse, the incident was forgotten. Ted felt his hand being squeezed gently and he knew that the signal meant it was time to go. A simple tea was waiting, followed by an evening playing floater in front of the fire. As soon as they entered the yard at Number Eight, Ted went to the netty leaving Bertha to open the house. There was a note stuck in the sneck of the back door addressed to Ted and covered in coal-stained fingerprints. It was only a folded piece of paper but it was addressed to her husband and it was not her place to open it so she took it into the house with her and laid it on the kitchen table while she banked up the fire and put the kettle on to boil.

Ted came into the house all smiles, rubbing his hands together in anticipation of his tea. She nodded to the note as she cut the bread into thick slices and he read it with apparent glee.

'Champion!' he said, 'just champion!' He showed it to his wife.

In a scrawling, untidy hand, it said simply: *Uniforms in, get this Sat. H.G.*

'What do you think of that, pet, eh? Pick my uniform up on Saturday and next week's Sunday walk you'll be arm in arm with a real soldier! What do you think of that, eh?' He lit a tab and inhaled deeply with great satisfaction.

The evening was pleasant enough but he did not notice his wife was quieter than usual.

Chapter 11

Langley Park, Colliery Village, Monday 6th April 1914

The next morning at ten to six Ted was standing at his back door saying goodbye to his wife. He had a pint of hot tea and a crispy bacon sandwich in his belly and with the prospect of being a uniformed soldier one day nearer he was as happy as could be.

Suddenly, from a few doors up the street a muffled scream rang out and a deep voice began to shout. It was Cockney Joe Simpson. The words were too muffled to be heard but there was no mistaking the enraged tone in his voice nor Lettie's frantic pleading. For a few moments they were both to be heard together in a heated argument that rose and rose in hysteria to cease suddenly with the stomach-churning crunch of fist on flesh and the sound of Lettie collapsing into the house like a broken doll. The gate slammed hard against its sneck, followed by Joe, still muttering obscenities to himself, storming angrily up the street to the pit.

Neither Ted nor Bertha realised that they were hugging each other so tightly as they stood in their own doorway, hardly daring to draw breath. For a long moment silence hung above them like a shroud until the keening of an infant invaded the air with heart-wrenching misery. A pitiful sobbing joined the sound and after a few moments they faded away together as the hapless Lettie picked up little Sarah and quietly closed the door on their misery. Ted suddenly felt his wife shiver in their embrace and she buried her face into his chest and clung to him as though she would never let go.

He gently began to disengage himself from her and after a moment of hesitation she allowed him do so.

'I'll see you a bit later on, Bertha, eh?'

'Aye pet, I'll nip up to Lettie's afterwards and see if I can find out what's going on, shall I?'

Ted snorted and placed a tab in his mouth, 'I reckon we know what's going on, pet. Cockney Joe's in the shit. He can't pay his way. He's been a funny bugger for a couple of months now, working every shift he can put in and he reckoned down the Star the other night he only joined the Territorials for the money.'

He lit his tab and exchanged a forlorn smile with his wife and, slamming the gate behind him, set off up the street to work. A few people were stirring by now and despite the early hour a steady stream of men were making their way to the pit.

Now that Ted had gone, Bertha took down his Sunday overcoat from the hanger behind the stair door and put it on over her woolly shawl which in turn covered her nightdress. She pulled the cracket up to the fire and poured herself the dregs from the pot of tea. It was stewed and over-strong by now and not as she preferred it, but it was hot and welcome and as she stared into the flames of the fire she thought hard about the incident that had happened a few minutes before. The wailing of the little girl haunted her and over and over. In her mind she could hear the sickening sound of that punch. Where had Joe struck her? How badly was she injured? What had Sarah seen, poor little bairn?

About half past eight, while she was in the middle of possing Ted's shirts in the tub in the yard, Harry Fairbairn came down the street and leaned on her gate.

'What cheer, flower. Doing the washing are you?'

She looked up and said 'Yes Mr Fairbairn, I am.' She paused to brush a stray lock of hair from her face, 'Have you got any post for us?'

'Naw, just stopped for a bit of crack, like. Cannot walk past a bonny lass like you without saying hello, can I?'

Bugger off, will you!

Bertha refused to look up, staring hard at the shirts as they foundered amongst the suds at the bottom of the tub. Eventually, she heard a sigh as he detached himself from the fence.

'I see Number Twelve has got itself an eviction notice on the door. Ta-ra flower.'

She hated him, how she hated him, with his big nose and his smelly postbag. How dare he fancy her! Anyway, he was gone now. She leaned on the poss stick, weary with the exhaustion of trying to ignore the postman.

It was true, then; Cockney Joe was being evicted.

This was all because of those bloody tick men, they had no business pestering honest folk and tempting them with money. *Forgive us our temptations.* Isn't that what the Lord's Prayer said? Well Lettie had been tempted all right. And it turned out that what she had borrowed was more than she could pay back. Of course, she had done so without Joe's knowledge and when he found out he had been rightly furious; but the damage was done. Within a month of handing over the loan the tick men would be back for the first of the repayments. Then it dawned on you that you would be repaying a damned sight more than you borrowed and if you couldn't repay that they would either loan you even more money or extend the repayment period and before you know it you would owe five or six times more again. Then they would come for you.

If you couldn't pay they would take your valuables and your furniture and sell them for a fraction of what they were worth and you would still be in debt to them for the balance, and the interest was mounting. If you still couldn't pay they would inform your employer that you were a 'bad debt' and your employer would 'help' you by giving half your wages to the loan firms direct and you would be severely admonished for dragging the name of your respectable company through the mud... And you were still in debt. And at the last, came eviction.

This is where the colliery finally saved you from yourself. The rent for your house was deducted from your wages at the Colliery Offices, and an eviction would mean settling your family with relatives (or in the workhouse) and you could live with whoever would keep you, thus releasing the rent money for the loan companies. The fact that it also released the house for another miner to rent was bye the bye. Bertha closed her eyes as she remembered the great handful of money the tick man had shown her just before Christmas and thanked the Good Lord for giving her the common sense to resist such temptation.

She had rinsed the shirts and was hanging them on the line when Lettie came to the gate with little Sarah in her arms. Her top lip was split open in the middle and her cheeks were swollen. Blood was crusted around her nostrils and grief haunted her eyes. Bertha motioned her indoors and broke open the damped down fire to put the kettle on.

So began the ritual. Eviction always took place at noon on a Friday, and now there was no stopping it. Rare though the occurrence was, a grisly ceremony had grown out of it during the short years of the village's life.

On the Monday previous to the date of the event, the notice to quit was pinned onto the defaulter's door. There would follow a sinister, silent stirring in the community. Eddie Todd, one of the carpenters at the pit and a cousin of the fish shop owner, was the first to visit the hapless household and would always be seen to leave with a satisfied smile on his bovine features. More vegetables than usual were being harvested from the allotments belonging to the families in the street and the shopkeepers would note a fall in trade from those same families. During the week, black-faced men would come straight from their shift at the pit to the unfortunate family's door, with coins jangling in their blue-scarred fists. A bargain would be struck, hands spat upon and shaken. Then whatever furniture or meagre valuables had been purchased would be spirited away. Money from such deals was given into the safekeeping of a friend until after the bailiffs had been so there was none to be had in the house; but you couldn't hide a dining room table or an English oak press.

The day of the eviction arrived. It was well before nine o' clock when any unsold items of a size to be carried away were brought into the yard to form a pathetic pile of jetsam ready to be sold off for coppers. A chamber pot here or a good gully knife there: anything that would add to the money the victims would need after they became homeless.

Bertha, who had been looking after Lettie all that week, could not resist the temptation to go up and join the small crowd forming at Number Twelve. Ted was at work and Robert was asleep so she had no one to answer to. She made up her mind to go but she still felt guilty, even though she had looked after the lass over the past few days, making sure her injuries were clean and that little Sarah was fed. Wrapping herself in her shawl, Bertha left Number Eight to join the little knot of women gathering in Lettie's yard. She had a couple of coppers in her pinny pocket and if she saw something useful she might as well have it as anybody else. The stuff for sale was pathetic; it was nearly all junk and she could see at a glance there was nothing she wanted. Lettie sat on a wooden chair by the door with Sarah on her lap, staring uncomprehendingly through swollen, bruised eyes.

Bertha had not got out of her how much she had borrowed off the tick man but it had been enough to go to Durham on the train and outfit little Sarah like a princess, as well as buy her Joe the Christmas present of his dreams. He had always wanted a gold fob watch with a cover on the front and she had hunted the place down for the best one she could afford. Those she had been shown in the jewellers were lovely but a bit pricey even considering the amount of money in her bag, but the nice man on the market stall told her a tale to end all tales about this watch. It had belonged to a great Earl whose daughter had committed suicide whilst on holiday in Switzerland and that he had beggared himself trying to find out why. He had sold his house, his land and finally even this beautiful pocket watch in pursuit of his quest to solve the mystery of his daughter's death and eventually died penniless and of a broken heart. His body was found frozen to the ground on the pauper's grave, which was all that the Swiss authorities would allow as a last resting place for his poor child.

Bertha thought that if that doesn't tell you the bloody thing was bad luck then nothing would! But Lettie had been moved to tears by the story and was moved to tears yet again when, on Christmas morning gone she had dressed Sarah in all her finery and made her wake her Dad from his sleep to give him with the present of his dreams.

Joe did not beat her. Instead, in his rage he upturned the bed and smashed the blue-glazed washbasin and jug against the tea chest that served as a dresser. He left the house, returning some hours later blind drunk and in a terrible rage. Lettie could only watch as he sat on the rocking chair by the fire with his arms clutched around his middle. He was rocking backwards and forwards and humming tunelessly to himself. Every so often he would dart a glance at the frightened girl. She could make nothing of this. It was supposed to be a wonderful Christmas Day. She clutched Sarah tighter and tighter to herself, as the humming grew louder and more discordant. Tears were running down Joe's pockmarked cheeks now and he was shuddering violently as he rocked back and forth. Then he let out a cry such as Lettie had never heard. It was anger and frustration and impotence and rage all rolled into one hideous howl. He tore the watch from his pocket and held it out for her to see.

'You see this, you stupid bugger, you've sent us to the poor house with this. What was you thinking of? It's not even gold, girl; it's not even proper gold!'

He hurled the watch to the floor with terrifying force and Lettie stared, wide-eyed as it exploded into a thousand pieces. The little springs and cogs shot out like tiny, glinting raindrops, cascading all over the room.

Tears welled up in his eyes again as he sobbed to himself, 'Not even real bloody gold.'

Hardly daring to breathe, Lettie and her daughter stole out of the back door and down the yard. If they were gone for a while he might go to sleep and mebbes wake up in a better mood. Instead of Christmas Day being the most wonderful of her life Lettie Simpson was seen to be carrying her Sarah through the snow covered back streets of Langley Park until they were both frozen to the bone. Poor, daft Lettie, eventually the cold and the snow drove her home to her man where their fragile marriage was never to recover.

Bertha was jerked from her reverie by a nudge in the ribs from Jenny Timms, Walter's wife.

'He's coming.'

It was said loud enough for most of the little crowd to hear. The women with careworn faces stopped picking over the wretched leftovers of Joe and Lettie's life and came out of the yard to stare down the street as Eddie Todd rounded the corner leading the nag-drawn dairy wagon commandeered for a couple of hours and bearing a newly built two-wheeler handcart. His son, an ox of a boy at fourteen, accompanied him. Lettie stood just inside the gate holding little Sarah on her hip. Wordlessly, Eddy dropped the back and unloaded the little cart, which he left on the road. He and his son entered the house without so much as an acknowledgement of the hapless Lettie and came out first with the sideboard and then the bed.

Effortlessly loading their plunder onto the wagon they left as churlishly as they had come, the boy gawking shamelessly at the assembled crowd of women. Bertha had half a mind to go and fetch Robert from his bed so that he could wipe the filthy grin off the lad's face, but what would be the point. The wagon disappeared around the corner by the Blue Star leaving the little handcart, still unclaimed, abandoned in the middle of the street. The silence was agonising. It was eventually broken by Mrs Timms, who took hold of the cart and wheeled it towards Lettie's gate.

'Howay, pet. You show us what you want keeping and we'll give you a hand to sort it out.'

One or two of the women joined her and the rest began to disperse. Bertha couldn't face going into the Simpson's house and went home. Soon the handcart would be filled with what were known to the eviction board as 'private and personal possessions'. It would be left in the yard for inspection by the bailiffs and if they agreed that the contents were 'vital for the well-being of the transgressor and his immediate family' they would be allowed to keep them. In truth, it meant that they would only be permitted a few clothes and blankets to allow them to survive on the open road in case nobody took them in. Everything else would be sold to offset the debt.

Bertha went back to Number Eight. She was supposed to bake some bread and go up to the allotment for vegetables that morning but she couldn't be bothered. It should be the moneylenders that were to be punished for preying upon the weak and helpless. She could hear Robert snoring upstairs and thought to Hell with it! She would have a bite to eat and a cup of tea now and at twelve o'clock she would go into the street and watch the eviction take place and see if she could do anything to help, although she hadn't the faintest idea what.

After an eternity, midday approached. Bertha sighed and put down the cards. There was still no sign of Robert waking up so she put on her shawl and headed off down the yard.

There was always a crowd at an eviction, but mostly only from the street, the other villagers respectfully ignoring the event. Once the officials arrived, no one was seen to help or to extend sympathy, after all a debtor or a persistent lead swinger got what he deserved.

The bailiffs were first on the scene. They were big men looking like gorillas in their ill-fitting suits and bowler hats and they waited quietly at the back gate. Doctor Chrisp was next – he was the first member of the Colliery Board to arrive. The Board consisted of a body of three officials employed by, or affiliated to the management. They were always present at an eviction to see fair play. Fair play! Chrisp's face set in a mask of distaste at the thought of the phrase. Where was justice for these poor folk? They worked so hard for so little. He closed his eyes and groaned softly as he walked up the street. He saw the bailiffs and refused to acknowledge them, instead exchanging a few words with some of the women, inquiring after the health of their husbands and children. He saw Bertha and nodded politely. An awkward silence fell for a moment and Chrisp was relieved to see the colliery under-manager and pay office secretary approaching the scene from the top of the street. They touched their hats to one another and a few stilted words about the weather faltered into silence as their attention was drawn to the pit end of the street. The massive and unmistakable silhouette of Constable Healy was positioned in the middle of the road, staring down towards them. His head turned in the direction of the pit as he was joined by another figure, that of Joseph Simpson. Together they walked slowly and with dignity down the middle of the road to join the crowd outside Number Twelve. Joe was as black as the Ace of spades, having come directly from his shift at the coalface and the whites of his eyes were a startling contrast to the rest of him. As they approached, the big constable touched his helmet respectfully to the officials before speaking gently to Joe.

'In you go, son, and bring your family out so's we can see them, eh?'

Joe nodded meekly and went to open the gate. As he did so the bailiffs made to follow him up the yard but were stopped in their tracks by Healy, who informed them that although the presence of an Officer of the Law was not a legal requirement at an eviction, he considered it a good idea as it prevented shite like the loan company reps from becoming over-enthusiastic in the pursuance of their duties. Particularly as such over-enthusiasm could lead to use of the minimum necessary force to prevent any such action. There was something else about tearing out their liver with his bare hands, but anyway, they stayed where they were.

A minute later Joe backed out of the house, clumsily manoeuvring the little handcart they had bought so dearly from Eddie Todd. It wasn't even full to the top and was covered with a woollen blanket. He pushed it to the gate and clattered it down the back step into the street. The bailiffs, with one eye on Constable Healy moved towards the cart.

'Stand still!'

Big as they were, the two men stopped dead. The smaller one spoke. 'We've got a right to search it, we've got a right. They're only allowed to take what's vital and that's all.' His voice trailed off as the massive constable sailed straight towards him. Even Joe backed away. Healy was practically nose-to-nose with the bailiff, his huge moustache quivering, and without taking his eyes off the trembling man he addressed Joe.

'Mr Simpson, is there anything in that cart that isn't vital to your well-being?'

Joe's voice was a near whisper as his frightened eyes darted from the bailiffs to the policeman and back again.

'No.'

Healy's voice boomed out. 'Well that's settled then, bonny lads, nothing that's not vital. So I'll thank youse two to stay away from that cart while Mr Simpson goes indoors and brings out his lady wife to listen to the legal goings on with these proper officials.' He inclined his head to the thoroughly intimidated colliery representatives.

Cockney Joe stood arm in arm with his wife while the pay office secretary read aloud from a khaki coloured card to the effect that the couple now owned only what was in the cart and every other possession was to be cleared from the house by the bailiffs to offset the disgraceful amount of debt they had accrued. Somewhere along the way little Sarah, who was being held by Mrs Timms, burst into tears which set Lettie off to crying as well and one by one all the women present, including Bertha, began to shed quiet tears too. Throughout this ritual humiliation, Constable Healy never dropped his gaze from the two bailiffs, who stared back insolently, though with fear lurking in their eyes.

When the ordeal was over the Colliery Board Officials touched their hats to one another and went their separate ways, leaving the wailing clutch of women standing outside Number Twelve. The bailiffs had not moved, however, and neither had Constable Healy. It was obvious they were not going to let the Simpson's cart get away so lightly. Healy sighed a great sigh that blew the ends of his moustache up into the air.

'Look lads, why don't you get about your business raking over the stuff in the house while this man and his missus get on their way, eh?'

There was an uneasy silence but the men made no move to do as the policeman suggested. He sighed again. 'Joe, you know where I live, lad. Why don't you take your cart and park it in my back yard until you and Lettie get yourselves sorted out a bit. Just tell my missus I said it was all right, then you can get yourself back to work, eh?'

Dumbly Joe nodded and with a furtive glance at the bailiffs and then at Lettie, he set off up the road with the little cart. One of the men started to follow him but he was stopped by a great wooden truncheon smacked smartly across his chest. He gasped as much in amazement as with the shock of blow. He hadn't even seen the constable draw the weapon. When Healy spoke, this time the mock joviality had gone from his voice, which was now hardly more than a whisper and positively exuded menace.

'I'm through being nice to youse bastards. You get the stuff in the house and you get out of my village and if I hear any more from you I'll chew your bollocks off myself. Do you both understand?'

They said nothing. Silently and with many a backward glance they edged up the yard and entered the house to list all of the pitiful valuables left there prior to collection and eventual sale.

The little clutch of women was dispersing and for now Mrs Timms had taken Lettie under her wing. She put her arm around the hapless girl's shoulder to lead her and Sarah away from the vacant colliery house that for a few short months had been her family home.

Bertha did not know when she had felt so depressed. She turned to set off back to Number Eight and was surprised to see their Robert standing at the gate. He must have been there all the time, watching. She cursed under her breath. Now he would see that she had been crying. Oh, what the Hell! So what if he did? She straightened her back and marched down to the gate where he politely stepped back to let her pass. He softly cleared his throat and spoke.

'I just thought I might be needed, you know, like... Anyway, I've put the kettle on for a cup of tea, I thought you might want one.'

She looked up at him and smiled through her tears, even punching him playfully on the chest. God, he was so like her Ted – peas in a bloody pod were the Sunniside Smiths.

'Yes, our Robert, I could just fancy a cup of tea.'

* * * * *

Half past two that afternoon Ted fairly skipped down the street and into the house. Obviously a backbreaking shift down the pit had done nothing to dampen his high spirits at being a uniformed soldier in a few days' time. He bathed in front of the fire and ate his meal of tatie pot with relish. Suppressing a belch he pushed the empty plate away and looked at Bertha.

'Joe went missing off shift today for a bit, never said a word neither. Any bread and gravy?'

'There's a bit left in the pot, help yourself, pet.'

Bertha couldn't be further from sharing Ted's mood. She had wanted to bring up the subject of the eviction but was unsure of how to begin. She knew Lettie Simpson was

at the Timms' house with little Sarah but she didn't know where Joe was going to stay. It couldn't be at Number Eight, not with our Robert here, but she knew Ted would offer without hesitation or thought. She could feel her eyes filling with tears again as she recalled the day's events. She had to tell him: Joe was his mate. It would be just awful if her husband found out from anyone else.

Ted sat in silence, smoking a tab as his gravy went cold on the plate while Bertha unfolded the details of the works of evil men upon the innocent. His mind was in rags as he tried to reconcile the triviality of getting his uniform early against the dreadful tragedy that had befallen the family of his friend. So that was what the lads were muttering about on the way home. He had half noticed something was up but was too full of himself and the DLI, and looking forward to his dinner. He hardly felt his wife's hand rest upon his own and her voice gently invade his colliding thoughts.

'There's nothing we can do, pet, except trust in the Good Lord to see that they'll be all right.'

The hand squeezed firmly but gently and the spell was broken. They talked for a while across the table about how it was amazing that nobody had seen it coming, what with Joe's increasingly bad temper and eccentric behaviour. It was funny how when a thing finally came to pass it seemed to have been so obvious all along. It was amazing how a load of little things suddenly fell into place, and it was equally amazing how the more they did so, the more the gulf between the enormity of Joe's debt and the inadequate means available to him to try and pay off the tick men, became obvious. It must be like trying to shovel shit with a stick. As Ted lit a second tab from his first there was one thing the couple agreed on. There was no blame attached to the Simpson family, however sackless Lettie was or however quick to anger was Joe. It was directly down to those bastard tick men that scuttled their way through the colliery villages like the vermin they were, preying on anybody and everybody who was short of a bit of cash. God! Wasn't that all of them?

Chapter 12

Langley Park Colliery Village, Saturday 11th April 1914

The week dragged by as if fettered in great chains. Joe Simpson never missed a shift and never said a word. No one else was much disposed to speak either. Lettie and little Sarah were still at the Timms' household but nobody had a clue where Joe was staying, nor were they inclined to ask. He looked more and more unkempt as the week wore on and he worked like a demon. Just before dawn on Saturday morning of the 11th there was a stirring in the village as all the lads were getting ready to set off for Burnhope and the weekend camp. As Ted was saying his goodbyes at the back, he and Bertha were startled by a shuffling at the bottom of the yard. It was Cockney Joe standing outside the gate. He was clean and properly shaved, but his clothes were crumpled and he looked gaunt and hunted. His attempt at a smile failed as he asked if there was a quick cup of tea on the go before they set off. Ted was somewhat taken aback by these words from someone he hadn't heard speak for a week but Bertha was quicker off the mark.

'Of course there is, Joe. Howay in and have a warm while I pour you some.'

Ted's eyebrows lowered and he began to shake his head. The DLI lads had organised to meet at the catwalk steps in about five minutes and were going to set off without waiting for stragglers and to be honest nobody had expected Cockney Joe to turn up at all. Bertha ignored the expression and pulled Ted back into the house. 'Come on in, Joe.'

The gate clicked open and Joe's boots clacked up the yard. The man who used to walk straight into the house with a cheery smile hesitated in the doorway, but Ted was up to speed now.

'Don't just stand there, man, come on in by the fire, we've got a few minutes.'

Bertha handed an enamel mug of stewed tea to Joe as she expertly scanned his person. He had his best boots tied by the laces and slung around his neck and a crumpled brown paper bag with what looked like a couple of apples inside for his bait. She exhaled impatiently, and quickly fetched the loaf from the scullery. 'Ted, get that old flask my Dad gave you, it's in the table drawer in The Room... come on we've only got a couple of minutes, man.'

She busied herself making up a couple of thick pease pudding sandwiches. This alarmed Ted, as the pease pudding was a treat he had been looking forward to when he returned from camp; he knew better than to say anything though. Within a minute both men were at the door again but Joe was now equipped with a flask of tea and a decent midday meal. Ted hadn't the heart to tell his wife that you get fed at camp anyway and took his own lunch as a luxury supplement to eat on the way. They were on their way up the street again in short order and the silence was agonising, Joe not inclined to say anything and Ted bursting with questions but aware he would be intruding if he so much as opened his mouth. The noise of the shunting yard just over the line increased suddenly as they rounded the corner at the top of Railway Street. As they approached the community washhouse the half-light revealed a crowd of men smoking tabs or pipes and talking in low whispers. Heads turned at their approach and the reaction to seeing Joe was uncomfortably mixed. Some stared in unfriendly silence at the wife-beater who had let his shift down and disgraced the village, whilst others looked with pity at the hapless victim of the unscrupulous moneylenders who had forced him into the humiliating position of not being able to keep his family together. It seemed to Ted, however, that the odd, quiet, 'How do, Joe' or 'What fettle, mate', outweighed the hostile silence of some of the group and Ted was relieved when John Merrigan came to stand beside them, staring defiantly at anyone who would meet his eye. He was also surprised to see the uniformed figures of Jimmy Barker and Harry Clarke. He had supposed they were long gone by now along with all the other uniformed men for the early parade and camp set-up.

It was Jimmy who spoke first. 'Howay, bonny lads, get yourselves up onto the catwalk and form line three abreast and we'll get on our way, eh?'

The instruction wasn't given loudly or sharply but with just enough volume to be heard over the clanking of the endless belts as they fed coal to the disintegrator shed, and most of the group moved off amiably enough in the direction of the steps.

'Hey, Jimmy, who voted you Kaiser?' Several pairs of eyes closed at once as the voice of Billy Robson grated on the morning air like fingernails down a blackboard. Jimmy was already halfway up the wooden steps when he suddenly stiffened. He turned around, using the extra height to meet the gaze of every man in the group. When he spoke, it was with patience and clarity, as one equal to another.

'Look lads, I'm not here this morning to lord it over you. I know there was some cock-ups last weekend but Sergeants Hanson and Malone were fairly impressed with the lot of youse. To move things on a bit they asked me and Harry, asked, mind you, if we wouldn't mind using the time it takes to get to camp to sharpen up your drill a bit on the way.' He paused as a relief valve somewhere let off a piercing shriek that lasted ten or twelve seconds – no point in even trying to talk over that. 'I know we don't outrank you but me and Harry have been in the DLI for nearly a year so let's have no daft carry-on eh? Just do what we say, like.'

There was a mumbled assent and the odd reprimand aimed at Billy but in the main the lads got themselves sorted out. Jimmy and Harry were methodical and professional in their organisation of the little company and all of the 'proper' orders they issued were given in as quiet a voice as all the clamour of a pit running at full pelt would allow.

Fat Harry spoke up. 'Hey Jimmy, can we still smoke while we're marching, like?'

The answer was 'yes' which was greeted with a general murmur of enthusiasm, and emboldened by this informality Billy Robson spoke up again. 'Hey Jimmy, while you're in charge of us do we have to call you 'sir' or anything?'

Dicky Howell joined the conversation before any reply could be made.

'Go easy, man, 'sir' is on my bloody shift down the pit, aren't you, sir.' The ensuing laughter was stilted and uncomfortable and soon died away.

'Lads!' The sudden severity of the words made the company jump. It had been spoken by Harry Clarke who had obviously had enough of the banter. 'Give you bastards an inch of rope and you'll manage to hang your bloody selves with it! Get it into your thick heads will you. This isn't a game. You're here to learn to defend your country in the event of a war. That means killing people and getting shot at. If you piss about on the battlefield you'll be first to hit the ground. Now can we stop all the bairns' stuff and get on our way. *Please.*'

This last word was said with such venom that there was no room for misinterpretation of the courtesy. There was a second's pause before Private Harry Clarke barked out the attention. He gave the men a couple of seconds before giving the at ease.

'Right then, let's have no more shite. Yes, you can smoke. Yes, you can talk amongst yourselves quietly unless ordered not to do so. If there is something you need to bring to our attention you address Jimmy as Private Barker and me as Private Clarke. Now get lit up, we're late.'

Within half a minute the men were marching along the catwalk towards the Lanchester Road. There was no conversation at all for quite some time.

Watching the body of men disappear into the morning mist was Lettie Simpson. She had been hiding in the gap between the two top netties on Railway Street.

The hour's journey up to Burnhope passed quickly enough. The lads soon settled into the rhythm of the march and behaviour was passable. It had been a good idea of the two uniformed men to allow talking and smoking. The lads kept up the step with fine fettle and obeyed the orders as they came. It was a beautiful morning and the brisk pace kept them warm and in good cheer.

Just as the squad turned off the Lanchester Road towards the Old Castle ruins there was a small clearing for stagecoaches and omnibuses to meet and exchange passengers. It was here that Private Clarke shouted the halt. They were left-turned and dismissed while they were instructed to swap their work boots for the polished ones and given a couple of minutes to relieve themselves in the bushes. It was only when George Moody accidentally pissed on Ted's boots that he thought it might be an idea to do things the other way around next week. When they re-formed, not a man spoke, not even Billy or Dicky. This was a different affair to last time. This company was not a soaking wet rabble without any idea of what to expect, but a group of men bursting to show off their newly acquired drilling skills.

Tabs were extinguished and they left the clearing with nineteen pairs of heels hitting the road as one man and it made their hearts soar. The uniformed privates began to bark their orders with more volume and authority and no one objected; it would all add to the impression they wanted to give on their arrival at camp. Dicky let out an especially extended fart that elicited howls of dismay from his comrades. His defence of 'Better out than in' fell on deaf ears and Privates Barker and Clarke let it pass, thanking God that the incident occurred on the road rather than the parade square. The flag hove into view, not the drenched and lifeless rag of the week before, but the Union Flag of The British Empire rippling crisply in the morning breeze. The camp looked different, too. The parade square lines were sharp and well defined. The company of uniformed men was being drilled by the instantly recognisable Scottish burr of Corporal Lawrie. They were practicing rifle drill with pickaxe handles and looked like they had been doing it all their lives. The two tents, one large and one small, were set up to one side of the flagpole, and the awning covering the kitchen area, all looked as if they had been there since the previous Saturday. The women preparing the food looked just as miserable. The only difference was the addition of a big green tent behind the kitchen and a motor lorry parked beside it. Somewhere behind Ted, Tom Dodds piped up cheerfully, 'Hey! That'll be our uniforms, lads. They'll make soldiers of us yet.'

'QUIET IN THE RANKS YOU MONGERS! SQUA-A-AD... HALT!'

The order came like a thunderclap. The men halted correctly but instead of staring resolutely ahead began looking around to see where such a shocking order could have come from.

'Look to the front, you bunch of useless twats. Who told you to move? Private Barker, Private Clarke... to me.'

Then they saw him. He was little terrier of a bloke who must have been a full head shorter than Ted. He marched to the front of the company and looked at them as if he was about to explode. He was wearing the double chevrons of a corporal and his uniform, though clean and smartly pressed, looked like it had been cut down to fit.

Jimmy Barker had been heading up the company and was already abreast of the corporal so he remained at attention where he was, while Harry doubled to the front and stood ramrod straight next to his comrade. Both men towered over the little figure but there was no hint of anything other than iron obedience in their demeanour.

'Privates Barker and Clarke, get to the armaments tent and draw a rifle each. Then get back here on the double. Move yourselves! The rest of you stand still.'

Ted's heart sank. Out of the corner of his eye he could see the Stanley lads grouped in front of the kitchen, mugs of steaming tea in their hands and grinning like Cheshire cats. He was burning with embarrassment at the thought of being humiliated in front of them again. How did they get here so bloody early? The little corporal stared at the company, trying to catch an eye and failing. After a few moments, Jimmy and Harry arrived back at the double with a pickaxe handle each and without waiting for an order snapped to attention. The silence was crippling. The sounds of the drill NCOs putting the other squads through their paces seemed to recede into the distance.

'Right, you bunch of useless bastards, since when does a squad of private soldiers in the Durham Light Infantry waltz up to a weekend camp chattering like a bunch of fucking lasses? Anybody want to tell me?'

So appalling was the onslaught that no one in the squad moved a muscle. No one did anything to draw attention to himself in case he came under attack from the furious NCO.

'You bunch of fucking cowards.' The voice was lower now and more menacing. 'Has nobody got the bollocks to defend their company? Isn't there one of you got enough guts to stand up and be counted?'

After a second's pause Jimmy Barker's voice rang out, 'Permission to speak, Corporal.'

'Shut up! Just fucking well shut up!'

What happened to the 'no swearing' stuff? What have we done now?

'I was talking to this bunch of pansies you are supposed to be training. I was talking to this bunch of nancies that you are supposed to be instilling discipline into. In short, I was talking to the monkeys, not you two useless fucking organ grinders.' He turned his wrathful gaze away from the pair of hapless private soldiers and back onto the main company.

'You bastards have let the side down! You have let your NCOs down, you have let your squad down and worst of all you have let me down. And I do not like being let down, men. I do not. When you march, you march in silence. Discipline demands it. So, for the last time, what was all the chatting about?'

The silence was only a couple of seconds long but it seemed an eternity. Then Tom Dodds cleared his throat loudly and clumsily before speaking in a shaky voice, 'Permission to speak, er, Corporal, sir.'

Before any reply could be made a voice rang out loud and clear across the parade ground. The lads recognised it as at once as Sergeant Malone.

'Corporal Huddart!' None of the lads moved so much as an inch. They had learned that lesson all right. 'Your presence is required in the outfitting tent. Would you go along immediately please?'

The corporal looked as though he was going to choke but came to a smartly to attention as the big sergeant approached.

'Thank you, Sergeant Malone.'

He turned his gaze on the lads who were as still as statues. 'Another time, men.'

He did a cracking left turn and marched around the parade ground to the big tent behind the kitchen. Sergeant Malone stood at ease and watched the diminutive figure recede, before turning an expressionless gaze towards the lads.

'Who was talking?'

Tommy's shaky voice answered. 'It was me, Sergeant... sorry, like..,'

'I watched youse lads as you came over the hill. I was quite impressed. Considering you couldn't put one foot in front of the other last week I thought you looked a bit professional. I take it this is due to the support given you by the two privates here, would that be right?' The voice was quite conversational. 'I asked you a question, Private Dodds.'

'Yes, sir. Sergeant. I mean, sorry, Sergeant.'

'A word of advice lads, and it's not as if you weren't told last week either, isn't that right Private 2494 Robson?' Nobody moved a muscle but Billy Robson went redder than he had ever done in his life. 'What I want you to do is simple. Stop chattering in the ranks, respect Privates Barker and Clarke whom you've just dropped right in the shite. And try to stay in Corporal Huddart's good books. Think you can remember that?'

After a short pause he continued, 'I didn't hear a reply, lads.'

No further prompting was required as nineteen voices shouted, 'Yes, Sergeant,' in perfect unison.

Malone twirled the right side of his moustache and surveyed the company.

'Good, now go and get a cup of tea and a tab and wait for Lance Corporal Carter to form up your squads. Private Barker, you have the men.'

'Yes, Sergeant, thank you, Sergeant.' Jimmy smartly slapped his hand across his pickaxe handle in salute and about turned to look at the men. It was impossible to read the expression on his face but his voice was calm and clear as he ordered the men to march around the square and dismissed them at the kitchen tent. Even so, every soul in the company was well aware that they had let him and Harry down, and that somewhere along the way they would fall foul of Corporal Huddart again. They piled their boots and bait under the table, and queued up for a mug of tea. The Stanley Company greeted them warmly enough and showed no signs of capitalising on their embarrassment; after all, they were comrades now. The tea was stewed and had a funny metallic taste but at least it was hot. Ted exchanged greetings with a few of the lads who were in his squad from last week and so did most of the others. Tom Dodds, polishing his specs with great concentration, remained quiet, still reeling from the uncalled for onslaught of the little corporal and John Merrigan quietly smoked his tab while his eyes flitted from man to man trying to see if he could recognise his missing boots. He had thought to bring the matter up with one of the sergeants to see if they could help – boots weren't bloody cheap – but looking at the trouble caused by talking out of turn he could only imagine the stink that would ensue if he accused somebody of thieving. He drew smoke hard into his lungs and decided to let the matter drop.

In an exact repeat of the previous week the chatter died away of its own accord as Corporal Lawrie and Lance Corporal Carter approached the tent from the direction of the flagpole. As if on some silent command, everyone drank off their tea at once and took a last drag on tabs and pipes so that when the two NCOs arrived at the tent the men were more or less ready to be told off into their squads. They halted just in front of the group and most of the lads drew themselves to a self-conscious attention. Corporal Lawrie smiled at this and Lance Corporal Carter spoke first.

'Good morning, gentlemen.'

The ensuing two-second silence was enough to allow both groups of lads to recall what they had learned about army mentality last week.

A hesitant, 'Good morning, Lance Corporal Carter', elicited a faint facial twitch that they hoped was a smile. He opened the old leather-bound file he was carrying and scanned it rapidly.

'Right, Private Robson, you are marker for Number One Squad and Private Guildford, you are marker for Number Two Squad. Go and stand on the edge of the square, if you please.'

Billy Robson and Fat Harry trotted off without a word, to take up their positions, standing to attention with their toes just on the white line.

'Right, the rest of you, GET FELL IN!'

There was an instant explosion of movement as forty-odd men changed from an aimless, shuffling bunch into two reasonably neat squads of men all stood to attention and ready to receive orders.

The next hour or so was hard work but it was rewarding. Each squad did its utmost to out-march the other and at the end of the session everybody was sweating. They were now drilling like professionals. Ted thought they were at least the equals of the uniformed lads who had laid down their pickaxe handles and were seated cross-legged on the ground in front of the podium listening to Lieutenant Brass give them a talk on something or other. He was drawing stuff on a big blackboard and pointing to his sketches with a stick. It so much reminded Ted of school back in Sunniside that he couldn't help but smile. A sharp command to wipe that stupid grin from his face brought him instantly back to the present and, except for Jacky Tait turning right when he should have turned left and marching off on his own for a bit, all seemed to go well enough to please Lance Corporal Carter. He drew the squad to a smart halt in front of the kitchen and dismissed the men.

'Right lads, that was well done, well done indeed. If one or two of you would take it upon themselves to teach Private Tait his left foot from his right for next weekend I would be very grateful.' This raised a giggle amongst the lads that even Jacky joined in, relieved that his only punishment was to be a mild ribbing. 'Grab yourselves a tea before Corporal Lawrie gets here with his bunch then you've got a talk on history and tactics from Lieutenant Brass. I'll come and get you in ten minutes.' He 'about turned' and marched off in the direction of the big tent next to the flagpole and the lads all sighed with relief.

Some people queued for tea, some lit up a tab or a pipe and others trotted off to the dugout latrines. Cockney Joe sat down on the grass where he was and lit a tab. Ted stood in the line for tea when one of the Stanley lads called something or other Morgan came up to him and Jacky.

'What cheer, lads? We did canny on the square, what d'you reckon?'

'Except for me going off on me own, d'you mean?' said Jacky defensively.

'Naw, don't be daft, man. Lance Corporal Carter could have torn you to shreds but he didn't, did he? I reckon he's all right. Not sure about this Huddart bloke though, he's the one that took you apart this morning, isn't he? What the Hell was that all about, like?'

Ted took two mugs of tea from the little boy who stood behind the trestle table and handed one to Jacky. He thought about getting another and taking it over to Cockney Joe but decided to leave him alone. Jacky was explaining to the Morgan lad about their encounter with the little corporal and over the general hub-bub of the conversation Corporal Lawrie's voice could be heard as he marched Number Two Squad up to the kitchen and dismissed them for tea. This time the two squads didn't break up and re-form as the Langley-versus-Stanley gangs like they did last week but more or less stayed in their squads and even introduced some of the squad members to their village mates. Ten minutes after their dismissal, and Ted would have bet it was to the second, back came the two NCOs. All tea was drained and tab ends extinguished without a word.

'Markers to the line.'

Off trotted Billy and Fat Harry.

'Get formed up lads. Number One Squad, you will spend the next hour or so in the company of Lieutenant Brass, who will begin to teach you the rudiments of tactics and trench warfare. I will remind you that you will be in the presence of an officer carrying the King's Commission. If it is reported back to me that any of you have behaved in a manner fit to bring the name of Number One Squad into disrepute then those individuals will answer to me. Is that perfectly clear? Good. I will warn you in advance, men, that Lieutenant Brass is very fastidious and has an exceptional eye for detail. Do anything wrong, however minute, and he will spot it and report it to me. And I will deal with you. The lecture will cease at twelve-forty hours when you will break for your midday meal after which you will assist Corporal Huddart with uniform issue. Squa-a-ad Atte-e-en-shun!'

He marched the company to the podium where Lieutenant Brass was waiting. He was standing in front of the big blackboard and on a little trestle table was a cardboard box full of coloured chalks, all standing up. Lance Corporal Carter dismissed the men in front of the podium and sat them cross-legged on the grass. With a smart salute to the officer he about turned and marched off in the direction of the tent next to the motor lorry.

'Good Morning, gentlemen. For the benefit of those of you who don't know me, I am Lieutenant Brass.' He used a wooden pointer to tap the nameplate that was at the front of the little trestle table. Ted recognised it from the recruiting room of the chapel when he enlisted.

'I am a second lieutenant in the Eighth New Durhams and today it is my job to give you a little information on the proud history of your unit and its role in the development of affairs as they stand in Europe today. There will also be a short talk on trench warfare and its use in armed conflict. Please keep any questions you may have until I give permission to ask them, at which point those of you who wish to do so should raise their hands, so.' He raised his right arm into the air and kept it there for a few seconds. 'On a lighter note, it's nice to see some familiar faces amongst you. Some of you may remember me as one of the Recruiting Officers with whom you enlisted. And don't feel you have to sit cross-legged the whole time. Please seat yourselves as comfortably as you wish, just don't shuffle about too much.'

There was a small commotion as the men tried, as inconspicuously as possible, to seat themselves more comfortably. They were all aware that Lieutenant Brass was watching them and many were puzzled by the conflict between the apparent kindness of his words and the fact that, even though they were only doing as they were bid, they were somehow inconveniencing the young officer.

'Very well, let us begin. Today is Saturday, April 11th 1914. A rather better day than last Saturday, I'm sure you'll all agree.'

His smile was genuine enough and the lads laughed quietly and politely at the joke. It was obvious, despite his high ways that he meant well and as he spoke, the lads warmed to him. Ted tried to take it all in but his interest in World Affairs was sketchy at best and much as he began to like Lieutenant Brass he thought he was a bit of a boring talker. The first fact to stick in Ted's mind was that the DLI were known as the 'Dirty Little Imps'. It mostly went downhill after that but it was interesting that half the royal families in the world were all related, though. The bit about all the various treaties that bound this country to that and the obligation of nations to go to war in the case of somebody invading somebody else struck him as a bit mad. It sounded as if all it would take was for one bloody idiot to do something sackless and the whole of Europe would topple into all-out war like a row of dominoes going down. Then again, the people who were responsible for the welfare of huge countries, Prime Ministers and suchlike, were supposed to be sensible people and were brought up to do the job.

He half listened as the lieutenant droned on and felt pleasantly drowsy until a sharp dig in the back jerked him back to dozy awareness. He looked around to see Jacky drawing his leg back. Realising what had happened, he felt his stomach lurch as he snapped fully awake and looked to the front again to see, to his intense relief, that the officer was pointing to a neatly chalked list of countries allied to Great Britain in the event of a war and was completely unaware of the offence. Not that he was the only one, either; somewhere behind him a gentle snore was stopped abruptly, presumably by the same means that had saved Ted. After about half an hour the lads were given a five-minute break to stretch their legs and have a smoke. Ted took a light off a Stanley lad, and looked round the parade ground. Was this truly only their second week?

He was brought abruptly back to earth by a stubby finger being poked in his ribs. It was Billy Robson.

'Howay, dreamer. His Nibs is coming back.'

There was a gentle murmur and a few grunts and protests as the lads extinguished pipes and tabs and began to settle themselves again. Jacky's mischievous whisper came from behind Ted, 'Try and stay awake this time, dozy.'

A few stifled giggles ended abruptly as the lieutenant mounted the podium. He looked around the group, staring directly into the mens' eyes.

The second half of the talk was more interesting, possibly because it was a bit more like the stuff the men would actually have to do. It began with 'Defence of Localities', which was in Chapter Four of the Field Service Pocket Book as issued by the War Office. As the young lieutenant began to warm to his subject, he became more animated, scratching sketches of fire trenches onto his board with practiced ease and demonstrating some fascinating facts, like what a killing zone was. The men also found it interesting to learn that a trench was never dug in a straight line but had to be 'castellated to prevent enfilading'. Knotted eyebrows were obviously in the majority so Lieutenant Brass rehashed the phrase with the aid of a diagram. When the lieutenant moved on to 'Map Reading and Field Sketching' it was Billy's exaggerated intake of breath, presumably meant to convey sheer wonder that anyone could expound on such a complicated subject, that drew Lieutenant Brass' attention to him. He stopped mid-sentence and gaped at Billy, seemingly unable to know what to do next. For a few seconds an uncomfortable silence reigned as the officer stared at Billy, who hadn't a clue what to do either and sat open-mouthed staring back.

It was Lieutenant Brass who broke the stalemate. He nodded curtly in Billy's direction and spoke quietly, 'You there, the stout fellow, are you all right?'

Before Billy could reply, a sharp dig in the back from Cockney Joe's boot reminded him not to drop everyone in the shite. His mouth opened and shut a couple of times before he suddenly and vigorously began to rub his right leg with both hands.

'Sorry sir, bit o' cramp, sir. I get it sometimes if I sit still too long. Sorry, like.'

Another dig in the back.

'S... sir.'

Everyone waited with bated breath. Lieutenant Brass stared at Billy for a few seconds more then said, 'Well go and walk it off, man. Stay in ear shot and sit down at the back when you're ready.'

Billy stopped rubbing his leg and sat as still as if he was frozen to the ground until another dig in the back jerked him to his senses. He stood up to attention and his right arm flickered upward a couple of times as if he wasn't sure whether or not to salute. In the end he didn't and stumbled sideways over the crowd of seated bodies to perform a strange, exaggerated limp whilst making great capital out of rubbing his left leg as he did so. Ted closed his eyes in disbelief at the absurdity of his antics; he would surely get the whole bloody lot of them hanged if he carried on like that.

But Lieutenant Brass appeared content to ignore him and began to drone on about finding true north with a variation to the west and the crowd of seated men were all attention. After a few more overviews and a few more sketches, Lieutenant Brass said the word 'uniforms'. Ted jerked upright and began to listen hard. This was it, man!

'And since you will be getting your uniforms after your midday meal I'll give you a quick précis of your kit and what it means. I will say first of all that it is a rare privilege that is being afforded to you men. This is only your second weekend camp and normally kit is not issued until the sixth. But there are extenuating circumstances that can't be gone into here. So let us begin.'

This was more like it!

The issued kit was apparently divided into three sections: personal, public and necessaries. 'Your personal kit consists of your boots, caps, drawers, tunics, trousers, puttees, woolly gloves and suchlike.'

This apparently became your very own property. You could even keep it when you left the army for good. Canny, that.

The drone continued, accompanied by the staccato scuffing of chalk on blackboard.

The 'public' stuff was issued as required, like for a special action or a parade and had to be returned afterwards. This included greatcoats, full-dress headdresses, leggings and waterproof capes. Here, the lieutenant made a joke that these would have been handy if they had been issued last weekend and those who were listening laughed politely.

'Necessaries' consisted of badges, boot blacking, laces, braces etc. Amongst the more recognisable trivia were unfamiliar items such as button sticks, hose tops and even housewives! By now, everything the lieutenant had spoken about earlier had been erased by Ted's concentrated effort to try to remember what he had said in the last five minutes.

Eventually, the scuffing ceased and so did the drone. An almost inaudible collective sigh went around the group accompanied by gentle groans of relief as they shifted position to ease their stiff joints. Lieutenant Brass was standing with his hands clasped behind his back, surveying the men. He actually looked a bit uncomfortable, as if he wanted to put his hands in his pockets or something but felt as if he ought not to do it in front of the men.

'That would be it for today, men. Amongst next week's subjects will be Field Punishments, First Aid and March Discipline... very important in the infantry, so there's something to look forward to. Any questions? It's a couple of minutes to 1240 hours and your midday meal so try to keep them both brief and pertinent if you please.'

All heads immediately swivelled around to the kitchen area. Sure enough, the women were cutting bread and stirring broth, and what's more, the uniforms were already queuing. There was no sign of Number Two Squad, however, so they just might not be last served after all. Lieutenant Brass was bouncing impatiently on the balls of his feet and looking at the men.

'Any questions, then?'

What's a puttee? What's a button stick? How did you know the time so exactly when you didn't even look at your watch? What's the difference between a killing ground and a dead ground? How do you change centimetres to inches on a foreign field map? Would I be allowed a moustache like that?

There was a non-committal buzz followed by a silence Ted did not feel inclined to be first to break.

No. No questions.

Lieutenant Brass called the men to their feet and ordered attention. He then dismissed them to their midday break and left the podium slightly faster than Ted thought dignified. As the lads lit up their tabs and began to amble over to the kitchen area, Ted fell in with Jacky and Tom Dodds. They stood for a moment and watched the officer duck swiftly into the smaller of the two tents.

'What's his hurry, like?' said Tommy as the flap was dragged abruptly down behind the disappearing figure.

Ted took a long drag on his cigarette and grinned, 'I reckon he's got a lass in there, man. What d'you think?'

'What the Hell's the matter with you two, can't you tell when somebody's busting for a piss?'

Ted and Tommy frowned at Jacky and glanced involuntarily towards the latrine area near the wood. Tommy was the first to open his mouth but nothing came out. Then it dawned on them both together and Ted spoke with a smirk. 'He hasn't! He hasn't got a chamber pot in there... has he?'

The two-second pause seemed to stretch for two minutes before the three of them exploded into laughter.

'Too much tea and bought biscuits, that's what I reckon.'

'Aye, I'll bet they're them nice little crumbly ones you get at the Co-op.'

'Likely the ones with the currants in, an' all.'

'How many o' them do you think you can get on a saucer?'

'The whole bloody packet if you take the cup off.'

'Anyway, officers don't piss, they have a wee wee.'

The laughter continued all the way to the kitchen area where Number Two Squad was arriving. There was not a single smiling face amongst them.

* * * * *

They soon met up with the rest of the lads and got stuck into a surprisingly good broth that was doled out by a couple of disinterested middle-aged women. A young lad with all his hair shaved off, cut the bread into big chunks which he handed to the recruits. It was instantly obvious that the Number Two Squad lads had not had a good morning in the issue tent. They were grim and sullen and the name of Corporal Huddart wafted about the area like a bad smell. Nearly all conversation was in careful whispers because Corporal Lawrie and Lance Corporal Carter were stood at ease just under the awning, supervising the men during the break. When they had finished their broth, they washed and returned the mess tins and broke off into groups to find places to sit in the warm afternoon sunshine and eat their bait. Ted's group consisted of Jacky Tait, Tom Dodds, Billy Robson and John Merrigan. They could see Cockney Joe sitting smoking a tab under a tree near the latrines but thought it best to leave him be for the moment.

'Youse lot are pretty quiet,' added Ted. 'Not much of a day in the tent, then.'

'Naw.' John looked shiftily around him to see if anyone was in earshot before continuing, 'That Huddart is a right little bastard. If anybody else had spoke to me like that I'd have pushed his teeth down his bloody throat.'

Chapter 13

Burnhope Village TA Camp, Saturday 11th April 1914

Number Two Squad had indeed had a dreadful morning: not that their work had been in any way onerous. It had consisted of unpacking the various components that comprised the uniform of a private soldier and, under the malevolent stare of Corporal Huddart, arranging the gear on the rear of two parallel lines of trestle tables so that it was in the correct order to be issued to the men as they filed past in an orderly queue. There were boots to unpack and two pairs of laces to be dropped inside each right boot. The boots were then to be arranged in order of size (ascending) so that as a recruit came down the line he would be asked his size and the appropriate footwear could be issued. It was the same for all the other gear. The tables were set up in a 'U' shape so that you entered and exited through the same end of the tent. You picked up your trousers first, then a tunic top, two shirts, braces and so on until, boots last, you were in possession of the complete uniform of a soldier of the Eighth New Durhams.

Hardly onerous at all, in fact, it could even have been a pleasant experience were it not for the bullying behaviour of the little NCO. There were two young privates with Corporal Huddart and both looked about as downtrodden as it was possible to look. Even though it was obvious to all the men in Number Two Squad that the boys appeared to know what they were about, that did not stop him from abusing them at every turn. This was only the second camp for the Langley Park lads and although they were only just becoming used to the verbal onslaughts they received from the drill NCOs they at least understood that the reason they were being shouted at was to try to pull them together into a tightly disciplined group as quickly as possible. If they performed well they may even receive some encouragement – or at the very least be ignored – and they were only screamed at if they failed to come up to the standard required.

The dreaded Corporal Huddart, however, seemed to have a different idea of army discipline from any of his contemporaries. His chevrons appeared to award him the privilege of insulting and debasing anyone in sight who was not of equal rank. The squad was browbeaten into a fire-chain to unload the clothing from the motorised wagon and screamed at to unpack the crates and pile the gear onto the trestles. The two privates tried as quietly as possible to ensure that the lads were doing things properly but if someone made an error, like when John Merrigan got a bit too enthusiastic opening a crate with caps in and upset the whole lot onto the ground, the diminutive corporal seemed to appear from nowhere and loosed a volley of invective at him that even the ex-fisherman thought shocking. John held Huddart's eye though, and although he was standing rigidly to attention as ordered there was still something in his manner that said he would not be cowed by such an unnecessary cudgelling. Unabashed, Huddart began to harangue the young private, a lad called Sam Hurry, who had been put in charge of the section, practically reducing him to tears.

There was hardly a man in the tent that didn't want to beat the shit out of Corporal bloody Huddart but he seemed totally impervious to the wave of hatred aimed at him. If he noticed it at all, it spurred him on to new depths of depravity as he publicly humiliated the Hurry lad even further by ordering him to take up a pickaxe handle and run twenty times around the square holding it over his head for the apparent crime of being a cry baby and a useless fucker. Fat Harry Guildford was sent to make sure the count was right as Huddart apparently had more important things to do. Harry tried to stop the lad at sixteen laps but Hurry ran on to complete the twenty just in case they were being spied on from the tent.

Eventually, most of the gear was more or less distributed correctly. The rest would be done after the midday break by the other lads. Number Two Squad stood rigidly to attention with the young privates in the front rank whilst Corporal Huddart slowly and deliberately inspected every item laid out. He fastidiously flicked a piece of dust off a pair of trousers here and straightened up a tunic top there. Each time he made a minute and unnecessary adjustment he would turn round and scowl at the squad as if it were some act of great negligence. He could hardly contain himself when he spotted a tiny piece of soil with a couple of blades of crushed grass on it sticking to the corner of one of the trestles. He picked it up on his forefinger, walked slowly up to Sam Hurry and held it an inch from his nose. To Hurry's credit he didn't move a muscle but it was clear he was distressed.

Huddart tutted slowly and deliberately before flicking the offending mud from his finger and facing the squad square on. It wasn't his diminutive stature that made him look ridiculous, despite the best skills of the tailor to try to make his cut down uniform look as normal as possible, it was his whole attitude. He strutted and puffed like a pouter pigeon and George Moody was ready to bet he hated anybody who was half an inch taller than him for no other reason than that they were. It was still no excuse for picking on the lad, though; Private Hurry seemed a conscientious worker who laboured long and hard to keep Huddart off his back without realising that no amount of work would be sufficient. The squad had seen enough and the atmosphere was murderous, but no one moved a muscle and no one spoke a word. They stood as still as statues and stared directly to the front observing nothing. They let the torrent of abuse wash over them and thought that perhaps this Territorial stuff wasn't such a lark after all.

When they had heard for the thousandth time what a useless shower of mongers they were and that they couldn't be trusted with a bucket and spade, they were grudgingly dismissed to their midday break.

* * * * *

Ted lit a second tab from the barely glowing remnants of the previous one. A shadow had fallen over the little group and the conversation was half-hearted. Ted was a step further removed than usual because it was his first wedding anniversary the very next day. He had bought Bertha's present, a neck chain with a little brass bell in the shape of a teddy bear attached to it, and she would get it along with her card tomorrow when they visited Mam and Dad in Sunniside. He had organised with Robert that when he had been to see Louise the previous weekend he would nip into Bobby Stokoe's and get the old man to draw a card for him like the one he did for their wedding day. Bertha was so taken with the wedding card that it was still on the mantelpiece in The Room. They had to go to Blackhill first, to see Bertha's folk, but that was just the way the trains worked out, and with everything on Sunday Service, it would be way after eight before they got back to Langley and Bertha would just have to fix his tea late.

Ted was jerked back to the present by the voice of John Merrigan. The thick South Shields accent was overlaid with menace. It was a warning meant for them all although he was staring alternately at Billy Robson and Dicky Howell.

'That little bastard is out to get whoever he can. No clowning around, or you'll drop everybody in the shite. Just take whatever he chucks at you and get on with it, all right?' To his credit, the normally garrulous Billy just drew hard on his tab and nodded. Dicky just stared at the ground.

Suddenly the convoluted lecturing of Lieutenant Brass looked a rosy time indeed compared to the afternoon they would have to spend with Corporal Huddart.

Suddenly Dicky piped up, 'It's not me you've got to worry about, bonny lad, it's Cockney Joe over there. He's bloody loopy, man.'

Sure enough, as all eyes turned to the lonely figure they began to worry that Joe might indeed be the weak link. He was still sat near the latrines and although the smell must have been awful, he appeared not to notice. He was hugging his knees and rocking gently back and forth. Ted noticed that at least he had eaten his bait so he couldn't be that far gone.

'What was he like when you were marching?' asked John.

'Aw! Just what you see, man. He's behaved canny enough. He's just a bit funny, that's all.'

'All the same, keep an eye on the bugger. If he has a go at Huddart there'll be Hell to pay for the lot of us.'

The lads smoked in silence for a moment until a sharp expletive was heard from Joe's direction.

They all looked up, but John Merrigan was first to react, 'Aw! Bollocks!'

He leaped to his feet, practically trampling Ted as he tore off in the direction of the latrine area. A gasp of surprise went up and Ted's gaze followed the sprinting figure just in time to see Cockney Joe disappear into the woods at a run. He was on his feet in a second, closely followed by Tommy Dodds and one of the Stanley lads. There couldn't be much time left to the five-minute whistle, why the Hell did he have to pick now to crack up? Ted and Tom Dodds were level as they vaulted the low canvas windbreak and tore through the latrine area, raising vociferous objections from the men occupying the site. Ted actually leaped over the head of a squatting man and received a threat to his nether regions for doing so. He lost his cap as well.

If you haven't got your cap on you might as well be bloody naked.

He could hear the rest of the group galloping close behind him. He raised his voice a little but did not dare shout in case it drew attention to them. It was still possible that none of the NCOs had seen what was going on.

'Go back, Tommy, hadaway back and tell the others to as well. There's no need to land all of us in the shite.'

Tom Dodds ran on a few paces as if thinking it over and nodded, fiddling with his spectacles and slowing to a halt. Ted saw from the corner of his eye that he had turned around and was holding his arms out wide to stop the rest of the lads from continuing the pursuit.

Then he was in the woods. The pine trees were tall and thick and a permanent twilight reigned. He could see John's shadowy figure ahead of him but Cockney Joe was nowhere to be seen.

Follow John. The ground was treacherous, feet sinking into a thick carpet of pine needles that hid tough, stringy roots that were ready to trip in an instant. He heard John swear a couple of times and guessed that he had nearly stumbled as well. In the distance, muffled by the thick curtain of trees, Ted heard two whistle blasts, one long and one short, and his heart sank. That was the five-minute warning and here he was plunging ever further into the dark wood and ever deeper into trouble. Then it occurred to him that the uniforms might be in here too. They were on a map-reading exercise and the wood could be full of them. What if he ran into one? How would he explain his presence? He was edging ever closer to John and the fact that John had not eased the pace must mean that he had Joe in sight.

Keep up, man!

He was only a few feet behind now and the slight downward slope helped the pace a bit. His breathing was rhythmic and steady and his leg hardly hurt at all. He reckoned he could run for ages and in a perverted sort of way was beginning to enjoy the chase. If he reached out his arm he could probably touch John's shoulder – he toyed with the idea of doing so. Shit! John stopped suddenly and gasped as Ted ran right into his back and sent the pair of them flying head over heels to collapse onto the ground in a heap of blinding pain.

A split second later, both men were scrambling to their feet amid a shower of pine needles and curses. They both looked wildly around until their eyes focussed on Cockney Joe, his back to a tree and a formidable bough waving menacingly in his hands.

His eyes were wide and red-rimmed and his breathing was feral. It was plain that he could run no further and it was obvious that he meant to resist any attempt to return him to the camp. The only sound was harsh breathing and now that they had actually cornered him, Ted didn't know what to do.

John spoke. 'Come on, man, Joe, if we run we can make it back for forming up, don't drop us in the shite, mate, eh?'

'Leave me alone.'

'What do you think you're playing at, man, it's not just us that'll get into trouble, it's the whole lot of the lads. You don't want that, do you? Come on, Joe.'

The grip on the bough tightened and the red eyes fixed on John. Joe's breathing became easier but his attitude remained on the offensive. He hefted the bough menacingly, 'Just leave me alone. Come near me an' I'll have you, I swear to God, I will.'

John and Joe stared at each other and Ted's mind was spinning. Now we've caught the bugger what do we do with him? He felt totally helpless as he stared at the two men. Their eyes were locked into each other's and they were frozen into a stand-off. He cast his gaze around but the twilight and the noise of breathing was all there was. Then he saw John's cap lying on the ground in between the two men. Presumably it had landed there during the collision. He began to execute his idea the instant it entered his head.

'Just leave him, John, he's not worth the bloody bother.'

Ignoring Joe, he strode forward confidently and bent down to pick up the cap. As his hand closed around it he launched himself forward with all the speed he could muster, landing his head hard into Joe's belly. The man collapsed against the tree like a bag of slack and lay gasping for breath as Ted kicked the bough from his hand and flung it as far away as he could. Joe was fighting for the breath that had been knocked from his lungs and his face was a mask of agony.

He tossed John's cap back to him and through the silence of the moment they could hear in the distance two blasts of a whistle, one long and one short.

John was looking from Ted to Joe and back again. 'Well, come on some-body, say something. How the Hell are we going to get out of this, eh?'

With a painful grunt, Joe heaved himself slowly to his feet. All sense of menace appeared extinguished. When he spoke, his voice was a painful wheeze. 'You two just go. I'll follow.'

There was a pause, as the two men looked at Joe suspiciously.

'Honest I will. Just go back... now.'

Ted wasn't sure whether the tears welling in the wretched man's eyes were from the sudden winding he had just received or something else going on his tortured mind.

'Come on then.' John turned on his heel and strode back towards the camp, Joe staggering behind.

Ted watched the two figures for a moment, then loped off in pursuit. They reached the edge of the wood and the malodorous smell of the latrine area enveloped them. It was as if the camp had been frozen in time. Nothing seemed to move at all. Ted scanned the whole area as they came to the bottom end of the parade square and he was completely unnerved. Still as statues, and with their backs to the podium were the men of Number One and Number Two Squads.

All eyes were on the three men making their way towards the assembly. Ted wanted to run towards the squad, in order to shorten the time he was spending so conspicuously as the object of focus for all those pairs of eyes, but John Merrigan was in charge, and was marching with all the dignity he could muster towards Sergeant Hanson.

As the three men got closer, Ted saw that the men had not closed ranks but the spaces where he and his companions should be standing at rigid attention were left noticeably empty. Cockney Joe was standing as straight as his heaving lungs would allow as John came to attention in front of Sergeant Hanson. Ted was not sure whether he should do the same in front of Sergeant Malone but that would have meant marching over towards his own squad and there were enough eyes upon him as it was. He waited for John to say something that would formally announce their return but he just stood there, his eyes fixed on the gleaming, brass badge of Hanson's cap. Even Sergeant Hanson appeared non-plussed, as if he too was waiting to hear some kind of excuse for the absenteeism but when it became apparent that none was forthcoming he cleared his throat loudly and ordered John to get fell in. Ted was horrified. Apart from the malevolent stares of the men there was no obvious retribution and John was now safely ensconced in his place – which left himself and Cockney Joe stood in front of the wrong squad.

He stared around until he caught Corporal Lawrie's eye, specifically his right eye, which was hard to miss as it was practically bulging out of his head. His left eye was closed and he was staring straight at Ted. The single eye was alternately boring into Ted's and rotating to stare in the direction of Number One Squad. After an eternity he clicked. He hoped to God Joe would follow his lead as he did a smart turn to the right and marched as briskly as he could until he halted opposite Sergeant Malone. Thankfully, he could hear Joe halt just behind him.

He turned to face his NCO, whose face was surprisingly passive. Following John's lead he stood to rigid attention and said nothing, waiting for his sergeant to allow him to step into his place as quickly and inconspicuously as possible – but it appeared that he was not through being tortured yet. Ted was blushing fit to burst and he was acutely aware of being bareheaded, having lost his cap somewhere during the chase. He was dishevelled and covered in pine needles and wished the ground would open up and swallow him: and he was being bloody well ignored by the only man capable of relieving him of this horror. Was he doing it on purpose? Sergeant Malone's expression hadn't changed in nearly a minute, which felt like over an hour. Ted's mind was racing, had he missed something? What had John Merrigan done right that he hadn't?

Oh God! We're not waiting for Lieutenant Brass, are we?

He didn't need to look around at the faces of the men to feel the bile that was focussing upon himself and Cockney Joe. His world was caving in...

Malone said something which Ted missed. Suddenly Ted was back on the alert; but it was too late. Sergeant Malone's expression had changed to anger and the words came again, but this time a thousand times louder, 'GET FELL IN!'

No one jostled them and no one cursed them: the lads were far too knowing for that. Every misdemeanour, however trivial, would be visited by terrible retribution from Sergeant Malone. The squads were marched to opposite ends of the parade ground where the two sergeants handed over to the junior NCOs. Then began an hour of the hardest drill the lads had come up against so far. Of course they had no idea it was going to be an hour – the first ten minutes alone seemed like an eternity and the sweat was dripping down everyone's back. They marched and counter-marched and marched again. Then it was all done again at the double.

Most of them were fit enough to take the physical punishment but it was the dread of being the first to make a mistake, to put a foot wrong or set off in the wrong direction that terrified them. Every individual's greatest fear was that of being the cause of further punishment for the whole squad, and this was multiplied a thousand-fold for Ted, John and Joe.

Twice, there was the most awful uproar from Number Two Squad, as Corporal Lawrie took some individual to task. The second time it was Fat Harry's name that was screamed out. Eventually, the lads knew the session was drawing to a close when both squads began a series of circuits at the trot. Ted counted twelve and his leg hurt like Hell. He was gasping by the end of it. God knows how lads like Fat Harry and Billy Robson coped.

When they were dismissed, most of them just collapsed on the ground, while some stumbled dizzily off to the latrines. More than one of them had piss stains on their trousers but no one said anything. Ted slumped heavily onto the grass, taking long, controlled breaths in through his nose and exhaling through his mouth.

He looked around to see if he could see Joe and caught the eye of one of the Stanley lads instead. He lip-read the word 'twat' and the expression of sheer loathing took him completely by surprise. That wasn't fair! He had only tried to help his mate.

'Private soldier 2504 Merrigan; Private soldier 2505 Smith; Private soldier 3017 Simpson.'

Sergeant Malone's voice rang around the camp like a great bell. There was no instruction issued, no order given, just three names that hung on the air long after the sound had died away. The lads were on their feet in an instant. Ted hurried towards the little tent next to the podium, wondering vaguely why Cockney Joe's number was so far away from his own and John Merrigan's when they had all enlisted together. He had hardly gone two or three steps when he was deliberately tripped and stumbled hard onto the ground. Stanley bastards! He was up in a second and running again. He caught a glimpse of the offender and was utterly dismayed to see it was Tommy Raper, staring after him with an ugly expression on his face.

No time now.

Outside Lieutenant Brass' tent Sergeant Malone was seated behind a small trestle desk. The battered leather file was open and a list of neatly penned names and numbers were listed on the top of the ledgered page. There were several columns beside the names, all containing immaculate, pencilled ticks. All except the last column was completely filled in: even upside down, Ted could see the very obvious absence of two ticks.

Sergeant Hanson was standing to the right of Sergeant Malone and spoke with quiet authority. 'At ease men.'

The trio obeyed the order then Malone spoke. 'Right lads, who's going to start?'

The silence was agonising. After what seemed like an age, it appeared that no one wanted to explain the situation.

It was John Merrigan who spoke. 'We were skylarking and we missed the whistle... sorry, Sergeant.'

'Skylarking were you, son? Three 'Dirty Little Imps' just playing in the sun. And then you said you were sorry. I suppose that's all there is to it. Would that be right, Private Merrigan?'

The ensuing silence wasn't long but it was very, very deep.

Malone spoke first. 'You've let yourselves down, boys. You have let your squads down and you have let me down. I am not going to give you the whole lecture about being a tight unit or about being there for your comrades; you'll get plenty of that from Lieutenant Brass over the next few weeks. But you have dropped your comrades in the shite, gentlemen, and unless you have anything sensible to say in your defence Sergeant Hanson and I intend to mark you officially absent from parade. This will render you liable to field punishment. Do you understand?'

None of them did, but all three muttered a desultory, 'Yes, Sergeant,' anyway.

'You may, of course decide not to accept our punishment, in which case we refer the matter to Lieutenant Brass on his return. Would you prefer that option?'

'No, Sergeant.'

Very deliberately, and without taking his eyes of the lads, Sergeant Malone leaned forward, took a wooden pen from its groove in the desk and dipped it into the small bottle of ink.

Slowly and deliberately, he drew two indelible, black 'O's into the vacant squares on the pencilled list. The significance of the ink wasn't lost on Ted. It could not be erased. That 'O' was on his record for ever. Sergeant Malone gently blew on his handiwork to make sure it was dry before turning the page to uncover an identical sheet of paper with one tick missing. He glanced up at Sergeant Hanson who nodded. A third 'O' was added alongside John's name. It was frightening how, on a sheet full of identical grey ticks your eye went straight to the black noughts, to the names of the people who had let the side down, to the people who weren't dependable.

'Punishment, Sergeant Hanson?'

There was hardly a pause before the reply came, 'Clean up the shithouse area.'

* * * * *

Ted's spade bashed another sod into its place over the ordure beneath. Even as he patted the turf down he was careful to leave it about three inches proud of the surrounding earth as he had been told last week. This was all so bloody unnecessary. There were still at least three hours to go before dismissal and the six original trenches were easily capable of coping with the amount of shit that would be deposited by then. Ted straightened up and surveyed the area left to be done. John was on his second trench already and appeared to have settled grudgingly into his work. With no specific instructions issued, the lads had decided to take two trenches each. They were about six feet long, a foot wide and a bit less than two feet deep. Urination simply required aiming into the trench but if you needed a shit you had straddle it so that the spoil would be deposited below ground level. Newspaper for wiping was kindly supplied by His Majesty's Armed Forces and was to be found on a tree stump, weighted down by a brick, at the entrance to the area.

When the operation was complete you had to use the spade provided to cover the deposits with the earth originally excavated, which had been left in a neat line alongside the trench.

'Get stuck in, Ted, will you, man?'

Suddenly jerked from his reverie by John's harsh instruction he stopped thinking and worked with a will to finish filling in his trench before digging the fresh one next to it. He cast a glance at Joe who was working steadily, muttering under his breath. It was almost as if he were actually holding a conversation. Ted decided to keep a closer eye on him. If he went daft again they really would be in serious trouble. The whole time he was working Ted kept casting about him for his lost cap. It was embarrassing being bareheaded and he was also afraid of any retaliation being visited upon his missing headgear. The three men worked in comparative silence, settling into the pattern used when working deep underground hewing King Coal. You saved your breath and got on with it, only speaking when the need arose. That way you kept your breath for working instead of pissing it away on small talk that could cost you an extra couple of shovels-full by the end of the shift. Translate that into money and it came to a few extra coppers come pay day and that was always important.

Cockney Joe finished his second trench first, but Ted and John weren't far behind. About three quarters of the way through the last trench, they were aware of Sergeant Hanson watching them from the other side of the square. They did not increase their pace – they were old enough hands at manual work to know that if you did, it would seem obvious to any onlooker that you weren't working your hardest previously. The uniforms were starting to return in dribs and drabs and of course the first thing they did was make for the latrines.

'What cheer, lads,' beamed a short private soldier with a ruddy complexion. He dropped his trousers, confidently and abundantly defecating into the trench Ted was just finishing off.

'I've never had a new trench all to myself before. This is champion, this is. Hand us that shovel, bonny lad.'

Speechless, Ted did as he was bid. What the Hell, he had finished the trench anyway. Another couple of uniforms, deep in conversation about metalled roads and precipitous grounds, casually urinated into Cockney Joe's trench without taking the blindest bit of notice of the red-eyed man with the spade who was watching them. John was watching Cockney Joe, too, just in case he decided to take exception to the intrusion. Joe met his gaze, however, and did nothing beyond jamming his spade into the neat pile of earth that ran beside the trench.

There was no sign of Sergeant Hanson and the only other person in authority that could be seen was Corporal Lawrie, who was drilling Number Two Squad into the ground. Obviously Lieutenant Brass had finished his lecture and Corporal Lawrie had decided to restore the men's circulation.

Sergeant Malone's voice crashed across the parade ground. 'Latrine party to the supply tent... NOW!'

Without a word, John stabbed his spade into the ground and set off at a lope up to the white line that began the square. For one horrible moment Ted, who was a couple of paces behind him, thought he was going to cross the square but he veered off to the right and skirted the line. Joe had fallen in a step behind Ted and, more or less together, the three of them trotted to the entrance of the big, khaki tent where the sergeant was waiting in his customary, stiff-as-a-board, at ease position.

The lads stood to attention without any prompting and awaited whatever fate the NCO was about to visit upon them.

'I'll leave it to youse lads whether you consider yourselves lucky,' he began. 'That is, whether shovelling shit is better than being under the tender care of Corporal Huddart or not. Personally, I couldn't give a damn about any of you. You let Privates Barker and Clarke down this morning before you even arrived and you let the rest of us down just now by buggering off into the woods for a skylark when you should have been ready for duty. Now, I'm going to say this once, so pay attention, especially you, Smith. Piss the army about any more and your arses won't touch the ground for the rest of your career. Do I make myself clear?'

Why me, what the Hell did I do? I want my cap.

Without any hesitation the three replied together, 'Yes, Sergeant.'

'Right. Wait here. Your squad will be out in a minute and you can join them for uniform issue. God help you if you are brought to my attention again.'

Without even waiting to hear the half-hearted 'Yes, Sergeant', he smartly brought himself to attention and marched off in the direction of the podium and the tent beside it.

The 'minute' turned out to be nearer five, but none of the lads moved a muscle as they waited at an uncomfortably strained attention for whatever was about to happen, when the voice of Corporal Huddart vomited from the confines of the supply tent. You couldn't have said that the lads were eavesdropping, but canvas isn't exactly the best barrier for preventing the escape of profane language. The final order to dismiss was followed by the shuffling of feet and the emergence through the now uplifted flap. The tall, spotty lad who couldn't march was first out followed by Tommy Raper and Jacky Tait. Dicky Howell was next and as soon as he saw the trio he silently mouthed the most obscene of oaths. It was instantly obvious why he had not done so with his usual gusto as Lance Corporal Carter was immediately behind him. He saw the three men and moved to stand in front of them. Ted tried to stand even more to attention but it was difficult when he was straining every muscle in his body to the limit already.

Suddenly there was only Lance Corporal Carter in the whole world.

'Well, well, well, if it isn't the three naughty boys. Come to say 'sorry' have we?'

Nobody said a word and the silence hung loud in the air. Suddenly Ted hated Carter's thick, Yorkshire accent, but he blurted out a quick, 'Yes, Corporal, sorry we let you down, Corporal.'

Carter slowly shifted his gaze to Ted but said nothing for a long time until the tent behind him had finished disgorging the remaining men of Number One Squad. He slowly put his whistle to his mouth and Ted could not help focussing on the word 'lusty' stamped into the chromium, it was the same sort as Mr Jobling the greengrocer used for refereeing handball. The screech of the long blast was excruciating, filling Ted's ears with pain; but not to the extent of causing him to miss the all-important second blast when he leaped, with the rest of the lads, to take up his position in the squad. In creditably few seconds, they were formed up on the edge of the square where they waited while Number Two Squad was marched towards them and halted to their right. Corporal Lawrie and Lance Corporal Carter took their places front centre as Sergeants Malone and Hanson walked together from the tent next to the podium to join them. Carter stopped in front of Number Two and Malone faced Number One.

'Private soldier 2505 Smith. To me!'

The words were like a fist to the pit of his stomach and Ted's heart sank for the thousandth time that day. How bloody much more? He left the comfortable anonymity of the centre of the squad and marched as smartly as he could around the outside until he drew level with the big sergeant, where he stood briskly to attention. He had had enough of shit for one day in every possible sense but he was damned if anyone would see it on his face. Sergeant Malone reached into his tunic pocket and withdrew a battered but thankfully unmolested flat cap, which he held out.

With an embarrassed nod, Ted took it and placed it gratefully upon his head, instantly feeling more secure now that he was no longer bareheaded. Should he thank the sergeant? Too late. He was dismissed back to his place in the squad and both units were drilled together while Corporal Huddart supervised the setting up of a trestle table outside the supply tent by his unhappy pair of boys. Bits of uniform appeared on it and eventually the two squads were halted facing the little NCO. Further along at the kitchen area the uniformed soldiers were being doled out tea and leftover bread. They were in good cheer, grinning and pointing in their direction, obviously well aware of what was coming next.

It wasn't as bad as the lads thought. Huddart was an evil little bastard but here he was in his element, ruler of all he surveyed, which put him in what passed for a good mood. He asked for a volunteer and when none was forthcoming he chose the lanky kid who couldn't march and made him stand next to the table and strip naked. A few embarrassed chuckles went round but not much more. The men had already deduced that Huddart could switch moods in a second and no one was prepared to risk being a target for that. The kid, who was made to introduce himself and told not to be shy, pronounced himself to be William Maddison from West Stanley.

Immediately seizing the opportunity Huddart proceeded to refer to the boy as 'Big Willy' much to the amusement of the audience. He kept the lad standing naked and to attention for far longer than was necessary while he explained about the uniform they were all going to be proud to wear, and was endlessly amused by Maddison's breaking voice, even to the extent of imitating it like a Music Hall turn. Ted began to wonder about Huddart's motives for this, bearing in mind that his two helpers were of a similar age.

He began with 'drawers, cotton', which didn't look half as serviceable as pit long johns but the Maddison lad was more than grateful to cover his nakedness, only to discover he was to disrobe again in order to demonstrate 'drawers, woollen'. It was obvious the lad was in desperate discomfort but that was not going to stop the unsinkable corporal from trying to wring the last ounce of humour from his predicament. The final straw came as the corporal hefted a pair of 'trousers, service dress' and after a brief description of flies, braces buttons and turn-downs he decided it was too warm for the woollen drawers and perhaps Big Willy would be more comfortable in the cotton version, so would he strip again. Close to tears but with his face a mask of determination Maddison did so, standing to a gawky attention at the end. The laughter was non-existent now. The joke was long over, except, it seemed, for Corporal Huddart. Ted risked a glance sideways and saw Sergeant Malone staring expressionless at the demonstration. That was all right, then; he didn't like it, either.

Suddenly aware that his innuendos were no longer eliciting any kind of amusement, Corporal Huddart changed tack and for the rest of the demonstration was all brisk efficiency. The two young privates handed him various bits of gear, which he described, demonstrated and handed to Maddison to don. Every so often he cast a sidelong glance at Sergeant Malone, who was staring unblinkingly back. Was he there to make sure the little corporal didn't go too far in his abuse of the men?

In a short time, Maddison was standing in the at ease position, wearing the uniform of a member of the Durham Light Infantry. The last article of clothing to be demonstrated was the soft cap. The lads were assured that this was the most important piece of kit they would be issued, on account of the badge. Any silly bugger could wear the uniform but the badge was important. The badge was unique. The badge marked you out as a privileged person, a soldier in no less a brotherhood than the Durham Light Infantry. He held the cap aloft in one hand and the badge between the thumb and forefinger of the other. After a quick demonstration of how to affix the pair together using the locating holes and the split pin he perched the finished item upon the head of Private Maddison. Ted thought he made himself look ridiculous, having to reach up so far to place the headgear on the tall boy's head. If it were up to him, he would have picked somebody shorter.

He didn't actually look too bad at all. The trousers were a bit short but once the puttees were applied they looked fine. The spots on his forehead stood out a bright, angry red and he positively reeked of mothballs but, in the main, even this gangling youth was made to look a bit dignified by wearing the King's uniform. He was stood to attention and made to march up and down a bit, the better to show the kit off, then stood to attention once again and forgotten whilst the lads were ordered to form an orderly queue outside the tent that held the kit ready to be issued. Talking quietly was allowed until you entered the tent. Ted was eighth or ninth from the tent flap, which he thought was grand. Just close enough to the front to hear what was going on so he wouldn't make any mistakes, but not too far back that he would have to wait ages. As soon as the first man went through the flap a weak voice shouted, 'Name and Number.' It must have been Sam Hurry or his mate. Just then, Ted received a painful jab in the kidney, which made him gasp aloud. It took him a moment to recover from the pain and surprise and he turned his head to see one of the Stanley men in his squad staring hatefully at him.

'Just a reminder, bonny lad, You dropped us in the shite. Just watch your back, eh.'

Ted stopped himself launching a fist by an effort of sheer will. It would be just his bloody luck to have a go at this bastard and get caught again, further reinforcing himself as a troublemaker. He decided it would be best left alone, and turned his back on the man.

Another jab and tiny lights spun in the air in front of Ted's eyes.

When he had recovered, he adopted what he hoped looked like a casual manner and turned to look into the eyes of his attacker. Aware that all eyes were on him, he managed a half smile.

'Try that again, and I'll flatten you,' he promised quietly, although the force of his intentions was probably quite clear to everyone.

Suddenly, he was at the flap and almost missed the reply of 'any time' as he entered.

'Name and Number!'

It was Sam Hurry standing behind an empty trestle. To the rear of the boy was another trestle laden with trousers. The pattern was repeated all around the inside of the tent until it reached the flaps again. The first man in was still only halfway round though, so half the issue staff were just stood waiting.

'Smith, Edward. 2505, Private.'

Hurry ticked off the name on a clipboard list and looked Ted up and down with a practiced eye. He turned to choose a pair of 'trousers: service dress' from the neat piles behind him. Motioning Ted to put his arms out in front he unceremoniously dumped the garment onto them, at the same time jerking his head to the right, indicating that he should move on. Hurry's mate looked Ted up and down in an identical manner and dumped a 'jacket: service dress' on top of the trousers.

As he moved on, Ted listened carefully as his assailant gave his name and number: Private 2806 Christopher Turner. He was determined to take his revenge on Christopher *bloody* Turner at the first opportunity that didn't land him in trouble again.

Moving along the U-shaped queue, he collected an ever-growing pile of clothing and gear and was surprised to discover it even included the likes of braces and hairbrushes. By the time he had gone round to collect his 'cap, soft, service with badge' and finally his 'boots, ankle' (which were the only items for which he was asked the size) he was beginning to feel almost buoyant. This was the moment he had waited for and if it weren't for all the misfortune that had befallen them that day he would have felt absolutely elated. He emerged from the tent and followed the queue up to the kitchen area where people were finding themselves a space and cramming their newfound treasure into the kitbag provided. Why the canvas bag had been issued halfway around the queue instead of at the beginning or at the end was dismissed as one of those army foibles they would just have to get used to.

Ted knelt down to fill his bag, and was shortly joined by Jacky Tait who was grinning like a Cheshire cat. It was a bit hard that the women had packed up early so there was no tea, because everybody was parched, but that was that. While the lads were packing their kit the uniforms were striking the supply tent and packing the surplus items of gear into various crates and boxes. The NCOs wandered amongst the men giving pointers or reprimands where required and eventually everyone had their kit more or less stowed. The men were put into their squads on the edge of the square, each man keeping his kitbag beside him.

Sergeants Malone and Hanson were back in charge now and things felt a bit more like normal. They were given a talking to about how the kit was now theirs but more importantly was their responsibility. By next week it was to be cleaned, where necessary altered to fit and the boots worn as often as possible to get them broken in – and they were to have a shine on them like a shithouse door on a frosty morning, or else. Apart from that, they had done a good day's work.

The uniforms had finished packing the gear onto the motorised wagon and were then formed up and marched once round the square to be halted in front of the lads where they stood to attention.

Sergeant Malone spoke. 'Now please note, gentlemen, that these uniformed soldiers have done a longer, harder day's work than you have and are still a presentable body of men. This is the example they have set you and this is the example you are to follow to the letter.'

He was right, as well. Ted could see the boots were scuffed and scratched by the day's toil but underneath the mud the shine was so deep you could just about shave in it. The cap badges shone and the creases were still evident in the trousers and sleeves. Each man's clothing fitted like a glove. Bertha would have her work cut out this week and no mistake.

'Private Barker, Private Clarke. To me.' Sergeant Malone's voice boomed out and Jimmy and Harry left their positions to stand to attention in front of the NCO. Harry was seconded to Number One Squad and Jimmy to Number Two.

Lance Corporal Carter then spoke. 'Right lads, this looks like a repeat performance of last week, doesn't it? What is it about you mongers that you just can't bloody well behave? We seem to have improved, gentlemen. This week I have not one group misdemeanour to deal with but two.' A frozen pause hung in the air that no one felt the urge to break. 'So! We have a bunch of schoolboys who like to go for a skylark instead of being on the square...'

That's not fair, we've been punished for that!

'... and a fight in the ranks during supply parade.'

Ted's stomach lurched. He hadn't fought, just given a warning, surely.

'... and what, gentlemen, or should I say who, is the common denominator in these two most deplorable incidents? Private 2505 Smith. To me!'

Fighting back his rage at this injustice and blushing fit to set himself on fire Ted did as he was ordered. He was about turned so that he faced the fellow members of his squad and then Lance Corporal Carter really got stuck in. He summarised the events concerning the incident with Cockney Joe as a playful bunking-off episode and described the attack by the man who had turned out to be Christopher bloody Turner upon Ted as a minor scrap that both parties should be thoroughly ashamed of. Since Ted was a party to both incidents he was to be made an example of. And here he was, burning with shame and fury. Ted hated Lance Corporal Carter and he hated his stupid Yorkshire accent. He hated Cockney Joe and he hated

Christopher *bloody* Turner. He was dismissed back into his place and the order was given to the worst squad on parade that day. Clean up the shithouse area.

* * * * *

The march home was a quiet one, for not even Billy or Dicky seemed to have much to say. To be fair to the lads, they left Ted, John and Cockney Joe well alone, so by the time they had crossed the catwalk they were just a straggling bunch of men. Harry Clarke looked at Jimmy Barker to check whether or not to pull them back into marching order but Jimmy just shook his head. Best let it be for now; they were nearly at the community washhouse where they would be dismissed and it would be best to let the whole thing drop and start off fresh next time.

'Er, dismiss, lads. See youse all later, eh?'

With that, he looked about him for a moment and turned to go home. Some of the lads did the same whilst others dumped their kit bags on the black ground and, lighting tabs, got themselves into little groups for a natter. Ted looked around but could catch no one's eye so decided to go straight home. He didn't want to talk to anybody anyway.

Bertha heard the gate crash and knew her man was back. She had made a barley broth with dumplings today so that if he was delayed it would keep and taste just as good later on. He opened the door and her smile widened to a grin. The grin faded when she saw the expression on Ted's face. She couldn't quite place it, but something was wrong.

Rallying, she said, 'How's my Dirty Little Imp, then?' and gave him a hug and a kiss that were only perfunctorily returned, so she tried a new tack, cocking her head towards the kit bag and saying, 'That's nice pet, you've brought me a present, shall I open it now or after you've had your dinner?'

She was relieved to see his weak attempt to smile as he let the bag fall carelessly to the scullery floor, and was surprised at the intensity of the hug he gave her.

'Let's have our dinner, pet, we'll have a look afterwards.'

He ate heartily enough but remained quiet and Bertha didn't push him. He would come around in his own time. She was pleased that Robert had already left. He had finished his shift that afternoon and was now on the bicycle heading for Sunniside and his Louise. After a bath in front of the fire and a couple of tabs he took up the bag and displayed the contents on the floor, explaining as he went. She could sense the lack of enthusiasm, though, and when he had finished, he declined her offer of a cup of tea and a couple of games of floater, in favour of going to bed early. Bertha stayed up for a while, saying that she had some darning to finish and a handful of baps to make which would bake by themselves in the cooling oven, then she would bring him a nice mug of tea when she came up. She was less than an hour, and half of that was examining Ted's newly acquired equipment. She held the tunic up to her nose and gently inhaled. The smell of the naphtha spun her back to Consett and to Crozier's, and to trotting around the streets in the cart in the sunshine collecting and delivering laundry. She buried her face in the coarse, khaki material, shuddered, and breathed in deeply. Her past was so alive, so immediate, there was Tappy Lappy, gurgling fit to bust, and there was Gabriel and all the children smiling and waving.

Dear God, how I miss you all.

But her man was troubled and she must go to him so she made the tea and went upstairs, leaving his kit where it was, spread out on the floor. He was snoring gently, and the fresh stains on the pillow showed he had cried himself to sleep. Bertha bit her bottom lip and restrained herself from running her hand through his tousled hair. She got into bed as quietly as she could so as not to disturb him and sipped her tea in the dark. He was so like a bairn sometimes. No! All the time. What had upset him so much? She would likely have to wait until tomorrow to find that out.

Chapter 14

Langley Park Colliery Village, Sunday 12th April 1914

The rain-soaked chill of April passed into a breezy May and on into June. Ted's wounded pride was short lived and healed quickly enough as he grew ever more confident in his abilities as a soldier. There wasn't much bother with Christopher bloody Turner at camp. Once he tried to trip Ted during a mapping exercise and was rewarded, quick as a flash, with a blow to the chest followed by an iron grip to his throat and the threat of never making it back to camp again. From then on, they gave each other hard stares whenever their paths crossed but that seemed to be all.

Cockney Joe's house, once it had been stripped bare by the bailiffs was given to a newly married young hewer called Willy Reid from the village. He had been living with his skinny wife, Alice, who looked about fourteen, at her Mam and Dad's house in West Cross Street and Ted had never once seen him in the pub. It was less than three days after Joe and Lettie's eviction that the Reids moved in and the lad was in the Blue Star the same night. He drank two pints of ale, struggling with the second, and to everyone's great amusement, practically staggered out of the place. It was Jacky Tait who had remarked with a grin that it must be grand to be out from under the thumb. Ted had silently wished the raw young'un more luck in his new house than Cockney Joe and Lettie and little Sarah had ever had.

Joe was no longer living rough but was sleeping in the cloakroom of the Salvation Army hut by the allotments up at South View. He was on his honour to Captain Forsyth to leave the place every day as he found it and to bring no hard liquor onto the premises; and, if he so wished, he might join any of the meetings or services that he chose. When Joe received the offer of the stark, bare floorboards of the Sally Ann hut, he swallowed what little pride he had left and thanked Captain Forsyth with all humility. He chose to attend none of the prayer meetings but just to be on the safe side obeyed the first two instructions to the letter. He scrounged a hot meal at the end of the shift where he could and mumbled monosyllabic thanks as he left immediately afterwards, shunning all requests to stay on for a bit.

Robert and Louise were finally to be married and time was moving on. They were into the first week of July now and arrangements were well under way for the forthcoming ceremony, which was to be held at the Primitive Methodist Chapel in Tow Law in August. Robert had a spring in his step that was hard to hide. He was up to Sunniside a couple of times during the week now as well as on Sundays and sometimes he even used his hard-earned money to go on the omnibus instead of using the bike. Bertha wondered how that clapped out old contraption managed to stay in one piece. She remembered the bike fondly. It had been given to the Smiths by old Bobby Stokoe the day he was sacked from the pit and it was the main reason Ted was able to get up to Blackhill so often when they were stepping steady. It all seemed so long ago. They had only just had their first anniversary and already it was like ancient history. Anyway, it was Robert's turn now and about time too. He was practicing a lot on his violin so he could do a turn after the ceremony and at Bertha's request he had included 'Danny Boy' which still brought her to tears (much to Ted's amusement) whenever he played it. There was still no sign of a house in Langley, though, and time was running short.

But Ted had problems of his own this week. The first was that next Saturday's camp set-up was now down to his squad so they would have to be at Burnhope for 0600 hours instead of 0800 and of course they would finish and get home that much later after striking camp and packing everything up. Then again, the officers and NCOs were there at 0600 hours every week.

The second was the increasingly pessimistic subject matter droning out of Lieutenant Brass' lectures. The last one was the worst. It was grand to learn all the facts and oddities about how to fight a war, even though you were only given a pickaxe handle instead of a 303 rifle, except the 'World Affairs' bit was not only depressing, but the urgency imposed upon it had become downright alarming. Lieutenant Brass had picked up on a minor article in the previous week's *Advertiser*.

On Sunday, the 28th June 1914, Archduke Ferdinand of Austria–Hungary had been assassinated whilst he and his wife were on a state visit to Bosnia. A madman had shot them dead in their motorcar. Now, the madman wasn't from Bosnia, he was from Serbia, but since both Bosnia and Serbia were on our side and Austria–Hungary was one of the opposing Central Powers, it was making some decidedly nasty noises about invading Serbia as punishment. Serbia apologised and shouted its innocence to the world saying that just because the assassin was Serbian you can't blame the whole bloody country, but Austria wasn't listening.

Lieutenant Brass reckoned it was just the excuse they needed to invade and occupy Serbia, which they had had their eye on for years. The trouble was, because Serbia was on our side, France would have to help which meant Germany would come in against France. Belgium was in there somewhere and if anybody touched them, Great Britain would defend them like a shot. And Russia... Russia? Somewhere about three quarters of the way through this explanation Ted – and most of the other lads as well – gave up. The upshot was plain to see however: unless something very drastic happened, the whole of Europe would topple into an all-out scrap.

Everybody knew that Germany was the real pain in the arse – they were the ambitious buggers – but all these treaties that everybody had with everybody else seemed to mean that if any one country picked a fight the whole of Europe would wade in and there'd be Hell to pay. Mind you, he was assured it would be a short war and at the end of it the air would be cleared and all the nations would know exactly where they stood. It annoyed him a bit that every time he got home and tried to explain to Bertha about the Central Powers and the Allies and what the latest moves were, she seemed to know as much about it from the papers and nattering to her pals as he did! What's more, Lieutenant Brass had told all the lads in the greatest of confidence that this was restricted information and was not to be bandied about in public, as there were spies everywhere. They must be working for the *Durham Advertiser*, then.

Anyway, the consequence of all this appeared to be that far from leading the safe and simple life of Territorial soldiers who would remain in England and defend the shores of their country, they must now consider the possibility of being on active service alongside their regular brothers-in-arms in the European Theatre of War. This was a great honour and every member of the DLI who so served would be anointed with glory.

That was all very well, but was he going to tell Bertha?

This was exactly what she and her Dad had predicted would happen and here it was... bugger! What's more, due to the deteriorating situation between Austria and Serbia (or was it Bosnia now?) the lighter duty Summer Camp to Scarborough was to be cancelled and replaced with the rather more onerous war training course in Morfa Camp in Conway, North Wales – date to be announced, but imminent. The march home that Saturday was the quietest yet. Each man occupied not so much with thoughts of fighting on foreign soil, but, after weeks of both looking forward to sunny Scarborough and making light of the whole Territorial business to their wives and mothers, they would now have to deliver the news that they would most likely be an integral part of the British Expeditionary Force to Europe. There was hardly any banter and it seemed to come as a relief when they were finally dismissed outside the community washhouse. George Moody, who had a further couple of miles to go home to Witton Gilbert, inquired if anybody fancied a quick pint in the Blue Star, but only a handful went along, the rest overcoming the anxiety of confessing to their families that the great lark that had been joining the Terries had finally congealed into the stark reality of a fighting a war in foreign parts.

Ted saved the news until after dinner that night so as not to spoil their enjoyment of the meal. As was to be expected Bertha made great capital out the event. Not in any hysterical or shrewish way but with the keenest of sharp phrases. Where Ted had expected a scene there was only a quiet conversation across the kitchen table, but you could have cut through the pauses with a gully knife.

'So, no more Scarborough?' she said eventually.

He couldn't tell whether she sounded happy or sarcastic or what. He thought hard to come up with a reply that would make him appear both nonchalant and informed.

'No pet.'

She drummed her fingers on the table for a while before replying, 'You don't have to go, do you?'

Ted knew there were ways out of it if he really tried, like he could swing the lead about his broken leg not being up to it, but he didn't want to. Plus, he could already hear the sniggering of his comrades for being under his wife's thumb.

'Well, I suppose you'd better go then.'

Relief flooded through Ted like a bursting dam, tempered ever so slightly by apprehension concerning the tone in which his release was delivered.

'I suppose so... it's just if things get bad, like...'

'For God's sake, Teddy, things *are* bad. You've just got to look at the papers, man... there's going to be a war and I don't want you in it. Can you not get that into your skull! This isn't a game, man. Once you go across the water you could be shot and killed. Yes, you!'

As if to make the point, she jabbed him hard in the chest with her finger. He felt the force of the thrust on his breastbone. The pain was hard enough for him to involuntarily cover his heart with his hand. He felt exposed somehow, defenceless, like.

All his arguments about glory and the short duration of such a conflict fell to the floor, scattered like a pack of cards and he hadn't the faintest idea how to pick them up.

Chapter 15

Langley Park Colliery Village, Tuesday 21st July 1914

The cage clanged to a halt at the surface and the bright, early afternoon sun was dazzling to eyes that had spent hours straining to see by the light of a dim lamp.

The jack engine relief valve outside the cage suddenly let off a howling scream that made the miners jump. It didn't usually do that, and for about half a minute the banshee wail drilled through to the bones of the men as they left the cage and began to shuffle down the boarded walkway to set off home after their shift.

There was no thought of conversation with that uproar going on and Ted actually felt the noise vibrating through his teeth. The clamour stopped as unexpectedly as it started but all the men were temporarily deafened and the only thing inside their heads was an infernal ringing that made any crack impossible. Ted was with Jacky and John as they stepped off the ramp where a couple of blacksmiths were trying to calm down a hysterical pony, obviously upset by the racket, before stepping into the cage. Their ruddy expressions, brought on by spending lives in close proximity to the red-hot forges, never ceased to be a source of wonder to Ted. He lived in a world where men were either white as snow or black as coal, depending on whether you were starting a shift or finishing it. For a brief couple of weeks in the summer when the pit was closed everyone managed to go a shade redder when exposed to the summer sun while they either lazed away their days or toiled in their allotments, but these iron workers always had an appearance of rude health about them that somehow made him jealous.

His back was aching and his leg hurt. Would the damned thing ever heal properly and give him some peace? He followed the example of every other hewer around him and loudly hawked up a great load of black mucus and spat it out onto the ground before ascending the open stairway to the catwalk. The jack engine shriek had been replaced by the crashing cacophony of the endless belts overhead as they carried the fresh-hewn coal to the Carrs disintegrator shed. He licked his lips but could still feel the dust scrape along his tongue and so spat again. There had been a crackdown on spitting on the catwalk and notices were up all over the place informing every employee to 'expectorate with due care for other members of the company and to keep the elevated walkway clear of phlegm at all times' – which the lads had rightly translated as not gobbing where the office workers could step in it.

Still quiet, the group of men re-formed into a caterpillar-like column as they shambled along the catwalk towards the village on the other side of the line. Pipes and tabs were lit up and inhaled gratefully. Ted narrowed his eyes and gazed off to the right towards the Ottos, the huge, beehive-like coking furnaces cocooned in clouds of perpetual smoke. Even in the daylight, you could see the faint red haze that, when the sun had set, became the crimson glow of Hell that marked them out for miles around. An official of some sort was striding towards them, clad in a black overcoat and bowler hat, and carrying a shiny new leather brief case. To a man, the entire column of hewers moved respectfully to one side to allow him to pass, touching their caps as they did so.

He repeated, 'Good afternoon, good afternoon,' several times and Ted wasn't the only one to wonder at his obvious youth and his pitiful attempt to grow a pencil moustache that had all but failed. At least his passing provoked the men into conversation, if only to deride him behind his back for his lack of years, and to wonder which office worker's son he might be to get such a leg up as to be wearing a bowler hat at his age. Anyway, Ted was convinced he could grow a better moustache than that.

As the group descended the stairway to the washhouse, many a toothy white grin broke across black faces at the sight of the children stubbing out rolly tabs and wafting the air with their hands to clear the smoke. Then the notice pinned to the wooden wall of the washhouse caught their attention. The unmistakable Crown and Bugle of the DLI crest was printed Centre-top and underneath. Hand-written in bold, confident capital letters was the single word, 'URGENT'.

This immediately divided the men into those who needed to know the latest developments and those not involved with the regiment, who either carried on home or went to the Blue Star. Not everybody remaining could read, so it ended up being Fat Harry's job to broadcast the contents. Relishing his momentary importance, he cleared his throat loudly and spat out a great dottle of black before he began.

'It is the duty of all members of the Eighth Durham Light Infantry, who, upon

learning the contents of this brief, do consider themselves duty bound to pass on such information as is contained herein to all other members of the Eighth Durham Light Infantry who lie within their ken.'

He paused as the little crowd grew restive, with murmurs of, 'Get on with it, man, Harry. I want my dinner while it's still hot, man,' and 'Cut the shite out and just tell us what the gist is, will you?'

A little offended by this less than enthusiastic reception to his public speaking capabilities, Fat Harry attempted to continue reading the notice word for word until Billy Robson let rip with a fart both long enough and loud enough to get the attention of half the village. His equally strident voice sailed over the mutters of disgust at his behaviour, as he said, 'We only want the gist, Harry, all right?'

Conscious of his moment of fame having slipped away, Harry silently admitted defeat and scanned the rest of the notice, his lips moving wordlessly as he absorbed the information. After a few seconds he spoke.

'We're off to Conway on the 25th... next Saturday... for two weeks.'

It was as if a great cloud had descended over the lads. Two weeks... two weeks! The shit would really hit the fan now. Suddenly every mind started to race at once.

How far is it?

How do we get there?

What about work?

How does the family get paid?

What about the allotments, the pigeons, the Leek Show?

Are you allowed to drink ale?

Suddenly Ted heard Jacky's voice muttering in his ear, 'Handball semis are on Sunday 26th, day after we go.'

Bugger! Half the teams would be missing so the whole thing would be a shambles. Ted lit another tab and shouldered his way through the thinning crowd to read the notice for himself. The upshot was that the Langley Park contingent would parade at 0650 outside the Blue Star where 'duly appointed officers or NCOs' would march them to Durham Station to embark on a troop train at 1010 hours. They were to be in uniform, carrying full issue pack and have enough food to last for one day; and they were to miss the semi-bloody-finals of the handball league as well! Ted was in two minds whether to go for a pint as he trudged miserably alongside John and a silent Cockney Joe to the top of Logan Street. They parted company with a nod and Ted thought better of it. The fact that he had to walk past his own house where Bertha could see him might have had something to do with it. As luck would have it, she wasn't in the yard but there was a load of washing on the line so, slamming the gate behind him, he carefully negotiated the sparkling white sheets so as not to get coal dust all over them. Nothing was worth that.

Bertha seemed in a canny enough mood as he undid his boots at the door; she had just whitened the step as well so he took exaggerated care to avoid getting black on it. He stripped to his combinations in the scullery and loped into the kitchen to be handed a mug of strong, sweet tea. The tin bath was ready in front of the fire and the smell of stew and dumplings was mouth-watering. There was an enamel tray of scones cooling on the hearth and an empty plate on the table by his elbow displayed evidence of crumbs, which prompted him to mischief.

'Who's been stealing the scones, then pet?'

The reply was just as cheeky. 'Cat next door. You can have one with your cup of tea if you like, or you can keep it 'till after you've had your dinner.'

She knew the answer before he could acknowledge the statement and he grinned as she went to get the butter. The grin faded as she continued, however, 'The rest's for Jenny Timms and Lettie. I'll take them up while you're in the bath.'

She deposited the freshly buttered morsel onto the crumby plate and put it back on the table beside him. She also handed him a grubby, folded piece of paper.

'This was stuck through the sneck when I came back from the allotment.'

She said no more but sat purposefully down across the table from her husband and looked straight at him. It was folded into quarters and bore the name 'Ted S' on the outside. Ted was sure she would not have read it even though he wouldn't have minded if she had. She was a bit stiff-necked sometimes, was Bertha, but that didn't stop her waiting patiently until he came in so she could share the contents. He thought about a bit of monkey business where he would say he might open it after his bath because his hands were covered in coal dust, but one look at the fingers drumming on the table was enough to make him think again.

It turned out to be from John Brannon, the landlord at the Star, informing him that due to the present circumstances the handball matches due to be played on the 26th of July would now be brought forward to Sunday the 19th and he hoped Ted would be able to compete. Could he please let him know as soon as possible.

Bertha let out a sigh of relief, 'Is that all? I thought it was the DLI come to haunt us again. Well thank the Lord for that. I'm off to Jenny's now.'

She stood up and took her shawl down from the hook on the back door and, tipping the scones unceremoniously into the armadillo basket, blew a kiss towards her husband. 'I'll be back in time to scrub your back, pet.'

Ted took the quickest bath he could, because he knew bloody well that Bertha would come home from the Timms' house with full knowledge of what was happening to the Durhams. It wasn't that he hadn't told her deliberately, but she was out of the door before he had got round to it, that's all. He was naked and vulnerable in the tiny bath and he didn't want to be in that position when she flew through the door demanding to know what was going on. He had meant to tell her as soon as he stepped over the threshold, honest!

He managed to scramble, still mostly damp, into the clothes that had been laid out over the back of the chair to warm by the fire. He even managed to empty the bath into the yard, taking the utmost care not to splash the sheets on the line, and hang it on the nail on the netty wall. The expected storm did not, however, materialise. Instead, the door opened quietly and the sneck was dropped gently into place.

Bertha took in the room at a glance, noting her husband's casual, cross-legged deportment as he smiled up at her from his chair. It was no good, she couldn't be angry with him. She couldn't help a thin smile as she took off her shawl and, rolling it into a bundle, threw it at the gangling, puppy-like creature sat in the chair.

'Come on then, Mr Smith. Out with it.'

While she dished up the stew, Bertha listened quietly as he related all he knew about the camp at Conway. It wasn't much more than she had heard from Jenny Timms and he could not answer the questions she asked of him, like what was happening to the pay? With no bairns to feed yet, they weren't doing too badly but the thought of no money coming in from the pit for all that time did worry her. What must it be like for those families with lots of mouths to feed? She suggested he might go and see Harry Clarke later on and find out if he knew any more. Harry had, after all, attended previous annual camps so he might be able to shed some light on the situation. There was a moment of panic when she mentioned Robert's forthcoming wedding, until they worked out that he would be back a good few days before the event. Still, he felt secretly ashamed that the wedding had not entered his head until the subject had been brought up by his wife. Ted was thinking on his feet now. He used the last of the bread as a shovel to pick up the remains of the gravy from his second helping as he planned the rest of the day. If he went to the allotment this afternoon, he would have to go to Harry's in the evening. Harry always went to the Blue Star in the evening and anyway, didn't he have to see John Brannon about the handball?

It was all very well John saying he hoped everybody could attend the new date set for the semi-finals but Ted was supposed to be working this Sunday and nobody just takes the day off, not unless you want to lose a day's wages. You can't very well plead illness either – not if you're going to be seen jumping about like a silly bugger in the handball court with everybody and their granny watching.

Get our Robert to swap shifts... that was it!

By the time he had helped clear the table it was all sorted in his head. Bertha had just got a new bag of seed taties from Jobling's greengrocers and Ted was to take them to the allotment and trench them in after he had set some of the bigger carrots into new cramps. Bertha had said that Walter Timms, Jenny's man, had just had a load of fresh horse manure delivered to his allotment which was only three gates down from Ted's so if Ted gave him a hand to shift it, mebbes he could have a bit for the taties as well. Robert was working two extra half-shifts today and tomorrow in order to cover for somebody or other's injury and would be in at six o'clock tonight, so if Ted got home at the same time they could all have a bite to eat together. He thought better of bringing up the idea of exchanging shifts whilst eating in case Bertha had something to say about it, but there was nothing wrong with taking Robert with him when he went to see Harry and John and having a word over a couple of pints of ale.

With any luck, by the time he went to bed tonight he would have the allotment ship-shape, all questions about Conway answered, handball sorted out for next weekend and two or three pints of ale in his belly. Nowt the matter with that!

He grabbed the big shovel and the garden fork from the coalhouse, and also took the opportunity to wear his army boots to soften them up a bit more. His wife handed him some fresh tea in the enamel flask and a surprise scone she had saved him from her baking. Normally they would have gone to the allotment together but what with all the flat ironing to do and Robert's tea to see to, for when he came in, she had plenty to deal with. She stood at the gate and watched her man walk up the street back towards the pit and thence to the allotments further up the line past the Ottos. Her keen eyes crinkled with amusement as she watched him eat the scone in one mouthful. It was supposed to be for his break but she knew it would never make it out of the street. He was a silhouette against the sun now and that made his limp all the more obvious. It was only slight but it gave him a rolling gait, like a sailor, and she knew it would never get better. As she walked back up the yard, she absent-mindedly felt the washing hanging on the line. Just right for ironing: thanks be to the Good Lord for this July sunshine.

But first, she would tidy up Robert's room and see how many cups he had under the bed.

* * * * *

Ted's plan had worked a treat and he had rarely felt so cocky. Here he was in the Blue Star with a tab in his mouth and a pint glass in his hand. The conversation was flowing as freely and pleasantly as the beer, and all was right with the world. Indeed, things had panned out even better than he had hoped. When Robert had come in from his shift he brought some news of his own. The shift deputy had called him up before he got into the cage and told him to get straight to Mr Swallow's office.

Thankfully, he was clean, as he had been summoned before he had started his shift. He stubbed out his tab with his heel, took off his cap and opened the door to the main office. Two or three young lasses and a boy sporting the lamest moustache Robert had ever seen were sat at little desks writing things in ledgers behind a great wooden counter. An older lady whom he recognised as Mrs Sanders who ran the office, got up from where she was sitting behind a much bigger desk and came towards him. A couple of stifled giggles from the girls had been cut short by a severe glance and she listened patiently as Robert explained that he had been sent to see Mr Swallow, the colliery manager, but he didn't know why.

She asked his name and payroll number then turned to a highly polished wooden mail cabinet. Her fingers hovered for a second over the little piles in the 'S' pigeonhole until she extracted a half foolscap brown envelope and handed it to him without a word. Robert read the neat, italic script on the front in the hope that it would give him a clue but all it displayed was 'Smith R.T. LPCPRN 00663.'

At a loss as to what to do next, he decided to leave and read the contents in private but he was stopped by Mrs Sanders who politely requested that he open and read the letter here and now. He did. The recently vacated miners' residence at Number Ten George Street was his if he wanted it. He couldn't stop his hands from shaking as his face split into a broad grin. All troubles over, all problems solved. The lady was grinning as broadly as he was – she had bloody well known what was in the envelope all along! There were a couple of forms to read about conditions of let and rent arrears and such stuff, then he had to sign them and she signed after him. She conveyed Mr Swallow's apologies that he could not award the property in person but was rather busy at the moment and wished Mr Smith well in his new home. Champion!

So here they all were in the Blue Star with lots to rejoice about all round. Robert had bought the first round for Ted, Harry and himself to commemorate the fact he was now an official resident of Langley Park with his very own house.

Robert easily agreed to swap shifts so that Ted could play handball next Sunday, so Ted was celebrating. They were both relieved that the news about Louisa finally moving to Langley had put Bertha in such a good mood that she positively pushed them out of the door to go to the pub, but don't forget to bring her back a bottle of stout. The real icing on the cake for all of them was that Number Ten George Street was practically dead opposite Ted and Bertha's out the back.

They were on their third pint now and had been joined by a few of the lads who all wished Robert well in his new home and then tried to find out what they could about who was available for the handball so they would know where to bet their coppers.

Morfa Camp, in north Wales, was generally accepted as an act of fate and like it or not they were going: pity it wasn't Scarborough, though. Harry Clarke had put everybody's mind at rest about pay by telling the lads that their wives would get a money order in the post from the army every week they were away. Naturally, the pit would pay you nowt for the duration.

On the international front, it looked like the assassination of Archduke Ferdinand was about to have the grim implications that Lieutenant Brass said it would at the last camp. The Austrio-Hungarian government was having none of Serbia's entreaties that the murder was nothing to do with them and nobody was in any doubt that they would invade; it was just a question of when. The first pint, burdened with such news, was a quiet affair, but the third, with all the good stuff about the handball and Robert having a house to live in prior to his wedding next month, lifted the mood no end.

Suddenly, over the general uproar, a high-pitched yapping announced the arrival of Clementine, the little sausage dog, and Fat Ena, come to the bottle-and-jug for her jar of ale and nightly argument about how she was always cheated out of the full amount. Patrick rolled his eyes Heavenward but business was business and Fat Ena was a regular customer, even if he did wish she would fall into the Browney and drown... along with her yappy bloody dog.

'Don't forget the change Patrick,' shouted his Dad as the lad headed reluctantly off to the bottle-and-jug counter.

Handball forgotten for the moment, the crowd's noise abated slightly for the nightly entertainment of Fat Ena trying to cajole an extra couple of mouthfuls of ale from the ever more hard-hearted young man who would have none of it. Eventually she left, grumbling and bemoaning the ways of this cruel world to Clementine who, catching her mistress' mood, yowled back in sympathy.

That's where everybody in the place would join in the yowling and John would shake his head once again and carry on pouring pints.

'Last orders in ten minutes, lads. Are you listening?' John's strident voice reached into every nook and cranny of his public house and upon repeating the instruction a second time he was joined by Caesar's sonorous bark from somewhere out the back. The cleverer ones took this as a cue to nip round to the bottle-and-jug entrance to jump the queue and collect a drink for their wives as a peace offering for being late in. Others took the hint and set off home. Ted was deep in conversation with Jimmy Barker about the merits of how much horse shit to mix with straw to make the best manure, when a tug on his elbow took his attention. It was Robert, who shoved some change into Ted's hand with the curt instruction to get his arse round to the bottle-and-jug quick and get a couple of ales and a stout for Bertha while he ran down to Todd's Fish Shop for a parcel of chips. Timing was everything – it was 'beat the queues' or forget it. Ted downed the last dregs, handed the empty glass to a smiling Jimmy and dodged out of the door and round the corner to find there were only a handful of people in front of him. He was behind old Freddy Wardle.

'Canny night, Freddy,' he said genially.

'What's canny about it? Look at the state of the place.'

It took Ted a moment to recover from this minor assault; he was only trying to be pleasant.

'What do you mean by that, like?' He looked around. 'What's the matter with it?

'Not Langley, you daft bugger, I mean the world.' Suddenly Freddy burst into a fit of coughing so furious everyone in the small queue turned around. He wheezed and gasped for breath, spitting great dottles of black into an already black handkerchief. 'Youse buggers think this is all a lark don't you... I'll tell you this for nowt... Germany doesn't!'

Aw! Not now Freddy; I'm having a canny night, man.

'Aye, I suppose you're right. It looks like Serbia's had it anyway.'

'Never mind them lot, it's Germany you've got to watch. You mark my words.' Freddy was wheezing as if he was about to expire. He looked down at the soaking black rag in his fist. 'You got a clean hanky, Ted?'

Reluctantly, he pulled a crisp cotton handkerchief from his pocket and handed it over, wincing as Freddy hawked a load of black phlegm into it. He'd work out what to tell Bertha later. She wouldn't miss it until the next lot of flat ironing anyway. The queue shuffled along and a load of latecomers joined on the end. Little Alice Reid walked out sporting a cracking black eye, and carrying a basket containing three bottles. She and Willy had moved into Cockney Joe's house after he was kicked out. Ted wondered fleetingly if it was the house that made the men beat their wives. Patrick's voice could be heard requesting the next order: canny lad, Patrick.

In just a couple of minutes, Freddy got his bottle of stout, nodded his thanks and turned away. For a second his gaze took Ted straight in the eye.

'Keep your head down 'till you're told otherwise, son. No volunteering and no daft bloody heroics, they'll only get you killed. Understand?'

With that he lumbered off coughing into the night, leaving Ted wondering what all the urgency was about. Freddy knew a thing or two and had a chest full of medals to prove it, but it wasn't as if Ted was off to war tomorrow.

This train of thought was interrupted as he came to the little hatch, which framed Patrick Brannon in a rectangular halo of light and smoke. He was in the middle of ordering his booze when Robert appeared at his side with a newspaper parcel that dripped hot fat and vinegar from an ever-widening stain and smelled absolutely bloody delicious.

Robert put the chips on the draining board while he took his boots off and Ted set the bottles down on the table, taking care not to disturb the three neat piles of carefully ironed clothes that were ready to go upstairs. Bertha smiled at the boys and, putting her darning down, got up from the rocking chair and started to cut some bread. They were all agreed the only way to eat chips was in a decently buttered sandwich with loads of salt and vinegar. Ted poured the ale into mugs and for a few moments there was no conversation at all as the three of them tucked into their treat. It was Bertha who broke the silence.

'Well, what's the crack, then?'

The conversation remained amiable and mostly centred around the forthcoming wedding of Robert and Louise and their house over the road. At Bertha's request Robert went upstairs for his violin and played a couple of quiet tunes including, naturally, 'Danny Boy'.

Eventually, the music and the conversation dried up and everyone caught the yawns off everyone else. Bertha was the first to go to the netty, ever mindful of the consequences of following two half-cut men, and her absence was just long enough for the lads to extinguish all the lamps. Ted hid behind the back door and Robert crouched down at the far side of the rocking chair where the glow from the fire wouldn't catch his shadow. They both thought it was amazing that Bertha never noticed the absence of the lights, she just breezed back in as if it was broad daylight and before Ted could jump out at her she was round the door and firmly pushed him over on his arse.

'Our Robert, turn a lamp up... now!' He did as he was bid. 'Ted, get yourself to the netty, I'm going up... and don't forget to damp the fire down.'

It was a bit overcast but promised to be a canny morning. Bertha had got up early to see Robert off to work for six o'clock and had taken a mug of tea each up to the bedroom where Ted was still snoring gently. They had precious little time to themselves these days and one of those rare private moments was now. She shouldered the door open quietly and smiled as she saw her man, flat on his back with his mouth open. He was unshaven and his beard was still soft and downy. His hair was tousled and he looked about twelve. Quietly, she placed one of the mugs on the floor beside him before tiptoeing around to her side. She climbed in and couldn't resist running the back of her hand gently across the fluffy stubble. He didn't stir an inch. Bertha smiled as she focussed on his open mouth. She took a deep breath and blew sharply, then creased with laughter as Ted awoke with a cough and an expression of utter confusion. He blinked furiously a couple of times as sleep fell away and after a few seconds was back in the land of the living.

'Has our Robert gone to work?'

'Yes, pet.'

There was a short pause as this information worked its way into his still sleepy brain.

'Can we have a cup of tea, then?'

'The Tea Fairy's already been. It's beside you on the floor, pet. Drink it while it's still hot. What time do you have to be at the handball, pet?'

'Sign on at half past nine, don't know what time we're playing, though.'

'That's plenty of time.' Bertha plucked the half-empty mug unceremoniously from Ted's hand and deposited it on the floor alongside her own.

* * * * *

It turned out that Ted wasn't playing until quarter past eleven, but that would give ample time for his breakfast to go down. He had had a bacon sandwich this morning with a bit of leftover mashed tatie fried into a fritter just how he liked it, all crisp on the outside so you could pick it up – not that he was allowed to, of course.

Jacky was there and in good fettle and the gathering crowd was mingling and chatting in the yard of the Blue Star and the street outside. Already the bairns were stotting balls off the gable ends of Railway Street and Logan Street and old Freddy Wardle was enthroned on his cracket, pencil and notebook ready to take bets from anybody daft enough to part with their coppers.

Caesar had been tied up by the door to the bar and many an eye was scanning the court to ensure no stray dog shit was hiding where it could scupper the chance of a win. Jacky Tait's incident in the previous league had risen to the ranks of fable – and the ribbing had started already. Mr Jobling had arrived with an old shoebox in which he kept several of the new India rubber balls. You needed a few spares because they bounced so high they could clear the wall and disappear altogether. Most folk said bring back the old hand-sewn corkys but Mr Jobling said rules were rules and progress was progress. First up were the Wall Nook lads, Davey Preston and the Hoggard lad who had cheated their way to victory last time round. They were up against a new team: Danny Collinson, the boy who had tried to enlist when

Ted had joined up, and his cousin from Witton, Andrew, nearly ten years his senior, tough as nails and a canny football player as well.

A cheapjack had set up his barrow outside the Blue Star gates and was busy selling sweets and little toy birds made out of clothes pegs decorated with brightly coloured feathers. The mood and the decent weather had settled a near-carnival atmosphere over the event. Mr Jobling blew a long blast on his whistle for silence then announced the competitors in the first game. The teams went onto the court and took up their positions. To be honest, the Collinson lads looked like they were going to get hammered but then again the looks on their faces meant they weren't going down without a fight. An unexpected rustle in the crowd took everyone's attention, jarring uncomfortably like it shouldn't be there. Ted allowed his gaze to detach from the four lads to Bertha, standing on the edge of the crowd. Her head was moving this way and that. She was looking for him. Her hair, usually up in a neat bun, cascaded about her shoulders and she wasn't wearing her shawl. Why was the black face of Cockney Joe beside her? He should be at work. He should be at work with Robert.

Ted screamed his brother's name and began to tear his way viciously through the stunned crowd of people. It seemed a path suddenly cleared for him like the parting of the Red Sea in the Holy Bible story and the only thing in his vision was the ever nearing, tear-stained face of his wife. Her mouth opened and closed and even though no sound came, he knew she was repeating his brother's name over and over again. Without a thought, Ted grabbed her by the shoulders and shook her violently.

He felt red-hot tears spring into his eyes as he yelled at the top of his voice, 'Where is he? Where is he, man?'

Suddenly he felt strong arms grab him from all sides and he was wrestled away from his stricken wife. Cockney Joe's face swam into his vision, all pockmarks and coal dust and fear: he smelled of coal and firedamp and his black hands were tight on Ted's shoulders. His lips were moving but no sound seemed to be coming out of his mouth but then, from a distance and out of synchronisation with the lip movements, came a faint, tinny travesty of his voice.

'There's been a fall. It's Bob. You have to come now, Ted. Now!'

Then the whispering started, coming in from all points of the compass and overlapping as the crowd regurgitated the information.

'Tow Law Bob's been in a fall.'

'Tow Law Bob's been buried.'

'Their Robert's been injured.'

'Bob Smith's dead in a fall.'

Suddenly, Joe's voice jerked back to normal as he shouted above the racket, 'It's your Bob, Teddy boy. You have to come now.'

Ted shook himself free in one angry, brutal jerk and, pushing his way through the encircling crowd he broke away towards Railway Street and ran as fast as his legs would carry him towards the pit. He gave not a single thought to the wife he had so roughly handled, as he sped up the street, his breath coming in great, gasping sobs.

He was vaguely aware of Cockney Joe following hard on his heels as he passed the community washhouse and thundered up the steps onto the catwalk. Out of the corner of his eye he saw Deputy Goodenough on the collier's cart disappear around the corner shouting curses at the pony, which was dragging him at full speed down to Dr Chrisp's house at Wall Nook.

* * * * *

He was at the cage of Number 3 Shaft now. A trapper boy was the only occupant and as soon as Ted clattered onto the platform the lad pushed the brass lever to tell the operator in the shed to begin the descent. Joe landed on the platform a couple of seconds after Ted and the lad clanged the gate shut. They were on the way down. Joe took hold of Ted by the shoulders again, though gently this time, and looked hard into his eyes.

'Ted, are you listening?'

The clanging of the great wheels on the headgear gradually diminished along with the drumming of the endless overhead belts as Joe spoke of how Robert had gone up into a narrow seam. It was hardly bigger than a foxhole and was only shored at the opening. You had to crawl into it on all fours and any coal you pulled out had to be put into a flat rope basket and dragged back to the tub. Ted and Robert had swapped tokens so that any coal Robert won would be Ted's and vice versa.

Ted had told him it was hard work up the seam but the winnings were grand. Why hadn't he kept his bloody mouth shut!

* * * * *

They told Ted how the lads were working the main face when, from the foxhole came a bright blue flash followed a split second later by a whoosh.

Everybody's heart had stopped.

That light was gas.

Gas killed.

For a few seconds they froze. Nobody dared to move. Nobody wanted to draw the attention of the gas. It was everywhere, it always was, and it had to be treated with the utmost respect or it would slay you. Look at West Stanley pit, back in 1909. Two explosions a minute apart heralded the deaths of 168 men and boys. It was a strange death. Above ground didn't look that much different, telling nothing of the carnage below. Two explosions a minute apart. How long had gone by since that first whoosh? Every man was sweating buckets and still nobody moved a muscle. One minute? Two? John Merrigan's eyes met Joe's and they both looked at Tom Dodds.

Slowly, deliberately, the men picked up their lamps and headed towards the seam entrance, stepping carefully over the tub rails. The darkness was hardly dispersed by the feeble light of the Davy lamps but, reluctantly, the shoring swam out of the gloom to reveal that there was no longer an opening behind it. A smooth, solid shiny face of coal covered the entire entrance, as if it had never been hewn. John kneeled down slowly and ran his hand over the surface. There was a few seconds of silence when even to breathe loudly seemed intrusive.

'It might just be a couple of feet this end. Mebbes he's all right, just a bit stuck, that's all, man.' It was Tommy Dodds who spoke, but he was fooling nobody. John turned his gaze on Cockney Joe.

'Go and tell Ted, and see that the deputy fetches the doctor.'

Joe nodded silently and backed away from the blank, staring face of coal, as if he did not dare turn his back on it. As his footsteps faded into the blackness John had said, 'Let's go and get the lads.'

* * * * *

When Ted arrived there were eight or nine hewers at the face. The tiny shoring had been cut away and new beams at nearly four feet high were ready to gully into position. Two lads were on their knees, hand hewing the original entrance and carelessly throwing the coal behind them where a boy was transferring it to a tub that had been drawn up for that reason. There was no one in charge, nobody giving orders, but every man had a purpose and the work went on grimly and silently.

A couple of canaries in cages were silently watching. They were present for the purpose of detecting the gas, for they fainted away at the tiniest whiff, long before a man could become aware of its insidious presence.

As soon as the two lads at the entrance saw Ted, they stopped. One of them offered his cuddy bar. He took it with a nod, acutely aware of how incongruous he must look in his white shirt and creased trousers and waistcoat, all ready to create just the right impression when he stepped onto the handball court.

Well, not today. He knelt down beside the other hewer and attacked the coal with persistent, mechanical strokes. Not hysterically or in anger, but with the carefully measured blows of a man who knows how to conserve his energy and beat his opponent down through sheer resolve. His brother was on the other side and he was here to get him out.

An hour passed and then two. Deputy Goodenough had arrived with Doctor Chrisp but made no move to organise the men into a more efficient team: they knew what they were doing. The hewer who was working alongside Ted had been relieved three times and finally Ted had to admit defeat and allow himself to rest. He moved away from the face which was a good two feet back from when they started, but it was still solid. That was a worry. At some point it had to give way to fragments, be they coal, rock or clay, but solid coal meant a downward displacement and nobody could even guess how far back that went.

Everything was done in near silence. The hand hewers moved away to allow the shoring to be reinforced and then, without a word got back onto their knees to begin the agonising slog of attacking the face yet again.

They had been there for four hours now. Deputy Goodenough had a shift to run, so was unable to stay but every so often he would return to see if there was any change. The last time he brought a zinc bucket full of clean drinking water and a ladle. When Dr Chrisp had first arrived he offered quiet words of encouragement to all, but soon ceased to do so. His only real action was to insist that Ted rest more often, which he did... reluctantly. And so they continued for a further two hours until Ted's partner, a lad called something or other Abbs smashed his bolster rhythmically into the solid surface of the face and whooped with shock as the bar practically disappeared out of his hand into the opening beyond. They had reached the end of the solid slab and were now into rubble. Without a word, all efforts were redoubled.

Nobody knew where the extra energy came from but these weary men had a goal now and for better or worse they could see an end to their labours. In less than fifteen minutes the stubborn, solid coal slab was demolished and the lads were clawing at the fist-sized lumps of coal with their bare hands and hurling them rearward in an effort to further penetrate the tunnel. No one wanted to stop in order to allow additional shoring to take place but John Merrigan insisted and a protesting Ted had to be pulled gently away to allow the operation to continue. The lads got the side beams positioned in short order but the lintel proved a bit troublesome so Tom Dodds went forward to help whilst Ted sat apart clenching and opening his fists in an agony of impatience. A hand fell upon his shoulder and he looked up to see the concerned face of Dr Chrisp. There were no words, but the touch of the man seemed to calm Ted down a little. He felt his shoulders relax and the agonies of cramp in his forearms seemed to ebb a little. For the first time in nearly seven hours he thought of Bertha, and the way he had so cruelly handled her before he threw her aside to run to the rescue of his brother.

Robert was trapped somewhere in that black Hell because Ted had wanted to play bloody handball and persuaded him to swap shifts.

'Ted, I think you'd better come.'

He had no idea who had spoken but the tone of the voice chilled him to the marrow. Needles of ice stung his blood, and his cheeks were suddenly hot then cold in quick succession. He tried to get to his feet but the ground seemed to rotate and sent him crashing to the floor. He was unaware that he had gashed his arm as he tried to stagger upright and head for the tunnel. It seemed to mock his efforts, rotating first one way and then the other to send him deliberately off balance. The tears came again as he fended off helping hands and headed up the slope into the newly shored space where he came face to face with Martin Fletcher, a lad who normally worked in another part of the pit. Fletcher would not meet his eyes at first and when he did, Ted followed his gaze to a point about a foot below the roof where, amidst the chaos of rubble and dust you could, if you focused properly in the gloom of a lamp, just make out the still, cold fingers of a hand. They were black and without nails and they were bereft of life.

What the Hell was Robert doing up there? Ted didn't know what to do. The only sound he could hear was a sort of high-pitched whistle inside his head and he wanted to be sick. He crawled up the sharp fragments of coal, oblivious of the pain in his bruised and torn knees. He stared dumbly at the fingers as a detached part of his mind wondered how much pain his brother had suffered in losing the nails, how desperate had been the attempt to dig his frantic way upwards to freedom only to be thwarted by a solid lump of coal weighing several tons. He noticed a pair of chubby hands appear beside him and begin carefully to remove fragments of coal from around the hand exposing it as far back as the wrist.

It was Doctor Chrisp. He worked slowly and respectfully and after a few moments held the hand in both of his own. He was a strange sight, this portly, middle-aged man in his smart waistcoat and once shiny shoes, kneeling on a sloping carpet of coal hundreds of feet beneath the surface of the earth. That detached part of Ted's mind suddenly remembered that he, too, was dressed in his best, all ready for handball. They must be the two best-dressed swells ever to grace a coalface. He stared at Chrisp. In other circumstances, the incongruous, black stripes of smeared coal dust across his balding pate would have been amusing but not now. Chrisp let out a sigh and shook his head. He released his hold upon Robert's hand and Ted lip-read rather than heard the murmured regret.

There was a whisper of movement as everyone stirred at once. Robert was dead. This was no longer a rescue so there was no urgency any more. Rough hands patted Ted gently on the shoulder as the miners mumbled their condolences. They shuffled off into the murk back to their places of work to leave Ted, John, Joe and Tommy with the task of extricating Robert from the fall. There was the best part of a shift's worth of loose coal to tub up as well. Coal was money – the more you hewed the more you earned – but when a life was in danger, coal was just an obstruction to be hewn out of the way and discarded. Cockney Joe came to kneel beside Ted and wordlessly began to pull the black fragments away from around the body, casting them behind him where they tumbled down the slope to John and Tommy who collected them up, and deposited them in the tubs. In such circumstances, the bulk of the coal would go to the family of the injured or deceased and it was up to them to decide whether any reward from such a windfall would find its way back to the men who, at the cost of their own wages, abandoned their legitimate workings to take part in the rescue. Sometimes it did, sometimes it didn't: either way, nobody made a fuss.

Minute after long minute ticked by and gradually the remains became more and more exposed. Ted was trying to work in calm isolation, deliberately burying his rage that such a thing should happen to his brother and the devastating guilt of being the reason that it had. It was when the head was exposed, nearly hairless, presumably burned away in the gas flash, with one lidless eye and a mouth crammed full of black dust, that the fullest extent of the agony of Robert's demise was revealed.

And all for a game of handball.

Ted had continued to work in silence but now began shuddering almost uncontrollably. Tommy had folded up his jacket and placed it under Robert's head as Joe and Ted were tunnelling down either side of the body.

Another half an hour revealed the further horror that the legs were trapped below the knee by another, smaller solid block that had to be hewn away. The left leg was crushed and mangled to a bloody rag. As the body was finally released and towed gently down the slope, the leg flowed sickeningly over the contours as if it were liquid, the ragged boot swivelling obscenely this way and that. Deputy Goodenough was back, crouching beside the doctor. In front of him was a stretcher. Gentle hands and kind whispers came out of the darkness and Robert was turned face upward to be lain upon it.

Ted stared at his brother in disbelief, his lips moving in utter silence. Deputy Goodenough moved unobtrusively to stand beside him and placed a hand gently on his shoulder. This was where they sometimes went mad and had to be restrained. The old man had been down the pit for more years than he cared to remember, and had seen his share of shocking tragedy. Disbelieving sons recovering the bodies of their fathers, or fathers embracing the lifeless husk that had been their child and, rocking gently to and fro, crooning a nearly forgotten lullaby and running black fingers through tousled, lifeless hair.

Today it was brother grieving over brother. Will King Coal ever be satisfied? Is it not enough to take years off a man's life without having to take his life as well?

For a moment anger supplanted sorrow in the old veteran's heart but he showed none of it and stayed by Ted. Grief can take a man an infinite number of ways.

Ted suddenly stiffened. Here it comes.

'Where's his cap?' He began to cast his gaze around, 'Has anybody seen his cap? He's not bloody going up like that... where's his cap, man?'

He wrenched himself away from the old man and began scrambling around, digging amongst the rubble with his bare hands, the tears flowing freely now.

'He's not bloody going up like that.'

It was Tom Dodds who gently restrained him. He spoke quietly and kindly, 'It's all right Teddy. Here man, he can have mine. Just for now, like. Here.'

Everyone remained motionless, like a tableau, as Ted stopped scrabbling and stared up at Tommy. Nothing moved for an eternity until Ted whispered, 'No. It's my shame. He can have mine.'

The numbing, anaesthetising shock that had kept Ted driving himself on was wearing off. He was wild-eyed and tear-stained. Shocking white channels ran down his black face from his eyes to his chin. He was staring at Robert, the black shell on the stretcher. And all for a game of handball. He screamed a terrible scream, a lonely, guilty scream that shocked everyone who heard it. From cold numbness he suddenly began to hurt everywhere. His knees gave way and he sank, sobbing, to the ground beside the body. Hands came out of the darkness to touch and comfort him but even as he asked the Lord God why this awful death had been visited upon his beloved brother, he knew the answer.

He did it for you Ted, and all the cocky little buggers like you.

Regimental photograph at Prest Street School prior to leaving for France. Taken April 1915.

Robert Smith, Ted's brother.

*Louise Blenkin-
sop (standing),
Robert's betrothed*

The 'Onward'

*London Bus convoy through
France/Belgium.*

Ted Smith

Ted as POW - 8th from right-rear

Edith Smith. (Ted's Mam) and brother George.

Harold Smith, Ted's brother,
Royal Northumberland Fusiliers.

Walter Smith, Ted's brother, Royal
Northumberland Fusiliers.

Langley Park 1906.

The Second Battle of Ypres [ca. 1915] after Richard Jack A.R.A.

Chapter 16

Durham City Station, Tuesday 4th August 1914

The first troop train back from Morfa Camp at Conway was slowing to a halt none too gently as it passed over the Durham viaduct on its way into the station. The guard had wound down the brakes with a bit too much enthusiasm and all the carriages bumped and clattered as the coupling chains suddenly reached full stretch. The abrupt change in motion woke nearly every soldier on board, including Ted, who had endured much of the journey on the floor of a compartment underneath the window. He had spent most of his time trying to fend off Fat Harry's legs on one side and a lad from Waterhouses on the other.

The lad was sound asleep, cradling his rifle awkwardly so that the muzzle was pointing directly at Ted's right temple. Making a distasteful face he pushed the barrel away with his finger. There were thirteen people in the eight-seater and the place stank of tobacco and body odour. The train itself was designed to carry around three hundred passengers in reasonable comfort and not the five hundred or so presently on board, who were crushed together like pilchards in a tin. The second train following an hour later with the remainder of the company was just the same. It was just after midnight on August 4th, and they had been on the journey back from Conway for what seemed like days. He stretched out his bad leg, trying to avoid the sea of khaki puttees and started rubbing his thigh. His mouth was dry and raw from smoking too many tabs to pass the time and his water canteen had been empty for ages. Harry stared down at him with red bleary eyes and obligingly moved his legs to give Ted a bit more room before rubbing the window with his battledress sleeve and peering out.

'Home sweet home – and it's spitting on to rain.'

Somebody farted and sleepy moans of disgust drifted impotently through the air. It was no good, he had to stand up or he would get cramp. Drowsy objections were raised at the commotion until Jacky chimed up with the fact that the train was drawing to a halt anyway and they were all going to have to move their arses regardless. With some reluctance the whole compartment stirred and the tangle of arms and legs seemed impossible to solve. Somebody heaved the sliding door open and a couple of seated bodies in the corridor fell in with obscene cries of objection. A few curses later, everybody managed to get upright and more or less organised.

Ted turned around and stared out of the window behind him. It was nearly a full moon. The curve and elevation of the viaduct approach was such that the streets of Durham appeared to roll out underneath the train like a great map. It was just like looking down on Langley from the Board Inn on Esh Hilltop. Immediately below, Crossgate Peth was black and shiny in the rain. Shimmering rainbow-like halos formed around the gas mantles of the lamps that flanked the thoroughfare as it disappeared towards North Road and into the City Centre. At the bottom of the valley the river was shining like wet slate as it wound around the spit of land that held the cathedral and the castle, both exploding out of the thick clumps of trees surrounding them and utterly dwarfing the buildings of the city. All eyes turned to stare out of the opposite windows where the train was finally drawing to a halt at the platform. Slightly above them rose Wharton Park with its forbidding battlements and the muzzles of a couple of cannon, relics from the Crimean War, poking menacingly through the gaps in the glistening grey stone. After having been deafened by gunfire at Morfa for the past couple of weeks this unwelcoming view held a new significance for the weary soldiers.

Shouldering their rifles they began to shuffle off the train and the blast of cool air and drizzle brought gasps and unfavourable comments while the platform slowly filled with men milling about to no apparent purpose. Within minutes, however, instructions were shouted across the length of the station as the NCOs disembarked and rallied the men into some sort of order.

The first voice was reinforced by a second, then a third, until the noise on the platform resembled a parade ground. Basically every man had to go to the baggage wagons and retrieve a kit bag – anybody's kit bag – and make their way immediately up to Wharton Park where they were to be formed up for an address.

Ted couldn't care less. He was bone weary, his leg hurt and his head was still full of Robert and the accident and the funeral and Louise's hysterical attack upon him in the little church in Sunniside. He would never forget the sight of her struggling to be free of Mam and Bertha and Vera, her hat hanging off the back of her head by the pin, as they dragged her outside and tried to calm her down.

He would never forget being called a murderer.

He had endured agony and humiliation – and still was – from the second Dr Chrisp had pronounced his brother dead down the pit to the bringing home of Robert to Sunniside and the distraught wailing of Mam and the grim silence of Dad.

Nobody but Louise blamed him, but he would never forget.

* * * * *

He did his duties at Morfa Camp well enough. Bloody awful place: it was built on boggy ground where the chill wind from the sea permanently lashed them with wet face-slaps, even in July. They were accommodated in decrepit old bell tents that let in more than enough wind and water, and had seen their best times years ago.

Conway? Never saw the place. A mysterious walled city hundreds of years old and most likely full of pubs and fish-and-chip shops. It was visible off to the east through the drizzle and might as well have been as far away as Jerusalem. They were at Morfa Camp, not Conway, and at Morfa Camp they would stay. He learned how to fire his Short Lee Enfield rifle. He was tongue-lashed along with his mates for not being capable of firing fifteen rounds a minute, which nobody could – the best being ten or eleven – and he learned how to bayonet suspended straw dummies where he was complimented on the ferocity of his outlandish scream as he did so, indeed he was held up by the NCO in charge as an example for all to follow. The NCO would never have guessed in a million years that Ted was bayoneting himself.

Morfa had been tough all right, much tougher than anyone had anticipated and the unrelenting sense of foreboding never let up. They learned the geography of trenches and the different sorts that were made for different purposes. Then they dug trenches, filling bag after bag with the dull, sandy earth and piling them up fore and aft of the excavations as they were instructed. Then they dug more trenches whilst under fire from blanks and then yet again under live fire from hand held weapons. Mud spouted up around them and though they were constantly reassured that the explosions were a safe distance away it still all seemed a bit bloody close as far as the lads were concerned. They were taught the rudiments of First Aid and Field Dressings by young Lieutenant Stenhouse of the Medical Corps and his team of orderlies. All constructive stuff, until the end of the first week when they had to fill all the trenches in again and empty the sandbags ready for the next intake.

They were then moved further west along the coast to another site where the trenches had already been built. This time they were complete with duckboards, timber linings and well-equipped dugouts lined with wood and lit with candles. The men were informed that this is what trenches at the front would be like, and when you go to war there's nowhere safer. They had to attack a couple of ruined farm buildings that were held by 'the enemy' which meant a new sort of trench digging, the sort where you lay on your belly in an open field under fire and dug a ditch using the excavated earth as a crude breastwork. It was commented upon more than once that if digging trenches won the war the DLI boys would be up for a medal each.

* * * * *

When they left Morfa Camp they were as ready to fight as they could be. The men had been organised into companies and Ted was in 'D' Company under Captain Bradford who was assisted by Lieutenant Brass and the freckly young Lieutenant Wood, amongst others. Pretty well all the gang were also in 'D', so that had worked out all right.

Then suddenly they were back in Durham.

'C'mon, dozy, get up that hill, will you?'

A hand placed itself firmly on Ted's shoulder and suddenly he was on the station platform again. As he turned, a kit bag was pushed into his belly. Instinctively, he enclosed it in his arms and looked at Tom Dodds, who was in the act cleaning the rain off his specs with his fingers prior to hoisting a bag onto his shoulder.

'C'mon bonny lad, let's get over with, eh!'

They trudged out of the station and up the hill to Wharton Park. Such was the discipline instilled into these tired men over the past fifteen days that in the early hours of Tuesday morning, which might as well have been the middle of the night, just over two hundred of them paraded in the drizzling rain as smartly as if they were showing off their standards to the King. A small commotion off to the right resolved itself as the two officers on the battlement area turned and saluted smartly. A second group of officers stepped up and stood facing the men who, although already at the attention, managed to squeeze a little more rigidity into their backs at the sight of such an eminent assembly. An imposing man of just over six feet tall took a couple of steps to the front. It was Lieutenant Colonel Blackett, the GOC, or 'Big Bill' as he was irreverently known. He looked up and down the ranks for a moment, nodding approvingly whilst obviously marshalling his thoughts prior to beginning. He tapped his cane on his leg, clearing his throat a couple of times and finally, after scratching his moustache, began speaking in a firm, clear voice.

'Good morning, men. It's a shame to see such a wonderful turnout wasted. Should we perhaps wake up the Lord Mayor and have him come and inspect you?'

A polite ripple of laughter echoed around the formation and, thus encouraged, Lieutenant Colonel Blackett carried on.

'I have just come from the station master's office where I have been on the telephone to GHQ. It would seem that troops of the German Army invaded Belgium yesterday. The occupation was completed during the hours of darkness last night, while we were all entrained and heading for home. Now, it says something about the reputation of my Dirty Little Imps that when the Kaiser orders such a cowardly attack, he does so while we're all stuck on a train that won't stop until it gets to Durham.'

More shallow laughter.

'He made damned sure we were well out of the way, and after observing your intensive training over the past fifteen days I can't say I blame him.'

Even Ted managed to raise a smile.

'But the point is, men, that everything has changed in the few hours we have been travelling. When we embarked on our train at Morfa Camp we were at peace in a world slowly toppling into war. Well, the invasion of Belgium changed all that. We have a Treaty and a friendship with the Belgians that stretches back I don't know how many years. When they call upon us for help, we will aid them with all of our might. Men, the government and people of Belgium have called upon Great Britain for assistance to rid them of their German aggressors and we will do just that. War has not yet been officially declared between ourselves and Germany but it is only a formality: only a matter of time. You are soldiers of the King. You are soldiers of the Eighth New Durhams. When we are called upon – and I assure you it will be soon – you men, each and every one of you, must give the best account of yourselves in the forthcoming conflict that you possibly can. Will you give your best?'

The cheer that went up was amazing. A few moments ago, this was a group of travel-weary men with no other thought in their heads but to walk home through the rainy night or bivouac where they could until daylight and then set off. Now they were soldiers of the King and ready to fight Germany with tooth and claw this very instant. Hurrahs went up, some caps were waved in the air and the lads were absolutely ready to march off to war. Lieutenant Colonel Blackett nodded slowly and approvingly as he looked round the assembly, smiling and catching an eye where he could. He held up his hands for silence and it came quickly enough.

'I know that you were supposed to be going home tonight, by whatever means was available to you, but I'm sorry to say, that for the present at least, this has had to be changed. In a few minutes we are all marching to the market square where arrangements have been made to fill you with hot food and get you bedded down for the night. As soon as things become clearer we will better know what our next move shall be. But for the moment we must keep you together as the fighting force you have proved yourselves to be, ready to meet the enemy as soon as you are bid.'

Not much cheering this time.

* * * * *

It was a short but miserable march along North Road and the steep, narrow confines of Silver Street. They ended up on the slick cobbles of the market square, dominated by the magnificent statue of that bastard the Marquis of Londonderry and his charger, high on its giant plinth. To the lads' surprise a better than average soup kitchen had already been set up in the covered market, which was an amazing enclosed subterranean area next to the main square where stall holders – for an extra premium of course – could set up their barrows and sell their wares away from the often inclement weather. The men were marched down the short tunnel into the covered market and dismissed. The skeletons of wooden stalls ran in little streets across the stone floor and a detail began distributing oil lamps amongst the company.

Since no instructions were given to bivouac in any particular order, the troops divided themselves into groups of comrades and settled themselves for the night. The food beat the shit out of Morfa. There was beef broth and boiled potatoes with bread and all the butter you could spread on it. There were even apples. You couldn't go back for more but there was always a few secreted tins of bully beef in somebody's pack that had been 'borrowed' from Morfa, where it seemed, that was all there ever was to eat. The tea had the same stewed, metallic taste it always had in the army but it was hot and this time you got to put your own sugar in. It took no time at all to divide the men into two camps: the ones who were going to make it home that night, including all the Sacriston, Witton Gilbert and Langley Park lot, and the lot who thought they were going to camp out, cold and hungry, overnight and then set off for home the following morning. Well, nobody was going home now but at least the lads were inside, out of the rain. It was a bit of a surprise to find that sentry details were being set up and two armed guards were placed on the exit tunnel to the market square.

'What the Hell's that in aid of?' piped up Billy Robson, 'Are we expecting the Kaiser tonight, then?'

'It's not to keep the Kaiser out, you silly berk, it's to keep you in.' Cockney Joe, looking as hunted as ever but at least joining in a bit lately, continued, 'It was all right being as far away as Wales but we're nearly home now and half of these lads could be in a warm bed in an hour. It's a bit tempting and we don't want any deserters, do we?'

It was obvious he wasn't including himself as a potential absconder; everyone had received a letter or two whilst they were away, and had written home as well, but not Joe. The little group fell silent for a moment and the conversation was closed with 'Well I'm buggered,' from Jacky Tait.

About an hour later the contingent from the second train arrived and the comparative luxury of space was eroded as the men reluctantly rearranged themselves to accommodate the rest of the company.

Pipes and tabs were lit in sober silence and those who weren't ready for sleep got out dog-eared cards or dominoes to pass the night gambling by the poor light of the lamps. Tom Dodds was looking through his Wills Cigarette cards. He was proud of his collection from the 'Physical Culture' series, which numbered twenty-two, with nine extra duplicates for exchanging. There were fifty in the set and he was determined to complete it.

This was where Ted found himself guilty of the sin of avarice. He wanted Tommy Dodd's collection. He liked the slim, muscular young men so expertly painted, performing all sorts of acrobatic feats on modern gymnasium equipment like the parallel bars, or the suspended rings. Tommy grinned and waved a hand close to Ted's face, which had the effect of making him jump, so intense had been his concentration on the colourful cards. Tommy continued to grin as he spoke.

'You look like your tongue's going to hang out all night, you daft gowk. Here.' He thumbed through his duplicate set and after a bit of rearranging, handed Ted four of them. 'That'll start youse off, but any duplicates you get I want to see them first, mind. Mebbes I won't have them but I want first bagsies, all right?'

Ted couldn't believe it. At first he got embarrassed and tried to return them but Tom would have none of it. 'Hadaway, man! That'll give you a good start. Now let's see if you can catch me up, eh?'

After a while, the games became listless and the conversation more desultory. A few of the company were Durham City born and one such lad, called Charlie Wilson, joined Ted's lot and was greeted amicably enough. It was amazing how a fortnight in the wilds of Wales brought men together, and they listened as he told the tale of the wonderful statue outside. Of course, nearly everybody in the Company knew it from when they were bairns, when they had visited the market on a Saturday and gazed in wonder at the giant hussar on his horse. Opinions were divided over whether he was a friend to the miner or a deadly foe. Some said he provided free houses and education for his employees but it was also a known fact he forbade trades unions and incarcerated agitators and strikers at will. Either way he was long dead.

Eventually, the whole place fell still and the only commotion to be heard was the hourly changing of the armed guards at the exit. There was many a disgruntled group that night that thought of this as their first night as prisoners. Ted didn't join in the conversation or the games and by now his friends knew well enough to leave him on his own. Robert had been a popular fellow in his own right and was missed by them all but none of his friends could convince Ted that his brother's death was just a tragic accident. It was dreadful to see him so heartbroken and full of guilt but he had absolutely convinced himself that it was his own machinations that had brought about the death of his brother... and all for a game of handball.

The morning dawned and the sun began to stream in through the roof windows that lit the covered market during the hours of daylight. It was just after six o'clock but no reveille had sounded and no sergeant's barking voice had yelled at them to get on their feet. The honey-coloured light bathed the men benignly in its glow as they slowly roused themselves and stretched into wakefulness. Two armed guards still stood by the exit tunnel and one or two NCOs were standing talking together near them. There were no officers in sight and it transpired they had been billeted in the luxury of the Rose and Crown Hotel at the top of Silver Street, about a hundred yards distant. Eyes were casting about to find any evidence of breakfast being served up but seemed this was not to be. One or two of the soldiers had approached the guards in order to leave the building and get an early start home but since no orders had been given, the answer was 'no'. One was bold enough to enquire of the little group of NCOs and was told sympathetically but firmly that until the officers arrived with further orders then the entire company was staying put.

It was just after seven o'clock when a couple of officers marched down the tunnel. The sentries snapped to attention and the NCOs saluted. The men were given no orders to form up but they all got to their feet and milled into a quiet group facing the arrivals. They were Lieutenant Brass and Lieutenant Stenhouse and it was bloody obvious that they had had breakfast.

It was Stenhouse who spoke up. 'Good morning men, I hope you slept well?'

The embarrassing silence did not last long as the officer carried on regardless, 'It would seem that, in the absence of any further instructions from GHQ, we are to remain here until orders arrive stipulating precisely what action we are to take. We have awaited information regarding our position with Germany and as yet nothing is forthcoming... so here we stay.'

A murmur began to grow amongst the men and Lieutenant Brass began to look visibly flustered. Was he blushing? It was plain to see that the Rose and Crown lot had sent their youngest out to deliver the unpopular news that the lads were going nowhere. A stentorian voice barked for quiet and the order echoed around and around the cavernous space. Brass jumped but quickly regained his composure, they glanced at each other and Stenhouse beckoned to the burly corporal who had just ordered the men to silence. They spoke in low tones for a few seconds, whereupon the corporal saluted smartly and the officers left the building. Almost at once all the NCOs made a beeline for the corporal and an animated conversation concluded with Sergeant Coates of 'A' detailing a load of his lads to get properly dressed, collect their rifles and then trot up the tunnel out into the market square.

What the bloody Hell was going on? Suddenly, the murmuring started again but quietly this time, and with a watchful eye on the NCOs who were studying the men equally carefully. It was Sergeant Hanson who took charge. He stood in between the two sentries flanking the tunnel and his voice boomed and echoed as he spoke.

'Right... just listen you lot. In future when an officer addresses you, you will keep bloody quiet until he's finished... Do you all understand?'

The absolute silence that ensued was answer enough.

'Right then, you've got fifteen minutes to get yourselves made presentable. Then you can file out smartly to the square where breakfast is being prepared for you. You will go out in squads with intervals in between to make sure you don't look like the shower of shit you resembled yesterday when you got off the train.'

One brave soul stepped forward and raised his hand for attention.

'YOU! Put that bloody arm down and follow orders. What the Hell do you think this is?'

That, obviously, wasn't a question and with no further ado the men prepared themselves for breakfast and whatever else the day was going to hurl at them. Soldiers behave best when they are busy and the company was kept busy all that morning. The first thing that happened was that the armed sentries at the tunnel entrance were stood down, which relaxed the lads no end. It was amazing how the freedom to walk up the tunnel into the fresh morning air, under orders of course, made a difference to the mood. Boots were bulled and buttons were polished with a will, both to remove the travel grime from the dreadful train journey of the night before and in anticipation of emerging into the sunlight for a grand breakfast. Actually, it wasn't that grand. In fact, it was exactly the same fare as last night – probably the leftovers. The only fly in the ointment was the embarrassed-looking armed guards standing at every road that left the market square, effectively sealing them in. Still prisoners, then.

The morning wore on and at about twenty to twelve the sentries on the Silver Street picket snapped smartly to attention and Lieutenant Colonel Blackett, Big Bill himself, came striding into the square. He was accompanied by Lieutenant Brass and young Lieutenant Wood, who were obviously there for a lesson in how to talk to the men. All the seated lads stood up and he nodded affably to everyone he passed. He waved his cane at the NCOs to prevent them forming the men up and made his way towards the statue of the Marquis. There were a few steps leading up to the plinth and he planted himself firmly on the top one and waited until all the men had formed a quiet group in front of him. He proceeded to inform them that nothing had been heard from GHQ therefore none of them, officers and men alike, were any the wiser as to the country's footing with Germany. Since the day was wasting away and the Eighth New Durhams had better things to do than entertain the good citizens of the city with their prowess at marching and arms drill, they would all be stood down for the day and those who wished to could make their own way home to see their wives and sweethearts, though for the sake of propriety not both at the same time. There would be no records taken and no issue of chits. The men were on their honour to return to the market place for parade at 0900 hours in the morning. Those with too far to go were welcome to the freedom of the city and would be fed and watered and allowed to sleep tonight in the covered market. He touched his cane to the peak of his cap in acknowledgment of the murmured assent and stepped off briskly back the way he had come towards the hotel, followed by the younger officers.

Chapter 17

Langley Park Colliery Village/ Whitburn, Tuesday/Wednesday, 4th/5th August 1914

'Sarah will you stop that racket, man, I can hardly hear myself think!'

Bertha was trying to do a dozen things at once as the little girl looked up at her, all tears and snot, and burst into a fresh wail. She was sat on the floor next to the rocking chair with a half-eaten soggy biscuit in one hand and a wooden cup-and-ball in the other. Bertha was only half way through the flat ironing and the new baps were ready to come out of the oven. She had sent Lettie up to the allotment for some taties over an hour ago and had no idea where she was. Dinner was yesterday's broth that would be thickened up with the taties... if they ever arrived! She was seriously beginning to regret offering to take the hapless Lettie Simpson off Jenny Timms' hands for a few days and now that she had, she wondered how Jenny had coped; the woman must be a saint.

Lettie was over the moon when she was informed she would be moving in with Bertha, but not quite so enthusiastic when the first night consisted of a hot bath and a good scrub for her and her daughter. Over the first few days Lettie was tutored in the fine arts of keeping a house. Warm-hearted as the Timms family might be, they weren't shining examples of Cleanliness and Godliness, and some of the language that came from little Sarah's mouth had to be heard to be believed.

But Bertha had a mission – she would take Lettie under her roof while Ted was away in Wales and knock her into good, housekeeping shape or die in the attempt... and things weren't looking good. Lettie proved herself to be listless, sackless and permanently distraught. She was as distracted today by the shame she had brought upon her husband as the day they were evicted. She absolutely couldn't concentrate for more than ten seconds at a time and burst into tears at the drop of a hat.

Right, that's the baking sorted, now to finish the ironing in time for the water to be hot enough for the poss tub.

Standing the iron on the grid in front of the fire Bertha wrinkled her nose suspiciously and narrowed her eyes at Sarah. The lass was two and still doing a dirty in her drawers. Bertha closed her eyes and whispered a quick prayer for patience. For the hundredth time she looked out of the window and down the yard but there was no sign of Lettie. The smell grew stronger and Sarah began to wail again. Bertha closed her eyes, tightly this time, and slowly breathed in and out three times.

Her mouth had stiffened into a thin line as she leaned over the kitchen table and slid the sash window up. It moved easily and silently now.

As soon as Ted had been fit enough after his accident she had insisted that he clean and lubricate all the windows until they moved at the touch of a finger. She stopped, paralysed for a second as she was reminded of the second time the window had been used as an emergency exit. That was when their Robert had been brought back from the pit in a casket less than a month ago. This time there had been no scrabbling to free the sash lock and no broken fingernails as the frame struggled with the layers of paint to free itself. This time the window had opened easily and silently to allow Robert to come home for the last time; and he left by the same means when the undertakers came to fetch him away. God! This house was so full of Robert.

When Lettie had come to stay, Bertha put her in the brass double bed with Sarah and moved herself into Robert's room. She was in the middle of giving it a good clean when she came across his violin under the bed, wrapped in a bit of thin oilcloth to keep the dust off.

Lettie was standing beside her ready to take the sheets and bolster case to the poss tub in the yard when she saw Bertha suddenly sag and bite her lip, her eyes brimming with tears as she hugged the instrument hard to herself. It only lasted a second and Bertha had put it carefully down on the bare mattress and had taken Lettie down to show her how to poss the sheets... again.

Where is that bloody lass? If she didn't turn up soon, Bertha was going to have to change Sarah herself for no other reason than she could no longer stand the smell.

When she did arrive nearly half an hour later it was with the news that she had been talking to Fat Ena and Clementine. Her son, Tommy had sent a letter home to his wife saying that Wales was a terrible place where it rained nearly all the time, even in July, and his wife had replied that it was lovely and sunny here in Langley and it served him bloody well right. Lettie found this funny and laughed as she passed on the news to Bertha. Then she went quiet and the two women stared at each other for a while.

'Bertha, will youse write a letter to Joe for me... please. If I tell you what to say, like?'

Bertha looked long and hard at Lettie, who was hardly any younger than herself but was so weak and vulnerable. Her eyes glanced quickly at the plaster Alsatian dog on the mantelpiece. She had decided that it was under here that letters from her Ted would be kept. But between the plaster base and the wooden mantle there was nothing. Ted simply hadn't written any letters, or if he had she had not received them. Although now she especially looked out for the odious postmen and steeled herself to be pleasant to him should he start to walk up her yard where the bicycle was still propped against the fence.

'Yes pet, of course I will, but you have to peel some taties this minute and get the broth on for dinner while I start the washing, all right?'

That evening, with Sarah tucked up in bed there were just the two of them sat drinking tea in front of the fire. They discussed the letter back and fore for a bit before going to the table where Bertha wrote it down and read the finished article back to Lettie for her approval. God knows it was simple enough: just a heartfelt plea for Joe to forgive her all her stupidity and a firm promise that she would be a good wife in future. There was no mention of where they were going to live or how they would pay for it while the crippling debt from the moneylenders lay upon them but the appeal was sincere enough and if they at least got back onto speaking terms, Bertha thought that would be a start.

Lettie suggested that they play a couple of hands of floater before going up to bed and Bertha agreed, not that she could really be bothered. Lettie had struggled a bit when first learning to play but proved surprisingly quick to learn and once she got the hang of the game the lass actually started giving Bertha a run for her money. Over the few days she had been at Number Eight, Lettie had improved no end in all things except her own spirit. She missed Cockney Joe Simpson terribly and would always bear the scar of her own folly, livid across her soul, for losing her home and her husband. It was coming on for midnight and had started to rain, not heavily, but enough to drum on the windows. Both lasses wondered if it was raining wherever their men were.

Lettie thought about how Bertha had been kind to her. Bertha was her best friend, but she couldn't solve her problems. She couldn't make Joe love her or make them a little family again, living happily ever after. That night, as Lettie rolled quietly into bed so as not to awaken Sarah, the tumult that was her thoughts began to gel, and for the first time she grasped that even the most innocent of actions can have enormous, calamitous consequences... and there was no way back. Gently she sniffed her daughter's freshly brushed hair before she cried herself to sleep, listening to the rain, completely unaware that just across the stairs Bertha was doing exactly the same thing.

The next morning, the sun shone down upon Logan Street so brightly that last night's rain might as well have been a hundred years ago. It was shortly after six and bright beams of light pierced the thin curtains of Number Eight, lighting the place up like a lighthouse.

As she pulled the shawl over her nightie Bertha could hear children already playing in the street. The familiar 'Coming by 1-2-3', echoed with unnatural loudness as they began a game of blocky. These were from families with too many kids: they were nearly always Catholics. Bertha thought they were all like Old Mother Hubbard, those Catholic families, with so many children they didn't know what to do. Bertha rapped on the bedroom door before opening it and went across the room to open the curtains. 'Come on youse lot,' she said brightly. 'You can't lie there all day. Lettie, make sure Sarah does a wee in the pot or you'll be washing them sheets again.'

Whereupon, she breezed out as quickly as she had breezed in, but once outside she stopped and waited silently at the top of the stairs, then smiled to herself as she was rewarded by the sleepy tones of Lettie cajoling her daughter into wakefulness and shoving the protesting little girl out of the bed. The now familiar hissing of Sarah urinating into the chamber pot was a relief in more ways than one, mostly for Lettie as Bertha had been quite strict about who was to wash the sheets after a little accident. It did the lass no harm either and Bertha went downstairs quite pleased with herself.

An hour later, the threesome had breakfasted on toast and jam, and gallons of sweet tea, and Sarah was playing in the yard. The street had fairly come alive now. One or two traders could already be heard pushing their barrows and hawking their wares. The kids were still playing as it wasn't school time yet and you would think it was a Saturday afternoon, what with all that racket going on. It amused the lasses to watch little Sarah, who was dragging the broom behind her up and down the yard. Every time she got to the gate she looked out. This was a daily ritual and it turned out she was waiting for the knife sharpener so that she could giggle excitedly at the fountain of sparks that leaped from his grinding wheel. But it was not to be today, so she went up and down the yard until the broom got tangled up with Robert's bike and it fell on her causing a cloud of short-lived tears. Once Sarah had been calmed down and was sitting cuddling into her Mam, Bertha announced that it was such a bonny day they were all going up the allotment for a bit of make-and-mend and they would take a picnic. Sarah squealed with delight and clapped her hands at the wonderful news.

The allotment was about ten minutes' walk from the house, a bit on from the brickworks and just past the far end of the Ottos. The little plots of land were laid out in much the same way as the terraced cottages of the village. A muddy path led down the middle of two streets of plots, each about twelve paces wide by about fifty long. Those on the right ran to the railway line and those on the left backed onto Esh Farm fields. There was no fence cutting one allotment off from the next, just a little fallow pathway and complete trust, although a post-and-wire barrier separated the far end of the right hand lot from the railway line. Ted and Bertha's was Number Sixteen and it was little Sarah's delight to stand on the wire fence looking over the shiny, parallel rails to the colliery opposite.

Either side of the line was awash with splashes of railway weed, bramble blossom and bright yellow dog roses. She would watch the shimmering heat haze given off by the Ottos as they turned coal into coke and she would listen to the crunching roar of the Disintegrator Shed as it pulverised King Coal into fist-sized nuggets.

Heaven was when all of this excitement was topped by the sudden whoosh of a locomotive passing in clouds of smoke and steam just a few feet from her face.

When they were first awarded this little bit of land it was Ted's idea to use it only to grow vegetables because now that he was a married man bringing in a wage and keeping a wife, the whole business of the cost of things hit him with a bang. It was all right when you were little, you just came to the table when you were called and ate everything that was put in front of you – or else! Once you had to pay for it yourself that was different.

Then he had his accident and it was left to Bertha to do the growing and tending. She, however, had decided a few flowers here and there would not go amiss and Ted had been both surprised and delighted on his first visit during his convalescence, to see the pathway flanked by alyssum and down on the right at the railway end was a raked area ready to seed for a tiny lawn.

It had all moved on now, of course: the lawn was lush with short thick grass and it was reasonably hidden from the passers-by by a curtain of lupins assisted by an ingenious arrangement of maypoles for the peas. It was Bertha's idea to plant sweet peas in the same bit so that you got the flowers and the scent as well as the produce. Beyond the peas, up by the main path were the gooseberries and blackberries and all down the left-hand side were potatoes, carrots, beet and the bracken cramps where all the harvested stuff was stored.

Sadly, there were plenty of dandelions too. Those little buggers would live anywhere they liked and if left for too long would grow roots the size of fists then you would never be rid of them.

So, today was a weeding day, and both lasses removed their shawls and hung them on the wire fence. Bertha got stuck in around the potato trenches where there was a lot more strange looking greenery than there ought to be. She left Lettie to cut back the gooseberry bushes to make sure they didn't overrun into the carrot patch. Little Sarah helped her Mam for about five minutes before wandering off to play on the lawn and look for trains. It was hot work but neither of them complained. There wasn't an oven, flat iron or a poss tub in sight, which counted as bliss.

'What cheer, lasses. Keeping busy then?'

They both looked up at the greeting and it was old Freddy Wardle shuffling along the path to his allotment a few down from Ted's. His cap was on the back of his head and he was holding his face up to the sun.

'Hello, Mr Wardle,' replied Bertha. 'Aye, we have to keep the place tidy, don't we?'

The old man grinned and waved as he shambled past. Bertha took this as a sign for a rest. Straightening up, she put her hands into the small of her back and arched backwards to get the stoop out of her body before turning to Lettie. It was all she could do not to laugh out loud. The girl was as red as a beetroot and her long hair was everywhere but where it should be. She looked flushed and flustered but was struggling away with a particularly stubborn tangle of brambles and it looked like a fight to the death. To her credit, however, there was a respectable pile of thorny twigs and branches in a heap behind her and there was a good clear foot to the carrots. Their eyes met and Lettie gasped a smile and blew a stray strand of hair from in front of her face. Naturally, it fell back out of place again.

Bertha had done well, too. Four buckets of dandelions and other non-desirables had been emptied into a heap ready for burning and the tatie trenches were looking a bit more respectable. Bertha's hands were black and Lettie's were covered in scratches, so it really was time to stop for a bit. They sat on the lawn and Bertha rubbed hard at the rapidly drying film of soil on her hands to remove as much of it as she could before passing out the biscuits. They took turns drinking from the water bottle. Sarah ate her biscuit and swore shockingly when she was refused another but then a passenger train filled their world as it clattered past and all was forgotten. Lettie looked embarrassed and watched her daughter running up and down the path chasing a butterfly.

'She can't help it, man, Bertha. Walter swears all the time, even when he talks to Jenny and I can't stop her hearing him, can I?'

'I know, pet.'

In the silence that followed, the sound of Freddy coughing the black out of his lungs was loud and intrusive, as was the loud hawking as he spat the residue onto the ground wherever he stood. He was a canny old soul and had been good to Ted, so best to ignore it.

'How there! Do youse lasses want a cup of tea, like?'

The sound of Freddy's voice rasped through the air. She looked in his direction to see him sat on an old dining room chair that had seen grander days. A small campfire was crackling in front of him. He had an old zinc bucket that was punched full of holes around the rim and was placed upside down directly onto the fire. A knackered old kettle was perched on it and steam was singing merrily out of the spout. Lettie's eyes met Bertha's and they grinned and nodded to one another. Bertha waved and shouted her thanks.

Just imagine, a cup of tea outside in the sun, and all this way from home! Her face fell a little when she saw the old man chuck a handful of tea leaves straight into the kettle but tea was still tea and beggars can't be choosers. Keeping an eye on Sarah the two lasses made their way up to Freddy's plot. Sarah was chasing something imaginary up and down the path and didn't want to come but they could see her well enough.

'There's only one spare cup so youse'll have to share, and I've got no milk mind.'

They both grinned and nodded their assent, kneeling down on the rough grass by the fire.

Freddy's allotment was what Bertha imagined Ted's would look like if he were left to his own devices. It was dead rough and ready but she guessed it had everything it was supposed to. It just lacked a woman's touch, that was all.

She knotted her eyebrows in puzzlement as Freddy wrapped what looked suspiciously like one of her best hankies around his hand prior to grasping the hot handle and pouring the tea, leaves and all, into two battered enamel mugs, one of which he handed across to Lettie. Sarah took a small linen parcel from her pinny pocket and unwrapped the last two biscuits. She held the offering up to Freddy whose face broadened into a gap-toothed grin. With a muttered 'thank you', he scooped both biscuits up and began to eat them together. Lettie frowned but at a glance from Bertha she demurred, so they watched as he noisily chewed his treat and beamed at them through rheumy eyes. For the first time she noticed that the thumb of his left hand was missing. He made no further attempt at conversation and, lighting his pipe, occasionally hawked and spat contentedly into the fire.

Eventually, it was Lettie who broke the silence. She had been admiring the tea caddy that was lying in the grass next to his feet. Although it was worn and battered with age it was the shiniest black she had ever seen and all its sides were covered in figures dressed in strange clothes of red and silver and gold. Silver trees with golden blossoms grew in the background and the lid was adorned with sinister looking flying birds with long necks and sharp claws. Then she remembered why it was vaguely familiar – it was like Ted and Bertha's mantle fringe in The Room at Number Eight, the one she had got off her Mam for a wedding present. The one that came from China.

'Excuse me Mr Wardle, is your tea caddy from China?'

He looked at her for a second and blinked. 'Why, yes it is... you're a clever lass, pet.'

As the girl blushed, Bertha suppressed a grin: she was bloody sure that it was her hanky as well, and was going to count them when she got home.

They ambled back towards Logan Street and Bertha was quietly thinking that Lettie would have to leave soon because although she did not know exactly when her man would return. She knew it was imminent and she was sure that he would not approve. Best get the house looking like it had never happened. She noticed Lettie's expression change as they walked past the Timm's back gate at the top of George Street. The look of contentment faded from her face as she remembered the smelly couch, and the dirt and the bad language, but she said nothing. The gate of Number Eight was ajar. Probably that bloody Harry Nelson – he shouldn't be allowed to be a postman.

Perhaps it's a letter from Ted!

Her heart began beating off her ribs but Bertha deliberately didn't quicken her pace, which would be unfair to Lettie. It was little Sarah who ran in through the open door first and the excited squeal and cry of 'Dada' stopped both women in their tracks.

The door was two paces in front of her and she daren't go in. This was her house and she daren't go in! She shut her eyes and, breathing in quickly, pushed the door wide open and walked in to be confronted by two unshaven soldiers sat at the table, drinking tea and smoking cigarettes. Their tunics were undone and two rifles were propped up next to the boiler. They still had their boots on and there were muddy marks on the floor. She stared from Ted to Joe and back again. Why did he look so different? Sarah was standing next to her Dad, who had draped his hand across her shoulder, his pockmarked face like thunder.

He stared unblinkingly at Bertha as he spoke in little more than a whisper.

'Thanks for the tea, comrade, got to go.'

He threw his tab in the fire, slung his rifle and walked out of the house. He stopped dead as he ended up face to face with Lettie, whose eyes were brimming with fright and tears. Sarah tried to follow her out of the house but Bertha held her. They watched, mesmerised, as Lettie slowly raised her trembling hands and placed them hesitantly, almost delicately, on his chest. Their eyes were locked, hers pleading and his unfathomable. For a moment that stood poised on a knife-edge, Lettie mouthing her husband's name repeatedly, tears flowing down her cheeks. Without uttering a word or taking his eyes from hers, Joe slowly placed a hand on her shoulder and firmly pushed her to one side. He had begun to shake. Suddenly galvanised into motion he swept past her and set off at a quick walk towards the gate, ignoring the now screaming woman who was holding on to his tunic and being dragged down the yard after him. He shook her off and disappeared, leaving her kneeling, hysterical and screaming on the road. Bertha watched, horrified, as Lettie screeched the name of the man she loved one last time and seemed to collapse inwards into a shuddering, helpless heap. She could sense Ted standing behind her and passed Sarah to him as she walked down the yard to put her hands gently on the weeping girl's shoulders. She looked up and down the street at the still, quiet figures of the villagers.

'Come on, pet.'

Lettie looked up and Bertha was shocked to see how old and mad she looked. She took hold of her and raised her to her feet, leading her back into the house away from the prying eyes of the passers-by.

* * * * *

Lettie returned reluctantly to the charitable Hell of the Timms' household so, in the early evening at Number Eight, Ted had shaved and bathed, and was sat at the table quietly playing draughts with his wife. They had eaten their meal of leek pudding and taties and Bertha had washed the dishes early so that the rest of the evening would be free. She knew by now that he must be off first thing in the morning and this short time was all they had. She was glad to have her man back but it was not as she had imagined. There was a distance between them that she could not fathom, a bit like the distance between his Mam and Dad, and it upset her that his homecoming had not been the great occasion she had hoped. She put on a brave face, and they spent what should have been a glorious evening together as if it was just any other day when he had come off shift for his tea.

She coaxed out of him something of the life he had experienced in Wales but he spoke without any gusto and of course he didn't mention the extra burden of Corporal Huddart or Christopher bloody Turner. But she was right in her judgement that her man carried with him the guilt of the death of his brother and was carrying it still. The business with Joe and Lettie hadn't helped either. He now had the same guilty, hunted look as Cockney Joe and she didn't want her Ted to go down that road.

He won the first game, but without much enthusiasm and she went into the pantry to fetch a couple of bottles of ale. With careful questions and the addition of a bit of gossip of her own, she eventually coaxed him into a better mood but was concerned that the reason he had little that was amusing to relate was that the oppressive severity of the camp had no amusing content to it.

They had never left the place and were worked like dogs from dawn to dusk learning God knows what awful things you needed to know about trenches and bloodshed and dying for the Colours. The only light relief from this tyranny, it seemed, had been two visits to the cinema and, one night in the second week, when one of the lads hopped over the fence, cap in mouth, and milked a few scraggy cows. Some of the men, including Ted, enjoyed the luxury of freshly drawn milk and boy, wasn't it grand!

The funniest bit came next morning when the farmer complained across the fence to a staff sergeant that he had attempted to milk his cows to find that they had already been done! Who was responsible? All the lads were paraded and it was difficult to keep a straight face but they all managed. When the disgruntled Welshman had left, the staff sergeant had looked hard at the men who feared a reprisal.

'You might have saved me some... greedy buggers. Di-i-is-miss.'

They both laughed quietly at this and Bertha refilled Ted's cup. He wasn't keeping track of the fact that he had had nearly all of the ale while Bertha was nursing the tiniest amount. Good. He was relaxing now. It was all she could do not to ask him why he hadn't replied to her letters. She had spoken to loads of wives whose men had written to them, twice, even. But now was not the time. Ted was mellowing and her only worry was getting upstairs to bed without him staring into the room that had been their Robert's for so long. Keep him up until he could stay up no longer then off to bed and straight to sleep.

Breakfast the next morning was a hurried affair. They had to be up at six and Bertha was surprised that Ted had managed it without the aid of a shove. She came downstairs to find the fire lit and her man giving his boots a shine.

'There's tea if you want some,' he said quietly, nodding towards the pot on the hearth. Despite feeling so depressed she put on a brave smile and replied that he could do this every morning if he wanted. Her heart leaped with relief as he smiled in reply. Was he back to his old self? Even just for this morning? Mebbes her prayers had worked after all. She busied herself with the sausages and cracked a couple of eggs into the pan. There was a jarring moment as he pulled his boots on at the table instead of waiting until he was by the back door and ready to leave the house but she let it pass. She wanted nothing to get in the way of their last hour together. They spoke over breakfast about the coming war about which, true to form, she seemed to know as much as he did but she ended up as frustrated as he was at the lack of knowledge about the impending movements of the Durhams. Then they chatted about the allotment and Freddy Wardle pinching both the biscuits. It flashed into Bertha's mind about the hanky, but she discarded the thought. Not now.

Breakfast went by amiably enough but she could still sense a remoteness: her man was harder, more cynical and twice had to stop himself swearing at the table. In what seemed like a few seconds he was standing at the door, rifle slung, ready to depart. He looked so different. Gone was the cheery, gawky lad in the too new battledress that was as stiff as a board. Something was missing in his eyes and she wanted her old Ted back. He stood, wearing his uniform with an easy nonchalance and she wasn't sure whether she should hug him or not. They regarded each other for a few seconds before he spoke.

'It's not you, pet. Honest.'

The corners of his mouth began to curl into a reluctant smile and he raised his arms towards her. She flung herself into his embrace with an intensity that took him aback. Gently, he crushed her to him and she buried her head into his chest. In an instant, she was cartwheeled back to that Big Meeting day when he had proposed to her, hundreds of years ago when they were both free.

'It'll come right, Bertha, pet. I've just got to sort myself out a bit, that's all. Come on, pet, I've got to go.' He gently detached himself and, holding her by the shoulders, smiled his old smile. 'I'll be back before you know it, mebbes even tonight. We're just waiting for orders, that's all.'

She closed her eyes and nodded. Then heard the back door sneck go up. They were in the yard, bathed in warm, dawn sunshine. They were at the gate listening to the children playing in the street. He was striding out manfully as he made his way down the middle of the road towards the Blue Star where the lads were assembling. A couple of urchins were marching after him, saluting and giggling. Then he was gone to war.

The lads no sooner reported back at Durham than they were marched to the Railway Station at North Road and put on the train for Sunderland. It was the same train on which they had travelled across from Wales and it hadn't been cleaned, either. A small detachment under Captain Smeddle of 'F' Company remained to tidy up and to organise the transport of the tools and equipment.

All were pleased to see that Corporal Huddart was part of the detachment, particularly Sam Hurry and his mate who were on the train and free from his tyranny for the time being at least. It was a short journey to the little coastal town and it was such a bright day the windows were down and nobody minded the breeze. They disembarked on a platform not much bigger than the one at Witton Station, but it backed onto a marshalling yard ten times the size of the Langley's. The first thing that struck Ted was the air. It wasn't humid and grit-laden like at home, but sharp and tangy like at Morfa.

They spilled out of the station onto the cobbled street and by nature sorted themselves into their companies and squads so that when the NCOs formed them up it was done quickly and efficiently. The officers were having a parade of their own in an ornate wrought iron entrance leading into a little shopping area over the road. They were being handed bits of paper by Captain Stevens, the adjutant. Lieutenant Colonel Blackett was slightly apart, holding his stick behind him in both hands, watching the officers and men.

The senior officers communicated instructions to the junior officers, who instructed the senior NCOs, who ordered the junior NCOs, who shouted at the men. It was Corporal Lawrie who shouted at 'D' Company. Apparently they were here to defend the industrialised heartland of the north-east of England against attack and invasion by Germany, which might be imminent or might not. It was the responsibility of 'D' Company to build and hold defences from Seaside Lane down in Roker to the Gasworks up at Whitburn.

This was starting from now and the situation was sufficiently urgent that they were bloody lucky they didn't have to march double time to get there. It was only a couple of minutes to Seaside Lane and everyone filled their lungs with the crisp, clean sea air and gawped with boyish glee at the unfamiliar sights. Little cottages jostled with timber warehouses, chandlers and shops of every sort and size. Then they saw it. Rounding a corner of a disused gun battery, every man gasped together at the sight of the open sea. Grey-blue and flat as a millpond, it stretched out in front of them. The two encircling arms of the harbour walls swept out and away into the sea forming a haven for boats coming back from fishing trips or bringing in cargo from the Baltic. Right in front of them, a short pier ran a little way into the harbour and the lads marched straight onto it, scattering a few truant children with a scraggy dog as they went. To the right, the River Wear finally disappeared into the sea; and to the left, filthy black sand had ebbed in to form a tiny beach where a few small boats lay in a film of scummy water. An old man was sitting on the stern of one, gutting fish. He looked up to see the column of soldiers, spat, and got on with his work.

The lads at the front of the column were getting a bit worried now. The end of the pier was looming closer and nobody had called the halt. But His Majesty's officers and NCOs weren't the sort to needlessly drown their men, so the order was shouted and all was well. The men were turned left into line and the junior officers marched down the pier to stand in front of their respective companies. They were told where they were, which part of the town they were going to and what they would do when they got there. For the most part, it was to dig trenches to confound the enemy and to dig foundations for gun emplacements and searchlight towers to confound them further. A host of sideways glances and raised eyebrows indicated this sounded like a lot of digging.

When the junior officers were finished, the men turned left into reverse column and marched off the pier and up the coast road. Every so often, they were halted and a company of men would fall out as they reached their designated area of defence. Then they would march off again. Seaburn looked nice but another detail got that. Naturally, 'D' Company had the furthest to go and were all that remained of the battalion when they halted at Whitburn Village next to the gasworks, about four miles up the road. Mind you, it was interesting to see the difference four miles makes. They were on a straight road heading north with the sea on their right. That bit hadn't changed a bit – it was one, long, mucky beach littered with little rowing boats both serviceable and wrecked – but the further they marched the less town-like it became, culminating in little clumps of five or six single-storey cottages which Ted presumed had once been whitewashed. The big gasometer loomed up ahead of them and the familiar noise of a marshalling yard once more overshadowed the silent work of the fishermen and their wives.

Lieutenant Brass addressed the men, announcing that the honour of defending the Gas Works had fallen to them. First, they would break for the midday cold rations, then they would be told off into parties for individual duties, the first of which was to be the raising of a marching camp as soon as the bell tents arrived.

'Midday rations! Does he mean the leftover bread and butter that we didn't eat last night? Tight buggers, good job we've got a couple of tins of bully.'

Fat Harry lapsed into silence and he wasn't happy – come to that, nor were most of the lads strung out along a hedgerow behind the gasworks. There was an hour's break before Lieutenant Brass told off the various parties to their individual duties, so most settled down for their meagre rations and a smoke. John Merrigan went missing five minutes into the break and left the lads to their grumbling. Ten minutes later, he returned with an unfamiliar grin spread across his craggy face.

'On your feet lads, who wants some proper dinner?'

They all looked perplexed but one by one the lads stood up, brushing the stale crumbs from their tunics and half a dozen intrigued soldiers followed John down onto the boat-littered beach where, a short way off, a couple of fish wives had lit a fire with some driftwood. They were obviously mother and daughter but there was no difference in the way they were dressed. Long cotton skirts, shawls and headscarves meant that if you didn't look carefully you wouldn't be able to tell them apart. The young lass looked every bit as careworn as her Mam as she expertly gutted and headed a bucket full of fish and laid the fillets onto a dirty steel tray.

Wrapping her greasy shawl about her hands, she lifted the tray and placed it squarely over the fire in the drum. Her Mam had cleared all the heads and guts back into the bucket and walked down to the water's edge where she flung the contents into the sea. The gulls screamed and fought over the remnants, leaving the little party alone for a while.

Soon the hiss and crackle and smell of grilling fish made everyone's mouth water. The fish was ready. The two women wrapped their hands in their shawls and expertly lifted the hot metal tray onto the sand and stood back.

'Hands in pockets, lads. A ha'penny each'll do nicely.'

John took off his cap and went round collecting the coppers, and handed them to the older woman who bobbed a clumsy courtesy in return.

'Well, dig in then.'

Billy had grown a proper walrus moustache while they were at Morfa, and was pleasantly engaged combing the fish scales out of it with his specially modified moustache comb. When he had finished he tapped the resulting formation gingerly with a finger and raised his eyebrows in surprise at the result.

'Hey! It's gone hard, does it look all right?'

Tommy tapped it as well.

'Aye, canny. Must be the fish oil or something.'

Billy grinned, well satisfied with the results of his grooming and completely ignoring the fact that he reeked of fish. He beamed as he felt his moustache again.

'That's even better than chip fat, that is.'

Ted and John stood in silence for a few minutes until John pointed up the beach towards the north. 'See up there, about another five miles is South Shields. That's where I'm from. I was a fisherman until I came to Langley Park.'

He gestured again towards the scattering of folk who punctuated the boat-ridden landscape. 'See this lot, I was just like them until one day, when I was just turned thirteen, my Dad took my kid brother out and didn't come home from a fishing trip. I would have been out as well but Mam wanted a load of wood chopping. A few days later the boat came in on its own. Mam never went in it again. There's no bloody charity here so we were starving. In a couple of weeks, this drunken bastard moved in and kept beating shit out of Mam and me. Fed us, though, had his own boat, see. Anyway one day while he was out Mam made me up some bait in a towel, pushed a couple of coppers in my hand and sent me on my way. If I ever set eyes on that bastard again I'll kill him.' He pulled his watch from his pocket and sniffed loudly. 'Time to get back.'

Without waiting he strode up the shingle back to the gasworks leaving a silent but well-fed string of soldiers to follow.

They worked until 2000 hours digging trenches. Not just trenches but foundations for defensive walls. They also dug foundations for towers that would hold lights that would cast artificial moonlight out to sea in order to detect the enemy all the quicker. By the time they were called to a halt, nearly three miles of coastline had been utterly transformed, and that was just 'D' Company's two pennyworth. The locals hated it and one or two of them approached the lads to say how they were ruining the town. The weary soldiers were quick to retort the Kaiser would ruin it a bloody sight more if there were no fortifications at all.

Stand down was 2030 hours and the men were allowed to do as they wished until curfew, which was 2200.

Although the men had the freedom to visit the public houses and fish shops if they so wished, few did that night. After the evening meal, which was a watery tatie pot, there was a good-natured scramble to bunk in with mates and once squatting rights had been established most of the lads were content to assemble around the fires and yarn, or walk up to the road and sit on the little sea wall smoking tabs and pipes whilst watching the surf pound its way up the beach in the dim moonlight.

Next morning at 0530 sharp, the bugle could be heard all over the site. There was a curious echo to the penetrating din, which turned out to be not an echo at all. As he slowly climbed into consciousness Ted realised it must be the bugles of the other companies to the south of them, blowing at the same moment but not quite in time. Anyway, no time for any of that. Shit, shave and morning parade first. He climbed over the protesting body of Jacky Tait and lifted the tent flap. Surprisingly it was really misty and not very warm. After yesterday's grand weather it would be a shame if it was going to change for the worse. He shaved in a little tin bowl of cold water, kneeling down on the grass and without a mirror, and once he was sorted moved out of the way to let the next man in. He lit a tab and walked up to the road. The mist was so thick you could hardly see the sea and he suddenly shivered.

'Don't worry, it'll soon burn off. It'll be a canny day again – apart from the digging.'

It was John Merrigan. Ted thought he had changed since he had come out to Sunderland. He had always been a bit quiet but now he seemed uncomfortable somehow.

Breakfast was porridge so thick you could wave it around on your spoon but the tea was canny. Then it was back to digging and sure enough the sun came out. Late that morning Captain Smeddle and his rearguard party from Durham caught up to them with a mule train and some horse drawn wagons. They arrived with all the heavy tools and equipment necessary to construct the formidable defensive barriers necessary to repel an invasion. That afternoon the timber and corrugated iron sheets arrived. They were to be deployed into the raw trenches and machine gun emplacements, when the easier work of reinforcing and fettling would begin. That would be a doddle after the digging and the lads were looking forward to it. The biggest laugh was the two wagons full of sand that had been requisitioned – as if there wasn't enough on the beach over the road. But such is the army and at least it amused the lads. It amused them even more when they found out that evening that the sand was for filling sandbags to help protect the sea front buildings from shelling and that it had been requisitioned by none other than Corporal Huddart who had been bollocked rigid by Captain Bradford himself for the error. Serve the little monger right.

* * * * *

Today, dinner would be a peppery sausage stew, and tea as well, but followed by apples. By now, the company was settling into something like a routine.

The days passed quickly in a confusion of work and food and sleep and suddenly two weeks had passed them by and it was a Saturday. By way of reward, they were to stand down at 1300 hours and the rest of the day was theirs to do with as they pleased. It was mid-morning and Ted was teamed up with Jacky, Tom Dodds and a couple of others, fettling some timber reinforcements. They were working with a will and singing some ribald songs as they toiled, completely immersed in what they were doing.

It was with a shock like a blow to the stomach that Ted suddenly realised that today was Saturday all right; it was Saturday the 15th of August and it was Robert and Louise's wedding anniversary. He screwed his eyes up tight as he fought to prevent the tears from streaming down his face and he felt his mouth go slack. He turned and leaned on the planking, his breath coming in shuddered gasps. His workmates were alarmed and dropped what they were doing to rush to the aid of their comrade. He managed to stutter out the reason for his behaviour with an apology. He took some deep breaths and steadied himself, aware of how he must look, and embarrassed by his conduct.

'It's all right man, I'm all right, honest. Just give me a minute eh?'

He had bloody well forgotten, hadn't he?

He had forgotten about his brother.

* * * * *

Ted felt deeply ashamed that the burdensome regime of work had driven all thoughts of Robert from his mind. He had written a short note to Bertha the other day, promising a longer letter later. He considered that would do for now and he swore to himself he would write properly as soon as they all got back after dismissal but fatigue took over and he went straight to sleep. If he kept thinking about Robert then he wouldn't be dead. How dare he stop thinking of Robert? Mebbes he wouldn't go to the pub with the lads this afternoon, he should just stop in the camp in front of one of the bonfires and concentrate on his brother, who would be alive today if he hadn't been such a selfish little bastard.

He was in control now and worked fiercely until the end of the shift, saying nothing to anybody. When the whistle blew for stand down he pulled his braces back over his shoulders and flung on his battledress top. The men were paraded and dismissed, and he went back to the tent surrounded in a cloak of silence so tangible that his comrades could not have comforted him if they tried.

Strangely enough, it was the reclusive, unpredictable Cockney Joe who penetrated Ted's armour. He watched him as he entered the tent and lay on his camp bed. Ted felt his arm held in a firm but surprisingly gentle grip and Joe's cold, flint eyes were looking into his own, piercing their way into his very soul. He felt hot tears rise.

'Not now, Teddy.' He felt his arm being shaken. 'Not now, comrade. You listening? Eh?'

For a second the whole universe was filled with Joe's eyes, and then everything snapped back to normal: the pockmarked face and the tobacco-laden breath, and behind him the embarrassed figures of his friends trying desperately to look as if they had noticed nothing.

With an effort he somehow made the tears subside stillborn and slowly nodded as he whispered, 'Aye Joe. Let's go out. Just a couple of pints eh?'

The grip on his arm slackened.

Chapter 18

Whitburn, Co Durham, Sunday, 16th August 1914 to Sunday 18th April 1915

That morning's reveille sounded ten thousand times louder than normal. Ted thought his head would cave in with the racket. Where the bloody Hell was he? Where was Bertha with his tea? He managed to open one bleary eye and was shocked to see the writhing bodies of men moving around him in the tent. He lay dead still, not trusting himself to move in case he was sick. A face swam into view then a voice drilled its way into his head: it was Jacky's.

'He'll be all right, just a bit worse for wear, man.'

'Still, get him outside in case he throws up again.'

There was a pause that allowed him to concentrate on how vile he was feeling then calloused hands took hold of him and helped him to his feet. He protested that he couldn't stand up straight without his head spinning round and round, out of control. He was led, bent nearly double, out of the tent to where the distant voice of John Merrigan suggested he be taken up to sit on the sea wall for a bit of fresh air. It was cold and Ted wanted to die but in his heart he had to admit the sharp sea air was marginally better than the fug of the tent. He was left alone for a while, staring into the mist and at the vomit on his boots, and conscious of others coming along and seating themselves on the low wall. Some had plates of solid porridge or thick slices of bread and jam while others simply smoked. A wave of nausea shuddered its way through his body but he was not sick. After a while the familiar figure of Jacky sat down beside him, negotiating two enamel cups of tea and a huge hunk of bread and jam. Ted thought he would faint at the sight.

'Not for you, bonny lad. The tea is though, best get it down you.'

Deathly ill as he felt, Ted drew meagre comfort from holding the hot mug in the palms of his hands. Bursts of memory from the night before came and went. What was the pub called? The Board? It was a dingy place with a low ceiling of bilious yellow and it stank of fish and oil lamps. That's it! That's why he felt so ill. It was the smell of the oil lamps. They didn't sell proper ale neither, not like the Sun Inn and the Blue Star. It was the same as that stuff they drank at Consett, bloody rubbish. Jacky lit two tabs and passed one over. It was good to get the smoke back into his lungs. He inhaled gratefully and began to sip his now lukewarm tea, staring out at the morning mist over the sea.

Suddenly a breeze drew away the mist like a curtain and, for an instant, great black shapes were visible. The nearest two were low in the water, like immense, floating cigar tubes. Further out, two more shapes were momentarily evident.

Battleships?

Battleships! The huge silhouettes were jagged and spiked with great guns and towers. Then the mist closed in again and they were gone. A mutter ran along the line of men on the wall. It started incoherently but soon took form.

It's the Germans.

It's the bloody Germans!

Concerned glances were exchanged up and down the line of men and, as if by some unspoken consensus they all arose at once and began trotting over the road back to camp. As soon as an officer or NCO was spotted the men would make a beeline for him to report that the German fleet was just off the coast, hiding in the mist. Reports differed widely as to the number of ships and submarines but enough men were witnesses to prove the danger was real and present.

Word got to Captain Bradford who telephoned Lieutenant Colonel Blackett. Meanwhile somebody was banging the warning triangle and the din was like the bells of Hell. The men were armed and forming up; they were told off to defend the raw trench works they had spent the last couple of days digging. Ted had managed to drag himself back over the road and was forgotten in the melée. He was content to remain anonymous and dying, sat doubled up on the sandy soil fire step of his trench. Twice more the wind stripped the mist away from the fleet, the first time to reveal the behemoths for no more than an instant and the second time for nearly half a minute. This was ample time in the ever-strengthening sunlight to see the Union Jack flying stiffly from the nearest submarine and high up on one of the battleships.

A sigh of relief a thousand soldiers deep ran through the defences and the men relaxed, only to be screamed at by the NCOs to maintain their positions until ordered not to do so. Sure enough within a quarter of an hour runners were trotting up and down the line with instructions to stand the men down and informing them that the proper morning parade had been put back half and hour so that they could finish their interrupted breakfast. Ted had no idea who took his rifle back to the stack and was simply grateful to be left alone to die at the bottom of the trench until it was once more inhabited by his mates so that the digging could go on.

By noon the fleet had departed and the men of the DLI were now fully aware of how easily they could be sneaked up on by thousands of tons of sea-going steel and how small and vulnerable they really were in the face of such armament.

The next day, Monday, saw the rough earthworks and the sandbagging finished and all was ready for the timber and corrugated iron sheets to go in to complete and furnish the defences. After days of solid digging the lads were looking forward to this. Any silly bugger could shore up a revetment, or run a telephone cable, but a rumour had started going around that they were soon to leave. The rumour didn't last long. An instruction was passed down the chain to the effect that as soon as they were finished digging the foundations they were to depart: the following morning the Third Battalion Cheshire's were marching in to complete and furnish the system. Meanwhile, the lads were to be sent off to Boldon to dig some more defence foundations.

This didn't go down well at all. It would seem that the Durhams were to do all the digging and donkeywork while some other buggers could swan in afterwards and do all the easy fettling.

They vacated the locality and marched the four-odd miles to Boldon where they were billeted in an identical set of tents on an identical campsite, but without a gasworks. It was late afternoon so they were stood down on arrival for make-and-mend, letter writing and suchlike. But no leave; there was a war on. This time Ted wrote to Bertha and Mam. On Tuesday morning, the Eighth DLI began the arduous work of digging defences yet again. These were second line defences and took a bit longer. Once more they were moved on before their work was complete. This confirmed it for the lads. They were to do the grafting for some other bugger to breeze in and do next to nowt and this wasn't right!

They were shifted to Gateshead and then to Ravensworth Castle grounds, which at least was a canny location and at complete odds with the grubby towns and resentful inhabitants they were used to. Ted thought it was grand, a champion building with big square towers and a huge wall all around and it was hundreds of years old. It was blessed with forest to one side and fells on the other and was a beautiful spot on a sunny day. You could see for miles and miles. Closer inspection, however, showed the dilapidation of the place with great cracks appearing in the overgrown, ivy infested walls. A Saltwell lad said that it was the property of a family of mine owners who were so greedy that against advice they had the coal mined from under the building itself in order to grasp every penny, with the result that the place was slowly subsiding into the earth and serve the greedy buggers right.

The men were to be encamped in front of the gates on a gentle slope that looked like it might once have been a lawn or park but, like the rest of the place, had seen better days. There were no tents this time, just row upon row of pegs with unit numbers fluttering on tie-on labels at the head of every strip. Apparently, the tents were to arrive later on in the afternoon, but they didn't, so the lads had an opportunity to practise their bivouacking skills. It was a good job the weather stayed fine. The map reading had come in handy, too. Some of the lads had asked to borrow the locality maps and were enthusiastically working out how far they were from home and, at just about four miles an hour on the march, how long it would take for them to get there.

Ted was thinking that this was a bit more like proper soldiering. It did wonders for the lads' confidence that they could actually build a decent bivouac when they had to, or read a map, or charge at a straw dummy, bayonet fixed, and do it well enough not to get a bollocking off the corporal. Yes, this was more like it!

The night was warm and the lads were full of tea. Ted lay on his back on the short grass with his overcoat pulled around him like a blanket and tried to squint past the glow of the campfire, which was obscuring the stars a bit. Robert, and Bertha, and guilt drifted in and out of his mind, but not so intensely as before. He hadn't had a letter from Bertha this week but the battalion had been moved from pillar to post lately so it was probably still catching up. Her last one was a surprise, where she passed on the news from his Mam that both Harry and Walter had joined the Northumberland Fusiliers, responding to the new appeal by Lord Kitchener. So one Saturday morning they had set off by train to St. George's Drill Hall in Newcastle and when they got home half-cut on Saturday evening, they were both soldiers of the King. Apparently, hundreds of thousands answered the call in a panic because the war would be over by Christmas and nobody wanted to be left out. He patted his breast pocket and was comforted to feel the crackle of paper containing his wife's words.

The next thing he knew was when Tom Dodds shook him awake the next morning. The lads soon got the hang of breakfast. The field kitchen detachment was up and about long before reveille and the rows of cauldrons were steaming merrily away over the fire trenches while most of the battalion still slumbered. No one objected to the odd group of men shuffling up to the kitchen to have their breakfast early – in fact, it was a few less mouths to feed when the camp was truly awake.

The whole battalion had settled down to life as soldiers and longed, more than anything, for battle. A change seemed to have come over the company. A few weeks ago, the whole point of joining the Territorials was that the regular army would go off and fight on the battlefield while the lads would defend the country in case of invasion. But now, constructing and manning defences wasn't good enough. There was no honour in that.

What do you tell your kids?

'I defended a half-finished trench at Whitburn Gasworks... against the English Fleet'?

The British Expeditionary Force had been in France for a couple of weeks now and were advancing along the Mons canal, killing Germans at every step. If the Allies kept going at that rate the war wouldn't last five minutes. Even the Royal Flying Corps was out there backing them up, though what use a few flimsy aeroplanes were, was anybody's guess. The Germans were proper bastards too, not caring a hoot about their enemies. Weeks earlier they had beaten the Russian army and apparently had thousands of them crucified along the streets. They murdered children and thought up the most ghastly tortures for the prisoners. Rumours abounded about burnings, scourgings, nailing prisoners' boots to their feet and even staking the poor sods out on the ground and leaving them for the rats.

Ted was puzzled when he found out that the Mons area was industrial and full of coal mines and slag heaps just like Durham. That surely meant that it must be full of miners and their families who, logically, would likely have pigeons and allotments and probably play handball. That didn't seem to tie in with the Germans being the monsters, not if they were miners. Surely not. Well, whatever the case they were the enemy, and here were the lads at Ravensworth Castle, unable to get at them.

When the lads weren't digging ditches for somebody else they were practicing every manoeuvre in the book just to keep themselves occupied. The Kaiser was supposed to be building a fleet to rival the Royal Navy and ravage British coastal defences with it, but nobody had seen hide nor hair of it yet. In the early afternoon, the tents arrived and it was just as well because that night it started to bucket down with rain and it didn't let up for days. The whole place ended up a quagmire. The training went on though, day and night, regardless of the thick, sticky mud. Kitbags were exchanged for backpacks, which were made into either marching packs, which saw the men loaded down worse than the mules, or battle packs which dispensed with some of the less necessary equipment to make progress a bit faster. There was map reading, defence of columns, attack manoeuvres (both in line and skirmish), hand-to-hand fighting, raft building and God alone knew what else. The lads were, however, as content as they could be under the circumstances and for the most part spirits remained high.

Ted received a couple of letters from Bertha and wrote back in turn. Even Joe got a letter, which he read with a glowering expression; but he didn't throw it on the fire as most of the lads thought he would. He dared any of them to meet his eye as he shoved it forcefully into his breast pocket and squelched off into the rain, the mud sucking at his boots.

Mebbes he was on the mend. His army pay didn't come to any more than he would have got down the pit but he had volunteered to continue to have the moneylenders' dues deducted from it, and he didn't scowl as much when any of the lads offered to buy him a pint on their rare evenings off camp. Mebbes Ted was on the mend as well.

In a gas-lit pub with low beams he caught himself telling the story of how Robert broke Harold's thumb when they were bairns. They were taking turns bashing Hell out of one of Farmer Keenlyside's fence posts with an old claw hammer they had found, when Harold placed his hand squarely on the top of the stump and dared Robert to hit it... which he did. Ted was playing draughts at the table with George when they came in. Dad was off shift and Mam got a wet cloth to drape carefully over Harold's hand, which had swollen to twice its size. Dad glared at Robert and slowly and deliberately unbuckled his belt.

Harold became alarmed at the thought of his brother taking a beating for what was only a prank after all. He yelled out, 'I didn't think he would do it!' while Robert parried, 'I thought he would shift!' Dad looked from one to the other and his menacing stare changed to a grin.

'Pair of daft buggers,' he said as he rebuckled his belt. 'You're as bloody sackless as each other.'

A gentle laugh rippled around the listeners.

Harold was young and his thumb soon mended, mebbes a bit crooked, but the story had been retold many and many a time.

Ted found he was beginning to remember his brother fondly now, and he considered the words of the padre a couple of Sundays ago when he was preaching about coming to terms with the loss of comrades as they fell in battle and left you to stand and fight alone: 'Carry them in your heart, not on your shoulders.'

The training continued and the time passed. As the days were eroded away, the men were allowed weekend leave in rotation just a few at a time, though Ted and the lads hadn't been picked yet. There was no transport available either, so if you lived miles away it was hard luck. Eventually they were all sent back to Boldon to do more work on the defences.

They were well into the September of 1914 when they were moved back to Ravensworth but at least the rain had gone. The Second Battalion Durhams had been shipped out to France about a week ago and the lads were fully expecting to follow on but no word came so they carried on training. It was here, the following month, that Lieutenant Colonel Blackett said his farewells to the battalion because, sadly, he was unfit for overseas duties and would instead stay at home to raise another battalion of men to fight the Hun. He smiled fondly as he stated the family name would be well represented by his son, Captain Blackett, officer commanding 'E' Company. His own place was to be taken by Lieutenant Colonel Turnbull who had commanded a few years ago. The assembled parade stood to attention and half listened as the words of the high-ups washed over them. The comings and goings of senior officers meant little to the men, until a thought struck the lot of them all at once: why would Big Bill be leaving because he was unfit for overseas duty if the Eighth DLI wasn't going overseas?

This was a different bag of coal altogether, but if the lads had thought they were primed and ready for action with the British Expeditionary Force in France they had another thing coming. The NCOs certainly didn't appear to think so. Training was stepped up and in November they were moved into billets opposite Whickham Road in Gateshead: proper ones this time and just as well because it was really beginning to freeze. They were hastily constructed long wooden huts which stank of drab green paint but there were two pot-bellied stoves in each and they slept eight men apiece down each side in proper beds. Ted wasn't thinking quick enough when they moved in and he ended up with the bed two up from the door. Fat Harry and Billy Robson managed to get a bed with their feet opposite one of the stoves, jammy sods, while Harry Clarke and a suspiciously young looking lad from Waterhouses got the other. The parade square was a bleak piece of waste ground that fatigue parties had to clean up first and even at its best looked dreary and depressing after the splendid views from Ravensworth.

All through winter they stood to. They had the skills right enough but the NCOs were now working on stamina. A forced march through snow, then up the dreaded Lobley Hill or Chowdeane Bank, often at double time, weeded out many a man who thought he was at the peak of his fitness. The best way to improve? Do it again!

The billets were adequate and certainly an improvement on the tents, considering the chill weather. As winter groaned on and Christmas approached, the expectancy of leave was cruelly shattered. It was still the dribs-and-drabs method of a few at a time and if your turn came later rather than sooner that was tough luck. The German advance had been halted at Marnes but at the dreadful cost of hundreds of thousands of French and British lives. Now trenches on both sides faced each other from Switzerland all the way to the North Sea. The German fleet had finally shown its teeth in cowardly attacks on Hartlepool, Whitby and Scarborough, killing hundreds of civilians. There was a war on all right.

Ted had made it home a couple of times along with some of the lads from Langley Park and odd places along the way. Cockney Joe had been picked as well but declined to leave the camp. Bertha was in apparent good spirits and gave him all the gossip, and not a little 'confidential' military information, while he told her how things were stepping up and the rumour was that they would be gone before long and glad to see the back of the constant snow that blighted the season.

* * * * *

Christmas came and went with no leave but a delicious slap-up Christmas dinner, served by the officers in the big marquee tent and accompanied by plenty of beer. Next morning Lieutenant Stenhouse had quite a few hangovers on Sick Parade and they were dealt with by the simple expedient of handing them over to the duty NCO who drilled them until they were on their knees before sending them to assist with looking after the mules.

The war did not come to an end as expected, however. Indeed, it seemed to be more of a stalemate than ever. The Western front line of trenches had forced a complete deadlock onto the situation. Individual acts of heroism by Allied troops were plentiful – along with abundant confirmation of atrocities committed by the enemy – but nowhere was there evidence of the breakthrough, the victory that would turn the war to the Allies' advantage. This was a two-edged sword to the men. They were trained to the limit and the rigorous regime they were subjected to had made them fit and strong. Not only could they double up Lobley Hill in battle pack, but now they were capable of it after a day's training or even a three-day trek. They wanted the war to end but not until they had done their bit, met the enemy in France and beaten him fair and square. In January came the news that the cowardly enemy was now targeting civilians on British soil by deploying Zeppelins to drop bombs all over East Anglia. Bastards.

On a blustery day in early April of 1915, news came that they were to be given the opportunity to strike back. The following Sunday every man jack of them was to be marched to Newcastle Central Station to board a train for Folkestone where they would embark for France and the war. This was it. They were off.

Ted had spent the last couple of weeks or so growing the pencil moustache he had always wanted, and he was correct in his assumption that it made him look every bit as dashing as Lieutenant Brass. On a rare three-hour stand down a couple of days ago he had even gone into Gateshead to find a photographer who had been more than willing to immortalise him and mount the finished portrait in a real silver locket on a chain for not much extra. Ted reluctantly agreed the price and handed over a lot more cash than he had intended but when he returned a couple of days later to collect his prize he was more than delighted with the result. The photographer showed him how to snap the locket open and how to insert a future portrait of his lady wife into the empty space in the lid. Champion! Rather than post it, all he had to do was find the most opportune time to present it to Bertha, whenever the Hell that would be with the way things were tightening up.

* * * * *

It was Sunday 18th April 1915 at 0530 hours and there wasn't a soul on the camp who hadn't been awake for ages. Boots were bulled, buttons were polished and creases were knife-sharp. The Transport and Machine Gun department had left for Southampton during yesterday's rain but today was fine and the camp smelled all the sweeter for the fact the mules were no longer immediately upwind of Ted's billet. Breakfast was at 0600 and morning parade at 0800. The reason for the start was that the catering lads had to feed everyone and get the equipment cleaned and packed away in plenty of time to move out.

They were striking camp at 0930 and marching as a body to Newcastle Central Station where a fleet of trains was ready to take them to Folkestone in order to embark for France. In a couple of days they would be fighting the Hun and about bloody time. They had already had the lecture about how they, like any other new unit, would be let in easily, with their first tour accompanied by a seasoned unit to show them the ropes. They would then be rotated well behind the lines and gradually, as their experience built, they would be flung at the enemy with all honour and glory. To tell the truth this annoyed the lads a bit. They were fit, skilled and raring to go and were in no mood to be babysat by anybody when it came to engaging the enemy. They could cope all right. There was a palpable buzz around the camp. Everyone was on edge, but in an exited way.

This was it!

Breakfast was a bit hurried and at the end of it, each man was issued a travel ration consisting of a corned beef sandwich in thick sliced bread, a tin of McConachie's pork and beans and an apple, all in a waxy brown paper bag. They were also ordered to ensure their canteens were filled before the parade. Ted also supplemented his breakfast with half a tin of ox tongue shared with Tom, who seemed to have a never-ending supply of the stuff. He felt ready to march all the way to France now.

For the umpteenth time he fingered the hard outline of the silver locket containing his photograph in his breast pocket, all shone up and wrapped in a bit of tissue paper ready to give to Bertha as he embraced her on the platform prior to boarding the train for France and the war.

The battalion was assembling on the miserable parade ground with its views of nothing in particular but even the depressing vista couldn't keep the men's spirits down. Each company was formed up in lines about fifty deep and four wide before being stood at ease and allowed to talk for the moment. The NCOs fussed and clucked over their charges until every last man was just where he should be. Colour Sergeant Adamson bellowed the attention and nearly a thousand men moved as one. Ted's heart wasn't the only one to soar. Crisply, one unit after another led off in column, dressing to the right, and marched off the square and onto the adjoining road. The lads could feel their hearts thumping against their ribs as Sergeant Malone gave the order to march in the wake of 'C' Company.

They were off!

This really was the life. This was what they had joined up for good and proper! Ted thought it was a pity there was no brass band but this was a minor shortcoming. As the column marched down the gentle gradient of Ellison Street, it was clear to all that this was a big spectacle for the locals. Lads and lasses waved and cheered while older men touched their caps or nodded in tight-lipped approval. Little ragged lines of people were scattered along the route and had clearly turned out just to see the lads off. They were onto Askew Road now. Down to the left, in the distance, was the mighty River Tyne and on the other side the even mightier city of Newcastle, rose up out of the murky, busy waters as if by magic.

The road was empty of traffic as the march to Central Station had been well co-ordinated with the authorities. Black-clad policeman stood at intervals along the way to make sure it stayed empty. A small detachment was running ahead of the column ready to assist in the removal of any offending vehicles that might cause an obstruction. If they came across any, it wasn't obvious to the marching column, which seemed to proceed as if it were unstoppable. Everyone was aghast at the numbers of folk lining the route. There must have been bloody hundreds: couples and families, all smart as carrots. Some waved their headgear and others waved flags. There were cheers and 'Godspeeds' and now and again even a few flowers thrown into the marching body of men.

Ted had seen nothing like it in his life – and it was all for him. How he wished his Bertha could be here to see what a success he had made of his life as a soldier of the King. And his Mam and Dad. And his brothers. He wondered what Robert would think of him now. Was he watching?

Just over half an hour brought the battalion to the High Level Bridge. Ted had never crossed it. It was a cracking piece of work, constructed in two tiers so that rail and road traffic could use it simultaneously. The top level was for the train while the underneath section was for the horse drawn stuff.

Here it comes! Ted was about to set foot in the great city of Newcastle upon Tyne for the first time in his life. Officially the DLI were banned from entering the city from their camp in Gateshead on account of the fact that it was the territory of the Northumberland Fusiliers and although rival battalions were brothers-in-arms on the battlefield they were usually deadly foes off it, often to the point of testing each other's battle skills in the middle of a street or a public house bar. The ban wasn't enforced that heavily and provided you weren't stupid about it the odd trip into the 'Toon' was met with a blind eye. It quietly amused Ted that two of his brothers were in the Fusiliers and probably got the same lecture about Gateshead. The company ahead of 'D' was marching down the gradient and was just about to enter the dark rectangle that formed the covered entrance to the lower part of the bridge when something happened to its step. The entire journey out had resounded to the crisp left-right, left-right of hobbed boots on tarmacadam but the lads in front had somehow lost the metre, though not the pace, of the march. Khaki capped heads were bobbing and weaving in a haphazard fashion that had no timing to it. For some reason the whole of 'C' Company had broken step.

Sergeant Malone's sonorous voice rang out loud and clear through the melée.

'D' company! Keep your positions and keep up the pace... Bre-e-eak Step!'

They'd never heard this one before! They were good soldiers, however, and didn't panic. Ted wasn't the only one who had difficulty in trying just to walk when he should have been marching. At first everybody did the 'change step' at the same time so they were still all in unison but now on the other foot. That's when some of the lads started to box clever and stayed walking on the step they were now in and let the others change again. That was better. The column had reached the entrance to the bridge now and it was quite plain that the company in front were simply walking through the tunnel but keeping their formation tight. 'D' followed suit. It was cool and shady on the covered-in roadway, and quite wide enough for two carts to pass each other if they were careful. It was quiet, too, since the crowds of well-wishers were apparently not allowed onto the bridge itself. The tunnel wasn't completely closed in and lateral archways with ornate cast-iron patterns framed the outlook down to the river and onto the quayside opposite.

Ted was on the right of his formation and the view of the river and its quayside took him completely aback. Down to his immediate right he could see the jolly, orangey-red of the swing bridge. The bright colours made it seem like a toy, spanning the river not much above its busy surface but just high enough for the little tugs to beetle underneath it on whatever urgent errand they were on. If a taller ship needed passage the entire structure rotated around a central pier in the middle of the river to allow access. It must truly be a wonder to see it in action and many a man in that great procession wished with all his heart that it would do it now. Surely there had never been a waterway so hectic. Even though it was Sunday it was alive with craft of every kind. In the middle of the river a little paddle steamer was being followed by a line of dirty barges that looked so low in the water they might be in danger of sinking. On both banks, tall ships were secured and tiny figures scurried up and down gangplanks loading or unloading God knew what. A modern steam-driven ship with a sleek green hull and a single funnel was being carefully berthed alongside the steep, stone wall of the jetty next to an area that was covered in by a great corrugated iron roof where stevedores fussed over cables or waved their arms as the ship glided gracefully into place.

The difference between the buildings on both sides of the river was never so apparent to the men as when observed from up here, so high in the sky. The Gateshead side was all warehouses and factories with company names, such as 'Sutherlands', painted in huge letters onto tatty, corrugated roofs. Factory chimneys belched black smoke everywhere and many of the buildings ran down to the river, indeed seeming to sprout straight from it. The Newcastle side, however, had a fine, wide promenade as far as the eye could see. Set back from it were great and stately buildings, hardly any of which were fewer than four or five storeys high. The ground floors seemed to be all shops and public houses with great big windows, some ornamented with swirling designs. The shops themselves were closed today but the quayside market wasn't and in between this ornate architecture and the busy workers on the edge of the quay there were tight little groups of citizens.

From this height, they were all just miniature caps and bonnets but everyone was in their Sunday Best, jostling amiably this way and that along the waterfront. Here and there, men were standing on little platforms to raise themselves above the throng. Some had banners and some waved books at the crowd. There must be every kind of God-botherer down there, thought Ted, smiling at the thought of Captain Hooker, the chaplain and the battalion's very own Devil-dodger. He had stood on the edge of the parade this morning obviously put out at not being allowed to give a short service, especially as this was a Sunday morning, but troop trains wait for no man and he would no doubt have plenty of time when they got to France.

Suddenly, a terrific roar filled the tunnel and the whole place seemed to vibrate. It immediately turned into a loud rat-a-tat-tat, thundering overhead and causing little shreds of muck to drift down. Everyone looked up and Sergeant Malone's voice rose even above the frightful din.

'Keep your formation tight, you mongers. Haven't you ever heard a train before?'

The noise was gone as quickly as it came, fading into a rattle, then a hiss and then nothing. They were at the far end of the tunnel now and a roar that was obviously a second train was rising in volume as the bright rectangle of the exit approached. Sergeant Malone had stopped to watch his men and as Ted's rank drew level with the burly sergeant, he noted out of the corner of his eye that Malone was red as a beetroot and watching the lads' feet like a hawk, his eyes twitching rapidly from right to left.

'Back into step on my command, lads... By the left, qui-i-ick march! Left, Left, Left-Right-Left.'

There was a quick scraping of boots on tarmacadam and within a couple of steps every heel was hitting the deck together. Heads went high and chests were stuck out as the men marched proudly out of the twilight of the tunnel into the sunshine of the city of Newcastle upon Tyne. They were on a cobbled street now and their boots sounded like thunder. There were vast crowds of flag waving citizens as far as the eye could see, and that roar wasn't a train at all. The noise as they left the bridge behind was like the din at the Blue Star when a team scored the winning Ace at handball, only ten thousand times louder. Ted had no idea people could make such a racket.

On they marched, company after company, up the slight incline onto Neville Street and past a great statue of somebody or other, until on the left they could see an enormous, magnificent structure. It looked like a temple or something from Ancient Rome but in reality it was the Great Entrance to Newcastle Central Station. Above their heads was a complex spider's web of tram wires, and the road in front of the façade was broad and traffic free with a number of policemen patrolling the perimeter. The pavement areas were jam-packed with well-wishers of every shape and size. The columns were almost hemmed in as they marched along, the crowd so close you could nearly feel their breath. Ted could see a grinning little lad up ahead punching the legs of the men as they processed past him. His Mam stood behind him smiling benignly as if such behaviour was acceptable.

Bloody well better not do that to me!

Billy Robson managed to fart at him as he went past.

How the Hell does he do that?

He felt the little blow as he passed. Didn't hurt anyway.

It got a bit more interesting as they marched underneath a huge overhanging Bovril sign where a group of tarty looking, but very comely, young ladies were making the sort of suggestions unheard of in the open air and were being looked at very disapprovingly by the adjacent Womens' Institute group.

Up ahead the voice of some NCO was calling 'A' Company to a halt, it sounded like Sergeant Coates but Ted wasn't sure, and not many seconds later 'B' did the same. In less than fifteen minutes the entire battalion was drawn up impeccably in front of the station. They stood stock still for five minutes in the glorious sunlight, absolutely resplendent. There were no speeches and no one came to inspect them. They were simply on display as the flower of England's youth ready to go and fight for His Majesty against the evils of the Kaiser.

Somewhere inside the Great Entrance a band struck up. The boisterous crowd grew quiet as the strains of *'Onward Christian Soldiers'* floated out of the gloom into the sunny morning air. As the last noted died away someone in the crowd whipped up three cheers and although the first one was a bit quiet it took no time at all for the succeeding ones to reach an unbelievable volume. The cheers ended up being six or seven but nobody was counting.

Ted, like everyone else, was so proud that he thought his heart would burst with the joy of it all. If only Bertha was there... and Robert. Like everybody else on the parade he faced rigidly to the front but his eyes were everywhere looking for his wife. He had no idea if she would even be there because with typical army secrecy the lads weren't told what they had been practicing for until a couple of days before, but with equally typical civilian knowhow everybody and his granny had turned up on the day. Now they were slow marching under the great central arch of the station façade and back into the same gloom as the High Level Bridge. It was impossible to consider that such a magnificent structure was built simply to keep the rain off the gentry as they alighted from their cabs to catch a train. They must have money to bloody burn!

The change as they entered the main concourse was unbelievable. Nobody spent this much money on a railway station, never in a thousand years. The sunlight inside the station was as dazzling as it was on the road outside, cascading in through the glassed roofs that stretched the entire length of the complex in a colossal, graceful curve that mirrored the platforms beneath. A delicate tracery of steel rods and wires suspended lights and great clocks that all said ten minutes to eleven. They looked as if they were simply floating up there, suspended in mid-air. Streets of little buildings, all in matching dark wood populated the wide platforms and sold everything from daily newspapers to hot snacks. There were waiting rooms for First Class Ladies, First Class Gentlemen, then Second and Third Class, all separate. There were milliners, hosiers, bookshops and even a florist. The background noise was predominantly the hissing of the fleet of trains waiting impatiently along several platforms for the battalion to embark for Folkestone and somewhere, muted in the background, the brass band played on. There was more going on in Newcastle Central Station than the whole of Durham City – and that was without the trains.

The lads were paraded on the main concourse, one company at a time and then dismissed to where a network of officers and senior NCOs would channel them over the wide footbridge to board to whichever train they were allocated. Either civilians were allowed to mix with the men or everyone was turning a blind eye, but it seemed like half the local population was mingling with the soldiers right up to the carriage doors. Jacky Tait caught Ted's eye and inclined his head towards Cockney Joe, who was walking straight ahead, looking neither right nor left. They shrugged at each other resignedly. The throng was mostly women with a smattering of elderly men, probably seeking out a son, but wives and sweethearts seemed to be the order of the day, mostly flitting from place to place with an anxious look as they sought out their loved ones. One or two jammy buggers seemed to have found their partners and passionate kisses and embraces were exchanged; or tiny tots received their final hug and told to look after their Mams.

Fat Harry dug Ted in the ribs and directed his gaze to Tom Dodds who had ditched his specs and was in an ardent clinch with somebody who was definitely not his wife. Ted recognised the young lady as one of the group of girls under the Bovril sign back up on the road. Well, no harm in a stolen kiss... as long as Mrs Dodds didn't tap him on the shoulder in the middle of it.

The view from the footbridge was stunning, looking down on so many platforms and the small town that constituted the concourse. He wished he had a few minutes more just to drink it in but an imperious wave from an elderly officer moved him towards the steps down onto the far side. While he was still up in the air he took the opportunity to scan the crowd for Bertha but he couldn't see her. The throng was getting denser now with well-wishers everywhere and it was becoming difficult to keep up. The officers and NCOs were looking a little more harassed and were waving more frantically. Eventually, the lads were shepherded to Platform Eight where a big green 4-6-0 was chugging belligerently in front of a long line of coaches. Someone had chalked 'Look out Fritz' across the tender and the one on the next line down said, 'Berlin Express'.

Where the Hell was she? He was on the platform and heading for a carriage at the tail-end of the train with John and Jacky and it was like being caught up in a wave. He fingered the locket in his pocket.

Please be here.

The mass of soldiers was so dense it was impossible to try and go against the flow. One or two couples were desperately trying to hang on to each other and the lads passed one heart-rending scene after another, as young men tried to disentangle themselves from their lasses. The train was being systematically filled from the guard's van end to the tender, and as they were shuffled down the platform, the squat figure of Corporal Huddart was slamming a door on the last soldier into a coach. Tommy went to move past him but the little man put his hand out and blocked his way.

'Not so fast soldier, I'll tell you when you board this train.'

He started to walk backwards down the platform with one hand on the coach, occasionally looking over his shoulder but otherwise never taking his eyes off Tommy until he reached the next door; which he opened and gestured to Tommy to get on board.

'Fill it up from the tail-end and don't piss about. Get on board, then!'

As soon as they were beyond the clutches of authority the fun started. This was exactly the same set-up as on the troop train to Morfa. The carriages were all little compartments, linked by a long corridor down the far side. They bundled into a compartment, expertly stowed their gear and crowded around the entrance in order to try to make it look jam-packed. The never-ending line of soldiers kept moving down the corridor, took one look into the 'overcrowded' compartment the lads were in – and filed past. Soon the tide of men had passed them by. It was nearly five past eleven and they were supposed to be on their way to Folkestone at eleven sharp. Ted shouldered his way past his mates to where he could see the platform. There were few civilians now, but none of them was Bertha.

A piercing whistle screeched its way through the train and a lurch was felt underfoot. They were off. If Ted pushed his cap back and put his cheek to the window, he could see forwards as far as the footbridge where the train was now slowly heading. His eyes were moving rapidly now, scanning shawls and bonnets, coats and bags. The footbridge came level and the steps were packed, but only with strangers. Jacky vied with Ted for the best viewing place for he had not seen his lass either.

There was Mam! Dad was standing behind her on the next step up, and next to him was Bertha.

She came!

So had his brother George. Half the clan had come to see him off and he had missed them altogether. He banged on the window with the palm of his hand and shouted with all his might, startling everybody in the compartment; but from outside nothing could be heard. He would have looked like a goldfish in a bowl just opening and shutting his mouth for no reason. Jacky was first to spot why he was so agitated but the train was beginning to gather speed and the forlorn little group would soon pass from sight. He pushed Ted unceremoniously back off the window and undid the big leather strap that held it shut. The window dropped immediately and Jacky made way for Ted who stuck his head out and shouted at the top of his voice.

He had clambered nearly half way out of the window and was waving his cap as if he was demented: but she looked! It took her a split second to register. Her face split in a wide grin as she jabbed Dad in the ribs and pointed. It was nearly too late as the curve of the platform was whisking him away out of sight but the whole lot of them were waving frantically now.

Then they were gone.

* * * * *

The turbulent clamour of the station vanished in a few seconds to be replaced by a teeth-jarring rattle as the train passed over the myriad points that comprised the far end of the criss-cross system of rails. In a few moments it had settled itself down into the steady, repetitive rat-a-tat-tat of the main southbound track. The train was getting up to full tilt now and Ted was sat back in his seat, his cap perched on the back of his head and an unlit tab in his mouth, not sure whether to be disappointed that he had spotted his Bertha so late or elated that she had seen him and waved. And Mam was there, and Dad. Was his moustache whiter? Moustache! Had Bertha noticed the fine pencil moustache on his lip, or had there not been time? Did George have a moustache? He hadn't noticed. But he had said 'goodbye' and he was off to war.

Fat Harry wasn't happy. The window was still open and he complained about the draught, but since nobody else moved to close it he eased his bulk out of the seat and lumbered across to do it himself. At that moment there was a sudden loud swish as another train flew past in the opposite direction. The carriage rocked sideways for an instant and Harry's cap was gone, sucked clean off his head by the draught created by the passing train. There was no sympathy of course and the hapless Harry received advice and jibes in equal measure concerning knitting himself a new one sharpish and avoiding Corporal Huddart like the plague or risk the firing squad. He plumped down in his seat red-faced and angry, and resigned himself to landing in France bareheaded.

The banter settled down as the lads got into the rhythm of the journey. They had learned by now that the best way to pass the time was to ignore it, so the conversation became desultory as each man was slowly lost in his own thoughts. Fat Harry read his book and Tom Dodds was thumbing his way through his collection of 'Physical Culture' cigarette cards. Since he had twenty-three now and six swaps as well, he reckoned there must be somebody in the entire British Expeditionary Force who could help him complete his set. Ted was mildly jealous. After all, it was Tom who had started him off on the same collection by giving him four of his very own cards. He wondered how to go about getting more when the sliding door swished open.

They all looked round and Cockney Joe, tab in mouth stood looking in.

'Room for a little'un, comrades? I've just left the biggest bunch of tossers in the British Army. Utterly bloody boring.'

Without waiting for an answer, he strutted into the compartment and closed the door. In just under two hours the train slowed down – then speeded up again. A great wooden sign with the word 'Lincoln' flashed by.

Billy Robson was getting a bit frantic. 'Is this France? Bloody Hell, are we here?'

A few grins were exchanged but nobody put him out of his misery.

Ted thought it looked pleasant enough, just a bit hilly.

'Are you sure this isn't France? We've been on the train for ages.'

It was John Merrigan who put him straight. 'It's Lincoln, Billy. Which part of France do you think that's in?'

Billy blushed but said nothing, engrossing himself in lighting a tab. Jacky tried to start a game of 'I spy' but was threatened with actual bodily harm. At various points, any of the lads would begin to eat their travel rations, or converse quietly or just doze the journey away. Billy had woken from a light sleep and gone off to the toilet at the end of the carriage. Without warning, the train slowed down and came to a halt in a station about the size of Durham. The signs said the place was called March and after registering this fact every soldier on the train went back to whatever he was doing with no further sign of interest. After a few moments there seemed to be some sort of commotion on the platform: a porter walked past the window pushing a little wooden cart but looking back the way he had come. This broke the monotony! George Moody clenched his pipe firmly between his teeth and hauled himself up to the window. He pressed his cheek to it to see if he could see further up the platform and couldn't, so he opened the window and leaned out.

This let in the sound from the outside world and it was predominantly the agitated voice of Billy Robson, who had clearly alighted, demanding to know whether or not they had arrived in France. The station porter thought he was taking the piss and went by trying to ignore him. This reinforced Billy's conjecture that obviously the man didn't reply because he couldn't speak a word of English! He set off in pursuit of the beleaguered porter but was brought to an abrupt halt by the voice of Sergeant Hanson bellowing at him to stand still and shut up. By now, as many of the lads as could get to the window were there, all stifling giggles. Sergeant Hanson was bollocking Billy rigid for getting off the train without permission and just about anything else he could think of.

By now, several more NCOs were moving about on the platform and keeping a weather eye on the carriages just in case anyone else decided to go for a wander. Billy was sent back on board with the biggest flea in his ear it was possible to imagine and by the time he arrived, red-faced, back at the compartment the window was back up and everyone was sitting quietly as if no one had noticed the incident. Billy said nothing and bunched up in between Tom Dodds and Jacky Tait. The silence was excruciating. Fat Harry caved in first by making a farting noise with his lips and it took all of about three seconds for the lads to collapse in fits of laughter.

Jacky, with tears in his eyes said, 'Hey Monsewer, parley vous?' and that set everyone off again. To his credit Billy took it all on the chin – he pretended to ignore the remarks whilst using his special comb to groom his ever-thickening moustache. By the time the train set off again, now re-coaled and topped up with water, he was aware that about twenty miles of English Channel stood between him and France and everyone promised faithfully to let him know when he was about to set foot on foreign soil.

It was dark when the train stopped again at Liverpool Street Station and everyone had been dozing on and off for ages. The lamps in the carriages had not been lit, so as the outside world grew dark, so did the little world that was the compartment full of weary soldiers. There was little interest that they had arrived in London. So what! It was just another stop. Except for Cockney Joe, who was looking wild again.

Ted noticed the change in his friend and commented quietly, 'Everything all right Joe?'

He wasn't prepared for the violent look that punched into his eyes. But it went as quickly as it came and Joe lit a tab, inhaling hard.

'Yeah, fine my ol' mate. Right as rain, I am.'

There was a long silence while Ted plucked up the courage to continue. He hesitated again before he spoke. 'You were going to jump, weren't you?'

The expression might have belonged to a statue. There was not a trace of movement or emotion to be seen: just the eyes boring into him like hot coals. Suddenly a grin split his pockmarked face from ear to ear but Ted noticed it was not reflected in his eyes.

'Too clever by half, you are, Teddy boy. Don't miss a thing do you?'

The compartment was silent for a long moment until he spoke again in a voice that was barely audible. 'I could disappear here and nobody in the entire British Army could find me. Not one single, solitary geezer. I could start afresh, I could. No wives or kids. No debts. No nothing.'

Then Joe simply stubbed out his tab with the heel of his boot and pulled his cap down over his eyes then, leaning back in his seat, shut out the entire world with a wall so palpable it might as well have been built of brick. Ted looked around in the gloom and caught the eye of John Merrigan who was staring at him. Almost imperceptibly, John shook his head, warning Ted to pursue the subject no further, and the train lurched into life once more.

Nobody had the slightest idea what time it was when they started to slow down but the change from the regular rhythm was enough to shake most of them out of their fitful slumber. It was pitch black and the compartment stank. The only heat came from the bodies of the huddle of men and it wasn't enough. Snorts and sighs vied for attention as eyes were rubbed and limbs were stretched to shake off the slumber. The train did stop, but right in the middle of nowhere.

Sleepy eyes stared out of the window onto the featureless landscape that could have been anywhere and suddenly the dark was shattered by a train going in the opposite direction. The dim gaslights were illuminated showing that it was full of servicemen.

How come they had lights? Why were they going the wrong way?

Within a couple of minutes the increasing rhythm of the monotonous chugging sound was accompanied by a moderate lurch as the wheels slipped on the track and they got underway again. People were beginning to move up and down the corridor and voices could be heard as well as compartment doors sliding open and shut in the distance. Everyone was wide awake because clearly something was brewing. Harry got up to unfasten the window at the same time as Joe reached out his arm to open the compartment door, but it was already being opened from the outside. The bulky silhouette of Sergeant Malone filled the opening as surely as his gruff voice filled the air.

'God! You people stink. Collect your stuff, lads, and be ready. We're all going for a boat ride.'

He was gone as quickly as he came and the train carried on at a steady walking pace.

It turned out to be around 2300 hours, but a cloudy sky conspired to hide the details of what the place looked like. All that could be made out through the now open window was that the train was clacking through a little town. A few desultory streetlights failed to illuminate drab looking buildings until they moved over a beach area with a lot of little boats moored, slapping and chopping against one another in the dark.

The train lurched through a station out to where nothing could be seen on either side except the ocean and a few weak lights trailing behind them.

Billy was getting agitated again. He had not long been educated into the existence of the English Channel but had been assured that they would traverse it by ship: now here they were steaming straight to bloody France on the train! All of a sudden, the view from the corridor window was blotted out by a wall of black steel and they ground to a gentle halt, pulling painful faces as the locomotive let out an ear-piercing jet of steam. In less than half a minute the place was alive with men alighting into the dark.

The train had indeed travelled out to sea. They had stopped on a cobbled pier not unlike the one at Sunderland except that the railway tracks ran along its entire length. In front of them was the massive shape of the troop ship 'Onward' looming tall and sinister out of the choppy sea. Two planks ran at alarmingly steep angles from the pier to the deck. The lengths of rope that accompanied them as crude handrails gave the men no confidence in their ability to get aboard. Behind them, the empty train was already reversing towards the town, letting a cold sea breeze loose on the crowded jetty and causing everyone to shiver at once.

'Come on, bonny lads. Welcome to sunny Folkestone. Get your arses on board that boat sharpish or you'll be swimming to France. Come on now, move yourselves!'

There was no forming up, no ranks, files or companies. Just a great crowd of travel-weary soldiers flowing towards the gangplanks and gingerly ascending the slippery wooden surface in tiny, unsure steps until, on reaching the thankfully firm rail at the top they jumped down the short drop to the deck. Once there, a couple of NCOs and one of the crew moved the troops away from the opening as quickly as possible to make way for the next lot. Nobody gave any specific directions, just move fore or aft and stay out of the way.

Billy was having none of it. There wasn't a cat in Hell's chance of getting him to go up that plank. It was a bloody death trap. It was, however, amazing what a bit of threatening from a senior NCO was capable of achieving and Billy was even proud of himself once he was safely ensconced on board, twitching his great moustache with pride. Ted was shuffled aft along with the rest of the lads and managed to get himself a bit of rail to lean against while he had a tab and looked down on the busy scene below. A third troop train had now come onto the pier and was spilling men untidily onto the jetty. Down below, the mass of men wearily converging on the gangplanks looked as lethargic as he felt.

He was off to France to fight against the Hun: the greatest adventure of his life... and right now he couldn't care less.

He took in the dim outlines of the two steam cranes lying idle in their sidings and the diffuse lights in a small hut, which must be some sort of office. Any other time the superstructure of the ship would have fascinated him. It had two masts, one at the front and one at the back, and two great white funnels in the middle. Now that he was on board it didn't look that big. The tide was obviously high which just made it float all the higher in relation to the pier. He drew distractedly on his tab and thought of Bertha, watching the ever-dwindling band of soldiers down below turn into the ever-swelling one on board. A dig in the ribs from Jacky Tait followed by a pointing finger drew Ted's attention to one of the flatbed trucks that was disappearing into the dark... it still had the tool cart on it! They weren't the only ones to notice but it is not the business of the private soldier to question such oddities as the disappearance of the tool cart back into England when the rest of the battalion was heading to France.

Chapter 19

Langley Park Colliery Village, Co Durham, Monday 19th April 1915

Bertha sighed and put her pencil down for the umpteenth time, watching it roll across the table in the twilight. She never put the mantle lights on until the last moment and she thought to herself it was a silly bit of prudence, as it would do for her eyes one day.

This was her third go at writing Ted a letter. Yesterday had been so busy, what with his Mam and Dad and their George and the trip to Newcastle. It had been pulled from the brink of failure by a glimpse of Ted hanging out of the carriage window, waving his cap like a lunatic. A smile flickered briefly across her face. She knew about the goings on at the front as well as anybody and wasn't fooled by all the bunting and brass bands.

His Dad and George had been taken in, though many a knowing look had passed between Ted's Mam and Bertha. It had taken her nearly a fortnight of letter writing to get the little group together for the send-off. She had prepared tram, omnibus and train times and the journey would have gone like clockwork if it wasn't for the fact that half of County Durham, and Northumberland as well, had headed for Newcastle Central Station at the same time. The smile came back again as she remembered her man leaning out of the window waving madly.

Then he was gone.

They spent the rest of the day looking around the shops, which of course were shut because it was a Sunday, but that didn't matter. They had a light lunch at Allison's on Grainger Street, which George had insisted on paying for.

Dad said the scones were nice but he would rather have gone for a pint. Anyway, goodbyes were said and promises of further visits made, then suddenly she was walking up the yard, past the old bike, and into an empty house without a fire on.

Now she was sipping tea with no milk because she had forgotten to get some yesterday and staring at the gift of tobacco she had been unable to give her man – and the two brand new cigarette cards from the 'Physical Culture' series she had managed to scrounge for his collection. Lastly, there were the few pathetic lines she had scrawled onto the writing pad.

It was no good, staring at the page didn't fill it up with news and to be perfectly honest she couldn't be bothered. She was quite a prolific letter writer but that didn't mean it came to her easily. It was more like it had always been her job. She was well aware that the two families wouldn't be half so close if she didn't keep up the correspondence. Just like the older folk! Just because Sunniside was five miles from Langley didn't put it at the ends of the earth. Blackhill was ten miles and Bertha still got to see her Mam now and again. It was the men who were the worst. What was it Ted had been called when they first came to Langley? 'Tow Law Ted' and then Robert was 'Tow Law Bob'. Joseph Simpson was still 'Cockney Joe' but that was fair enough because London was hundreds of miles away.

Why was there this innate mistrust of strangers, of anyone from outside of their own village? The world was getting smaller. There were trains and omnibuses and trams now, people could get from place to place faster and more comfortably. She briefly wondered if this mistrust of anyone slightly different from your own wasn't the cause of the war in the first place. She sighed again and picked up the pencil.

This letter was going to be hard. The one she had sent off just four days ago was so full of bad news it was unbelievable. She could tell from the way he had waved from the train that he had not received it but it would catch up with him soon enough. She would rather not be writing this present letter at all, never mind doing it so soon after the last, but what must be done must be done. Dreadful things, terrible things, but things she knew she ought not to keep from her man, however she wished to protect him while he was living a life of hardship and tribulation away in France. Her lips compressed into a thin line as she looked again at the cigarette cards. She had included one in the last letter but now thought the act entirely inappropriate.

Her mind began to wander. She could always tell her Ted about the grand day they had spent in Newcastle with all its wonderful statues and tall buildings. No, it would sound as if it didn't matter that they had missed seeing him. What about the blockading of all the German ports by the Allies? He might know that already and if he didn't it would get up his nose that he had been informed by his wife who was back in England rather than his own officers. No, couldn't do that either.

It would have to be all the bad news from the village then. He was to find out from the previous letter about the terrible death suffered by Fat Ena's sausage dog but now she must perform the onerous task of informing her man that the perpetrator turned out to be none other than an unrepentant Walter Timms, who was proud of the fact he had rid the world of a German!

The fact had only come to light a few days ago and apparently his wife Jenny had been driven demented by trying to hush it up but it had all started when someone had told Walter of the atrocities the Germans were responsible for. The simple soul had become so enraged he had taken revenge on the little dachshund with no thought of the consequences should his conduct come to light.

Stuff like that doesn't stay quiet for long, especially when the equally simple Lettie Simpson is your charity lodger and sure enough, she told someone – in the strictest secrecy mind – the whole terrible truth. Then it was out, and it was surprising how it divided the village. There were those who thought he should be tarred and feathered before Tommy Raper got back to avenge the suffering his Mam had been put through and there were those who thought a German was a German and they were a blight to be eradicated from the face of the earth, dogs and all.

Bertha suddenly realised she was sitting with her elbows on the table and her face in her hands. Thoughts spun round in her head like a whirlwind. The knock on the back door last night had been Lettie, carrying little Sarah and a pathetic bundle of rags in a knackered carpetbag. She had been kicked out of the Timms household for good and all, so fetched up at Number Eight fully expecting to move in for the duration. There was a look of puzzled hate and frustration when Bertha explained that this time she couldn't help. Lettie absolutely failed to understand the loyalty Bertha now had to display to her husband and his friends. Tears of frustration burst from Lettie's eyes and she even tried to push past a shocked Bertha to get into the house. She bloody nearly made it as well, but a quick arm across the doorway prevented her. By now little Sarah was crying too and neither of them were listening as Bertha suggested going to see Captain Forsyth of the Salvation Army because after all he had helped her Joe when he was in need. Lettie called her a fucking bastard and turned on her heel to stamp down the yard.

It might as well have been a blow to the heart, but Bertha had stood her ground and refused to let the tears come. This wasn't charity, this was cruelty, but what could she do? She had tried to make the sackless Lettie a better, more responsible person, and she had failed utterly. She closed her eyes and prayed to the Good Lord for the salvation of Lettie, and in the same breath she prayed for something happy to write to her husband about.

The page on the pad still had the same amount of scrawl on it as half an hour ago. It wasn't going to change tonight, so Bertha gave up. She thought about her Mam and Dad, and about Tappy Lappy the pony, and about her life in Blackhill that had gone forever. It was all so unfair. Perhaps she should shut up the house and go back to Blackhill until Ted came home from the war. After all, it wouldn't be much longer than next Christmas and they could start off as fresh as fresh, and this time her husband would be a war hero.

She stretched her arms up to the ceiling and intertwined her fingers. Go to the netty and lock up. Mebbes everything would be better tomorrow.

Interestingly enough, the very next morning two letters arrived through the letterbox at Number Eight, Logan Street while Bertha was out shopping. Good! She had missed having to talk to Harry Fairbairn. She still thought he was the worst sort of lecher and didn't trust him an inch. He had become worse since Ted had gone away and she had sworn to tell her husband on his return.

The man had had the audacity to try to invite himself in for a cup of tea, and him knowing that her Ted was off to war! Bertha knew damned well it was more than a cup of tea he was after – and him a married man as well. God! How she hated him with his red, runny nose and his awful smelling bag. Well, he wasn't getting over her doorstep, not over her dead body, he wasn't. Her Ted would sort the loathsome bugger out. Just wait until he got home. But Ted was not at home and Harry Fairbairn did make her a little afraid, all the same.

One of the letters was from Mam and the other was from Ted's Mam. No problem finishing her own letter now. There was all the news in the world to pass on.

From outside in the street came a terrible, agonising scream. It froze the very blood in Bertha's veins.

Chapter 20

S.S. 'Onward', Monday 19th April 1915

The gentle roll of the ship was almost soporific. The crew quietly got on with their duties and largely ignored the teeming mass of soldiers that surrounded them. For their part, the troops moved mechanically out of the way of the seamen when requested to do so. They were mainly a subdued lot, fatigued and bored by a long journey that was apparently far from over. Everyone tried to find a nook into which he could slide in order to sleep the weary time away. One of the exceptions was John Merrigan who, as soon as the last beams of the lighthouse had drifted out of sight and abandoned the 'Onward' to the open sea, seemed to have turned into a different person. He was no longer taciturn, no longer morose. Indeed, he was inhaling the damp, salt air to the bottom of his lungs as if it were good tobacco smoke.

About twenty minutes after they had departed Folkestone he seemed no longer capable of containing himself. Suddenly Ted, who was leaning half asleep on the rail, took a solid dig in the ribs and was invited to go 'for a wander'.

Why the Hell not? He had slept away a lifetime on the train and was bored rigid staring into the inky dark that surrounded the ship. It was a bit chilly so they untangled their overcoats from their packs and donned them, pulling the big collars up to keep the wind out. They made sure their packs were safe with a semi-comatose Jacky Tait and set off 'for'ard', as John said, in order to 'get the cut of the lass' jib'. Ted followed submissively enough, glad to have something to do other than sit and fester until the ship docked.

The 'Onward' was a two-decker with an extra superstructure traversing the front of the upper deck for the bridge. She was crammed with soldiers but the pair could still make their way about without much difficulty. They got for'ard as far as they could until they were halted by a metal railing that ran the width of the ship. Beyond it, several crew members were lounging about and smoking pipes in amongst the hawsers, winches and general paraphernalia that sprouted from the deck. Ted had never seen cables coiled so neatly. Every so often a level piece of deck was given over to a variety of ropes, large and small, all coiled and stacked as if ready for inspection. They gently shouldered their way through to the rail where John nodded to the nearest sailor who unsmilingly returned the nod. John leaned forward over the rail and began a desultory conversation with the man who, again without a smile, answered John's questions and eventually thawed to the point of getting up off the metal drum he was perched on and moving over to join them.

'Seafaring man, are you then?'

John shrugged and explained who he was. Apparently, the seaman was from Donegal and had been on the 'Onward' for four years. He was very proud of the fact that this was the first ship to ferry cars to France and back on a private basis. Unlike in Britain, there was no national restriction of twenty miles per hour on the continent so the well-heeled could take their motorcars with them on holiday and enjoy the freedom of travelling anywhere they liked and as fast as they liked. All right for some! After a little more conversation, the seaman took the unexpected step of inviting them over the railing to show off the winding mechanisms and mooring apparatus, all of which, after a recent refit, were as modern as they could be. After the short tour they were invited to sit on one of the large hawsers right up at the front and mostly hidden from the eyes of their fellow soldiers. The seaman beckoned to one of his mates who came over and produced a small pot flask. They took turns in swigging from it and it turned out to be whisky. Ted had assumed it would be rum.

Most of the yarning took place amongst the other three and Ted was quite happy to listen to the maritime chatter of his companions and let the alcohol warm him. After a while he felt a nudge and was suddenly jerked awake. He sniffed loudly and looked about him with bleary eyes. The seamen were no longer with them.

'How long was I asleep?'

''Bout half an hour. Come and have a look at this.'

John made his way towards the front of the ship, carefully picking his way through the equipment on the deck and, removing his cap, leaned over the railing as far forward as it was possible to go. Ted did the same. The creamy rush of the sea as it split and surged down either side of the prow was as beautiful to listen to as it was to behold. There were no lights this far forward but it took no time for eyes to get used to the inky blackness. The contrast between the slick, glossy surface of the sea and the creamy froth of the bow wave as it swirled and flew over the stem was hypnotic, the swishing sound almost dreamlike.

'This is all I ever wanted to do. All my life.'

John followed this with a long, bitter silence broken only by the hiss of the bow wave. They stood leaning on the rail, each lost in his thoughts. Ted was suddenly worried about John. He had always seemed invincible, but here he was with a fractured childhood and bitter memories from his past that would have beggared a lesser man.

Well, if he could shoulder his burdens and still conduct himself the way he did, so could Ted. He took two cigarettes from his baccy tin and offered one to John. The level stare he got in return was disconcerting but after a few seconds it turned into a faint smile and the man took the tab. They both turned their backs to the rail and jammed their caps on their heads. John spoke first, nodding towards the little knot of seamen playing some dice game or other a few yards back.

'Let's offer them a tab as well. They gave us the best seats in the house, didn't they?'

Ted nodded and, with newfound nerve, walked confidently towards them. He stopped without turning when John spoke again.

'Thanks, Ted.'

So they sat and yarned and played dice to while away the time. Ted felt grand, and he had never seen John so animated. Here they were an élite amongst the soldiers on this vessel because they had the respect of the seamen. Ted could feel jealous eyes upon him from behind the metal railing that might as well have been the walls of mighty Troy, impregnable to all unless you were invited in. Cigarettes were exchanged for more pegs of whisky.

Eventually, at some signal missed by both Ted and John, the seamen packed in their gaming and shuffled off elsewhere, leaving the lads alone on the foredeck. It was time to get back over the rail. The privileges were at an end and they were private soldiers of the British Expeditionary Force once again. John faced down the soldiers in his way as he climbed the railing and, surprising himself, so did Ted. It took no time at all to get back to a snoring

Jacky Tait and to ensure their packs were in good order. Nobody asked where they had been. Half of Ted wanted to brag about their being invited into sailor country but he took a leaf out of John's book and said nothing.

Shortly, a half-dozing Tom Dodds cleaned his specs and peered ahead, swearing he could see a light in the distance. Dawn already? Everyone pulled out pocket watches but it was just before one in the morning. They all searched but could see nothing, except George Moody, who backed Tommy up. Tommy insisted however and sure enough, after a few minutes the lads were, one by one, able to see a speck on the horizon. They all agreed there must be something to wearing spectacles and for once nobody took the piss out of Tommy's eyesight. The dot of light grew to a smudge and there was a stirring all over the ship as if everyone had been made aware at once that their destination was looming. The 'Onward' chugged on and the light became brighter. Soon they had reached land, which was lit up like daylight. Billy Robson was getting agitated again but was assured that this was definitely, honestly and finally France: Boulogne, to be exact. They were soon steaming in between two giant wooden wharfs that funnelled them into the docking area. Once again the soldiers moved out of the way of the seamen as they busied themselves tying up the ship. One of the crew with whom Ted had been sharing whisky and cigarettes, passed close by and Ted flashed him a grin, but it was as if they were total strangers. They locked eyes for an instant but there was no hint of recognition from the sailor. For a second Ted was angry. Then he let it pass.

The 'Onward' was now moving slowly sideways towards the brightly lit landing stage. This was different altogether to leaving Folkestone under cover of darkness like a thief in the night. Every detail of the docking area stood out as sharply as if it were under a summer sun. A little knot of men in khaki was standing beside a pile of bales of hay... and there was Major Ritson right by the quay, fists on hips and legs apart, looking as confident as if he were back on the square in Gateshead.

The seamen both aboard and on shore were working expertly towards setting up the gangplanks and in a few minutes the men were disembarking to set foot in France. Half the docking area was covered in goods, machinery and artillery and half, disturbingly, was covered in wounded soldiers. For the most part they were muttering quietly amongst themselves and ignored the odd, cheery wave or halloo that the disembarking men threw their way. They just stared momentarily at the newcomers and withdrew into themselves once more. The screams were few and far between but when they came, they curdled the blood of the Durhams: shocking outbursts of agony that could not even be guessed at. Mule drawn ambulances and GS wagons were plodding back and forth along the entrance to the dock to deliver yet more of them. Red crosses on white circular backgrounds were in evidence everywhere. Under the lee of a wall were several neat, orderly lines of stretchers filled with wounded men covered in khaki blankets to keep out the cold. The walking wounded were huddled down beside them or grouped into little knots, smoking and talking quietly amongst themselves. Ted immediately recognised the pattern of the stretchers as the same sort upon which he had spent the first nights after he had broken his leg.

At least he had both his legs. As his eyes scanned the rank and file of stretchers it was obvious from the contours of the blankets that many of these poor souls were in a worse state than that. He had to look past the geometrically neat rows to the individual men in order to see the horrors perpetrated by the barbarian Hun army. Blankets flat along the stretcher where legs should have been. Stumps of arms accentuated by the red and white of blood-soaked dressings against the drab of khaki. Heads swathed in bandages appeared twice their normal size, sometimes covering the eyes as well. God alone knew what was underneath all that. They were all so exposed on this brilliantly lit landing stage and Ted wondered what would have happened to them if it were raining. The men of the Eighth DLI disembarked as they had climbed aboard, anyone, in any order. When sufficient of them had reached the tarmacadam surface of the dock, the NCOs barked orders and soon formed them into their companies. There was no rest now.

There was the briefest 'Welcome to France' speech from Lieutenant Colonel Turnbull who added that now they were part of the 151st Brigade under the command of a Major General W.F.L. Lindsay. That made all the difference, that did.

No sooner were the men formed up than the order to march was given and off they went out of the docks, past the lines of silent, staring, wounded men. It was the sheer scale of the operation to deliver the wounded to the ship that struck the newcomers. This was not just the Durhams marching off to war. Half of England must be here and there were just as many wounded leaving the place as there were men to replace them. How many of the Durhams would be back here in a few days or weeks lying on a stretcher? Would they be bereft of legs, or both arms like one poor bugger who sported two pink-bandaged stumps and stood with a fag in his mouth waiting for his mate to light it? How did he go for a piss?

Almost immediately, they began to ascend a ramp, and shortly after, they left the harsh illumination behind and were once again plunged into darkness. The march through the town was gloomy, and poorly relieved by the meagre gas mantles that served to light up the place. As they marched up the long unmade road, more GS wagons passed them in the opposite direction to deliver even more wounded to the docks.

They had been on the go about an hour, and all uphill. The marching packs were heavy and everybody was fed up. Apart from an old man leading a goat they met no one. His cheery wave and shout of 'Eenglish' was not reciprocated. They were on a hill above the town now and had come about four miles when one of the NCOs piped up that they were nearly home and would soon be tucked up snug in bed. This engendered quite a bit of interest amongst the lads, who started to take more notice of their surroundings. The made-up road of Boulogne had long since transformed itself into a badly wheel-rutted cart track through what looked like common land. No trees, just a few shrubs and the sudden appearance of a low wattle fence with a dilapidated, hand painted notice saying 'St. Martin's Camp'. There was no one on sentry and the entrance was a gap in the fence rather than a gate. The men eyed this new development suspiciously and continued to slog their way up a short rise to almost level ground. A collective gasp went up as they breasted the rise and saw row upon row of eight-man ridge tents and the smell of fresh brewed tea assailed every nostril at once. Surprisingly, the muttered comments of 'That's more like it' and 'Just the bloody job' were not cut short by the NCOs who appeared just as relieved as the men to see something approaching a decent few hours of sleep coming their way.

If the terrain wasn't familiar, the layout of the camp was. Streets of tents for the men on three sides of the ever-present parade square, which was just an open bit of heathland, and a big barn-like wooden building on the fourth for the officers' quarters. Behind one of the rows of tents was an enclosure from which was coming the sounds – and the smell – of mules. Next to the barn was a mess tent with a row of cauldrons bubbling over a trench fire. The smell of tea was now in fierce competition with the aroma of bully-beef stew, which was being tended by a small group of men, some in khaki and some in Salvation Army uniform.

A hatless soldier in shirtsleeves was waiting on the square until all the men were halted. He was standing beside what looked like a tall bird table with two hurricane lamps hanging from it, and he was apparently oblivious of the fact he was improperly dressed. He walked up to the small group of officers and presented them with a crisp salute. A short exchange ensued and the officers left the men under the orders of the NCOs and made their way into the barn, where no doubt they were to be treated to better fare than a bowl of bully-beef stew and a mug of tea. The lads couldn't care less: there was nowt wrong with stew and tea. It was no surprise that it tasted the same in France as it did in England, but the bread, which came in long sticks instead of proper loaves and had a crispy crust, was deliciously different and well received.

After a few minutes of conversation between the NCOs and the half-dressed soldier, the men were addressed to the effect that they would first of all draw a bedroll from the stores tent and billet themselves by companies in the tents before returning to the square for rations. In less than two hours every man had a bedroll in a tent and a full belly and was delighted to hear that reveille was to be at the unheard of late hour of 0700.

Inside, the tents were grubby and smelly. Tab ends littered the grass floor and so did empty food tins and it was obvious they had not been cleaned since being vacated by the last body of men, or mebbes the lot before that. There was one hurricane lamp per tent and luckily the one in the lads' tent was still half full. The bedrolls were clean and there were few complaints about the untidiness of the previous occupants. It was champion to dump packs and weapons and stretch out for a decent sleep instead of being cramped up on a train with back and neck aching. There was next to no conversation as they settled down in the grimy tent. The nearest man doused the lamp and in a very few minutes they were all sound asleep.

It felt to Ted that he had only lain down about a minute ago when the strains of the morning bugle invaded his sleep. He was freezing. Grumbling and cursing the lads looked around through bleary eyes and took in their strange surroundings. Outside, voices were heard shouting instructions to the slowly waking army. Tom Dodds, who was nearest the flap poked his head through and reported that the camp staff were walking amongst the tents issuing instructions that a shirtsleeve parade was to be held on the square at 0745. That was bloody nearly now! These unfamiliar voices were soon joined by the familiar tones of their own NCOs.

Shivering and, half asleep, the Durhams assembled bareheaded and without tunics on the square.

The men were soon snapped to attention at the sight of Lieutenant Colonel Turnbull accompanied by his adjutant, Captain Stevens and the COs of the various companies who were approaching from the direction of the officers' mess accompanied by an elderly major who looked like he was wearing a slightly outsized uniform. They stood front centre of the parade and Lieutenant Colonel Turnbull bade the men a good morning and hoped they had slept well. He then stood politely to one side, facing the men, as the major spoke.

He introduced himself as the camp commandant, Major Dollond, and welcomed them to St. Martin's Camp, in the district of Ostrovhe, or 'Ortoshove' as the army affectionately called it because it was more easily pronounced that way. He described it as a transit camp for BEF soldiers making their way to the front. Only yesterday the Sixth DLI had passed this very way. Orders were received in the officers' club from down the line for each new body of men as they arrived. Such orders would enable the newcomers to be placed at their designated position at the front with expediency in order to progress the advance. Such orders had indeed been received relating to the Durhams and had been passed on to their officers. Major Dollond managed a weak smile as he continued that such matters were less important than breakfast so, as soon as the men were fed, a working parade would be ordered and they would receive their instructions on a full belly.

It sounded grand, and would have been if breakfast had not been yet more bully-beef stew and tea – but at least it had that nice bread, which was apparently known as 'bagget'. The Salvation Army men and women had brought out their musical instruments and were entertaining the men with a selection of the brighter tunes from the hymnary.

Naturally, it was Billy Robson who commented first. 'Do we have to have that bloody racket? I'm trying to eat, man.'

He was soon hushed up as most of the men were enjoying the show. This lot weren't pushy: nobody came around for a collection, nobody bothered them with a sermon and no one was asked to stand up and sing. It seemed that the Sally Ann was here purely to assist the army and to add to the comfort of the troops as they passed through the camp.

Most of the men had finished their meal and were cleaning their mess tins in the zinc baths provided when the band, after finishing 'The Son of God goes off to War' suddenly struck up 'God save the King'. Of course, everyone stopped what they were doing and stood politely until the last strains of the anthem faded to silence. Nobody knew who started the hesitant clapping but it was quickly taken up and the little group disbanded to warm applause and warmer smiles.

It didn't take long for everyone to get kitted up and Ted, John and Jacky were smoking a tab and looking down onto Boulogne and the sea. They had to admit that although the camp was as depressing as could be, the view from this shelf above the town was magnificent. But it was cold and windy, and the news that the Sally Ann lot had a rest hut of their own where you could get a mug of tea any time you liked was a bit more appealing. All the lads made sure their guns were clean and their marching packs were properly made up – just in case – then headed off to the rest hut for a bonus tea. They would have made it as well but for the voice of Corporal Tremaine thundering around them and telling everyone in hearing range, which must have been most of the camp, to return to their tents and clean up the litter in and around them. A stab of frustration pierced the lads: no bugger had done that for them!

The parade was at 1100 hours, and was more like a proper parade. The weather had warmed up a bit and the wind had gone down. The mules had already left and so had most of the smell. Some of the injustice at cleaning up the tents had been blunted by the anticipation of what was going to happen next. After they had been standing for a few minutes Captains Harvey and Bradford approached from the direction of the officers' club and separated to head their respective companies. Some of the other officers followed soon after. A smart salute from the NCOs turned the men over to their COs, who all said pretty much the same thing at the same time.

They were off to war. Now.

Chapter 21

Boulogne/ St. Marie Cappelle, Tuesday 20th April 1915

Their destination could not as yet be divulged but rest assured the Durhams were about to get their hands dirty at the front. Not to worry about marching all the way either. There was to be a rest and prep period of one hour, after which they would march to the station at Pont-de-Briques, about four miles up the road where they would join a train to take them on. Thanks were given to the staff of St. Martin's Camp for their hospitality: and would the men please leave the place as they found it?

As soon as they were dismissed, most of the men started a last brew of tea on one or other of the campfires that dotted the place. There was no point going to the Sally Ann rest hut as the queue was already a mile long. Ted stood with Jacky for a bit and reached into his pocket for a tab. His fingers immediately hit the hard metal of the silver locket he had never presented to his wife. He pressed his lips together and ignored it as he fished out his baccy instead and offered a rolly tab to Jacky. They gazed out over the sea at a small black speck that was throwing out a lazy coil of smoke as it made its way towards Boulogne.

'That'll be the next lot in, then,' muttered Ted.

'Likely. Well, we'd better get our skates on and put all the rubbish back in the tent, then.'

Ted's eyebrows knotted in puzzlement at Jacky's odd remark.

'Well, we have to leave the tents the way we found them, man. Captain Bradford's orders.'

* * * * *

The march out to Pont-de-Briques was uneventful and, thankfully, quite short. The men were halted on a flat piece of grassland on the side of the line opposite the dirty little station, where a train was already waiting and the little locomotive taking on water. A boy of not much more than thirteen or fourteen was holding the hose above the aperture. It was a funny sort of side tank 0-6-0 in a dirty, vomit-green colour. None of the lads recognised the type and they all laughed about the fact that they wouldn't be seen dead being pulled by a train that colour if they could possibly help it. Fat Harry laughed until he nearly cried, declaring the little locomotive to be the exact colour of his baby son's shite when he was first born.

The wrinkled face of the old driver however looked just like the driver in every locomotive in every pit in the north-east. The blue overalls, the flat cap and pipe, even the brightly coloured handkerchief around his neck were the same. Somebody shouted a greeting to him and it seemed strange that when he cheerily waved back his reply was in French. A grin of recognition crossed many a face and waves were exchanged when it was realised the machine gun lads were already on the trucks at the front. There were the Blenkiron brothers, and further back was Willy Maddison, as fresh-faced and spotty as ever, waving like mad to anybody who would wave back. They were sat with their equipment in open trucks of the same sort that worked the pit lines back home and apparently had joined the train at Le Havre, where they had landed after setting out from Southampton.

The lads, meanwhile, were looking up and down the train but could see only two carriages behind the tender, both full of officers. After the open trucks containing the machine gun detachment were loads of covered cattle wagons or horse wagons. Those at the back contained mules, obvious by the noise and smell. It dawned on the Durhams that the rest were for them.

The voices of protest were silenced immediately and the men brought to attention. They were then marched in file across the track in front of the locomotive and down the scruffy wooden platform to enter the first available wagon. It was marked in chalk letters: 'Chevaux 8. Hommes 40'. After about twenty sullen soldiers had filed in, the next man tried to move on to the next wagon only to be brought to the halt and told to enter the already inhabited one. With a bit of shuffling they managed to get the requisite forty men in the first wagon before they were allowed to move down the platform to the next. Ted's heart sank as his nostrils were assailed by the smell as he followed Freddy Laidler in. The floor was covered in straw and cow shit and stank worse than the mules. Thinking on his feet, he moved quickly to the front so that as the troops behind him entrained he had already bagged one of the corners. He took off his marching pack, dumped it between his legs and sat on it to watch as more, and yet more, men entered the truck. He was horrified when he realised the number of men boarding. They were packed in like pilchards and he had to stand up again or be swamped. There were little drop-down ventilation panels all around the top of the truck and the men opened some of them. The smell was appalling and more than one soldier commented that the mules were being better treated. A bit of pushing and shoving near Ted brought the bright red face of Billy Robson, accompanied by the unmistakable bulk of a hatless Fat Harry.

'What cheer, Ted. Room for a small one here, then?'

While the men were fumbling and fighting for space the door slid shut with a crash taking a lot of the daylight with it. Ominously, they also heard the bar drop which meant they were effectively locked in. A collective moan went up and hands were raised all at once to open the remaining ventilation panels.

Harry lit a made-up tab. 'Not exactly what I had in mind,' he said, offering the lit match to the others. 'Any idea how long this trip will take, anybody?'

'Too fucking long.' The answer came back almost as if it had been rehearsed by the crowd, followed by laughter that rang around the truck but was cut short as everyone was suddenly flung backwards.

At last they were off, and it was almost a relief. The temperature had risen in the truck in the few minutes since the door had shut but now that they were underway the breezes through the vents, though reeking, were a Godsend. Ted thanked his lucky stars that his plan had worked – get to the front of the truck so all the smell was blown away from you to the back of the train. Standing on tiptoe, he saw several pairs of eyes looking back at him from the truck in front. A hand came through next to one of the pairs of eyes and a 'How do, Teddy boy' floated across to him. He grinned anew as he recognised Tommy Raper, stuck his hand up to wave back, and promptly lost his fag as it was whipped away by the draught and flew back into the truck somewhere.

The train didn't seem to be travelling too fast and everyone was wondering why. After about fifteen minutes it stopped. The men in the middle asked what was going on and those on the edge near the vents said they were at a little station but couldn't see what the hold-up was. As the locomotive marked time with steam-laden wheezes a shouted conversation in French took place somewhere behind them. Then the train was off once more with a lurch that pressed everyone to the back again. This was repeated about ten minutes later and by a conversation relayed from truck to truck it transpired that the train was delivering stuff to each station and halt as it passed through. The first was a churn of milk, the second was a crate of chickens and the third was a ham wrapped in some net in a round hatbox. The journey continued, with stops at what appeared to be every couple of miles to deliver a pint of bloody milk or whatever, annoying the passengers.

The truck telegraph was working well by now, and it amused the men to pass insults to their mates in other trucks up and down the train, but time was passing and apart from resigning themselves to the fact there was obviously going to be no stopping for a meal, probably half the company needed to relieve themselves. Up to now, the sprinkling of NCOs had allowed the men to misbehave since it passed the time and they weren't really doing any harm, but occasional barked orders were now heard to keep them in order. As the journey progressed those orders became more frequent. It was close to 1700 hours when a message was relayed down the train.

'Next stop... piss stop.'

Suddenly everyone who thought they were going to urinate on the floor and try to miss everybody else's boots found the willpower to hold on a little longer and sure enough there was a gentle rumble as the train decelerated.

This time, when the locomotive hissed to a halt, the sliding doors were flung open, not on the platform side but opposite, where a great mass of desperate soldiers leaped down upon the greeny-brown marsh grass and relieved themselves where they stood. This was all much to the amusement of the four middle-aged ladies and two young pretty ones, all in trousers, who had opened the doors and were standing grinning like Cheshire cats. It was all too late for the embarrassed troops, who had more urgent things to think about than to determine the sex of their benefactors. They were unable to stop and so continued to urinate, blushing furiously, in front of the women.

Ted was as red-faced as anybody as he buttoned his trousers. He thought his neck must be crimson as he turned around to face the train again. Four of the women had disappeared and the remaining two were saying 'Tea, Tommy, tea,' and pointing to the sleeper-built platform across the line. This was a bit more like it.

The grassed area stank of piss and Ted picked his way carefully across the line, as there was the odd pile of shit to deal with as well. It transpired they had thirty minutes to drink their tea and eat whatever rations they had brought along with them, ensuring anyone without food would receive a fair share from their comrades. In reality the thinking was that anybody without food must have already eaten it, so serve the greedy buggers right. Swapping was legitimate though, and here and there amongst the groups of soldiers was somebody who had opened a seven-pound tin of bully doling out portions in exchange for baccy or chocolate or those bagget breadstick things. Ted downed his tea almost in one go and handed the enamel mug back to the pretty girl in trousers; he then fished a tin of Maconachie's meat and veg from his pocket. He felt a tap on his shoulder and turned to see Jacky Tait, chewing on a big chunk of dried beef.

'What cheer, Ted, come and have a look at this, man.' He turned to cross the platform and went out through a tattered wooden portal. The transformation couldn't have been greater. This wasn't the country halt they thought. They had arrived round the back of a bigger station on a bit of waste ground but once through the portal, the next platform was laid paving. In front of them was a faced brick wall with two ornate arches through which could be seen an elegant concourse that would have put Durham station to shame. They were on the outskirts of a city, or at least a big town, and turning around they could see above one of the arches they had just come through, the words 'St. Omer' and something else in French, carved into a stone plaque.

'It's just like Newcastle, man,' whispered Ted in awe as he pulled chunks of meat from the tin with his knife.

'Aye, but do you notice anything? Anything about the people, like?'

Ted stared around but it was just a busy concourse in a railway station. Impressive as Hell but just a big station nonetheless.

'No soldiers,' said Jacky flatly. 'Not English, not French, not nothing. Look around. You wouldn't even know there was a war on. Seems a bit funny to me.'

There was an uncomfortable pause for a few seconds then he broke into a grin and pointed over the station wall to where the tower of a great ruined church dominated the skyline.

'Let's go and have a look,' he said. 'We've got time.'

Ted wasn't so sure. He didn't like being away from the main body of the company for too long. In the event, the decision was taken for them by a piercing blast on a whistle followed by the strident voice of Corporal Lawrie.

'Smith and Tait, you pair of mongers... Get yourselves back here now.'

They both turned and Ted was about to double but Jacky put his hand on his arm to check him.

'Easy, Teddy boy. We don't have to make a spectacle of ourselves in front of the Frenchies, do we? Let's march back smartly now like soldiers of the King, eh!'

Ted felt every eye was upon them as they marched back to the archway and a slightly purple Corporal Lawrie. He was blushing fit to bust for the second time in twenty minutes but when they stamped to the halt in front of the NCO, the expected bollocking never arrived.

'New orders, lads we're to get back on the train pronto. We're off somewhere else. Move yourselves.'

That was it. Ted didn't want to lose his corner in the truck and trying to keep your place with your marching pack didn't work with everybody.

'Sorry, Jacky, lad, the tour will have to wait.'

A few paces and they were back amongst the men on the wooden platform wrapping up card games or exchanging cigarette cards. Out of the corner of his eye, Ted was startled to see a lanky private soldier with a big red scar under his right eye had a handful of Wills 'Physical Culture' cards, the same as his own and Tom Dodds' ones. He tried to remember the man's face so he could track him down later: might be a couple of swaps there.

* * * * *

Back on the train, it was as if they had never left. The gossip was that they should have spent an hour in St. Omer and had a decent ration stop but new orders had changed that. They were to proceed at once to a place called Cassell, which might be ten miles away or a hundred, and nobody knew anything more than that.

The mood was very different now. There wasn't much capering and the trucks were mostly quiet. *What new orders?* Everyone thought they were going straight to the front anyway and that's where all the previous excitement and high spirits had come from. *So what's changed?* Everybody knew that new troops were to be 'eased in' to battle and then rotated out for a bit. They'd learned all that to death before they left England and were pleased as punch at the thought of their first, quick tour of duty at the front being so imminent. Had all that changed now? Nobody seemed to know.

The train still kept stopping every couple of miles and now it seemed to labour as well because it was going up a long incline. It wasn't Fat Harry's idea of comfort considering they were packed like fish in a bucket and he made that clear enough, but never mind. It was about seven o' clock and starting to get dark when the train pulled up for the umpteenth time. The men were completely anaesthetised by now, and took no notice, but they were jerked back to a state of awareness as the bars were thumped open and the doors slid back. Ted rubbed his eyes and tried to stare out into the dusk.

Stone buildings, concrete platform, green wooden awning edgings and most importantly, men were opening the truck doors instead of women. Voices boomed out from all along the platform to collect kit, leave the station immediately and form up on the road outside. This was more like it. The whole atmosphere was charged with anticipation as the troops struggled away from the dreadful memory of the trucks and got down to the familiar task of becoming a company once more instead of being just so much livestock. They had no idea where they were but the assumption was it must be Cassel because that's where the orders said they were stopping next. Didn't look that impressive – more like a good-sized village with a half-decent rural station that was already closed and devoid of any staff.

Because there was only a deserted road outside they had to form up by companies only four men deep, which meant they were strung out for what looked like miles, but again it was nothing they hadn't practiced a thousand times so they were all organised in fairly short order. There were a few smiles when they heard the commotion from inside the station as the wagon handlers were trying to organise the mules that had obviously decided they were having none of it.

Once again, Captain Bradford, this time accompanied by Lieutenant Brass, addressed the men of 'D' Company. It appeared they were indeed at Cassel, that is to say, the station serving it, which was a couple of miles' march from the town itself. This was to be followed by a further couple of miles to the village of St. Marie Cappelle where they were to be billeted for the next few days for a rest period, whilst awaiting a decision as to what would be the best use to put them to. It was the usual speech with the usual attempts at humour but the men knew when to laugh politely and when to say nowt. So off they went.

Because it had been such a long day, discipline was relaxed and the men were allowed to talk and smoke in ranks if they so wished. A couple of attempts to strike up a song were stillborn and for the most part they marched in more or less silence. They were still going uphill though, and with marching packs. When they had trained at Lobley Hill they only wore battle packs and that was bad enough, but they knew better than to complain. All except Billy Robson and Dicky Howell, that is.

Lieutenant Colonel Turnbull, Captain Bradford and Lieutenant Brass were now mounted, having been reunited with their horses now that the mule and equipment detachments had caught up at Pont-de-Briques, and they rode up and down the length of the company cheering the men along. The distant lights on the top of the hill came steadily closer and once they were away from the town the road narrowed a bit and began to be flanked by tall, thin trees, not like the trees at home at all. Fat Harry asked Lieutenant Brass the name of the road they were travelling along. Without a second's hesitation the young officer replied that it was the Rue de Watten, a little to the rear it had been the Rue de Arneke.

'See Billy,' he shouted to his mate. 'I told you all the roads in France were Roody roads... Thank you, sir!'

A burst of laughter erupted from the men, but it was too dark to see if Lieutenant Brass was blushing or not. Ted smiled at the thought that he might be and was glad that, for a change, it wasn't him. Brass cantered back down the column and into the dark.

The higher up the hill they climbed the more the men became interested in some little red flashes of light that peppered the otherwise black backdrop of the distant landscape over the valley. Because of the crunching of boots on the road no sound could be heard.

When one of the men was brave enough to ask Corporal Huggins what they were, he replied, 'It's what you've come to see off, Briggs, it's the German Army firing on our lads.'

This spread through the men like wildfire and many a neck was craned round to watch the distant flashes of gunfire.

This was it.

This was real.

They reached Cassel shortly afterwards, and the lights of the town obscured the distant sparks where men on both sides were being blown to pieces where they stood. Abruptly, they were brought to the halt in a broad street on the outskirts of the town where at least they could form their companies properly. They were made ready as if for inspection and waited what seemed an age. A few strange British officers were about, mostly young'uns like Lieutenants Brass and Wood. All had red tabs on their lapels. That meant staff officers – the best of the best, men hand-picked to run the top end of the army.

They came and went while the men stood at attention, stock still. It was a bloody insult really, you didn't have to keep the men at the attention, not for this long. It was obvious to everybody that the Durhams were marking time until they found out what to do next and just because they had had a lie-in that morning didn't mean they weren't dog-tired now it was the end of the day. One young officer came to talk to Captain Bradford and he was a Lieutenant-bloody-Colonel! He looked about the same age as Ted and as he passed close to the ranks a glance showed he wasn't even shaving.

How the Hell does that happen?

Anyway, he was pointing and waving, obviously giving directions. Then the young staff officer thrust a fat brown envelope into Captain Bradford's hand and received a smart salute in return. The pair shook hands and the officer ambled off towards the centre of town and into the night. Eventually all the comings and goings of top brass eased off and the men were left in the tender, but at least familiar, care of their own officers and NCOs.

All would be revealed tomorrow but right now, the top of the list was the march to St. Marie Cappelle to get billeted up for a proper night's sleep. So off they went again around the outskirts of the town where they had to halt whilst an electric tramcar clanged its bell and whirred across the cobbled street they were marching down. Ted wondered if all Frenchy towns were so posh and so aloof from the war that was being fought just across the valley, where each little red flash meant somebody's death.

At least they were marching downhill now. They moved along the southern outskirts of Cassell and, as at St. Omer, they marvelled at how far away the war seemed. Soon they were out on unlit but reasonably well made up roads and to their left was a railway line. A talking point on the otherwise tedious march was the number of windmills they passed. They thrust up out of the top of hills and knolls all over the place, like stubby, ridiculous bird scarers. Ted remembered pictures in his schoolbooks. What was that story about the little Dutch boy who stuck his finger in a dyke and saved the town? But here they were for real. He had to include this in his next letter to Bertha, she'd be tickled pink.

Bertha!

Robert!

Instantly the ice-cold hammer thumped him in the heart. What could he have done to prevent it? Over the weeks, it had come to him slowly and with regret that praying seemed to make no difference. It began to shake his faith. So what was God doing? He was supposed to be everywhere, so what was going on?

Carry him in your heart, not on your shoulders.

Ted sighed a big, juddering sigh and gritted his teeth.

'Tired, bonny lad?'

He recognised the voice behind him as Harry Clarke.

'Aye, Harry. Clapped out and ready for bed, man.'

On they marched. There were two stops within ten minutes of each other, one at a junction where it was clear the officers were unsure of directions. They started off again and the gossip filtered down that the young staff officer in town had only arrived a couple of days before they did and hardly knew his way around himself. Bloody typical. Lieutenant Brass was sent on ahead at a canter to reconnoitre but a bend in the road by a thick copse made the order unnecessary. The lights of a good-sized village came into view and a tired cheer went up from the men.

It was a queer set-up, half farming village and half staging camp. The first of the column reached the village square, where a good many of the inhabitants had turned out and the smell of cooked food was most welcome, principally because nowhere in the heady mixture of strange aromas was there even a hint of bully-beef stew. The men halted smartly and the rest of the column filtered in behind and carried on until the entire area was filled with troops, though it was probably only about half of the battalion, so God knew where the rest were put. The 'at ease' was given and Lieutenant Colonel Turnbull addressed the men to the effect that this was a repeat of their arrival at St. Martin's Camp in that they would be billeted before they ate, so the sooner they got started the better and would the company commanders tell off their men now. Captain Harvey immediately stepped forward and addressed 'A' Company and, along with a genial looking villager sporting a huge moustache and a butcher's apron, they headed out of the square towards some farmland to the east of the village.

Major Ritson took 'B' Company, and walked alongside a small man in a black coat who looked like an undertaker. They headed in the same direction as 'A' but after a hundred yards or so took a turn to the left up a side road.

It was the turn of Captain Bradford and his guide, who looked so suspiciously like John Brannon of the Blue Star that Fat Harry swore that when they got back he would find out if the Brannons had any Frenchy relations. They left the village heading south-east towards some fairly flat land and in about fifteen minutes came to a good-sized farm that looked as if it had been almost entirely turned over to the army. Straw dummies hung from trestles in one field and low, sandbagged walls ran in rough parallel lines in another. The company was marched through the main yard, scattering the hens and a couple of screaming piglets before halting in front of the first of two barns. It was newish and in good order and obviously the animals had been moved out ages ago to allow accommodation for the great tide of the British Expeditionary Force. The smell was still around though, and the fact that the mules were put in a field immediately behind the building would ensure it didn't go away either. There was reasonably fresh straw, some baled and some loose, and above was a big hayloft reached by a stairway at the west side and two rickety looking ladders further round, tied off top and bottom. Best of all though, just outside the big double doors, two great cauldrons were simmering away and throwing out the most delicious spicy smell. On a trestle table was a pile of bagget bread and Captain Bradford positioned himself right beside it.

'All right men, find yourselves a bed space and deposit your gear. Sergeants Malone and Hanson will organise guard details now.'

The lads couldn't help but chuckle at the surprised look on the sergeants' faces. Malone reacted first. Gulping, he volunteered the nearest soldiers to him and when he saw Corporal Huggins smiling at their discomfort he put him in charge of organising the pickets. Sergeant Malone meanwhile had sent the remainder of the company into the barns and adjacent outhouses to stake their claims to a sleeping area.

The commotion died down within minutes and the NCOs were back in charge. The officers bade the men goodnight and set off into the large farmhouse. In no time at all queues formed up where a boy of about twelve stood at one cauldron and presumably his mother, also wearing trousers, stood at the other where they were ladling out portions of delicious smelling soup.

'All right, our Ted. How's it going then, comrade?' Cockney Joe unceremoniously pushed into the queue looking right into the eyes of the youth whose place he had taken. The lad said nothing. 'Bit of all right, this is. Decent food and decent fags; what more could a man ask?'

He offered Ted a cigarette from a blue packet with some Frenchy words on it and Ted knew better than to ask where they had come from. They tasted a bit perfumy but were canny enough. When they had collected their food they went back to the twilight of the barn where they joined some of the other lads, sitting on bales of hay and dunking bagget into their soup, which was full of funny vegetables and cut-up sausage. They unanimously agreed that Frenchy food was far superior to army rations, though not necessarily as good as home cooked stuff. After eating, some of the lads wanted to play cards or dice but the light was going fast. One enterprising soul plucked up courage to try to ask the woman who had been dishing out the soup if they could have a lantern, but all the arm waving in the world got them nowhere. She just kept shaking her head.

It was the little French lad who got what they were after and said something in rapid fire that none of them could understand. Eventually, he picked up a bit of straw off the ground and held it into the embers under his cauldron. As soon as it was aflame he said, 'Pffft! Pffft!' and, pointing to the barn, shook his head solemnly.

'Well, that looks pretty cut and dried to me,' said Jacky. 'The lad's Standing Orders say no lamps in barns full of straw.'

'Bollocks, he's just a kid. Are him and his Mam going to stop us?'

Of course, it had to be Billy Robson but, unluckily for him, Corporal Lawrie just happened to be right behind. The Scottish burr was unmistakable. So was the menace.

'There will be no lights in the barn, men. And there will be no discussion concerning lights in the barn. Any questions?'

He was looking Billy right in the eye.

'No, Corporal.'

Corporal Lawrie nodded and after a further beady stare at Billy, went on his way.

Dicky Howell piped up, 'Hey lads, there was no 'lights out' order, was there? No curfew, like. So who's for a trip back into the village? Mebbes there's a bit of grub left, or even a pub. What d'you reckon?'

There were some nods of agreement from the dog-tired men, but not many. To start with Ted was all for it as well. Mebbes he could find the soldier with the scar on his eye who was collecting the same cigarette cards. Mebbes he would get a few swaps.

Suddenly, Robert swam into view, limp and lifeless, with his mouth full of coal dust and no cap upon his head, and Louise was screaming at him again in the church, calling him a murderer.

He didn't deserve the cards. He didn't deserve anything. Perhaps he should just go into the barn and go to bed amongst the ghosts. He put his hand to his breast pocket and felt the hard oval shape of the locket he had yet to send home to Bertha. He was a bloody fool and he knew it. He had grown his moustache, taken the trouble to seek out a photographer and bought a posh silver locket to put it in. What was so hard about sending the damned thing home to his wife, to whom he had written about half as often as she had written to him? Well, that was what he was going to do tonight. *Tonight!* There was some light outside on the open space where the grub had been issued. The Frenchies all seemed to have those big bird table things with the lamps hanging from them so he went to his space in the cow stall and fished his notepad and pencil out of his pack. A scurry in one corner of the straw caught his attention, though it was gone before he could focus on it. Probably a rat. Well, he had seen rats before, last time only a day or two ago at St. Martins.

He remembered when he was a bairn in Sunniside somehow ending up at the entrance to Farmer Keenlyside's barn – he couldn't remember why he was there – but when he pushed one of the great doors open, the whole floor appeared to move away from the flooding light like a great carpet. He remembered his jaw dropping. Imagine... a whole floor of rats!

Well, it wasn't like that here, and the odd rat was no problem provided you kept your food well locked up. That reminded him, so as well as his pencil and paper, he also retrieved the half a tin of plum and apple jam he had left. Just something to chew on while he was writing his letter, like.

In the event, the lads were confined to camp that night and, truth be told, they were all done in anyway so nobody grumbled much. Ted's thoughts alternated between Bertha and Robert as he hovered over his letter in the fading light. He had written nearly half of it but had been dissatisfied on reading it back to himself: 'Got off the train. Got on a boat. Marched a bit. Got on another train. Marched some more'.

The only real highlights were the windmills and the tiny flashes of red across the valley, and they didn't make much of a letter. He tried again and managed nearly two sides this time. That was a canny start and he felt satisfied with his progress. Finish it tomorrow...

When he came back to the barn he could only just see, it was so dark. He stood in the doorway for a minute until his eyes became used to the gloom then he fumbled his way back to his space. Sometime around 0500 hours a lighter shade of gloom began creeping in through the big doors. Apart from snores and sleepy mumbles it was quiet enough. Ted was half awake but still fatigued after a rotten night of thinking too much and trying to catch up on his sleep at the same time. Whispering through the silence was a noise he wasn't sure whether he could actually hear. Was he making it up inside his head? It was the faintest pop-popping sound. Without opening his eyes he wrinkled his eyebrows and forced himself to concentrate. Was it the sound made by the distant red flashes of last night? Was it really artillery? There was too much commotion yesterday to hear the distant, muffled staccato – but here it was. It was somehow disturbing to be lying here and listening to the sounds of his brothers-in-arms fighting courageously to the death.

But in his heart there was none of the burgeoning excitement that had begun to surface throughout the battalion, just a numb obstinacy and a need to exonerate himself to Robert. His brother's memory no longer gnawed at him so fiercely, but the little knot of fire in his heart that kept Robert somehow alive had receded and begun to grow dim, and it left a breach in Ted's soul that would never to be filled.

Suddenly, another sound drowned out his thoughts. A sort of drone, like an insect. It was getting louder. The men were stirring from their slumber, disturbed by the now alarmingly loud buzzing. It was coming closer and closer and the vibration was sufficient to dislodge little pieces of muck from the roof. They were all awake now. With a mighty roar which shook them to the bone the sound suddenly began to diminish. Most of the men were up, all in various stages of undress. Ted joined the rush for the door, rifle in hand. If this was a trap he wasn't going to be caught in a wooden building full of straw, not bloody likely. Clad in only his socks, combinations and shirt, he burst into the weak sunlight as a second whoosh shook the building.

The noise was deafening. Straight ahead of him and coming this way low across the sky was a double-winged aeroplane. It was greeny-brown and had what looked like a ski or something strapped between its wheels. When it screamed overhead every man ducked or clapped his hands to his ears and turned to watch as it sailed over the barn, its wheels almost skimming the thatch on the roof and causing loose bits of straw to rise up into the air. There were two people on board, the rearmost was facing backwards and waving a genial good morning to the receding rabble of soldiers. Then they shot high in the air and the men watched them slowly turn into quiet, tiny dots as they gradually distanced themselves from the farm and made their way to the front.

The men all looked at each other and after a tense minute someone started to laugh.

'It's all right, lads. I think they're ours.'

'Bloody good job an' all. Bastards!'

More laughter and the men began to relax. Most of them returned to their bed spaces, heads full of the great adventure. Ted was curious to see Captain Bradford across the yard, bare-chested and half shaved, with foam still covering most of his chin and his pistol in his hand.

There was also an expectation of breakfast, which, sadly, was not realised. For some reason they had all taken for granted that a meal would be laid on, but nothing was stirring. At 0730 hours, the bugle split the air and there was still no sign of grub. The pickets passed on the word that morning parade was at 0830 hours and the men were to see to feeding themselves. That went down like a lead balloon, but at least Ted now had something thrilling to put in his letter.

The parade was to be done by squads as there wasn't enough space for the whole company in the yard, and they were a bit scattered about. The good news, however, was that they were to remain here for a few days. The aeroplanes that buzzed them were, apparently, from St. Omer and were 'often doing that, just for a bit of fun, like.'

Most saw the joke and a few didn't, but anyway, news got around fast that as well as training there was to be an inter-company soccer tournament, so would anyone interested give their names in to their company NCOs. If there weren't enough volunteers, not to worry because they would soon make up any deficit with pressed men.

Somehow the mail had arrived when no one was looking and Ted was overjoyed to be one of the recipients. He grinned as he felt the outline of the cigarette card through the envelope. *Good lass!* He roughly thumbed it open and within seconds the grin illuminating his features went out.

It was Jacky Tait, who had not received a letter this tide, who first noticed the change and looked concerned as he asked his friend if everything was all right. Ted simply handed the letter across and stood immobile as he read through it.

Dearest Ted,

Hello pet. I hope you are well. I wonder if I should ask you to sit down before you read this, as the news it contains is not the best. Your Mam has tried to keep in touch with Louise who is still grieving as we all are about our Robert. I think because of their relationship your Mam feels closer to Robert when Louise is about. She has been down for tea a couple of times but her family have put their foot down and sent a letter saying contact with us upsets her so it all has to stop. She has her family and her work and her church and needs nothing more, except time and God's good grace to make her whole again. I really like Louise. I hope we can keep in touch somehow. A terrible thing has happened to Fat Ena Raper. Her little sausage dog has been killed. It was a terrible thing. One afternoon it went missing and she was beside herself. That night there was a tremendous banging on Ena's door and when she opened it there was Clementine dead and nailed to the door. Who would do such an evil thing. The whole village is up in arms. Bobby Stokoe died a few days ago. He has been sick for some time and your Mam says they were expecting it. Poor Bobby passed away peacefully on his brother's settee where the family are still living.

The allotment is coming along a bit and the taties and cauliflowers are in and the cramps are still turning out good veg so that is a blessing. Everyone from both families wants to say hello and to pray for your safekeeping. Our Olive wants to know if it's raining and how many Germans you have killed. When I visit Mam and Dad I take your letters so perhaps you should tell little white lies if anything too awful happens, Mam worries so. Both Dads are the same as ever and pretend that everything is all right. I don't know where they get it from. It's been a bit miserable and drizzly for the past few days.

I sometimes feel you are on the other side of the world, pet, and I do wish you were home. But everybody I talk to thinks you are a hero (so do I) and we all know you are doing your bit. So are we here in Langley as well. I have never seen so many women working up at the allotments so we really are not helpless you know. We can muddle along all right without you men ha ha. Well I have the possing to do and sort the fire out. The dust from the pit is so bad at the moment I can clean the mantelpiece one day and write my name in the dust on it the next. Please write soon pet. Getting your letters and finding out how you are is a great joy to me. I love you.

Your loving and obedient wife,
Bertha.

Jacky stared at the letter for a long time, while Ted was casting an eye about for Tommy Raper, whom he saw standing with his hands in his pockets, smoking a tab and chatting to Fat Harry. Obviously, he had not got a letter and was therefore ignorant of the tragedy that had befallen his mother and her dog. He glanced at Jacky who silently handed back the letter and jerked his head in the direction of Tommy and Harry.

'You have to tell him, mate.'

Ted took the letter and sighed, nodding.

* * * * *

Some of the men had managed to bribe the young farm boy into reluctantly loaning them his knackered football and were alarmed at the amount of cigarettes they had to hand over in order to procure it. Hard little bugger, he was. But there was a tournament coming up soon and some serious practice had to be got in. The lads played in the bayonet drill area, using the straw dummies as opposing obstacles to raise the game. The weather was gorgeous and many of the men were quite content to laze about and feel the April sunshine on their faces. They were visited by the odd soldier from the other companies that were billeted elsewhere around St. Marie Cappelle and the story was pretty much the same as their own.

Ted had sorted his kit and uniform, and his boots shone like polished coal. He was sitting outside the barn with his head on a bale of hay. He had been watching a couple of old Frenchmen with hankies on their heads tied at the back who were mending the tiled roof of one of the outhouses. For such old codgers, he was surprised at their strength and agility. But now his eyes were shut and he was pretending he was up the allotment with Bertha enjoying the English sunshine.

The only disturbing element was the faint pop-popping of the artillery across the valley. It sounded like distant, continuous thunder and it was surprising how quickly you got used to the noise but the idea that this was the war, the real war where our soldier boys were fighting to the death whilst you were sat on your arse in the sunshine, took a bit more getting used to.

It would be their turn soon enough, anyhow. They would be 'eased' into the trenches for a short time as soon as they left the farm, more just for a look, really. Then they would gradually work their way to the front line over the space of a few days until they would take their long-awaited place opposite the Germans to fight properly for King and Country. And not too long after that they would be the veterans, introducing fresh-faced and scared young recruits to the glory of mortal combat. A stirring amongst the men made him open his eyes, blinking at the startling brightness. A tapping noise from the direction of the main yard drew everyone's attention. A bare-chested Sergeant Hanson was nailing up a notice on the thick wooden upright of the bird table thing that the lanterns hung from.

The lads crowded around to find it was the football fixtures for the next few days. Ted ambled over with Jacky Tait to be met by Tom Dodds and Fat Harry. The paper was headed: 'The Commander's Cup', and a list of fixtures was neatly written underneath. Good! Ted had not been picked. Just as well, because a further study revealed that Corporal Huddart was one of the referees.

Just then a stubby finger reached over his shoulder and pointed to 'A' Company's team where Christopher bloody Turner was playing. It was Cockney Joe.

'Pity I wasn't picked,' he said. 'There'll never be another opportunity like this to break both the bastard's legs. What do you say, comrades?'

Ted grinned. 'No,' he said eventually. 'Let some bugger else do for him, then we can just clap and cheer them on, eh?'

'Anybody fancy a walk around the camp, mebbes get some crack somewhere?'

A general murmur of agreement was countered by the fact that most of them were clad only in their long johns and might it not be a good idea to get dressed first? John Merrigan, who had silently joined the back of the little group, smiled inwardly and hoped that this change in Ted was a sign of his recovery from his grief at the loss of his brother.

Chapter 22

St. Marie Cappelle, Thursday/ Friday, 22nd/23rd April 1915

A pleasant walk around the edge of a mustard field behind the firing range put the little group onto a well-worn path that led to the 'A' Company camp. It was becoming a little overcast but still showed signs of being a fine evening as Ted, John Merrigan, Cockney Joe and Tom Dodds ambled on ahead of Fat Harry and Billy Robson. They heard the sounds of men laughing and shouting long before they came upon them and the noise reminded Ted of an enthusiastic handball crowd. The track was lined on one side with gorse bushes and a crude wooden fence on the other. Round a further corner was a small field where 'A' Company were taking the Commander's Cup very seriously indeed, playing on a proper footy field, complete with poles for corner flags and old-looking white lines to mark the edge of the playing area. Jammy buggers, they had a ready-made pitch all marked out for them by their predecessors. They had a better ball than 'D', as well. Lance Corporal Sherif was running the line on their side with Corporal Punshon as referee.

The little group was surprised to see young Lieutenant Wood, stripped to the waist like the rest, running down the far wing with the speed and grace of a deer, shouting his head off like any of the enlisted men and grinning all over his freckled face.

'Well, nobody wants to be an officer all of the time,' said Fat Harry philosophically. 'I expect the lad could do with a day off now and again just like every bugger else.'

'Bet he's in for a bollocking, just the same,' replied Billy, turning his attention to Lance Corporal Sherif. 'Hey, Freddy, where did your lads get a canny ball like that? Did you bring it with you?'

'Naw,' Sherif replied. 'We bribed it off that young French lad. Cost us a fortune in fags though.'

Incredulous looks were exchanged around the little group, which soon transformed into grins.

He'll go far, he will,' someone muttered as they strolled on their way.

An hour later and the lads had been right round the camp, stopping here and there for a tab and a yarn. As far as could be ascertained the young French lad had rented out five footballs. A surprise at the 'B' Company area was that the footy practice was being personally overseen by the smartly uniformed Major Ritson himself, shouting advice and encouragement to his men and pointing out opportunities with his riding crop. The lads could guess where the nearly new looking football had been procured. Along the way the odd quid of pipe tobacco was exchanged for a tin of jam or whatever and it was only when the lads were walking the quiet paths in between the company billets that the distant cracking of the artillery across the valley reminded them that they were on their way to war.

Ted had a wonderful surprise on the walk back in the form of Emmy Beckwith. He was sat on a log chewing a cigar with a few of his mates and running a candle flame up and down the seams of his uniform. That's where the lice laid their eggs and a quick heat with a candle soon fried the little sods. It turned out he was with the Stanley based 'F' Company and yes, he had been looking out for Ted as well and how the Hell had they missed each other all this time? After a bear hug, a fag and a chat about old times in Sunniside they arranged to meet that evening and go into the village for a look around and mebbes a pint. Then they moved on. At about 1700 hours the volume of the distant artillery suddenly increased massively and though still distant caused more than a little disquiet in the camp.

* * * * *

To the east of Ypres, the Allied front line trenches were occupied by a rich and diverse assortment of troops. The particular area stretching from the villages of Langemark to Poelkapelle was occupied by the elderly soldiers of the French Territorial Eighty-seventh Brigade, and to their right were the Forty-fifth Algerians, a North African unit of Zouaves, whose dusky skin and brightly coloured uniform gave them a startling and fierce appearance.

The late afternoon was warm and sunny. There had been a lull in the fighting and the French troops and their Zouave comrades were hoping it would last. The fierce artillery bombardment of the morning had been replaced by a languid truce and the French hoped that the Germans wished to enjoy the temperate weather as much as they did.

An unusual occurrence was the sight of a grey observation balloon ascending from behind the German lines upon which, after a few moments, three flares sputtered into incandescent life and died away again shortly after. All eyes were riveted onto the opposing trenches but no movement was seen and no shot was fired. Whatever it was it did not announce an imminent attack by the accursed Bosche. After posting sentries, both divisions settled down to preparing the evening meal and a peaceful mood was washing over the men.

At the centre of the system, Zouave Corporal Mahomet Fidale stood half-drowsing on sentry go. He was only slightly distracted from his duties by his little, wild looking terrier dog that was scrounging around the edge of the fire step searching for rats small enough to kill. More importantly, he was enjoying the aroma of the forthcoming hot meal his friend Private Kisher was preparing for both of them.

It was five o'clock of a nice evening. The sun was bathing the locality in a warm glow and a refreshing breeze had sprung up that was cooling the cheeks of all the men on the fire step. It must be the same in the German trenches. Didn't they enjoy a refreshing breeze?

Suddenly, two things happened at once. The distant sounds of the Bosche artillery magnified tenfold into a brutal barrage, though obviously the men in this part of the trench were not the target. It must be Ypres again, it usually was.

At the same time, a mysterious wall of dense mist was observed to have sprung out of nowhere and was obscuring the German trenches. It stretched as far as the eye could see in both directions. It looked like smoke but it didn't behave like smoke. It was a bit less than four feet high and drifted towards them driven by the gentle breeze. High above it the cawing of disturbed crows and ravens could just be heard over the artillery but there was no sign of the expected line of German soldiers following it out of the trenches. If it was to hide them from Allied fire it was unsuccessful: it simply wasn't high enough. The Bosche and their hare-brained ideas had failed again! Even so, the French officers ordered their line to be fully manned and at the ready. Reports were drifting in that the cloud stretched from Poelkapelle all the way to Lizerne – nearly four miles!

All eyes were on this strange phenomenon and an astonished murmur was heard as it suddenly began to transform, becoming taller and glowing a sickly greenish-yellow. Within a few minutes it was nearly twenty feet high and it swirled and roiled as if it had a life of its own. A wave of dread shivered through the superstitious Zouaves, but they stayed at their posts, partly out of fear of their officers and partly out of dread fascination.

Suddenly, they were in the midst of a plague of flies and bluebottles that seemed to materialise from nowhere and within a minute disappeared as abruptly as it had come. The men continued to stare at the cloud. Where were the Germans? Why weren't they firing through it? But no rifle fire came. There was nothing.

Fidale was puzzled by a strange rippling on the ground in front of the cloud, as if a film of some liquid were preceding it. Then the film resolved itself into a carpet of rats fleeing towards them. Another plague. The squeaking of hundreds of rats even managed to pierce the thunder of the barrage. Disturbed from their feasting on the dead of no man's land they were fleeing in panic towards the French line. The corporal felt his dog around his ankles again and lashed out irritably with his foot. A high-pitched squeal made him look down to see he had kicked a large black rat that was now defiantly baring its teeth at him. He gasped aloud with revulsion to see the trench floor was alive with yet more rats; they were everywhere and all fleeing from the bilious, yellow mist.

Several men began to experience a metallic taste in their mouths or started to rub their eyes. Somewhere off to his right Fidale recognised the sound of his terrier yelping in pain and terror. He tried to look for it but it was nowhere to be seen amongst the seething mass of rats that carpeted the trench floor.

Still the cloud advanced, borne by the gentle breeze that only a few moments ago had been so welcome. Now several of the soldiers began to cough and experience difficulty in breathing. What the Hell was going on? Along a four-mile stretch of Allied trenches the yellow-green cloud rolled inexorably forward and the mood of the soldiers was changing from trepidation to sheer terror. It was too thick to see through so they had no idea whether it was being followed by armed Bosche or not. Corporal Mahomet Fidale had fought many a battle and was no coward, his dark, lined face was a grim and fearsome mask as he laid his rifle on the smooth groove of the sandbag and made ready to repel the infidel.

Scores of men were collapsing back off the fire step, their seared eyes bulging and they clutched at their throats as the deadly gas burrowed and burned its way inside them.

Suddenly, there came a guttural command and the flat crackle of German rifles was heard all along the line. So the bastards had followed the cloud after all. Well, they would follow it no further! Without awaiting orders the Zouaves returned fire.

Then the cloud embraced the inhabitants of the trench. It slid effortlessly over the lip, turning the world translucent green as it clubbed hundreds of men to the ground in a welter of blinding torment. Everywhere the frightened soldiers looked they saw their comrades screaming and vomiting. Lungs were burned away as men shrieked in agony whilst frothing at the mouth and praying to God or Allah, neither of whom saw fit to save them.

There was only one thing they could do against such a ravenous and merciless foe.

They ran in their droves.

Officers, men and rats left the trenches and ran back to the rear. There was no order and there was no opposition. A few brave men, including Corporal Fidale tried to remain and defend their positions against the German attack but most perished miserably in a murky underwater world of green gas that burnt and drowned them from the inside, a poor reward for their courage. Fidale, trying to stand up out of the thick of the gas, fired continuously and although he could see nothing, stayed at his post longer than most, witnessing his comrades' expressions of disbelief as they saw, with bulging eyes, their badges, buckles and bayonets turning steadily from polished metal to a poisonous murky green as the corrosive fingers of the gas tainted them.

Fidale could feel his lungs filling with liquid and burning all at the same time. His skin was suffering the torture of the thousand needles and his eyes felt like they were being rubbed with sand. He was no longer sure what he was firing at, or why he was shouting at the top of his voice. He looked up and down the trench to see what the others were doing and gasped as he saw the trench itself heave and undulate like a gigantic serpent. Surely Allah the merciful and compassionate had not deserted him, his most true and faithful servant? Then the sandbags seemed to rise up from the breastwork and float before his burning eyes.

Was this a sign to flee?

Sensibly, in the end, Corporal Fidale retreated too. One man cannot fight such a plague and it would be nonsensical to die if you could fight again on another day. He never saw his friend again, or his dog.

The same gas enveloped some of the Canadian troops in the trenches to the right of these positions and sucked them down into the same agonising oblivion, but it was the French and Algerians who bore the brunt of the first chlorine gas attack of the Great War. Men died in hundreds even as they ran. They flung away weapons and greatcoats, even stripped off their clothing. Every ounce of their dwindling strength was devoted to trying to breathe. Singly or in groups the reeking, vomit-stained troops thrashed their way towards the rear. But the plague of gas did not stop at the trenches – the breeze bore it gently onward through the sun-dappled evening to embrace the farming communities, their children and their beasts. The gas was all consuming, welcoming anyone and anything that breathed good air. Within minutes, five thousand souls had perished and another five thousand, screaming in agony, wished that they had.

* * * * *

Across miles of blighted countryside, stumbled thousands of gas-stricken men, women and children. The troops to the rear were shocked by the appearance and behaviour of this hysterical horde but it was obvious they could not be pulled to order and so in the main they were let go. Gradually the story began to unfold and it dawned on the Allied High Command that not only were the Germans making use of a terrible new weapon but also the efficacy of the gas was such that it had cleared a four-mile stretch of trench in less than an hour. The line that had stretched from Switzerland to the sea was broken at last. The way to Ypres was open.

* * * * *

The same evening, St. Marie Cappelle was full of little strolling bands of DLI soldiers enjoying the rare treat of a time free from onerous duties. It was an agreeable little town and just to wander through the place was pleasant enough. Even though they couldn't find a decent pub, all of the cafés sold Frenchy beer, so that would do nicely. Everywhere else being full, they settled in a not too dingy establishment called the 'Café Montmartre', which had a pub sign depicting a load of steep, city streets lit up by Consett Iron Company lamp posts. The little group, consisting of Ted, Emmy, John Merrigan and Jacky Tait silently nodded agreement and went through the peeling, green door. A bell rang as the door opened and the inhabitants, mostly British soldiers in groups of four or five clustered around little circular tables, looked up for a second before returning to their beer.

It was pleasantly smoky with that aromatic smell you get from French cigarettes, as a little man in an apron showed them to a table near to the counter. The group on the next table were from 'C' and nodded their acknowledgement. They were playing draughts with a set that looked a hundred years old – the board was a solid square of wood and the paint was so faded that you could hardly tell the squares apart. The beer arrived in bottles but no glasses were offered. It tasted a bit perfumy, like the tabs.

The atmosphere throughout the whole café was one of quiet enjoyment, not like a pub at home where you stood with a pint and laughed raucously about the last handball match or good-naturedly took the piss out of your mates' misfortunes. Here it was more restrained, with the seated groups talking quietly, and only to those on their table. Ted thought about that as he smoked his tab and listened to John and Jacky discuss the possible fortunes of 'D' in the Commanders' Cup. After a couple of bottles he loosened up a bit and he and Emmy amused the other two with tales of their childhood pranks back in Sunniside. Ted pretended horror and embarrassment when Emmy told how he had fallen into Stanley Beck and landed, drenched, on the Dare Stone.

Amazingly, neither John nor Jacky had heard of Netty Pirates and were soon privileged to learn all about how to set somebody's arse on fire from a distance. Ted also asked the men at the next table if he could borrow the draughts board when they had finished. The answer was 'no' but he could challenge their champion for a bottle of beer if he liked. Ted didn't take much egging on and made short work of the game to boot! His opponent handed over the beer with a smile and a handshake.

Suddenly out of nowhere a pretty girl of about fourteen years old appeared and sang a song called 'Sweet little Polly Perkins' in a charming voice but with an appalling accent. The lads knew this one, it was a London song according to Cockney Joe, who sometimes sang it as they marched but everyone else knew it by its proper title of 'Cushy Butterfield' and it was a Durham song through and through. When she had finished she disappeared as quickly as she had come, leaving an embarrassed silence.

Joe spoke first, 'Very nice, like. I wonder how many German ones she knows an' all.'

And then it was midnight and the little proprietor was ushering everyone onto the cobbles while his staff of one old lady shut the establishment up.

Anyway, rifle range 0600 tomorrow and the St. George's Day Parade.

* * * * *

0600 the next morning arrived all right – with a headache and an ear-splitting bugle call, but the reveille was almost irrelevant, as the proper early morning call from the airmen of Number Four Squadron had already awakened the men of the Eighth DLI. This time fewer of them ran from their bed spaces to see the airmen pass overhead. Most of them moaned instead, clapping their hands to their ears and wishing they were back in England and in their own beds where there was a loving wife, a hot mug of tea and you didn't get woken up by devil-may-care, toffee-nosed maniacs flying so low that you had to duck or get your bloody head knocked off by the wheels. The officers were conspicuously absent from the roll call this morning and it turned out that whilst they were having their early morning tea there was a soot fall from the great chimney in the farmhouse dining room covering the whole bloody lot of them – and their tea – in clouds of the stuff. It was attributed to the buzzing of the buildings by the aircraft loosening the soot and it simply fell to the DLI to be the chaps who were there when it all finally gave way.

This cheered the lads up no end, and when the company officers finally did appear there was great fun to be had trying to spot if they had been blacked... Every one of them had missed a bit. Lieutenant Brass had great triangles of soot behind his ears, which prompted Jacky Tait to note that he was obviously never taught to wash behind them as a boy. Lieutenant Wood had a black tidemark around his shirt collar which incited the lads to bet he had only washed the skin that could be seen and was probably as black as the Ace of spades underneath. Even Captain Bradford had not escaped; although his uniform had been carefully cleaned it was definitely half a shade darker than regulation and the little black lines up and down the stitching and on top of the medal ribbons were plain for all to see. Many a grin on the faces of the men that morning suddenly went out under the baleful stare of a discomfited officer, only to illuminate once more when the stare had passed along the ranks.

It was cooler today and threatened to rain, and the noise of rifle range was a trial most of the men endured stoically whilst wishing they had consumed a couple of beers less the night before. But shooting practice ended, a cold breakfast was consumed and all preparations were made for the St. George's Day Parade at 1000 hours. It was to be held in a field about a mile southeast of the farm.

Every man who had spent so much time polishing his boots until they shone like mirrors groaned inwardly as he sank into the mud and fought against the suction to keep in step. It didn't take long for the battalion to assemble but it took bloody ages for the officers to turn up. Give them their due, though, when they did come they marched straight into the field and got their footwear just as mucky as the lads. Captain Blackett, Big Bill's son who commanded 'E' Company, went front centre and stood the men at ease. None of the officers looked comfortable and began passing comments amongst themselves. It became clear they were waiting, too. It was nearly 1040 hours and a light drizzle had sprung up just to add to the men's misery when Lieutenant Colonel Turnbull and Captain Stevens, the adjutant, both arrived on horseback. The lieutenant colonel was looking very serious indeed.

He didn't beat about the bush, either, first telling the men he would not insult them by inspecting what was obviously a first-class turnout and then saying that a serious conflict was developing east of Ypres and if the city was to be held against the German military then every available soldier in the British Expeditionary Force was to march and fight at once. It wasn't a long speech but it said it all. There was an apology about the cancellation of the Commander's Cup, and they were told to be ready to march out at 1330 hours. He handed over the companies to their respective officers and the St. George's Day Parade that never was, marched back to pack up their kit and set off for the front.

The place was buzzing! Despite the slight drizzle every man was excited as could be.

Ted was assisting the machine gun lads loading their equipment when a lone horseman was seen lazily clopping into the yard.

'Post.'

Young Lieutenant Wood ran out to sign for it. An officer had been sent for as soon as the man appeared but, either because he was the only one who was decently dressed or because he was expecting a letter from his mother, he ran in a most un-officer like fashion from the farmhouse to the yard. The rider gave a lazy salute and produced a pad of notepaper from his pocket upon which the lieutenant had to dash off three signatures on three separate pages.

The men were stood down temporarily and a hasty parade saw them get their letters. Then it was back to work.

Ted was most surprised to get a letter from Bertha because only the day before yesterday he had received the one with the news about the death of Bobby Stokoe and Fat Ena's dog. He recalled the morbid contents of the previous mail and only half smiled as he felt the familiar outline of a couple of cigarette cards through the envelope. Mebbes this one would be better news – he hoped so. He thumbed it open to find the '20 and 23' cards, ones he hadn't got, and they were brand, spanking new ones as well. The date showed this one had been written just a couple of days later, on the 19th, but the handwriting was all scrawly, as if his wife had tried to get the news down on paper as quickly as possible to get it out of the way. Amongst the news was that a man from the War Department had come to check Tappy Lappy, Mr Crozier's laundry cart pony, to requisition him for the army but having seen the glass tube that helped him to breathe the man declined to take him away, so that was a Godsend. On the other hand Gabriel, Mr Crozier's son, had gone for a soldier a week earlier and nobody had wanted that but he had gone anyway. It turned out that it was Walter Timms who had so cruelly killed Fat Ena's sausage dog. Last of all, there was the announcement that the morning after the Durhams had boarded the train in Newcastle, Lettie Simpson had deliberately poured petrol over herself and burned to death, screaming, in the back street.

Suddenly Ted felt sick and had to fight to control his heaving stomach. He looked around for Cockney Joe and saw him almost immediately, across the yard, hitching mules to the GS wagons with a couple of the lads.

Ted's head spun. Poor, sackless Lettie, who never meant any harm but who God had chosen to be a pain in the arse to everyone she came across. What the Hell had entered her mind to make her go to such a horrible death of her own free will?

Should he tell Joe? Should he tell him now? Should he tell one of the officers instead? Should he tell the padre, mebbes? Who should he tell? He had to tell someone... there was enough shit flying around in his head without suddenly being responsible for Cockney Joe and Lettie as well. But Joe was his friend. He might be a funny bugger but he had stuck to Ted through thick and thin. Suddenly the cigarette cards didn't matter. The letter didn't matter. The war didn't matter. With lips drawn tight and a shaking hand he put the crumpled paper into his pocket and got back to work. He had to think.

Chapter 23

Poperinghe/Ypres, Friday 23rd April 1915

1330 hours, Friday 23rd April arrived and 'D' was ready to go. They were addressed by Captain Bradford to the effect that they were off to defend the Ypres Salient from the might of the German Army. Ypres was vital to the Allies as it protected the seaports to the west and, since most of the country had been in the hands of the Germans since war broke out, this free city was the symbol of resistance to all the Belgian people and their allies. It would be no easy task – it was beleaguered on three sides by the cream of German artillery, but to see Ypres fall was to see the Allied troops demoralised beyond belief. It was their responsibility to ensure that the unthinkable did not happen and that this emblem of the Belgian people remained free and defiant. He went on to say that it was the duty of every man in the battalion – especially those of 'D' company for whom he was both responsible and proud to command – to be at the forefront of such a defence no matter what form it might take, and that he knew his men and he also knew they would never let him down.

There was an apology for the fact that they were not to be introduced gradually into fighting the foe but would be marching straight into the thick of the fray to face the enemy head on and Captain Bradford was confident in the ability of his men to play the game without flinching. Then they were off.

Company by company they marched through the thin drizzle until they hit the main road where they became one, grand procession of men, mules and equipment drawn out like a long, twisting cable being pulled across the map. Up to now, the German soldier had been an ape-like monster on posters or the child-killing beast that had ravaged his way through Europe spreading terror and torture wherever he went. Well, he was about to look the Durhams in the eye and get his arse kicked.

The men were allowed to talk and one or two songs had struck up which were lustily echoed around the column. *'Pack up your troubles'* vied with *'We're here because we're here'* and ever the most popular was *'He was saying goodbye to his horse'*.

As with all long marches, the euphoria of impending heroism in the face of the enemy soon gave way to chafing straps and footsore misery. The songs died away to be replaced by the dull tromp-tromp of a bored, mumbling column of men marching wearily towards the guns.

The sounds of artillery had gradually grown louder and more concentrated and the torpor of the dull march was being replaced by the activity that was burgeoning around them. Horse and mule drawn wagons and the odd rickety motor lorry were conveying large numbers of French troops across their path at every crossroad, heading north. It seemed that was a funny route as most of the noise seemed to be ahead of the Durhams to the east. Still, there were most likely plans afoot that were not for the likes of marching men. Generals and colonels did not confide the intricacies of their strategies to the plain, honest soldier. Some French troops were marching in little groups in the opposite direction to the Durhams and wearily stood aside to allow the great column to pass. There were quite a few refugees starting to appear too, scattered rags of humanity that gazed vacantly at the soldiers or glared at them with hate. Some had little handcarts piled with pitiable belongings and others had nothing at all. Men and women with small children clasped to breasts, or hoisted upon shoulders, or just dragged along by the hand, staggered by. There wasn't much room now as the road had thinned out a bit and had a watery ditch either side. There were fewer windmills to be seen and the road was once again lined with tall, thin trees with skinny branches that groped upward to the slate coloured sky. More and more roads were starting to look like this. A few of the Frenchies cheered the men on but many were silent and sullen. It seemed to Ted that all the colour had drained from the world.

The anticipated heroics had evaporated into a tedious footslog where, far from being joined by enthusiastic Allied soldiers, all he was witnessing was an undisciplined rush north and the odd group of suspiciously defeated-looking troops morosely eying the lads with the sort of look that makes you aware they know something that you don't. There were uniforms of every sort and men of every sort, from Indians in turbans to Moroccans in the most outlandish costumes. At least the Canadians looked like them, it was only when they opened their mouths it became apparent they were from halfway around the world. The Empire truly had pulled in every fighting force available to it.

There were also the wounded, and these were fresh wounded. These men were not like the British soldiers that had been on the dock ready to go back home on the 'Onward', all neatly dressed bandages, mugs of tea and cigarettes. They sported dirty blood-soaked rags and walked with the aid of their rifles or any bit of stick they had been able to pick up on the roadside. There were blindfolded men and men stripped of their clothes. Sometimes a horse drawn wagon full of injured or dead, driven by red-eyed soldiers would halt on the road and stubbornly stand their ground until the Durhams marched around them. Nearly all the lads wondered why they were being met with such suspicion. They were here to help, weren't they? Ungrateful buggers.

It was getting on for 1700 hours and the lads were hungry and weary. Through the light drizzle they had watched the road improve and widen, a sure sign that a town was coming up. There was some anticipation of a break and hopefully some hot food, not that anyone had said that would be the case, mind. They were at Steenvoorde, that's what the wooden sign by the road said and it was dawning on the men that most Frenchy townships were all more or less the same, a bit like all the pit villages at home. They skirted the place without stopping and went on to a large field to the east. Some quite big shell holes filled with stinking watery mud were now in evidence. They were in reach of the enemy's guns.

They were formed up facing the road and it was obvious by the trampled grass that this field had been used for this purpose many, many times. They were stood easy and allowed to smoke. When Ted finished his tab he flicked it to the ground and was surprised to see an identical but knackered tab end within an inch of where his had landed. It began to dawn on him that half the British Expeditionary Force must have marched this way.

'How far away is this Ypres, when it's at home then?' somebody behind Ted pondered.

'Dunno.' This was Tom Dodds. 'But you can bet your boots it's a long way. It's the capital of Belgium and we're still in bloody France, man.'

Ted wondered this himself but with his heart full of sadness at the death of old Bobby Stokoe, and Lettie Simpson's suicide, he had no inclination for other than a passing interest in their journey to fight the Hun, however imminent. Why Bobby Stokoe? Passing away in poverty whilst relying on the charity of others, was no way for a man to die.

He did it for you.

Then there was Lettie. Everybody knew she was a couple of pence short of a pound. But this! What had possessed her to visit such a horrifying death upon herself? In the midst of this turmoil it was only natural for his own guilt about the loss of his brother to bubble and surface once more. All this death! All this tragedy! And somewhere off to his left he could hear the voice of Cockney Joe fade into the conversation about Ypres – and he still did not know about the shocking tragedy of his wife.

'It's pronounced 'Wipers' so you've all learned something now, comrades. I thank you very much.'

'Doesn't matter a damn how you pronounce it, it's still bloody miles and I don't fancy walking all the way.'

'Well you could mebbes get back in one o' them pissy French cattle wagons on the railway if you like.'

The chatter went this way and that without Ted, and was eventually interrupted by a voice he did not know. It began quietly and incredulously somewhere behind him and to the right.

'Well, I'll go to the foot of our stairs! How lads! Will you look what's coming, like, over there from the town.'

The gasps were unanimous as all heads turned. The road from Steenvoorde was alive with a serpent-like movement. Through the drizzle it looked like a train, but it couldn't be because it was moving towards them along the road. It was bright red and as it approached, the blurring effect of the drizzle lessened and the serpent appeared to fragment itself into individual units. The excitement amongst the men was infectious and even Ted's melancholy was displaced a little.

'Them's buses, man. Look...them's bloody buses!'

Fat Harry's voice carried over the entire company and started off a cacophony of exclamations. Sure enough, as the units took on a more defined shape they emerged as bright red, double-decker, open top omnibuses: London omnibuses to be precise. The first of the unlikely convoy sailed past the lads and slowed to a halt a bit further down the road towards the head of the column, causing the entire line to draw to stop more or less altogether. It was a staggering sight. What the Hell were they all doing on a dirty country road in France? The bus opposite where Ted was standing was marvellous to behold. It was clean and bright, apart from the muddy wheels, and sported adverts on the side for Dewars White Label Whisky and Lucifer matches, just the same as on the Consett trams. On the front was the number '35' and the destination board said 'Elephant and Castle–Ridley Road–Walthamstow'. The driver was a uniformed man, but not the drab colours of the British Tommy – he was wearing the proper off-white jacket and cap of a London bus driver.

The line stretched back as far as anyone could see and with the odd exception of a drab grey or green vehicle the entire fleet looked as if it had been whisked away from England by a genie and deposited here fresh as fresh. It was such an incredible sight that more than one soldier was still gazing in wonder, completely oblivious of the ripples all around them as the NCOs told the men off to embark. Ted was instantly caught up in the swell of men crossing the field to the line of buses. He caught sight of Jacky Tait who was catching up on Cockney Joe and John Merrigan; and with a bit of diplomatic shoulder barging and a few apologies managed to meet up as they boarded the No. 28 for West Hampstead. Without exception the soldiers were grinning all over their faces, as amused as could be by this absolutely unexpected turn of events. Ted and the lads had shinned up the spiral staircase, being careful not to bang their rifles, and bagged grandstand seats near the front. They were wooden, slatted and uncomfortable but the buoyant troops couldn't have cared less. Apart from the fact they were to be transported in relative luxury – compared to the dreadful miles they had covered in the French trains – these London buses were a little bit of England, a little bit of home.

'Pity Cockney Joe ain't on this one,' smiled Jacky. 'I'll bet he knows every driver by bloody name.'

Ted was quietly glad Joe wasn't with them, as the image of Lettie exploded back into his mind. He would have to tell him sometime and the longer he left it the worse it was going to be. He forced himself to look around.

Being upstairs afforded a canny view. The drizzly rain had all but stopped but the lads turned their collars up against the breeze anyway and lit their tabs, pointing this way and that as something they saw caught their fancy. The breezy start didn't last long, though, because once out of the built-up areas the paved roads turned to country roads and then to glorified cart tracks. The speed was soon down to that of a marching man. At one point the word was passed along, apparently beginning with the driver, that to their left was the village of Abeele, which meant they were now on the France–Belgium border.

'That's the way to arrive in a new country, lads! In style.'

Despite their slow progress Jacky was still grinning. His cap was pulled low and he was trying to light another tab, obviously having the time of his life. Sometimes the convoy practically stopped altogether but the lads on the number 28 were still adamant that it was better than marching.

Shortly afterwards another piece of information reached them from the driver. It explained the erratic movements of the French troops and the increase in the numbers of wounded and refugees: poison gas.

It seemed the Germans had loosed tons of the stuff onto the Frenchies yesterday and there was no way to fight back so they had to flee or die. There were miles of unmanned trenches ready and waiting for the Hun to take and unless they were stopped, the way to Ypres was open. It was lethal stuff and would kill you in seconds. Thousands had died already, screaming and foaming at the mouth. It was also heavier than air so running into a dugout or hiding in a trench was no good. The gas would follow you. It was lurking in all the shell holes, anywhere you might hide from enemy fire. Clever bastards, the Germans – stick your head over the top and they would shoot it off. Try to keep down and you got gassed.

It was near dark as they approached a place called Poperinghe, skirting it to the south on what appeared to be a wide but hastily constructed dirt road. It was not so much a town as a whole camp now. A city of tents had grown up around the place and there were British soldiers to be seen, and others who turned out to be more Canadians, many of whom waved to the Durhams. Some of the buildings, however, were in a ruinous state, which spoke ominous volumes for its recent past at the hands of the enemy artillery. The lads could see lights away towards the centre and hear jumbled music. Well at least somebody must be enjoying themselves.

On the outskirts of the tents were the squalid encampments of the refugees. There were some dark skinned soldiers here too, dressed in what were once bright blue jackets and red trousers, but now faded and stained in a washed-out yellow. In the distance by a small copse, just about hidden by the near darkness were what looked like the outline of a pile of bodies and the weary movement of several burial parties. Ted frowned. The bodies appeared to be stacked in sets about four wide and four deep, and were layered at right angles. That was how you stacked railway sleepers back at the pit. That was no way to deal with people! Where was the dignity in that?

The convoy went past a field kitchen and the smell of bully beef stew floated into their nostrils, and here they halted again. This time the men could see officers disembarking and talking to the local brass. Likely more orders coming in. After a while they set off again – without eating. Now it was truly dark but the buses bumped on, their headlights illuminating a dangerously small area as they negotiated the makeshift road with its population of troops and refugees. That was when the lads had decided enough was enough and started to eat their rations. Everyone commented on the fact that shell craters were more numerous and some of the straight-up trees had bits blown out of them. Must have been some real action here, and not long ago either by the look of things.

There was no doubt, there was a big build-up of troops on the go, and once they passed a mule wagon stuck in a ditch with a soldier trying to cut the mules loose by the light of a single, pitiful oil lamp. The cargo of ammunition belts had slid off the side of the flatbed and they saw the silhouettes of a couple of men covered in mud from head to toe were wading in and out to retrieve them. Not much further on were two dead horses still in harness just off the road, illuminated by the weak halo of one of the few working street lights; and the smell, even in passing was disgusting. So were the glossy, red rats that crawled out of their bellies to see what was going on.

Once again the buses stopped and once again nobody was allowed to disembark. After about fifteen minutes they were off again. The not-so-distant boom of the artillery continued unabated and became disturbingly louder as they progressed. Rumours were now spreading that the noise was nearly all German weapons and that the Allies were hopelessly outgunned. How do rumours spread on a bus? Word had reached the lads, once again via the driver, that the target was Ypres itself, only about eight miles down the road. If the Kaiser couldn't have it for himself he would obliterate it from the face of the earth.

They swerved to avoid a crater and a communal shout went up as the men were pitched from their seats. They were now high enough up to see the pink flashes away in front of them from a different angle... more spread out like a map, and between the explosions of the guns and the flash of lights from the Verey pistols it was actually possible to trace by the row of lights what must be the front line. It was near enough straight except for a definite bulge dead ahead that looked oddly out of place.

This must be the Salient. This must be Ypres being pounded into the dirt. No wonder it was taking such a hammering. The whole geography of the place was a complete disaster. It was as if the entire plain surrounding the city was like a huge saucer, and the city itself was built into the little flat circle where the cup goes. The problem was that the Germans held damn nearly three quarters of the saucer rim and were having a whale of a time lobbing shells down upon the city from every direction. There was no conversation now. Everyone stared in fascination and horror at the story told in the flashes of light and the thunder of guns. And the buses lurched on through the dark. Because of the uneven road the headlamp beams dipped and rose, illuminating objects along the way in short flashes which gave a curious, jerky movement to whatever was lit up, a bit like watching moving pictures at the cinema. One such a shocking sight was the half a second's glimpse of a dead girl of about eleven years old lying at the foot of a tree by the side of the road. Her hands had been eaten to the bone by rats.

A collective moan went up on the bus and Ted's list of the dead had increased yet again. Our Robert, Bobby Stokoe, Lettie Simpson, the pile of bodies at the last stop and now some poor young lass who had done nowt to nobody. This wasn't the war they came to fight. Where was the magnificence in all this? He had an awful feeling that the dark was saving them from many a sight they would not have wanted to see.

It was not long before midnight when the convoy reached Vlarmer-tinghe and drew to a bumpy halt. The arcing headlamps and artillery flashes supplemented the moonlight in illuminating what had once been a pretty church that had had its steeple all but destroyed. Other than that, it was the same as any of the other villages, complete with its retinue of British Expeditionary Force tents pitched on every available bit of ground. It seemed to be run by Canadians. This time the camp was sectioned off by a barbed wire enclosure, about chest height, with gates at odd intervals. The place was huge, dwarfing the village on the hillside and a couple of the bigger buildings had been commandeered as a hospital for the gassed and wounded. Outside the barrier was a pathetic shantytown of cobbled-together tents and shelters, populated by refugees with nowhere to go.

There was the usual waiting about, presumably while the officers found out what was going on. Whatever it was, would likely be a quick decision because the drivers kept their engines running. Sure enough, within a couple of minutes the men were ordered to disembark. This time they weren't told to form into companies anywhere, they were just left milling about in the dim cloudy moonlight whilst the convoy of omnibuses moved on towards Ypres.

The lads were cold, damp and tired. They were also saddle-sore from sitting so long on the wooden slatted seats of the buses. John Merrigan lit a tab and watched them head down the bumpy road towards the sounds of the guns.

'What are they going to do... run the bloody Germans over?'

A couple of sentries pointed to some squat, derelict out buildings off to the right and said something to the NCOs in their funny drawl. The NCOs then came over to the column; they looked as knackered as the rest of the men. All eyes turned to them, awaiting the barked orders that never came.

'Over that way lads, to them low buildings... find a space and get some kip.'

Eyes met eyes then moved on. The agreement was unanimous and instant. The lads set off, filtering through the nearest gate. Ten minutes later they were huddled into a filthy stall and grouped around an upturned bucket with an oil lamp on it, sharing whatever rations were left to them and listening to the constant bombardment of Ypres only a few miles away. Carved into the rotten wood of the stalls was every sort of graffiti. Two fresh looking ones were next to Ted. One said 'Scotland forever' and the other 'Up the 9th'. The lads were all a bit smug at having got into shelter quickly because it was becoming obvious that there was nowhere near enough room to house everyone. The accommodation was a set of dilapidated outhouses for goats or cattle that apparently belonged to a nearby nunnery.

'Smells like it an' all,' muttered a disconsolate Tom Dodds.

'What... a nunnery?' said Billy Robson, opening a tin of bully.

'No you daft gowk. A stable, man.'

It was the gentle laughter that made Billy realise he had fallen for a joke so, blushing and muttering, he set about eating with his knife. A sudden blood-curdling scream ripped through the air from the hospital area. It died away to a pitiful gurgle and froze the blood of all who heard it. How could anyone scream like that? The sound of the shells flying overhead was almost a relief.

'I hate fucking bully, especially cold,' spat Cockney Joe after taking a swig from his canteen. Just then, a disturbance at the door was followed by a tired voice asking if another few men could be squeezed in as it was starting to rain heavily and the bivouacked men outside would get soaked.

A communal 'piss off' was immediately quashed by Sergeant Hanson who threatened the dissenters with expulsion into the worsening weather whilst the soldiers outside would take their places. It was nearly 0130 hours before everyone was settled down. They were all hungry and tired but the conditions made rest practically impossible.

Somebody piped up, 'I know a joke about nuns.'

Amid the collective groans were just enough resigned murmurs of, 'Howay, then' and 'Get on with it' to enthuse the comedian.

'There was this beginner nun, like, ran into the Mother Superior's office, and she was all scared, like. So the Mother Superior says, "What's the matter, my child?" So the beginner lass says, "Mother Superior, Mother Superior... I've just been for a piss and I found one of the toilet seats was up!" '

The silence was almost palpable, and was followed a few seconds later with various groans and threats – and objects – being hurled in the direction of the would-be joker.

* * * * *

It was a poor night. About two in the morning the mules and wagons caught up with the main body, and there was a commotion until the men and beasts were settled down: still no tool cart, though. Shortly afterwards a convoy of motorised wagons broke the fitful silence, and it turned out to be the London bus convoy heading back the way it had come. Once, the ground shuddered beneath them as a shell landed uncomfortably close by in between the village and the encampment. The men waited in strained silence for the next one but nothing happened.

'Must have been a stray,' whispered Jacky Tait.

There was precious little sleep to be had that night. The following day was to be not much better but at least the rain had eased off. The men were up for 0600 and breakfast was soup with no bread. It was made from dried peas which had not been soaked long enough prior to cooking. Consequently, the dish was little more than hard pellets in hot water. By 0900 there was still no word of a morning parade or any other kind of information for that matter.

'I've seen some depressing shit-holes in my time but this one takes the bloody prize,'

muttered Tommy Raper.

Before any reply could be made, the sight of three aircraft traversing the slate coloured sky took their attention for a while. The last unofficial instruction was to stay as close to their billets as possible in case of orders to mobilise. Ted took a light for his tab from John Merrigan. He supposed the village was once pretty enough, but certainly not now. Countless bales of barbed wire formed walls taller than a man's height, obliterating anything that may once have formed an attractive view of the area. The soldiers of the permanent detachment at Vlamentinghe were mostly Canadian who had little to do with the transit troops and went about their duties morosely. Armed sentries guarded equally tall walls of ration packs, and mule trains were constantly on the go, fetching and carrying all the paraphernalia of war. The refugees were kept at bay by a picket fence around the area where there were more armed guards to further discourage them. They were a pitiful bunch: people in rags who had lost everything to the Hun while British soldiers, their supposed allies and saviours, kept them at a distance by threat of arms.

At the far corner of the barbed wire wall Ted was startled to see a soldier bound spread-eagled to the spoked wheel of a gun carriage. Tom Dodds noticed at the same time and commented,

'Field punishment Number One. I remember that from Morfa.'

'Well, God help him,' stuck in Jacky Tait, scratching at the lice under his arm.

'What do you mean? He likely got nicked for stealing off his comrades, didn't he?'

'God help him, anyway.'

Jacky turned away disgusted as a stray shell landed nearer the village than was comfortable. The vibration of the ground beneath their feet ended the conversation.

They were issued a cold midday meal of tins of various foodstuffs and told to share it fairly amongst themselves and they were informed that, if they were still here in the evening, the meal would be soup. It started to rain again which slightly dampened the thunder of the artillery and they were still there in the evening. The meal was soup.

It was just coming up to 1800 hours and the men, totally disgruntled with the whole idea of war and useless bloody rations, were making their way back to their sleeping areas. Then the orders came and the Eighth Durham Light Infantry were to march into Ypres itself, right through the middle of the bombardment then onward to engage the Hun.

This was it, then. Form up and march off, like.

The men felt good to be back in ranks, back in proper formation. You knew where you were when you were marching down the road with an NCO or officer looming up into the corner of your eye. It was past dusk and they were progressing up a fairly steep slope. On breasting it an astonished gasp rippled through the column: it was just like the view from the bus the night before, but this time frighteningly close. They were looking down into the shallow crater with Ypres in the very centre on the flattest part. It was only a couple of miles away and enveloped in the fitful darkness of a blackout to make it less of a target. The strategy was useless, however, as the German gunners had the range down to the inch.

The city was visible in bright flickers as shell after shell rained down upon it, each one flashing its destruction through the wet evening air. The whistling of the shells could be heard quite clearly and it soon became easy to predict the resultant detonation. There were different sorts of whistles too, some shrill and others deeper. The deeper ones made the loudest bangs.

The refugees kept coming, too: a never-ending stream of human flotsam that drifted against the tide of the column, splitting against the bow and drifting down either side to disappear in the evening gloom. More curious, however, was the local population who were obviously standing their ground. There were a few houses and farms either side of the road where lights were blazing and it was obvious the inhabitants had no intention of leaving unless they were absolutely forced to. On the right of the column was a railway track and just behind it at one point Ted saw a woman hurriedly pulling a load of washing off a line and trotting through the drizzle back to her cottage with hardly a glance at the soldiers. He wondered why they were still here. Why would they risk their lives to remain in their homes when thousands were fleeing a city that was being systematically destroyed by an enemy that was inhuman enough to murder children in cold blood?

The road had ceased its downward gradient and had more or less levelled out now, and they were probably a mile or a bit less from the city and to be honest it didn't look too bad. Towers and spires still thrust upward into the rainy sky and against the flash of the shell bursts the silhouettes appeared to be a lot less damaged than the artillery would seem capable of inflicting. The men were getting nervous, though, and the ground beneath their feet was constantly humming and vibrating with every shell that landed and fleetingly illuminated the vicinity of its destruction.

It seemed a beautiful city, old and distinguished, and it reminded Ted of Durham, which had been around since the dawn of time. Ypres had a great wall around it, which told of a violent and chequered history, but the stateliness of the buildings had risen above that to give a dignity that even this relentless bombardment had trouble undermining. They crossed a bridge over a canal, then over a railway line and went into the city itself. Now they could see the damage. Whole fronts of buildings were collapsed into the streets by the remorseless shelling, revealing the wallpapered and furnished interiors. In other places, the frontages remained intact whilst the interiors had collapsed down into rubble inside them.

The shells were now exploding all around – at a distance to be sure, but no longer remote. The glare of each shell burst briefly highlighted the truth behind the apparent indestructibility of Ypres. The place was a skeleton. From a distance, through the curtain of rain, it might appear to be complete in shape and size but close proximity demonstrated that the flesh was being systematically stripped from the city's bones. The streets were littered with bodies, civilian and military, human and brute beast. Mules and horses vied in death with soldiers for a place to rot amongst the rubble.

They turned to the right off the Rue de Elverdinghe and then left onto the narrow Rue au Buerre. It looked just like North Road only half demolished and full of dead. It was funny how the street fronts had stayed up when the interiors and roofs had caved in. What looked like a normal frontage of shops and cafes was suddenly and horribly exposed as an empty cadaver.

Everywhere there were rats. Sleek rats, fat rats, rats as big as cats. In the distance they lent the otherwise still remains of the dead a ghastly shimmer as they skittered over them. Choosy rats, which did not have to forage but took leisure time to pick the best, most succulent remains on which to feast. There were dead horses harnessed to limbers and dead mules hitched to wagons. There were men, women and children, even little children, lying on cobbles or floating in shell craters. The body of an infantryman lay on the pavement beside them. He was lying face up as if in repose, except his skin was just ash and the rain was slowly sluicing it away to reveal the skull beneath. And he was wearing the same uniform as Ted.

Somewhere behind Ted someone retched and this was followed both by a quick complaint from the recipient of the vomit and the growl of an NCO as the now fragile discipline was brutally reinforced. They had to get through. Towards the end of the Rue au Buerre a mound of rubble stopped the column dead. A direct hit had caused a haberdashery shop and the above dwelling space to collapse clean across the street. The men were forced to scramble over the mess of demolished masonry and twisted wrought iron as best they could, and then form up on the other side.

The stench of putrefaction issuing from the rubble was overpowering, a noxious testament to the rotting dead within and the complete inability of any organised body to cope with restoring order. Grumbling and frightened the men scrabbled up the treacherous wet debris. Someone to Ted's left cursed as he began to slip back down. Ted turned and grasped the outstretched hand to halt the soldier's fall and was surprised to be staring into the eyes of Christopher bloody Turner. Turner regained his foothold and nodded curtly to Ted, releasing his hand.

It hardly escaped anyone's notice that the glistening white fragments amongst the sleek wet grey of the masonry were the bones of the dead picked shiny-clean by the rats. Scrabbling down the other side the men tried to reform the column but with the remains of the road so full of shell holes it was next to impossible. All that could be done was keep in as close a formation as the ravaged terrain would allow. The men's resolve was beginning to crumble but there could be no allowance for a weak stomach, even though not a soldier amongst them had seen a thousandth of the death that they were now witnessing.

The order had been given for silence. There was to be no talking or smoking from now on. This was where the training kicked in. This was where the discipline took over and got the men through. The mule train hadn't a hope in Hell of progressing by this route so it was left with a few scouts to try and find its own way, but not before the men were loaded with extra belts of ammunition from the wagons... just in case, like.

A movement up a side street caught Ted's eye and he turned his head to see a bare arsed toddler standing in the street by an open door. He had his thumb in his mouth and was watching the soldiers with interest. Suddenly a woman came out of the doorway and dragged the boy back inside. The slamming of the door was drowned out by the explosion of a shell a few streets away and again Ted wondered why these people were still here. A dig in the back brought him back to reality. It was Sergeant Hanson and it was time to get moving.

The burden was almost intolerable, as the ammo was in addition to the marching pack, ration packs and the weight of the rain, which was soaking into every bloody thing they were wearing. Drenched overcoats slopped against sodden puttees as the column approached the market place, a great open square, to the left of which stood the magnificent, ornate skeleton of what looked like the town hall. The superstructure was more or less intact but when the area was lit up by an explosion it exposed the building as the distressing façade it really was, empty and drained. There was nothing inside but a floor full of rubble and rats. The shells exploded, sending illuminated fountains of masonry high into the air and the men prayed and cursed in turn. Some shells landed nearby, covering them in sheets of wet plaster dust but by some miracle the column was complete and not a man had been harmed, except in their souls. They were covered in dust and rubble, and great sparks arced like fireworks over their heads, causing them to squint and duck but the shouted commands of the officers and NCOs took precedence over the assault of the Hun artillery. They marched through the lashing rain.

Left, right, left, right. Face the front. Ignore everything. Just march... just bloody march!

They had reached the Rue de Menin where a hospital a hundred yards or so to the left had been transformed into an inferno of fire and death. Horrible screams came from within and a mob of men and women were attempting to form a bucket chain from a nearby flooded shell hole. Gasps and sighs and profanities were wrenched from the hearts of the men and they were yelled back into silence. Several boxes of ammunition were burning bright pink in front of the building. The ornate main doors were a cascade of fire and little black darting shadows poured screaming out. It was only when the shadows moved into the darkness that they were seen to be ablaze themselves, screaming their way to death as human torches.

Ted's stomach lurched at the sight and Lettie Simpson crashed back into his mind, shattering every other thought into oblivion. Is this what her death was like? He managed to control the rising bile in his throat as he watched the hideous, twitching sprites that had once been human. Bad enough in the nightmare that was Ypres, how much horror must such a sight have caused in Logan Street?

'Tommy, Tommy. Help us. Help us, please!'

One or two of the men looked as if they might break ranks to do so and others gazed pleadingly at the NCOs and officers.

The order was reinforced brutally. 'Eyes front you bastards. March on. March on!'

Lieutenant Stenhouse, the medical officer, ran up to Lieutenant Colonel Turnbull and appeared to be having an argument with him. He kept pointing to the flaming ruins of the hospital but the senior officer shook his head and barked something, which snapped the young officer to attention.

He moved back to his place in the column but it was obvious he was very upset.

They moved past the stunned Belgians who could not believe they were being so callously ignored by the very men whom they had come to look upon as their redeemers. There was no more marching now. The road was too ruined with piles of rubble and gaping shell holes. The officers and NCOs were shouting themselves hoarse to keep the men in a semblance of order. Ahead, through the curtain of rain they could see a kind of cutting in the city wall that resembled the one where they had entered. Presumably this meant they had reached the far side of the city. Had they come through? Just off to the right a church with a beautiful tower was directly hit and blown to pieces in a torrent of fire that covered the men in fragments no bigger than gravel. It was raining gravel as well! One wall of the tower remained miraculously upright. It had no right to do so. Surely it must topple to the ground but no, it remained, fragile and defiant, standing tall in its wounded obstinacy; almost screaming its defiance at the merciless Hun.

The men moved on, grim faced. No one had been injured and no one had fallen out. Covered in dust and rubble, humiliation and fear, the men of the Durham Light Infantry moved onward. Ted was on the right of the column now, staring down a street that somehow seemed almost unharmed. He noticed curtains being opened across a window to reveal the silhouette of a woman looking out. They were hurriedly drawn.

They must be bloody mad!

They reached the cutting, where the road was flanked on either side by a pedestal with a stone lion on top. One was headless. They crossed a short bridge over a river full of unspeakable things and then they were out of the city. They had survived. There was no stopping, though, as the shells were still coming down and the column had to put some distance between themselves and the fiery Hell that was Ypres. As bad as the road was, it was now possible to form up in a reasonable manner and march off into the gloom and the rain. Miraculously there were no casualties. They had endured all that the horrors of Ypres could inflict upon them and had come through to a man. And to a man they would never forget what they had seen: or how very different it was to what they thought war would be like.

Chapter 24

Langley Park Colliery Village, Tuesday to Thursday, 20th to 22nd April 1915

Bertha had hardly slept – the dreadful images kept rolling up to her as she tried. There was Clementine, Fat Ena's little dog, nailed to the front door of her house, trailing guts right down to the step. The image didn't fade, rather it was overpowered by the sight of Lettie, ablaze and in agony, hands grasping thin air as she screamed. Suddenly she was a black, charred lump in the road, clothes and hair all but gone and red welts cracking out of the crisp, black flesh. A small crowd had gathered around the body and someone had gone to fetch Constable Healy. Bertha was struck dumb. She didn't feel strong or in charge or anything like that. She felt sick and didn't know what to do. One little toddler approached closer than the rest of the crowd and attempted to poke the body with a stick until he was whisked away by his Mam. Poor, sackless Lettie. Well, her soul was at peace now.

Somebody had the sense to bring out a sheet and throw it over her remains, but one black claw protruded from beneath it. The crowd stayed, forming a protective ring. The knife sharpener came around the bottom of the street pedalling his grindstone-tricycle and singing his heart out to advertise his services, only to be hushed at once and sent away. That was when Bertha noticed the claw, and her stomach revolted and threatened to vomit its contents all over the cobbles. Ever so slightly, the claw was opening and closing. It wasn't much of a movement but it was there. Somebody else noticed it as well and a quiet gasp rose and ebbed within the group. Lettie Simpson was still alive.

Far from being at peace, God alone knew what agonies were being visited upon her already tormented soul. Bertha flushed then felt icy cold half a dozen times in as many seconds. She really thought she was going to faint and clapped her hands to her cheeks, staring dumbfounded and utterly helpless, at Lettie's remains. From somewhere in the distance came a trembling, hushed whisper,

'Eeh! What are we going to do?'

The reply was much more direct. 'You do nothing at all, ladies. Just get yourselves off home and back about your business. Leave this to me, now. There's good lasses.'

Sailing through the group of women, Constable Healy was absolutely in charge from the moment he arrived.

'Can one of youse get me a couple of extra sheets, and Mrs Guildford, please could your lad run to the surgery and fetch Doctor Chrisp. Thanks, pet.'

There was a few seconds' pause while nothing happened at all until he spoke again, this time with an edge to his voice.

'Now, ladies... if you please.'

The spell was broken and the group began to dissolve. Bertha was on the verge of asking if there was anything she could do but her courage failed her utterly. She dispersed along with the rest and loathed herself for it. Despite her grand job with the Laundry in Consett she was now just another pit wife. Lettie's exposed hand was now, ever so minutely, trying to claw at the cobbles and Constable Healy's sharp eyes noticed the movement at once. With a small but deft movement of his foot the dirty sheet now covered the obscenity, and the policeman's eyes were boring into Bertha's.

'Go on home, bonny lass. There's nowt you can do for her now.'

In a few moments she was closing the back gate and Constable Healy was standing over what was left of Lettie Simpson, hands behind his back, daring anyone to even come near.

The image faded and Clementine was back, guts dangling but this time she too was alive and looking right at Bertha and whimpering.

Then old Bobby Stokoe swam into view, dead as a doornail on his brother's settee, white, sightless eyes staring at the ceiling. Then Robert with his mouth full of coal.

She sat up with a start, sweat dripping from her body, and she felt so cold. Mebbes she should break open the fire and make a cup of tea.

* * * * *

Next morning she gave the allotment a right going-over. She had deliberately chosen to go to it that morning; she had to get out of the house. She took the newly delivered letters from the two Mams with her in her pinny pocket to read again and roughly compose the replies in her head while she worked the vegetables. She was pleased she had been able to dodge Harry Fairbairn by pretending to be out when he came. He was starting to frighten her now.

It wasn't so cold that she needed her coat but she wore her shawl anyway. The sun, weak as it was, was warmish and welcome. In an hour she was sweating with the exertion of Dutch-hoeing the strip by the wire fence that separated the allotments from the railway – the railway that led to Consett then Blackhill and then home. She was sat having a rest when the dumpling figure of old Freddy Wardle turned up, wheezing and spitting. His rheumy eyes lit up when he saw her and he gave a happy nod, pushing his cap to the back of his head.

'What cheer, pet. Everything all right?'

It was obvious he had no idea about Lettie or Fat Ena and she was in two minds about whether to tell him but decided she would. So, over a cup of stewed tea made on his bucket stove, they sat for a full half hour and discussed the terrible events. Fred was scandalised, at first unable to believe he led such an insular life that such things would pass him by and then unable to believe that such things could happen at all. He rocked back and forth on his old dining room chair and shook his head, staring into the fire.

'Awful, awful. Poor little lass, poor little doggy.'

Bertha could only nod in silent agreement, feeling the tears fill her eyes for the umpteenth time. Then it all came at once and a great shuddering sigh tore her soul apart.

'And I do miss my Ted, Mr Wardle. I do miss my Ted so much.'

Then she was crying her heart out, her hands clasped tightly together as she sat with tears dropping off the end of her nose and the coke train thundering by on its way to the Consett Iron Company.

Fred watched for a few seconds before grunting and fishing a cleanish handkerchief from his waistcoat pocket and offering it to her. She recognised it at once as the missing one from her set at home but it was unimportant now, like everything else, except Ted being so far away and Lettie's terrible death and her own guilt that everything was her fault. A gnarled but gentle hand gripped her shoulder and she was staring into his kindly, baggy eyes. The smoke from his pipe made her eyes smart but she held his gaze.

'Lass, I know your Ted well enough and he's a canny lad with a good head on his shoulders. If any bugger is going to come back from this war it'll be him. You mark my words.

Now there's summat else troubling you, I know. There is, so out with it.'

Of course he was right and she confessed to her irritation about Harry Fairbairn turning into fear, as he grew bolder in his advances towards her.

He nodded sympathetically. 'Probably nowt, man. He just fancies his chances a bit, bonny lass like you. Just tell him to bugger off, like.'

He rose and stretched, signalling that the conversation was over. He announced he was off down to the bench outside the Blue Star for a pint and a bit of sun.

'There's always a bit of sun outside the Blue Star about now and I like a bit of sun.' He then went into a spasm of coughing that made him sit down again for a minute. He spat up great dottles of black, a reminder that even after years of retirement from mining coal it was always with you, always inside you, waiting.

She looked at this little walnut of a man with a heart the size of a hero and wondered if, one day, her Ted would be like this, all bent and broken by King Coal. Well, if he stayed the same man inside, like Freddy had, that wouldn't be so bad.

Chapter 25

Zonnebecke/Gravenstafel Road, 2000 hours, Saturday 24th April 1915

On they marched, away from the devastation that was Ypres and towards the lashing curtains of rain that weighed them down every bit as much as the excess of equipment they were carrying. There were fewer refugees on this road, or foreign soldiers either for that matter. Whether it was down to the rain, the time of day or to developments nearer the front, they did not know. Once away from the beleaguered city the men were given permission to talk and smoke but after the scenes they had witnessed there was little talking to be done. The battalion was shocked to a man and unanimous that this was not the war they had come to fight. Sodden tabs would not stay alight in the rain so the men laboured on like beasts of burden herded together.

There was some British activity further along the road however, mostly traffic going back towards the city. There was the odd mule drawn ambulance wagon and once two motorcyclists going in opposite directions waved at each other – and the Durhams – with quite some enthusiasm. The detonation of the shells was now comfortably behind them but the screaming caused by their passage through the air above the column was with them all the way, causing many a nervous upward glance.

One shell made a louder whistle than the rest and the noise kept on growing. Panic rose amongst the men and the shell landed nearby with a horrendous thump, The earth beneath their feet moved suddenly and the air struck the men causing them to stagger in unison as if punched by a huge invisible fist. Greatcoats lifted and hats flew off. Everyone's ears were singing. Automatically the battalion closed up and tried to quicken the pace.

'Drop of rain obviously doesn't put them off, does it?' muttered Tom Dodds whilst trying to clean his spectacles between his thumb and finger for the umpteenth time.

'You might as well just put them buggers away,' said Billy Robson irritably. 'Considering it's nearly dark and chucking it down they're no bloody use anyway, are they?'

Tommy sighed and stuffed them into his coat pocket, visibly wincing, as his hand was immersed in a cold puddle of rain that squeezed out of the sodden material.

A curious sight on the other side of the road, however, was a set of poles about nine feet high that had been driven into the ground in between the shot up trees. Sheets of tarpaulin and canvas were stretched between them to form a sort of screen. A few saturated soldiers were resignedly making running repairs to the structure under the command of a sergeant who looked old enough to have been pensioned off donkeys' years ago.

'What cheer, mate. What's all that about, like?'

Ted recognised Dicky Howell's voice as he loudly engaged the attention of one of the men. The soldier looked horrified and did not reply to the shouted question. Instead, the sergeant, who had a look of pure fury on his face, ran up to the nearest Durham NCO and muttered something quickly and quietly. The order was passed around for silence.

A few yards further on, another detail of screen repairers were trying to lash the soaking tarpaulins to the poles. Some were perched precariously on stepladders, their overcoats sloshing around them like wet curtains. One man glanced at the shambling column then left his work to run up to the lads and fall in beside them. He was obviously on the cadge but there was nowt the matter with that – provided he had something to trade. He was two or three ranks ahead of Ted, talking to Harry Clarke. Hands were moving and something was exchanged and then, after a few seconds quiet chat the soldier fell out and loped back up the road looking pleased with himself.

Word was getting around now, albeit at a low whisper. The reason for the screens was that off to their right was a bit of German high ground where this particular stretch of road was decidedly visible and in easy sniper range. Hence the screens to hide any of the troops travelling through, and the order to be quiet, so that they didn't make themselves a target. As well as the banshee wail of the shells screaming overhead they could hear another sound: the high-pitched whreee of rifle bullets as Fritz fired blind through the screens hoping to bag a Tommy.

Suddenly no one was disposed to talk any more and they marched through the rain in sullen silence through Pojitze, which was hardly more than a stinking pile of bricks and rubble and corpses, to Velorenhoek, where there was the usual waiting about whilst the officers did whatever they did to get further orders.

They trudged on remorselessly until 2300 hours when they were instructed to bivouac for the night on either side of the road. Cockney Joe was first to spot the thick overhang of brambles where the railway and the road met and he guarded it fiercely, with a foul tongue, until his band of comrades came to curl up within its meagre shelter and await morning. There was a blazing farmhouse just over the way which gave some scanty illumination to the scene.

Exhausted, the lads flung off their packs and extra ammunition belts, letting them lie where they fell as they attempted to shelter from the cold rain. This was bloody April! The rain had no right to be so cold. Granted they had suffered such drenchings during training both in Durham and at Morfa Camp but at this time of year at least it should have been warmer.

Rations were getting short and the men were hungry and depressed. The officers and NCOs were doing the rounds and trying to chivvy the men up a bit. It did raise the spirits to watch Lance Corporal Carter try to cheer them up when he was never known to smile of his own accord. It was obvious they were under orders to be cheerful because nobody in their right mind would be happy on a night like this. The younger officers were making a far better job of keeping a stiff upper lip – it was like it came naturally to them. The lads were stowed under the bramble shelter with soaking blankets over their heads, staring stared miserably at their feet. They were surprised by the arrival of no less than Captain Stevens, the adjutant, who gave them a polite greeting and, as they all began to scramble to their feet, gestured for them to remain where they were.

'Good evening, men. As you were.' He paused awkwardly before continuing. 'Found yourselves a cosy little bolt-hole I see. Well done, then.'

The few seconds pause was excruciating, the lads not knowing what to say and the young officer striving to find some common ground for informal conversation. The peak of his cap was dripping constantly as his eyes alighted on the huddled figure of Fat Harry, his blanket over his bare head.

'Private Guildford,' he smiled. Harry looked horrified. 'You will be pleased to know we are encamped just off the 'Rue de Zonnebecke.'

Another embarrassing pause whilst the captain awaited a reaction that clearly was not forthcoming.

He tried again. 'Another of your, erm 'roody roads', eh?'

This time the lads clicked what was expected of them and a nervous laugh ran around the assembly, which in turn prompted a more genuine, if relieved, grin from Captain Stevens.

'You caught Lieutenant Brass fair and square back there... with your 'roody road' prank... jolly good, Guildford.'

This was bloody awful. There might as well have been a million miles between them.

There was yet another pause that seemed a bit too long until Stevens bade the lads goodnight and just then seemed to notice Ted's pencil moustache, identical to his own, for the first time. He made no comment, but seemed to stare slightly too long before nodding politely and turning away to disappear into the rain.

It was John Merrigan who spoke through the near dark, lit only vaguely from the flames of the burning building nearby. His voice bore an invisible grin.

'You're in the shite now, Teddy, boy. Fancy copying an officers' moustache and reckoning you could get away with it.' His tongue clicked a few times. 'What will they do with you in the morning?'

Billy Robson tried not to laugh and snorted loudly instead. Somebody said 'shoot the bastard' and Jacky Tait joined in with a sepulchral, 'And the ghost of Edward Smith haunted the Roody... whatever it was... for evermore.'

A chorus of ghoulish voices all joined in at once with a whoo-oo-oo sound that was more comical than haunting.

Then in burst Corporal Tremaine who ordered them up.

'On your feet, lads, we're off to Zonnebeke... wherever the Hell that is... I SAID ON YOUR FEET!'

He was gone as quickly as he had appeared but his voice was still apparent, shouting identical phrases to other groups of men further down the line. It was Hell on legs trying to get up and moving. Dreadful as their resting places were, there was some degree of comfort to be had simply by sitting still, even if they were soaked to the skin. Now trying to get upright in a hurry and arrange backpacks and the extra ammunition belts with stiff, cold muscles was agony for every man in the battalion. It took longer than the NCOs wanted to get the men formed up and they made their displeasure manifestly obvious.

They were then given their objectives, which didn't go down well either. After all the painful footslogging to get into this war it appeared their first task under active service was to finish off some half-built (and half-flooded) trenches up near a place called Gravenstafel. They were given a guide, a Canadian corporal, to make sure they got there. Bloody great! Here comes the Eighth DLI, all ready to dig about in the mud finishing off some bugger else's job while all the action and glory went to the rest of the army. And they didn't have a tool cart. Or had that little detail not occurred to anybody? Then they were back on the march. The rain made smoking impossible and nobody was in the mood to talk anyway so when the order for no smoking or talking was issued it made no difference to the lads whatsoever – again!

This was just torture! Being told to get up five minutes after you've settled down and being weighed down with more gear than a man was ever supposed to carry was more than they could bear. The rain came down through the dark in sheets and the shells screamed over their heads. Behind them, each sharp crummp of detonating artillery chopped the stones of the beleaguered city a little further into extinction, whilst to the front, the different noise of men fighting was equally shocking. The flat cracking sound of rifles vied with the chatter of machine guns and the dull whoomf of artillery shells exploding where they landed several feet underneath the waterlogged earth.

Once again, marching was abandoned in favour of simply shuffling along, trying to keep pace and formation. At one point no less a man than Lieutenant Colonel Turnbull himself appeared alongside Ted's rank and shouted encouragement through the driving rain. He wasn't wearing a greatcoat and his uniform was running with water, but he seemed not even to notice. He just stood there with his walking cane under his arm as if he were on a Sunday morning parade and heartily cheered the men on. The lads weren't daft. They were smart enough by now to know what he was up to, setting an example, like; but they admired the fact he was trying. He was one of them officers who led from the front was Turnbull, and nobody minds a lad like that.

Ted's leg was starting to give him serious trouble now. The place where the break had been felt like it was on fire and he was limping noticeably. Thank God the conditions were so treacherous underfoot that actual marching was impossible. He was angry and frustrated. He had healed so well and so quickly that he had been on his feet and playing handball again before anyone could have predicted, and all the way through his training he had managed to hide the discomfort the injury had given him. He was appalled when Tom Dodds and Jacky Tait offered to take his extra ammunition belts for a bit. He declined abruptly and instantly regretted how discourteous he had been to his mates.

The going was poorer than ever now. The road was only obvious by its shell holes and the fields either side were more like lakes. Horrors abounded at every turn and even in the darkness of the small hours, the odd nearby shell bursts intermittently illuminated sights ever more shocking. There were upturned limbers and horses' legs black against the flashes of light, the corpses of men and mules in ever more unspeakable poses, a horse impaled up in a tree, a farm girl with her legs missing below the knees sprawled, hands outstretched towards the two dead cows she had obviously been herding. Then of course there was the smell, that sickly, cloying, sweet smell of death that even the rain could not wash away.

They reached Zonnebecke, which lay in corpse-strewn ruins and bypassed it to the north by following the railway line instead of the road. There was a narrow path here, protected by a small embankment about ten feet high and although it was only wide enough for two men abreast at least the turf was firm and progress improved. For one thing, it was on slightly higher ground and therefore less muddy and for another it relieved the men by blunting the sights and sounds of battle for a short while.

During the latest stop there was a commotion behind the lads as a runner made his way forward, pushing past the stationary soldiers until he reached the vanguard where a rapid exchange with Lieutenant Colonel Turnbull and Captain Bradford resulted in him returning down the line accompanied by an agitated looking Lieutenant Wilson.

'C' Company, who were bringing up the rear, had lost contact with the main body somewhere back along the road. Bugger! The men were told to stand easy but maintain position. Thankfully, the rain began to ease off a little. After about fifteen minutes, Lieutenant Wilson shuffled back along the narrow path and disappeared towards the front. Without awaiting the order the men sighed, retrieved their ammunition belts from where they had dropped them, laboriously placing them over their shoulders, each man assisting his comrades in getting the unwieldy equipment across the big backpacks. From way at the back, one of the mules was heard to complain loudly, probably about the same thing.

The order was passed along that 'C' was back in position and they were to proceed cautiously. After a while they came to a place where the railway crossed a road. The rain had lessened a bit more and odd signs of a watery three-quarter moon bled through the breaking clouds in an attempt to relieve the darkness. They had reached a small railway station and it was the same essay in death as everywhere else in this blighted land. They moved on until they came to a crossroads where they turned left. The dead were everywhere, but strangely, not many mutilated. It was a haunted road, populated only by the corpses and the DLI. Not a soul was to be seen anywhere. Did this mean that the refugees had all got out? Did it mean that the military were pushing forward? Was this desolation a good sign?

The noises from the front were definitely getting less and there was a clear gap between the big guns going off. Before, it had been so continuous it was like a rumble of thunder, but now it was disjointed, as if they were rationing their ammo or were just plain tired of the effort.

About fifteen minutes out of the station, a near-direct hit upon it lit up the sky and caused the weary soldiers to gasp. It was more likely to have been a shell that fell short than a deliberate attempt to destroy an already demolished target but even so it could have happened fifteen minutes earlier, or the companies could have been fifteen minutes later and just passing through as the shell struck. They laboured on.

The rain was definitely abating when they came to a crossroads where the guide took them left. The clouds were thinning and a bit of moonlight was straining to break through. For some reason the area did not appear so ruthlessly blasted as the rest, which seemed to make no sense at all as they were marching ever nearer to the front. There was something else as well – a faint but pungent smell. It was more than just a smell because some of the lads began to complain about dry throats or stinging eyes.

Was this the gas?

Was this what snuffed out so many thousands of lives without a shot being fired?

A ripple of panic began quickly to spread through the marching men. It was just as quickly pounced upon and quelled by the officers and NCOs.

'It's all right, men, it's only residual. Just a last remnant, nothing to worry about.'

They listened to the ever-diminishing volume of explosions and lessening sounds of rifles and machine guns. It was like hearing the death throes of a great monster, like the dinosaurs that used to roam Farmer Keenlyside's fields millions of years ago back in Sunniside, whose only remains were fossilised into the coal in the quarry by the river. Minute by minute the growling of the monster died away, grinding its way down to the odd shell or single rifle report.

The sky flashed red only intermittently now as a big gun was let off and made the cold illumination of the moon appear sallow by comparison. All up and down this section of the front line men on both sides were backing off from the fray, grabbing a rest before daylight when the slaughter would resume again. When the sun rose on this tragic land of flooded fields and floating corpses, men would hurl themselves and their machines at one another once again in an attempt to break an unbreakable stalemate. And where would the Durhams be when the fighting resumed? Digging trenches in the rain without a bloody tool cart.

*   *   *   *   *

About 0200 hours it started to cloud over and the rain began once more. This had the effect of erasing the smell of the gas but otherwise only added to the men's misery. After a while a couple of large, shell-fractured stone farm buildings loomed out of the darkness and the battalion was halted on the road alongside. A couple of important-looking officers left the building, walked up to Lieutenant Colonel Turnbull and saluted smartly. Hands were shaken and introductions made before the gaggle of officers entered the main farmhouse, which, although not marked as such in any way, positively reeked of being a military HQ. Oil lamps were lit in windows facing the road. Every detail of the interior was visible to the men now standing easy in the rain. They could clearly see the officers moving and talking.

'Canny target for a sniper, that is,' observed George Moody from somewhere up the line. 'I'd at least shut the curtains, like.'

They watched as a private soldier took in a tray of some steaming hot beverages with some glasses and a bottle, which the inmates accepted with nods of thanks. John Merrigan continued the conversation. 'Naw, man. They don't need curtains, any sniper would have to shoot through the shield.'

Eyebrows were knotted all over the place and it was Tom Dodds who asked the question, 'What are you talking about, man? What shield, like?'

'Us, you daft bugger, who do you think's standing between the Germans and the windows, eh?'

Two debates began simultaneously: one inside the building obviously to do with tactics, strategies and the deployment of the Durhams and a second one, outside in the pissing rain, about how grand it must be to have a commission and abandon your men to the elements with a possibility of a bullet in the back while you discussed their future over a nice mug of tea and a brandy.

In the event it turned out to be coffee, and their future had changed, though not necessarily for the better. When all the talk was concluded and hands were shaken once again, the British officers filed out into the rain to explain to their men that they had been engaged in tactical discussions with senior officers of the local Canadian contingent, Lieutenant Colonels Lipsett and Tuxford respectively, both of whom had more pressing need of the DLI.

Yesterday morning it appeared that the Germans had released another cloud of gas, this time against the Canadians themselves. They were hard pressed due to the previous attack disabling and killing so many thousands. The line was not yet consolidated and there were many gaps that the enemy would exploit if they got the chance. The Canadians were spread thin and desperately in need of reinforcements but had hung on tenaciously in the face of overwhelmingly superior numbers.

The men were ordered to reinforce and, if possible relieve, the soldiers of the Eighth Winnipeg Rifles to the north-east of a place called Boetleers Farm... right on the front line and immediately under the enemy's guns. Captain Bradford relayed this information to 'D' Company and away to their left Captain Harvey could be heard issuing the same instructions to 'A'. The transformation in the drenched troops was immediate. At long last, they were off to fight the Hun. They were off to engage him in a proper bloody fight, man to man, like.

For the umpteenth time the soldiers of the Eighth Durham Light Infantry had a last, vain scratch to try to alleviate the itching caused by lice, then assisted each other to shoulder the enormous burden of packs and rations and belts of ammunition, but just at that moment it didn't seem quite so heavy. Through the brightly lit windows, a couple of enlisted men were seen removing mugs and glasses and restacking maps into a neat pile. Captain Bradford appeared to notice this for the first time and the fact that all their high and mighty negotiations and drinking of coffee and brandy had taken place in full view of the men out in the rain made him look distinctly guilty.

On the advice of the Canadians, the mules were to be abandoned here because of the soft going, so the gear and belts of ammunition were redistributed amongst the men. The communal rising groan of the already overloaded troops was snapped into silence. With a wave of resignation the weary men began to shoulder the belts of ammunition as the lads in charge of the mule train issued them out. This was done from the rearmost troops, which comprised of 'C' and 'B' Companies and miraculously ran out near the end of 'A', meaning that there was no extra gear to burden 'D' Company at all. Even so, the lads knew better than to brag about their luck. All except Billy Robson, that is, whose stillborn smart remark died in his throat at the sight of Sergeant Malone, himself weighed down with extra bandoliers of ammo.

In the van, Lieutenant Colonel Turnbull was accompanied by Lieutenant Colonel Lipsett, who were so alike it was almost comical. Walking in front of the men, neither officer wore a greatcoat and they were strolling along, ignoring the rain as if they were on a Sunday walk.

Fortunately, Boetleers Farm was only another couple of miles along the road from the HQ buildings, which was just as well as the men were soaking, starving and absolutely knackered. Now that they had an objective that would consist of a built-up locality it was highly likely they could have a bit of a rest and some proper grub. It might even be hot grub if they were lucky.

The rain continued to fall though not so heavily as previously but there was no longer any moonlight because of the clouds. The closer the men got to their destination the quieter this section of the front became, though by the distant booms and flashes this was not the case everywhere. At a small rise in the road their guide filtered the battalion left so they filed down a short incline into a field, which took them out of view of the encroaching enemy lines which from here onwards commanded a good view of the Allied defences. Under strict, whispered orders to keep as smart a formation as possible they proceeded through the dark and the ever-lessening rain until at about three in the morning Boetleers Farm was finally reached.

And what a miserable objective it was. Through the darkness loomed a collection of bombed-out buildings that were fit for no purpose whatsoever. Most of the tiles had been ripped from the roofs by artillery blasts. In some bits, canvas had been untidily dragged across the spaces but for the most part the charred timbers just thrust naked, like ribs, towards the sky. The sandbags surrounding the buildings were not just there for defence, they were actually supporting the crumbling walls which would surely have crashed to the ground had they not been so reinforced. Low walls and hedges lined little paths that ran off until they were lost in the shadows, and clumps of trees were dotted about here and there in the gloom.

The farm was on a bit of high ground, which in peace time made perfect sense as it was good for drainage but when war was being waged it was all the more vulnerable. An easy target, it had been all but reduced to rubble. As the rain decreased, the lingering smell of chlorine reasserted itself.

Despite this, the farm was of strategic importance to the Allies and could not be abandoned. The ruined buildings had become dressing stations, housing the wounded and the gassed, who were comforted by untrained men because the medical officer was long since dead. The groans and screams seemed the same as everywhere else in Belgium and although the Durhams would never get used to such sounds they could at least thank the Lord they were not amongst the number of the unfortunate souls.

Lieutenant Colonel Turnbull summoned his medical officer, Lieutenant Stenhouse and after a brief conversation they exchanged salutes whereupon Stenhouse and his orderly, Lance Corporal Fish, trotted off in the direction of the dressing station.

Chapter 26

Boetleer's Farm, 0200 hours, Sunday 25th April 1915

This whole mess was down to gas attacks. The bloody Germans had killed and incapacitated thousands of brave soldiers – and innocent civilians – and had done so with such efficiency that four miles of trenches had been left undefended.

The Canadians were nearest and had to jump in and fill the gap before the enemy broke through. This they did with speed and courage but now that the positions were more or less consolidated it struck home how poorly defended the locality actually was. It was sheer guts that held that line, as there were nowhere near enough soldiers to properly man such a gap.

The Germans didn't know that, though, otherwise the defences would have been overrun in a shot. This area was not a solid chain of resistance, but more a series of one-offs that bluff and a great deal of determination had held against the enemy forces. But the thin line of khaki was growing thinner and now it was the turn of the Durhams to underpin it and at the same time prove that, although they had never yet fired a single bullet in anger, they were capable of doing just that.

To the left of the road the ground continued to fall away and here they passed to the rear of a series of not-very-well-built trenches. They were flooded with at least of foot of water which reflected the pale three-quarter moon. Instead of the solid, classic Morfa design the excavated earth – or rather mud – was slopped up in a heap on the facing side of the ditch in a poor attempt at a parapet. They held a right mixture of British and Canadians, but to a man they were grateful to see the lads turn up, showing it with smiles and quiet cheers. The Durhams however were snapped into precise rank and file by the NCOs and marched as smartly as the terrain would allow with eyes to the front until they were brought to a perfectly timed, if soggy halt and left at the attention in a field of trampled, rain-soaked corn.

Once again the custom of abandoning the men to the elements whilst orders were sought was put into practice, but this time the meeting between the inhabitants and the new arrivals was held in the open, in the rain, right in front of the men. Hurricane lamps lit the scene and an air of frustration was quite apparent in the officers' behaviour. Apparently, such was the speed with which the Canadian troops had been forced to fill the breach that there had been no time to chart the area and properly organise troop movements. Consequently there were no maps to refer to in order to best deploy the men and give their officers any clue as to how the surrounding area fitted in to the plan for defence. There was much pointing and gesticulating between the occupying officers and the Durhams and in the end they were all shouted down by Lieutenant Colonel Turnbull who silenced the lot of them as an NCO would shut up a bunch of raw recruits.

The conversation continued in a much lower key with Turnbull asking the questions and the others dutifully answering. It ended with a ten-second silence which seemed to last a lifetime.

More saluting, which always meant that some decision had been made, and the company commanders trotted through the rain back to their men with the junior officers right behind. Captain Stevens, the CO's adjutant remained with Turnbull and Lipsett and appeared to be receiving further instructions.

Captain Bradford planted himself front dead centre and spoke in a low voice, just loud enough for the rear rank to hear.

'This is it, men. This is what you have all worked so hard for these past few months. You are as prepared for war as the British Army can make you.'

There was a pause and the silence rang around the field.

'You men, and the men of 'A', are off to war now. This minute! 'B' and 'C' Companies are to remain and reinforce the Canadians, Middlesex and Monmouths who are manning the trenches by the road here. Because of the lack of knowledge of this area Captain Stevens has been given the job of trying to map it... And in this bloody awful weather, jolly good luck to him.' He was thankful to receive the hoped-for polite laugh from his men. 'We, however, are about to march forward to relieve some very brave men occupying a holding position right under the guns of the enemy. When we cross that road onto the open ground have no doubt in your minds that you will be fired upon by the Hun. Have no doubt in your minds that some of your comrades will fall. But above all, have no doubt that you must keep marching forward. Hold your line and hold your nerve. Do nothing without a direct order from your officers or NCOs. We've practiced this a hundred times. Now let's show the enemy that we can do it for real. Rifles at the ready? Good luck then.'

Bradford raised his hand for Captain Harvey to see, indicating that all was ready. Harvey did the same, but before the order was given to set off Captain Bradford heard his name being called in forced whisper. A young Canadian lieutenant trotted up and saluted smartly. The young man's left hand and forearm were covered in a thick, bloodstained bandage.

'Second Lieutenant Flett, sir. I've been sent by Lieutenant Colonel Lipsett to act as a guide to get you to the forward trenches and... begging your pardon sir, but the Lieutenant Colonel respectfully suggests you re-form your troops into column three men wide. There's a track that runs through the farm and just beyond the orchard, which will get us to the trenches quickly, and we'll present less of a target in column, sir.'

Captain Bradford was far too professional to let his annoyance show, but why the Hell hadn't Lipsett said all this before and not undermined his authority so publicly?

It made sense, though, and that was a damned sight more important than self-esteem.

'My respects to the Lieutenant Colonel and many thanks for his good advice.

Lieutenant Brass, Lieutenant Wilson, instruct the NCOs to re-form the men into column and Lieutenant Richardson, would you kindly pass Lieutenant Colonel Lipsett's instructions to Captain Harvey. It's getting uncomfortably light, gentlemen, so please make haste.'

The orders were carried out and a puzzled murmur from the men was cut dead by the NCOs. Ted was a bit agitated to find his comfortable position off to the left of the line at the back was now a distinctly uncomfortable one practically at the front of the column. He was sandwiched between Tommy Raper and Willy Maddison, with only one rank in front of them. About ten feet beyond stood Captain Bradford and Lieutenant Brass with the young Canadian officer.

Suddenly, a bunch of soldiers were jostling up to the Eighth and handing them petrol cans full of water for the Durhams and the Canadians they were about to relieve in the forward position. With a bit of reorganisation the cans were given into the care of the centre file who were allowed to shoulder their 303s but found it bloody hard to do so because of the ridiculous amount of gear they were carrying.

It was really starting to get a bit light now and the day's hostilities were about to kick off, with the Germans getting some target practice on a bunch of lads who were rapidly becoming sitting ducks.

The orders were given and the men set off through the rain at a quick march. There was a moist rustling of wet boots on crushed corn. They passed the ruined farm buildings on the left which served as dressing stations. The place was in a terrible state. Low moans could be heard, punctuated by screams, as the orderlies, now under Lieutenant Stenhouse, wrestled with the horrific work of caring for the wounded and gassed. The front of the column reached the road, the highest point of land. They were ordered to absolute silence because they were now in full view of the enemy guns. As booted feet touched as lightly as possible on the hard surface, Ted strained his eyes through the ever-brightening twilight to see what was ahead. He could just about make out a small orchard and a few fields bordered by hedgerows gently dipping away into the distance to what looked like a little stream. Beyond that, the land rose ever so slightly until it reached a small ridge that commanded a view of the whole valley. Even with his limited training he knew that's where the Germans were.

If he could see them, then they could bloody well see him. He reckoned it was about half a mile of completely open ground to that ridge. The fields contained corn only a few inches high so there was no cover and there was no sign of the trench they were to occupy.

The lads had seen some disturbing sights since disembarking in France, particularly as they passed through the horror that was Ypres. But they were totally unprepared for the orchard. It looked peaceable enough as they approached it but the strengthening dawn light revealed odd, lumpen shapes on the ground within. As they marched closer they were revealed as the bodies of men. They were sitting against tree trunks or lying in grotesque, unnatural positions and almost all had been stripped of their clothing. They had been partially eaten by rats, which scuttled away as the company approached, leaving the bodies to stare with eyeless sockets and grin with lipless mouths.

'What the fuck's been going on here?' grunted Tommy Raper.

The quiet of the column was broken as gasps and exclamations came from the men. The NCOs snarled them back into silence. No bullet had been fired yet and the tension was unbearable. If the Germans opened fire now at least the lads would know what was going on.

Is this a trap? Will the enemy open up in a few seconds and annihilate the whole bloody lot of them? Nobody marches across open ground in full sight of the enemy without being shot at.

They were through the orchard, leaving the obscene mystery of the naked corpses behind, marching through a field and heading to their right to join a dirt track, which, as far as Ted could tell took them onto clear ground and directly towards the enemy. Christ! They were marching through pouring rain, with no cover, across open bloody fields straight towards the Germans.

Why didn't they fire?

Discipline and fear prevailed and the men marched on in silence with Ted straining hard to overhear the whispered conversation between Captain Bradford and the young Canadian officer. Apparently the enemy should have opened fire as soon as the men had left the cover of the orchard and no, he had no idea why they hadn't. Perhaps it was to do with yesterday's gas attack or perhaps they were just keeping out of the rain. Captain Bradford seized the initiative and quietly passed the instruction for the companies to double their speed.

The silence was made all the more unbearable by the fact that the company should by now have been on the receiving end of withering gunfire from the German trenches. Some of the men actually held their breath as they trotted along. The common aim of every soul in the exposed company was to make as little noise as possible, do nothing to alert the enemy to the fact that two hundred mortal men were under their guns.

Ted was having an awful job, trotting along and trying to keep his rifle on his shoulder with his right hand while the rough metal handle of the petrol can cut into the palm of his left. The lad in front of him had lost his cap trying to push his rifle strap over his head so that it would be crosswise across his chest. He managed it with a grunt and, having ensured he would no longer lose his weapon he swapped the petrol can to his other hand. Good idea that! Ted waited a few paces to see if any of the NCOs would object and hearing no comment to the contrary did the same, whilst endeavouring not to lose his cap. The loudest noise seemed to be the sloshing of the water in the cans. The men were sure the noise was carrying right to the German trenches.

Ted's lungs were on fire and his leg hurt like Hell. The sloshing of water was joined by the rasping of breath as the men forced air into their lungs.

There was a trench just up ahead and to their left. They were home and dry.

No! Lieutenant Flett shook his head and they ran on towards the German lines.

The shell holes around the trench had been amazingly accurate. None of them were very big but they were clustered immediately in the region of the excavation, blurring its lines. Then the smell hit them, the sharp, sweet smell of rotting death, even through the rain. Quiet gasps of horror punctuated the rhythmic panting as the men stole a sidelong glance into the trench to see it partially flooded with oily water that glistened grey in the half-light. It was crammed as full with the bodies of Canadian soldiers as it could possibly be, almost as if a detail had been ordered to throw all of the corpses for miles around into this one trench. Ugly bodies, bloated bodies, bits of bodies, bodies missing eyes and limbs and with obscene black gouts of old blood around their mouths.

Then the Durhams were past and gasping for air more than ever. The German lines were as clear as could be. The ridge was in a crescent that surrounded them. They could be fired on from three sides now. They were running into the jaws of death and nothing was happening.

The corn had given way to marsh grass as they vaulted clumsily across the small stream, the squelching noise as they landed sounded loud in their ears but no shots came from the German positions. The tough, springy grass gave way to a mustard field that in turn became trampled mud. Shell holes – bigger ones – became evident once again. They were ill-defined and broken up. This was obviously a place that had been well and truly thumped. There was something wrong with the ground. It wasn't just muddy, it was undulating regularly as if they were running over giant furrows. The closer they got to the German line the more accentuated the contours became. It was because the shallow graves beneath their boots had been disturbed by shelling and the interred bodies were beginning to surface.

A few more paces and the dismembered, skeletal remains of dark men in strange, colourful clothes had been almost completely exhumed. Ted was momentarily fascinated by the mummified skull of a black skinned man, which somehow had held on to its thick moustache and red, flowerpot cap. He had to dodge around a bony forearm that was sticking out of the ground at right angles, still surrounded by a filthy blue sleeve. None of the men had seen anything like this and after Ypres, and the mystery of the corpses in the orchard, they were becoming uneasy. They ran on through the drizzle, crunching over bone, and the sound of sloshing water filled their ears while the cold hand of fear gripped their hearts.

None of this was right. Ted looked up to see a glint of something shiny on the ridge. Periscope? Helmet? Rifle barrel? Were the bastards lining up on him now?

Any second you'll hear the command to fire and it'll be the last bloody thing you'll ever hear.

The enemy trench was only about eighty yards away and there was no barbed wire in between, only mud and bodies and that was sod all use. They must know we're here by now. In a minute we'll be in amongst the buggers.

Then they arrived!

A khaki-clad soldier jumped up from nowhere and waved at the men, gesticulating wildly and silently for them to follow his directions. Captain Bradford hesitated for a moment but the young Canadian guide ran on and turned left, completely disappearing from sight. This galvanised Bradford to do the same after turning round to his men and wordlessly signalling them to follow on.

Lieutenant Wilson stopped suddenly and turned to wave the men past him. Ted and his comrades were the first of 'D' Company to enter the Canadian forward trench... and all without a shot being fired.

* * * * *

'Keep moving, keep moving. Keep goin' down. Keep goin' on down.'

The drawling voice was quiet, hardly above conversation level. Nobody wanted to attract the attention of the enemy that was so painfully close. Ted never saw the person who was speaking and he was only vaguely aware that he was running down a muddy slope into the side of a trench that was hardly more than a big ditch.

There were bodies everywhere. The fresh ones were Canadian and the older, decomposing ones were the strange dark skinned people in the bright clothes. Ted was half way up to his knees in water and it was very difficult to keep his footing. Sometimes he could feel duckboards under his feet but as he stepped on them they slid about. He splashed on, feeling other things that sent shivers up his spine. The trench wasn't deep enough to give complete cover – you couldn't dig a civilised trench in this land if you bloody tried because the water was never more than a few feet below the surface. Ingenuity had prevailed, however, with the displaced earth being made to form a half-decent breastwork with the odd loophole in it. The fire steps were reinforced with sandbags and bricks that were just under the surface of the muddy water.

Ted splashed on. They passed a few dugouts including one that had caved in, all of which seemed to be full of dead and wounded. In one, the bodies had been neatly stacked about four deep, like the railway sleepers at the pit, but mostly the dead seemed to have been left where they fell or pulled out of the way and just dumped.

'Look out, sir, it gets deeper here.'

It was Lieutenant Flett, nursing his injured forearm but still keeping up a good lick with Captain Bradford a pace or two behind him. The remaining Canadians had lined the fire step and were smoking and grinning cheerfully at the floundering, splashing boys who had come through the rain to relieve them.

'Hi guys, what kept you?'

'Good to see you boys.'

'Watch out for the puddles now.'

With a great splash Flett and Bradford disappeared up to their waists in water and waded strongly through the trench, which had narrowed considerably. Ted watched the three men in front of him slither down an unseen slope and just managed to get his balance right before he felt himself do the same. He cursed outloud but kept his feet as Tommy Raper grabbed his shoulder to remain upright. The shock of the sudden rush of water around his waist made Ted gasp, and he knew he wasn't the only one. He thought he had been cold and wet when they camped by the railway but he wished he was back there now with all his heart.

From somewhere close behind they heard Corporal Lawrie's voice. 'Get your rifles over your heads; hold them up out of the water!'

Bollocks! Ted knew this would happen. That was Corporal Lawrie doing the sensible thing when everybody had their hands full already. The column had reduced itself to a crude line one or two wide now and the lads began to struggle with their already soaking weapons. Ted had his hands full with the petrol can so he just splashed on holding it up out of the water, trying to ignore the dead rats and other, unidentifiable obscenities. After about fifty or so Lieutenant Flett started to emerge from the water as he climbed a shallow slope up into a trench similar to the one they had entered a few minutes before. Again they were welcomed by the grinning faces of the Canadian soldiers who were beginning to crowd the top of the incline. Captain Bradford was next up, the dirty water draining from his uniform in great rivulets. He exchanged a swift word with Lieutenant Flett who saluted and ran off down the trench. Bradford positioned himself on the fire step and waved his men through, at the same time barking at a few Canadians who were still on the trench floor to get up onto the fire step and out of the damned way.

'Come on men, one last effort. It's plain sailing now, let's show our friends we're up to the job.'

He waved them through enthusiastically and the company, trailing gallons of muddy water, emerged from the flooded channel and set off once again down the trench. Lieutenant Flett could just be seen just ahead clearing the Canadians onto the fire step to make way for the company. The same dead, the same rats and, in amongst the stink, the same welcoming smiles on the faces of the beleaguered soldiers.

Still trotting, the lads stumbled on trying desperately to avoid the bodies that lay where they had fallen but mostly having to run on top of them in the sloppy mud. They rounded a couple of shallow bends until they came to a right angle in the trench with a machine gun emplacement in it. At this point Lieutenant Flett turned and raised his hand for the company to halt. They were grateful to do so. The Canadian soldiers moved off the fire step to allow the Durhams to sit and willing hands relieved them of the petrol cans containing the much-needed water.

That was when everyone noticed it had stopped raining.

The officer in charge, a Captain McLeod, though thrilled to have his men relieved after they had been besieged for so long, was nevertheless dismayed to see such a bunch of fresh-faced boys as their replacements. He did not doubt their courage but to send such youngsters! His own men weren't exactly veterans but they had years on the Durhams.

Despite his confidence in Captain Bradford he felt he could not leave these boys alone to defend the area against such fierce odds so he decided to stay on with his machine gun crews and a couple of signallers. It was unfortunate that the machine gun ammunition brought by the Durhams was not the same pattern as the Canadian and was therefore rendered useless, but the gunners were not short of ammo so it was not considered a problem. With hearty thanks and a firm handshake, an appreciative Captain Bradford accepted the Canadian officer's gesture. The fact that the man was undoubtedly putting himself and his men to some considerable risk was not lost on Bradford, but not only did the offer swell the ranks of his men but also the expertise of the gunners would work wonders on the morale of his own untried boys. The steadying influence of the older men would be most valuable.

He decided to set up his headquarters in the dugout at the western extremity of the system. It was about two hundred and thirty yards from the enemy and although not central had served Captain McLeod well during his occupancy – he had situated his communications here and the right angle in the trench afforded a sweeping view of the German defences not only off to the east and 'A' Trench but a good way to the west and rearwards, though not as far as the farm. While McLeod didn't mention it specifically, it was not lost on Bradford that they were surrounded on three sides with little or no protection from the left, where the line simply faded away to nothing. And that was precisely where the strongest concentration of the enemy seemed to be.

Captain McLeod began to appraise Captain Bradford of the situation. The skies were clearing now and the dawn was bright enough to see all that was necessary.

'That train track over there is held by the enemy. It's the Ypres – Staden railroad. As near as I can figure it's about two miles away. You still see the occasional train go by but God knows what they're carrying.'

McLeod stood on the fire step alongside Bradford and was some minutes into a comprehensive briefing. Both men ducked down as a sharp crack was heard and the whine of the bullet a fraction of a second later whizzed overhead. It had certainly been meant for one of them. McLeod grinned, showing a set of white teeth with one of the front ones missing from the bottom row. The man was about thirty but Bradford thought he was older. He was unshaven and his eyes were red-rimmed but he appeared to be brimming with nervous energy. He was courteous but brusque, and had not gone into the horrors of relieving the trench system from the previous occupants; it would not help to clarify the present position so there was no point.

He explained that the colourfully dressed troops whose bodies were buried all around them were Zouaves. He had never met a live one, but somewhere, back in the short history of this trench, war must have been a more civilised affair than it was today. Once they had had the time to bury their dead decently, but recent shelling had disinterred more than a few. Then came the gas.

Chapter 27

Boetleer's Farm, 0330 hours, Sunday 25th April 1915

The lads were delighted to be offered strange cigarettes. Ted fought to extricate himself from his rifle strap and stared ruefully at the soaking weapon. Then the order came to divest themselves of all the extra ordnance they had carried for so long. An exhausted cheer went up that was uncontested by the officers or NCOs. Ted felt his shoulders rise as the awful weight was stripped away. He had never felt so light. He sat on the fire step and grinned at Willy Maddison, inhaling approvingly on a tasty, ready-made tab the scruffy young man had offered. The smoke hit his lungs and he exhaled gratefully, thanking God that they had made it to their objective without a scratch. He moved his right foot to make it more comfortable but it seemed to roll over something that came apart at the weight of his boot. He looked down and his eyes widened as he saw that he was resting his foot on the ankle of the bottom half of a body.

He had never seen entrails close up before, never mind rotten ones but what fascinated him the most was the fact that as he moved his boot backward and forward he could actually rotate the ankle he was resting on through 180 degrees. He was more fascinated than revolted and continued to rotate the foot, spellbound by the disproportionately loud sound of bone grating on bone. With a twist of his boot he could make the foot (why did it have no boot?) face either way he liked.

'Piss off Ted will you man?' It was Fat Harry, looking distinctly ashen as he watched. Ted shuddered as if he had just realised what he was doing and jerked his boot away from the body. 'Sorry Harry. Sorry, mate.'

He blinked hard and looked round the trench. A few moments ago it had been a haven. It had been somewhere to stop and rest and get your breath back after a run that seemed to take forever, where at any moment you could be shot through the head by a sniper or blown to bits by artillery. It had been a refuge from the storm of steel that had never come, and a place where grateful comrades in arms offered you a ready-made cigarette without even asking your name.

Ted closed his eyes, inhaled on his tab and pressed his lips hard together for a second before exhaling and opening his eyes once more.

What refuge?

The trench was filthy, flooded, rat infested and full of corpses in every state of corruption. The smell was abominable and the taste was worse. The lads were learning to recognise some of the odours now. The stench of old, black blood was sweet and cloying while mouldering flesh was sharp and pungent. Gas was in there too, giving the slight tingling in the nose, the faint drying of the eyes. It was the reek which terrified them more than anything else. They knew only too well that when it wasn't being blown along by the breeze it settled insidiously into low-lying areas and stayed there: areas like the deepest part of a trench, or in a dugout, the very places a man would hide himself away from the shells and bullets.

* * * * *

Suddenly, incongruously, the sharp, fresh scent of young mustard invaded Ted's senses and it was fresh and alive and intoxicating. For a second he was back in Durham as a child, racing through the fields at Grange Farm on some wild fantasy or other, where perilous beasts pursued the Sunniside Smiths who laughed in the face of such danger and still made it back to Mam in time for tea.

There were no beasts here, though, only men doing horrifying things to each other in the name of God alone knew what. God? God wouldn't allow all this shit! Maybe he was powerless to stop it or maybe he had just turned his back in shame, disgusted at the brutality men displayed towards one another. It was at that moment, with a shudder so small it would be imperceptible to anyone watching him, that Ted Smith first began to doubt the existence of the Almighty.

Without ever a shot being fired at him, in this remorseless, relentless and totally fucking pointless war with its dead horses that hadn't done anything to anybody and its fat rats and sleek looking bloody crows so gorged on human flesh that they could hardly fly, Ted felt a tear well in his eye as he surveyed the cold inferno. The shudder may have been small on the outside but it shook him to the very depths of his soul. He wasn't sure whether he believed in the Lord God any more and he didn't know what to do. He wanted Mam and he wanted Bertha to have her locket and he wanted to go home. He wanted to tell Cockney Joe about Lettie and he wanted his brother back. Suddenly a clammy, stinking body slid harshly down beside him, jerking him from his reverie. It was Billy Robson with a ready-made tab between his lips and an enamel mug full of strong, black coffee in his fist. Ted couldn't help but smile weakly at his friend who really did look like the cat who got the cream.

'This is the life, eh?' he said with a satisfying belch. 'I got this off my Canadian mate Peter, and he's a sergeant. What do you think off that, eh?'

He stood up again and raised the mug in a generous salute to someone further down the trench that Ted could not see. Then he farted loud and long as he spilled the coffee all over Ted's knees. The scalding liquid made him jerk to his feet as he gasped in pain but the sting was forgotten in an instant. He was about to remonstrate when he noticed the noise was coming from a gash in Billy's throat – it was like a small mouth and was expelling blood in a fine, gassy spray. Ted nearly gagged as he realised he was inhaling it. Billy's face was one of complete surprise as he slowly turned his head to stare uncomprehendingly at Ted. He collapsed like a sack of shit to lie face down at the bottom of the trench, dead as a doornail.

All the Durhams stared uncomprehending as the legs slowly stopped twitching and the body lay still. Everyone was aware of a faint whistling, like somebody was whirling a piece of rope around and around, then suddenly the noise turned into a series of sharp cracks and they knew they were being fired upon.

Nobody had heard the shot that ended Billy's life but the sudden fusillade that followed had the Durhams staring numbly around them. The Canadians didn't wait for the order but snatched up their rifles and leaped onto the fire step to man the trench.

'Fill the gaps, lads. On your feet and fill the gaps.'

The familiar borders twang of Corporal Lawrie punched through the staccato rattle of the rifle fire. Tommy was first up and grabbed Ted roughly by the arm. He had no time to protest as he was swung around and had to jump onto the fire step or crash his shins into it. He remembered to keep his head down, though. Out of the corner of his eye he saw Lieutenant Flett splashing back along the trench, darting nimbly around the dead and accompanied by a much older Canadian captain.

'Fire at will, lads.' It was Lawrie again. 'But don't waste your ammo, eh!'

Ted was dreadfully aware of the soft cloth cap perched on top of his head. He felt completely naked as he heard the bullets humming around him. If he listened carefully he could differentiate between the reports of the British rifles and the German ones, which seemed to be much duller. He fancied he could even tell the difference between the 303s and the Canadian weapons.

A violent punch on the arm snapped him back to the present.

'Shoot the bastards, will you, man!'

It was Tommy Raper, eyes all swollen and red with tears spilling profusely down his cheeks, but a look of grim determination was set into his face like stone as he pulled the trigger.

Ted felt his neck go red as he raised his head a fraction above the sandbag that topped the pathetic breastwork of sodden soil. About a hundred and fifty yards away across a field of trampled corn he could see a similar line of sandbags with the tops of helmeted heads appearing and disappearing in a curious rhythm that was somehow in tune with the crackling of the rifles. Why was there no barbed wire? He noticed a faint, slightly shiny groove in the coarse weave of his sandbag. This must be where the soldiers before him had rested their weapons to fire upon the enemy. But why weren't they here now? How many had died on this very spot? He stole a glance behind him at the remnants of the dead strewn on the trench floor but the jumble of bodies made it impossible to tell which of them had stood here to be struck dead by a German bullet.

Ted inhaled a deep, shuddering breath and raised his rifle to rest it along the glossy groove in the sandbag. He frowned as he noticed the bullet hole in the centre of the groove. The stock felt cold and wet against his cheek and he was worried that it wouldn't work after the soaking it had just received in the deep trench. Feeling very aware of his own mortality he squinted along the sights and took aim at a dull, grey helmeted head.

Here, in a filthy, flooded ditch choked with dead and wounded, 2505 Edward Smith, private soldier of the Eighth Battalion, Durham Light Infantry felt a lump swell his throat. For the first time in his young life he squeezed the trigger of his rifle to purposefully kill a fellow human being.

The report of the weapon seemed much louder and slower than it had ever been in training and he watched in fascination as the distant soldier rose up out of the trench as if being plucked by an invisible hand, his arms whirling in a strangely clumsy manner as he fell back and disappeared.

Ted's bottom lip began to tremble and hot tears filled his eyes. He crashed the bolt back and forward again, taking comfort in the familiarity of the weapon as it nestled against his cheek. Anger at the Germans swelled in him and he understood now why Tommy Raper was firing so determinedly beside him.

Ted cracked off another shot and turned to look at Tommy but he wasn't there any more: a grimy Canadian private in shirtsleeves and with his braces dangling around his trousers grinned back.

'There's never a good time to go for a shit, is there, buddy?'

Where the Hell was Tommy? Ted ducked down and stole a glance around. There he was, sat down on top of a couple of corpses with his back against the rear of the trench. His eyes were open and he had a look of complete surprise frozen to his face. He was stone dead. Ted's mouth fell open and he tried to say his friend's name but he couldn't. There wasn't a mark on the man; he couldn't be dead, not after Billy. *He couldn't.*

A loud whooshing suddenly noise filled his head and he felt hot then cold in quick succession. The Canadian soldier stooped down and firmly, grasped Ted's arm and shook it. He was looking right into his face and speaking gently. Ted smelled tobacco on his breath.

'You have to shoot back, son. You have to shoot back... OK?'

After a moment the dizziness passed and Ted nodded dumbly. The strong grasp on his arm lifted him firmly back up. 'You OK now?'

He nodded again.

'Don't think about it, son, just shoot. And don't get into a regular pattern or they'll pick you off like choppin' wood. Watch for anybody climbing out of the trench and take 'em down first, OK?'

Another nod. He felt faint and wanted to be sick. He was aware of the tears falling onto the sandbag to join the little puddle of water that the weight of his 303 forced up out of the weave. As bullets whipped and sang around him he began firing. He was not frightened, nor was he excited. He was a dull automaton whose job it was to inflict loss upon the enemy. He hardly took any notice as a German bullet plucked at the bag he was resting on and gently peppered his face with a tiny fountain of sand. The soldier to his right chattered the whole time, giving advice on staying alive during an enfilade and cursing the Canadian issue Model 10 Ross rifle for being bloody useless in trench warfare because it started to stick after too many shots. Sure enough, he struggled with a sticky bolt practically every other round – either it wouldn't withdraw or it wouldn't go back when it did. Ted realised he was firing three shots to the Canadian's two.

The man gave his name as Doody of the Eighth Winnipegs, otherwise known as the 'Little Black Devils'. Even under fire that made Ted smile as they grasped hands and he introduced himself as Smith of the Eighth Durhams... also known as the 'Dirty Little Imps'. They both grinned at the similarity of their titles and Doody said, 'Well we're all Boetleer's Boys now, buddy.'

In his unfamiliar, drawly accent the word seemed to come out 'Bootlace'.

He then said something about a bottle of rum in one of the dugouts and he fell back as a German bullet penetrated his brain and smashed its bloody way out of the back of his skull. He toppled down beside Tommy Raper. Ted fired on.

No one from the German side tried to leave their trenches and charge the Allied lines so Ted reckoned that they must have just woken up to the fact that reinforcements had arrived and they had to make a move to whittle them down a bit. He couldn't believe a trench could be so busy. Men were constantly running up and down, dodging the bodies or, where they were too thick on the ground, just hunching down and running along on top of them.

There were stretcher-bearers trying to dress the wounded. There were messengers shouting out the names of officers for whom they had instructions or information. There were runners in little groups following an order to fill a gap where too many soldiers had fallen and rifle fire was thinning noticeably enough for the enemy to spot. There were lads with tea chests full of ammunition, which they were distributing along the length of the trench as far as the deep channel and beyond that was 'A' Company – they had to take care of themselves. Teams of men with great bandoliers of machine gun ammunition wrapped about them came from both directions and went in both directions. What the Hell was that all about?

Above the shouted commands, directives, and encouragement were the awful cries of the wounded. How can so many sounds all be so neatly sub-divided and heard so clearly? There were shrieks and cries of pain and shrill screams of torture. Some were cut short abruptly and some faded in agonising torment. The despairing moans and pleas were the worst. Down to his left, a Durham lad Ted knew by sight, was sitting on the hip of a rotting Frenchy and mewling for his Mam. Both his arms hung uselessly at his sides and blood was bubbling from his mouth. There could never have been a lonelier sound on this earth than that boy's soft howling. Amid all the order and all the chaos, all the bullets and all the barked orders, that lad might as well have been on an island.

Somehow, there was a change. Ted didn't know exactly what it was but something had altered in the order of the trench. There were precious few men near him and he was beginning to feel terribly exposed when half a dozen Durham lads suddenly ran round the corner from the machine gun emplacement and jumped onto the fire step either side of him. There were Billy Trow and Arthur Davison, the two Sacriston lads, and the welcome, bespectacled face of Tom Dodds. He didn't know the others and he didn't care. He kept firing at anything that looked vaguely like it could be killed and tried to ignore the fresh piles of horror that were heaping up around him.

'Canadians are going!' It was Tom screaming the information unnecessarily loudly into Ted's ear. 'We'll be on our own in a tick.'

That was it! That was the change. All the orders and messengers and rearrangements of the men were to allow the orderly exchange of positions as the Durhams had manned the trench, allowing the Canadians to be relieved. Yes, that was it. There were only Durhams on the fire step now and the Winnipegs were down amongst the shit and death and filing towards the right, towards the place where the Durhams had entered not half an hour ago.

There were rapid farewells and Godspeeds, all done on the run, and Ted was jerked out of his concentration by a tugging at his tunic. A big Canadian gave him a broken-toothed grin and held up his slender, good-looking rifle.

'Swap you this for yours, buddy,' he said with an ill-hidden edge to his voice. 'She's a good marksman's weapon, better than your 303. I couldn't say how many Fritz's I've finished with her. Go on, buddy, I'll throw in a couple of packs of chaw. C'mon buddy, whadya say, huh?'

Ted could practically feel the underlying panic in the soldier's voice, since he was clearly uncomfortable about stopping when all of his comrades were bustling past.

'C'mon buddy. Please, huh?'

Ted didn't know what to say to the man, who was obviously ill-at-ease with his weapon and was desperate to possess a Lee Enfield.

Before he could reply Ted was relieved to hear the authoritative voice of a burly Canadian NCO scream at the man to rejoin the rest of his countrymen.

Ted breathed a shuddering sigh and kept firing. Soon there were mostly the Durhams and the dead left. For ten or fifteen minutes they fired on. The German enfilade had not lessened one bit when suddenly and faintly there came the echo of a collective cry of dismay from way out to the right of the trench system. All the lads turned their heads to see lines of tiny figures, just visible in the early morning light, in the open field, trying to make an ordered withdrawal. There seemed pitifully few now that they were no longer confined by the claustrophobic Hell of the trench. The little figures were attempting to fire and withdraw but even at that distance Ted could make out some odd behaviour. Some of the soldiers were stabbing their rifles, barrel first, into the ground and kicking down on them, or they had unfixed their bayonets and were smashing the heavy handle onto the firing mechanism. Something was clearly wrong and the knowledge settled swiftly on the dismayed Durhams like the Shadow of Death itself.

'Redouble your fire, lads. Draw the Hun's attention. Come on you bastards, FIRE!'

It was Lance Corporal Carter's thick Yorkshire accent and he was dead right.

Where was Corporal Lawrie? Ted fired.

Crash the bolt back. Crash the bolt forward. Change the clip when nowt happened and do it all again.

At least they had plenty of ammo. The whole line intensified its labours in an effort to draw the enemy fire away from the stricken Winnipegs who had thinned out in order to present a lesser target but had astonishingly still maintained a sense of order under the scornful fire. Then the unmistakable clatter of a machine gun erupted over the already jarring din and a cry of dismay rippled back from 'A' Company, who were nearest the Canadians. It echoed right down through the trench system to Ted and his mates practically at the other end.

The little figures in the open field were being contemptuously cut down like wheat, spinning, twisting, dancing and dropping as the blizzard of lead swept through them.

Not one of them turned and ran. Despite the mounting numbers of their dead and dying, everyone still on his feet continued to fire upon the enemy as they withdrew. Precious few of them survived, however, and it left a bitter taste in the mouths of the Durhams that the brave men whom they had relieved such a short time ago died so pointlessly.

With the slaughter of the Winnipegs the German fire began to dwindle and in a few minutes had virtually ended. There appeared to have been no ceasefire ordered but, apart from the odd crack of somebody taking a pot shot, the enemy seemed to have finished with the war for now. This was the bit at Morfa Camp where some NCO ran along making up a butcher's bill for the CO but apart from Lance Corporal Carter quietly telling the lads to pack the shooting in whilst keeping their eyes open in case the bastards try to charge the trench, it was as if the rulebook had been completely forgotten.

Ted looked blankly around and nearly jumped out of his skin when his eyes alighted once again on the young lad with the useless arms. He was still alive and looking at Ted with an expression of pure hatred.

What did I do?

Was it that Ted was unscathed? Was it that he had ignored the boy during the height of the gun battle? What the Hell had he done? The lad was trying to say something, his lips moving over blood-covered teeth as his glazed eyes bored straight into Ted's. It was no good. Ted shrugged himself off the fire step and tried not to stumble over the corpses as he made his way towards the stricken soldier. There was no apparent wound on the lad, which was unsettling considering he was blowing bloody bubbles as he breathed and his arms hung unnaturally slack and lifeless.

He offered a cigarette, which was always a safe thing to do. It was all so much simpler at Morfa, everyone did as they were supposed to do and it was absolutely bugger all like this. The lad shook his head, the least of movements, almost imperceptible, and the look of malice was as strong as ever. His lips moved as if he wanted to speak and Ted moved closer despite being nauseated by the sight of the watery, bubbling blood.

'What is it mate? What can I do, eh?'

The lips moved again and made a curious hissing sound but no sense came out. Ted moved closer. With a great effort the chest rose and fell and Ted overcame his revulsion and put his ear close to the frothing red mouth.

'Bastard!'

The word was a hiss but it was just clear enough. Ted started and moved to look into the youth's face just in time to receive a face full of thin blood as the lad spat at him. Ted gasped loudly and nearly retched with the sudden shock of this attack. His face was covered in blood and spittle and it smelled disgusting. He involuntarily ran his tongue across his top lip and it was all he could do to stop himself from vomiting. He shook his head and blinked. He didn't understand. What had he done?

Suddenly he was being shouldered out of the way as a couple of soldiers with a stretcher arrived on the scene and without a word unceremoniously dumped the lad on it and carted him off, slipping and sliding over the corpses, towards the centre of the trench system.

Things remained quiet for a couple of hours, which gave the men a chance to brew some coffee, a pleasant novelty for the inveterate tea-drinkers. For a while all was quiet apart from some subdued chatter and the occasional sound of vomiting.

It was coming on for eight o' clock and the trench was now in some sort of order. The men had been spaced as well as circumstances would allow and duties had been told off. An oddly familiar roar sounded above the trench and everything darkened momentarily as a shadow swept over the crouching men and was gone: an aeroplane. This time a German aeroplane swooping low along the trench. Was this why the enemy had ceased firing? The lads watched as it gained height, the engine making a strange, tinny noise as it laboured and sputtered under the pilot's instruction.

One or two bright sparks took a pot shot but with no effect. After perhaps a minute the aircraft returned flying in the opposite direction and along exactly the same path but now much higher. It was a strange looking thing, with only one set of wings instead of the usual two. They were designed more along the lines of a real bird, making it seem as if the lads were being stalked by some strange, man-made bird of prey. Then everyone noticed silver metal shreds floating down into the trench. In the still, early morning air it drifted down like snow, the bulk of it landing silently over the deep communication trench in the middle. Even in the midst of Hell the lads wondered what game the Hun was up to now.

Eventually it became obvious that they were up to nothing so a clear-up was ordered. Every second man stayed on lookout while the ones in between sank down onto the fire step and either lit a tab, closed their eyes or stared around in hushed horror prior to trying to make some sense of the carnage. There were new heaps of freshly slaughtered men that added to the ever-growing pile of corpses that was threatening to fill the trench to the brim and spill the living out onto no man's land. Ted inhaled hard on his tab, feeling the fierce heat of the smoke inside him. God, but it had gone quiet. Even the wounded weren't making much noise.

Ted slowly pulled a shaking hand across his face and stared at the broad red streak on his palm. He tried to put his tab between his lips but his hands suddenly began to shake uncontrollably. He doubled them into fists and after a while the shaking subsided.

A hand landed gently on his shoulder.

'Christ, Jacky, I thought you were dead, man. Where did you go?'

'On your feet, Ted, and look like you're doing something, will you, man? If any bugger catches you like this they'll shoot you faster than the Germans.'

The other Durhams were clearing the fire steps of dead and wounded, attempting to pile them up at the rear of the trench as protection from shelling. The original trench seemed to have no earth piled up behind it, which would make things very dangerous should a shell land there. Hadn't the Frenchies thought of that? Sadly the only material available to effect such protection was the dead bodies of their fallen comrades.

There was a dreadful air of tense uncertainty. No one had given any direct orders so none of the men knew whether what they were doing was right or wrong, but clearing the trench was sensible, wasn't it? Ted joined the lads, grabbing the arm of a fat Canadian corpse that was kneeling where it had slid down after being shot through the face. Ted stared with venom at the neat hole near the soldier's eye and his lip curled. *German bastards!*

As he tugged, the body fell back off the step and, with a loud gurgle like water going down a plughole, a couple of pints of dark red blood splashed out of its mouth in a fountain of stink. The blood was all over Ted's puttees but he was past caring now. He tried to lay the body on its back but the weight was too great and he just let it flop into a heap amongst the bodies and the spent shell cases.

With the odd snipers' bullet whining overhead, the same scene was being repeated all up and down this grubby scratch in the mud that contained so many more dead than living.

Chapter 28

Boetleer's Farm, 0830 hours, Sunday 25th April 1915

After a few minutes, distant voices were heard barking orders. From around the corner from the machine gun emplacement burst the wiry frame of Sergeant Hanson shouting for everyone to continue manning the fire step – a lull in firing lasting this long meant the enemy was up to something and the line should be at the ready, just in case. Hadn't they learned a bloody thing in training? At the same time the booming voice of Sergeant Malone could clearly be heard from the opposite direction commanding every second man to come down off the fire step to help see to the wounded, and hadn't they learned any bloody thing in training? Malone hove into view and for a few seconds neither NCO even recognised each other as they continued to bellow orders from about eight feet apart. They both became aware of the situation at the same instant. Their expressions were almost comical as they confronted one another in hostile silence, moustaches bristling. The showdown was to be stillborn, however, caused by the arrival of Lieutenant Brass who, for some reason, had divested himself of his jacket. Grins were instantly wiped off faces as the two senior NCOs snapped ramrod straight and saluted. Hanson was first to set the status quo straight.

'Sir. Awaiting your orders, sir.'

Lieutenant Brass's eyes darted rapidly from one to the other. He may have been young but he was far from green. In a few seconds he had gathered his thoughts and made his decisions.

'Sergeant Malone, Sergeant Hanson, let us make the most of this. Take a company of men and remove the dead from here as far back as the communication trench. Pile them up to the rear. I want a clear run for the men along the entire length of the trench...' He paused for a second as the crack from a German rifle was heard off to the left. '... well get on with it then.'

It all sounded such easy common sense, and of course he was right. The dead were dead and that was that. Never mind if Billy Robson and Tommy Raper were amongst them. Never mind if every one of 'the dead' had a mother or a sweetheart or a wife. They were in the bloody way and when the shooting began again the lads would be in a far better position to fight back if they weren't hampered by having to dodge round a load of bodies that could trip them up. Soon the two senior NCOs were barking orders and encouragement and the trench was gradually pulled out of the jaws of chaos. One or two of the fire step lads were even issued with periscopes so that they could keep an eye on the enemy safely. The wounded were taken towards the centre of the system and placed in the dugouts where possible.

Ted was put to repairing the breastwork with Joe Blenkiron, one of the brothers from the machine gun squad, and Charlie Thompson. Between the three of them they had to reinforce their section of breastwork that was sliding into the trench under the weight of the sandbags. It was slow, dirty work and you had to watch out for snipers but Ted was grateful for being in the open and not having to handle the bodies that the other lads were gradually clearing away.

Young Joe was a mine of information and gossip despite only having been in the trench the same time as the rest of the Durhams. Since the company had become parted from its own machine guns, which were still on a wagon somewhere down the line, the brothers had been sent to take over the machine gun emplacements from the Winnipegs, but because Captain McLeod had said his lads were to stay on, it left them a bit spare.

About ten yards to the right of Ted's working party, George Moody was taking an unofficial break from tidying up bits of bodies and was being sick as a dog when a low whistling noise filled the sky. There was no warning, no signal, just the plop of shells in mud and the eternity of a split second until they detonated with all the force that Hell and Germany could put together. Ted sat down hard on the fire step and froze. His mouth was open as he dragged in the air that punched and eddied around him. Only his head moved: but too slowly. He continually tried to catch up on where the nightmare was happening but he found he was repeatedly a second behind the disinterment of skulls and bones that leaped from the earth with new life at every explosion, only just catching the disembowelling of a Canadian machine gunner as his attention turned to the slop of guts that had landed, purple and writhing, on his knees.

The explosions were continuous now, like a long rumble of thunder. They were not all buried shells either: some exploded in mid-air sending lethal shards of hot shrapnel spinning and slicing through anything, flesh included, that lay in its path. He caught Dicky Howell, eyes wide and beseeching, sinking slowly to his knees, his arms reaching out towards nothing. Ted frowned. There wasn't a mark on him! Then Lance Corporal Carter pitched forward to reveal his glistening spine, all shiny reds and whites along with his still trembling lungs surrounded by the remains of his sodden, khaki tunic. There was a horrible farting noise, quite separate from the clamour of the shells as Lance Corporal Carter's bowels relaxed in death staining the already blood-soaked material even further.

This isn't it! This isn't facing the enemy across no man's land and yelling defiance as you advance!

A shrill scream, like a distressed girl, dragged his attention to Joe Blenkiron's last moments of life as he was nearly cut in half by God knows what and with his dying breath was trying to push his stomach back under his ribs. Charlie Thompson, who had been standing next to him, was a headless, twitching corpse.

The smell of shit and cordite was everywhere and Ted stood up at a crouch and bolted, scrambling over corpses and spent bullet cases. He had no idea whether he went left or right but he had to escape this Hellhole. He was conscious that there were other soldiers running the same way as him. Little gobbets of flesh continued to hiss around his face and the red mist was everywhere. Suddenly he went deaf and he could go no further as the group slowed to an abrupt halt.

A familiar voice rang out above the din. It sounded like it was far away, or under water or something. Then the borders accent clicked! It was Corporal Lawrie, somehow still alive. The words came faintly even though he was only a couple of yards to the front.

'Keep down lads. Just keep down. There's nothing we can do until the shelling stops. Just keep your heads down. Well done, Private Walton. Well done, Smith. Just stay low, lads.'

Well done? I was running away!

There was an eddy in the tangle of men as a couple of the Durham machine gunners forced their way through against the pack. They were laden with belts of machine gun ammunition and obviously destined for the gun emplacement next to where Ted had just been working.

The front soldier was the other Blenkiron brother, Robin, and as he caught Ted's eye he gave a brazen wink. Ted shook some life into himself and with an effort winked back, though he was aware he was not smiling and his mouth was still open.

Don't go... you'll see your brother...

What a fucking embarrassment! All this ammo and no machine guns. But the lads were showing the best of courage under their first terrible shelling, the accuracy of which was courtesy of the German aircraft and its silver foil markers. The lads were proving that they were all out to assist their comrades any way they could and even with no machine guns of their own were more than willing to risk life and limb supplying the Canadian soldiers with our ammo. Pity it wouldn't fit!

Suddenly Ted's attention was drawn away from the machine gunners and the shelling. As he kneeled in the red mud of the trench he saw something in front of him, in arm's reach, which was worth all the gold and jewels in the world. Everybody gets shot in the head. Everybody gets their head blown off. Half floating and half stuck in the mud as if it were a vessel that had run aground was an upside down Frenchy tin hat, exposed by the clearance of the corpses. Granted it still had remnants of hair and skin inside it but nevertheless it was a helmet. A spare one.

The noise of the shelling appeared to fall away as Ted concentrated on his newfound treasure, but before he could reach out his hand a huge explosion from the machine gun emplacement heralded the destruction of one of the weapons and its crew. The earth began to undulate beneath his feet. A direct hit on a nearby dugout had collapsed it completely, burying dead and living alike and sending shock waves through the ground like ripples through water.

Suddenly, Ted was back down the pit on the day of the tunnel collapse that had trapped him and broken his leg. Then he was down the pit again witnessing the fall that had killed Robert.

Earth was not solid stuff at all. It was as fragile as the clouds and capable of being tossed this way and that at the whim of the explosive artillery in the same manner as a breeze could toss a feather. That meant he wasn't safe in the trench and that in turn meant he wasn't safe anywhere. The sharp pain in his back was Corporal Lawrie hitting him with his rifle butt.

'Pull your bloody self together, you monger!'

The words were still distorted and distant but Ted straightened up. The rheumy, probing eyes of the NCO seemed to bore into Ted's own until, with a stabbing thumbs up, he patted him roughly on the shoulder and was gone. An explosion behind him tossed some of the bodies that had been heaped to the rear of the trench back into it. Ted stared at the tattered remnants for a few seconds and then felt the cold, damp stillness. The shelling had stopped. Now all he could hear was a ferocious whistling in his head.

The helmet! He turned, only to see a calloused hand snatch the trophy from the earth and a big, loping Durham running, stumbling, kicking up bullet cases as he headed in the direction of the flooded trench. But everyone else was running the other way, towards Ted. He recognised Jimmy Barker and a couple of the others and they were shouting something. Words came to him faintly but he got the gist of what was going on.

'The Germans are coming.'

As the men ran past someone grabbed him roughly by the arm and whirled him about. Suddenly he was clambering over the corpses again and heading back towards the machine gun emplacement up at the end. He was behind a soldier who was dragging a bandolier of machine gun shells behind him, mouthing every obscenity about the Germans he could think of in a shrill, hysterical voice. The bandolier bounced and snaked towards the machine guns as if it had a life of its own and he tried not to step on it. He risked poking his head up for a second and there they were: swarms of the buggers. He was shocked at how near they were. They had already covered half the gap towards him and because of the lack of wire and barriers in no man's land, were coming at a Hell of a lick and screaming like maniacs.

They were big sods as well, some in grey uniforms and some in blue. All had bayonets fixed and expressions on their faces that left no doubt as to the fate of the Allies if they made it into the trench. They hurled themselves onward, right into the teeth of the bullets. Were they bloody mad?

He ducked back down again. There was a sudden increase in gunfire ahead of the stumbling lads, accompanied by the unmistakable brattle of the machine guns as they opened up. He couldn't hear anything properly and it was a bloody nuisance. Hoping that remaining with the body of men would be enough to keep him out of trouble he lurched forward and rounded the sharp corner into the machine gun emplacements. The noise increased five-fold as the chattering monsters came in sight. Incredibly, one or two of the Canadian crewmen were smoking cigarettes as their machines spat death at the enemy. Corporal Tremaine waved them wildly to the fire step. In many places the corpses of their own men had reinforced the step but this was no time to comment. Cockney Joe was already there and so was John Merrigan, and further to the left were Harry Clarke and Corporal Huggins, all firing as fast as they could. They all had bayonets fixed.

The newcomers roughly barged their way in between the others and slapped their rifles onto the muddy remains of the sandbags. Ted was jolted on his right by the forceful arrival of George Moody grinning a toothy grin.

'Room for a littl'un, Teddy boy?'

Ted was glad to be next to his mate. George appeared to be eyeing up the approaching Hun with a detached air, squinting every so often. It was well known that he had the best eyesight out of all the lads and equally well known that he wanted it to be kept quiet as well. No sticking him on post duty where he could get his bloody head shot off, not if he could help it.

Ted stole a glance around the trench. Everybody seemed to be firing away so bloody calmly. Surely he couldn't be the only one horrified by the abominations he was witnessing, the only one whose head was ringing and whose heart was beating fast enough to burst out of his ribs? There was no lining up and taking aim here. There were so many of them it was down to just cracking off as many shots as possible into the wall of grey and blue to slow them down.

Crash the bolt back, crash the bolt forward.

The sudden increase in firepower halted the German attack less than twenty yards from the trench. This was different to sniping away at men in the distance. This was bloody butchery. Ted thought of it as a race. If you didn't bring them down they'd swamp the trench and it would be the hand-to-hand stuff. He didn't fancy that. Somehow, without a word, the firepower increased yet again as the men fell into their stride. There was a natural rhythm that went with this sort of shooting and it only came when the last dregs of conscience were drained from the men. The Germans had stopped being human beings and were now simply targets to be removed as rapidly as possible before they overran the stinking gash in the ground that was the lads' last haven.

It was as if the enemy had run into an invisible wall and man after man fell to the ground either screaming or deathly silent. Deep, guttural voices barked commands and amazingly, under the withering fire the Germans organised themselves into formation and retreated in half-decent order, firing rank on rank, until they were near enough to their own trenches to cut and run under a tremendous volley of covering fire that made all the lads duck down in shock and fear.

The ceasefire was called and a spontaneous cheer flashed across the Durhams that the NCOs could not prevent. A communal sigh of relief ran along the lines, which was washed away as they looked around and discovered the extent of those who had fallen during the attack.

Then the bird-like aeroplane came again, just to rub it in.

'Bastard!' spat George, looking up at the aircraft as it buzzed overhead.

'Where's our bloody artillery? That's what I want to know.'

Captain McLeod, Captain Bradford and Lieutenant Flett were at the extreme end of the trench, looking across to the German lines, alternately using a periscope and bobbing their heads up for a second. They appeared to be discussing some increased activity in that locality and it was not lost on the Durhams who were trying to follow what was going on, that there was an alarming number of dead Germans right at the end of the trench system and even a bit around to the rear of it.

They had seen the weak link! They had spotted the fact that the extreme left edge of the trench came to a dead stop and that there was nothing but fields all the way back to Boetleers Farm and the main Allied line. If the enemy got around the edge, the Durhams would be completely surrounded and done for.

Then they came again, charging and screaming.

That caught the lads on the hop good and proper but that was probably the plan. Ted had to hand it to them for being fearless sods. This time the attack was more to the left where the trench ended and the lads were hard put to keep the enemy out this time. Volley after volley, everyone firing at will, created a curtain of lead that the Germans simply couldn't penetrate, though it was not for the want of trying. There was an air of panic in the trench this time. The Hun had definitely spotted that the left end of the trench was vulnerable to attack and if it weren't for the Canadian machine guns and their crews every Allied soldier would have been mincemeat.

Not many minutes ago Ted had never taken a life. Now he had no idea how many people he had killed. Beside him, George Moody froze at the sight of a knot of Germans, apparently immune to British bullets, stampeding right up to the trench.

Ted managed to thump him on the side of the head with his elbow to pull him back into action immediately prior to thrusting his bayoneted 303 up and into the thigh of a big Hun in a blue uniform who was sailing over his head in a mighty leap. The man screamed as the bayonet ripped deep into the flesh inside his thigh and the momentum carried Ted over onto his back. With a bone-jarring crash he hit the corpse-strewn mud and blinked for a second before realising he was face to face with the soldier he had stuck. The man was huge, with a waxed moustache like the Kaiser's and hate-filled steel grey eyes. He mouthed something in his foreign tongue and struggled to lurch towards Ted, trying to heft his rifle up.

But Ted was faster. He tried to pull his rifle away from the Hun but it seemed to be stuck fast in his leg. Another tug brought a gasp of agony from the man and with the scraping sound of steel on bone. His bayonet was free.

A fountain of blood surged unbelievably high into the air, spraying everything with a shiny, new red as it settled like heavy rain. The soldier looked at his own blood gushing out of the wound. It was as if he was unable to believe so much could come out so quickly. He turned his gaze upon Ted, who watched the hatred in those steel eyes turn to disbelief and finally fade, like a lamp using the last of its oil. The light in the eyes went out.

The rest of the battle seemed like miles away until a bayonet flashed uncomfortably close to Ted's face and he looked up to see George Moody shouting at a big German who was scrabbling on top of him, trying to pin him down and stick him. George was crying copiously as, arms flailing helplessly, he shouted at the soldier, 'Gerroff me, you bastard. Gerroff me.'

There was just room for Ted to pull his rifle butt back. He did so and caught the German under the nose with a sickening crack. An oath exploded from the soldier as he dropped his weapon and stumbled backwards clutching his face, with blood gushing between his fingers. His arms fell to his sides as six inches of red steel suddenly erupted from his throat. With a scrape the bayonet disappeared and the big Hun fell sideways. Cockney Joe stood grinning at his mates – but only for a second before returning to the fire step to repel the already retreating enemy.

Ted and George joined him and fired at the retreating Hun. Again, they made an amazingly orderly retreat but this time not back to their old line. This time they were heading to the left of the machine guns where they seemed to disappear over a small rise.

Captains McLeod and Bradford were the first to sort out what was going on. Lieutenant Flett was dead with a bullet in the brain and Ted and his mates were spitting distance from the officers. Now that all was quiet again they fell to the task of getting the trench ready for the next attack. This time the use of German bodies to form heaps front and back of the trench made the danger a bit more immediate than previously. It meant the buggers had set foot in the trench. It meant that the trench was not impregnable.

The Frenchies had died defending it, as their rotting bodies had borne testament when they were disinterred by the relentless shelling of the Bosche.

The Canadians had died defending it as their gassed corpses bore confirmation.

Now the Durhams, it would seem, would die defending this redundant, useless, shitty piece of ground that wasn't even part of the proper line.

It was a vain, arrogant and completely pointless forward position that gained nothing for the Allies and cost the lives of brave men from many nationalities that had no knowledge of each other's heroic exploits against shells, shrapnel, bullets, bayonets and gas – other than from the corpses of their predecessors, disinterred or fresh on the ground to bear silent witness to inexorable death for nothing.

Ted was keeping half an eye on the two officers as he worked and there was a certain determined demeanour about the pair of them that wasn't there before the last attack. Captain Bradford waved at Sergeant Malone and Corporal Huggins, who joined him in the little group and went into deep discussion. It was coming on for midday now and the Germans seemed more determined than ever to try to take the trench. The shelling came once more, wreaking terrifying vengeance on the young English boys who had the gall to stand in the way of the mighty German Army. Then the shelling would stop, and for a second or two there would be silence until, with awful predictability, a guttural roar rang out from the German positions as they hurled themselves in sheer frenzy at the lads. Again and again they came but despite near misses they never managed to get a foothold in the trench. It seemed as if they couldn't believe that the Durhams had the fortitude, or the numbers, to see them off. Then they would retreat and the shelling would lay waste to the trench for the umpteenth time.

In truth, the lads had neither fortitude nor numbers, or anything else for that matter. If the enemy had been aware of the fact that they were down to less than half their number – and the survivors were demoralised beyond belief – then perhaps one more push would have seen them firmly in that Hellish gash in the ground, standing proud amidst the bloody rags that had once been 'A' and 'D' Companies, Eighth Durham Light Infantry. The telephone unit had been blown to bits along with its operators, and the carpet of dead was so thick it was difficult to walk upon it and still keep heads below the breastwork.

Then it stopped. The shelling ceased and the expected charge did not come. Nobody believed it, but the charge did not come. Surely the buggers were up to something.

Well, so was Captain Bradford.

When it became apparent that another onslaught was not forthcoming, a rapid exchange between Bradford and McLeod led to a shaking of hands and McLeod, with the last two of his signallers, stumbled through the trench in the direction of 'A' Company to the east in order to get back to Boetleer's Farm and report the position to Battalion Headquarters. Two Winnipeg machine gunners volunteered to stay and were made most welcome. McLeod and his courageous band had acquitted themselves with great honour and the three remaining men stumbled away, trying not to lose their footing whilst keeping their heads down. Someone started to clap. A single, solitary sound amongst the otherwise silent men. It was slow and not very loud, but then it was joined by another, and another until the trench was filled with the appreciative sound. Well did Captain McLeod deserve their thanks. If it wasn't for him and his machine gunners staying on, God knows what would have happened to the Durhams that day.

He was never seen again.

Chapter 29

Boetleer's Farm, 1300 hours, Sunday 25th April 1915

It was impossible to tidy up the trench now, for the dead well outnumbered the living, so what was the point. The orders went around just to keep heads down and try to grab something to eat. Within about half an hour some sort of order was restored and Captain Bradford had been back and forth through the system, encouraging his men and animatedly discussing plans with his officers. Ted was having a tab with Cockney Joe and Harry Clarke. None of them liked the way that the group of officers and NCOs were looking towards them as they spoke. Just then Sergeant Malone beckoned to the little group.

'I fucking knew it!' snorted Joe. But before he could say anything else he was curtly advised to shut it by Harry, who exhaled loudly through his nose and set off towards the group. All eyes were on Ted and Joe now, and it was amazing how, without their immediate neighbours moving a muscle, a clear space had miraculously appeared around the pair.

Eventually the group of officers dispersed, which Ted and Joe took as a sign that nothing further was to take place. Captain Bradford remained with Sergeant Malone, but just as Ted was breathing a sigh of relief, the officer beckoned them to join him.

With a barely audible, 'Here we fucking go,' from Joe, he and Ted stumbled over. The trench was a bit deeper here because of the machine gun emplacements so they could stand up more or less straight. The salute was returned and they were told to stand easy while the captain began to explain.

Apparently he was apprehensive about the area immediately to the east where a stretch of rising land fell away to form 'dead' ground of what might be some considerable area behind it. During the previous attacks Germans had appeared to come and go from this dead ground in significant numbers and it would be helpful to be aware of roughly how big an area this ground covered and how many of the enemy it might contain. If Sergeant Malone, accompanied by Privates Clarke, Smith and Simpson were to take advantage of the lull and reconnoitre the area, Captain Bradford would be very grateful.

The speed with which Harry saluted his willingness took the group a little by surprise. Ted saluted next followed a second later by an unenthusiastic Cockney Joe.

Bradford positively beamed at his volunteers and showered them with encouragement. He was big, bluff fellow who played rugby and cricket and was every bit as fit as the men he had trained so hard. Their task was to crawl up to the top of the rise, taking no chances, mind, and get back with a description of the lie of the land beyond and a count of the enemy.

That's it. Out and back. Shouldn't take half an hour altogether.

For a second they were plunged into shadow as the enemy aeroplane passed over them and was gone.

Then the captain was off, head down, towards the centre of the system on some other errand. The man never seemed to stand still for five minutes. Sergeant Malone waited until he was lost to view.

'Change of plan!' he said curtly. 'Private Clarke you remain in the trench. That's an order. It doesn't take four of us to count a bunch of Germans and you've got more experience than these two. We need you here.'

He nodded towards Ted and Joe. 'Right you lads, come on.'

Without even looking to see if his orders were being obeyed he climbed up onto the jumble of corpses, keeping his head low, and peeped over the lip of the trench. With a grunt he took off his cloth cap and held it about six inches above the ground, slowly moving it back and forth. After a few seconds he grunted in satisfaction and, cramming his cap back onto his head, crawled out amongst the dead. Ted and Joe were watching the exposed sergeant and the surrounding area like hawks. Malone crawled on his belly excruciatingly slowly to a position about ten feet from the lip before settling down and turning his head towards the waiting pair.

'Come on lads. You first Simpson, then you, Smith. Do what I do and you'll be fine.'

The hoarse whisper ceased and he faced forward again to set off slowly up the rising ground, staying stock still every so often and looking for all the world like any of the corpses that littered the rain-soaked ground around him. Ted watched a muttering, cursing Cockney Joe crawl about eight feet out, whereupon he gingerly followed suit. The few seconds getting out of the trench were the worst – he had never felt so exposed – but now he was face down on the pink mud, rifle in front of him, he felt a bit more secure. Where the Hell do you look? From his disadvantaged position he could just about make out Joe's heels a couple of yards ahead.

A breeze suddenly enveloped him. It was cold and fresh and smelled of hay, and all the blood and rotten flesh left his soul for a brief second. He tried to savour it but it was gone, and between him and Joe's heels was a bloated eyeless German soldier with a great gash in his belly and dried-up guts splaying out everywhere. The rats were no surprise any more, even when they emerged, red and shiny, from inside the bodies. The smell of blood and shit was back, and they crawled on. The sticky, cloying mud gave way to sparse earth and finally to meadow: proper meadow. The land was still blighted by German corpses and French skeletons though they seemed to grow sparser the closer the three got to the peak of the rising ground. This was not good. There weren't many Allied dead this far out to start with and the lads were beginning to stand out like sore thumbs. That bloody German aeroplane was still buzzing about as well. Joe started to crawl a bit faster and had to be hushed by Ted. Just because it seemed safe now didn't mean some bugger of a German wasn't going to stick his head up at the wrong moment and spot them.

Towards the top of the rise there were hardly any bodies and if anybody looked over the ridge that would be that. But they carried on, an inch at a time until Sergeant Malone, then Joe and about a minute later Ted, could see into the dead ground.

There were hundreds of the buggers, maybe even thousands. It was nearly like a proper camp with its mules and artillery limbers and motorised wagons and God knew what all else. With that many men they could overrun the trench in five minutes flat if they wanted to. But they hadn't, so what was going on?

They said nowt, but all three looked long and hard at the might of the German Army laid out in front of them. About half a mile beyond the camp the railway line was visible from the trench and a cattle train was pulling up. The three focussed hard and Ted wished George Moody with his hawk eyes was with them. The train stopped and within a few moments soldiers looking the size of ants began to disgorge from it and there were bloody loads of them.

'Well something's up, that's for sure,' muttered Sergeant Malone. 'And I don't suppose all this lot is for our benefit, either. Take a last look bonny lads, Captain Bradford will pick all our brains separately so make sure you've taken it all in.'

Ted was taking it in all right, particularly the little train in the distance. He remembered joking to Fat Harry back in Pont-de-Briques about the colour of the locomotive that took them to Cassell – baby-shite green. The tender was followed by two carriages and the rest were cattle trucks – in that order. Couldn't be... could it? Same train working for both sides? Must just be the way all Frenchies coupled their trains up, that was it. Anyway, now they were off back to the trench with information that would blow Captain Bradford's hat off. It wasn't easy going back, either. Sergeant Malone insisted that they crawl backwards this time because any dead Allied soldiers would most likely be facing the enemy, so if they were spotted and had to freeze they would look right. Also, their rifles would be pointing the right way if they were forced to fight. Ted and Joe thought it sounded bollocks but since they were going back to face Captain Bradford personally they thought it probably best not to argue.

So, minute by minute and inch by inch, they wormed their way back towards the trench. Just over half way they felt a bit more comfortable because there were so many more dead to hide amongst.

It was all going reasonably well until somebody grabbed Joe by the ankle. He froze immediately, gingerly looked round to find a young German soldier, tired tears of pain in his eyes, staring pleadingly at him. He was as young as it was possible to be and still be a soldier, and Joe was struck by the fact that he had attempted to wax his moustache into a faithful copy of Kaiser Wilhelm's own. Except that the lad's was more wax than moustache and the whole thing looked a bit pathetic, like Billy Robson's.

'Hilfe, bitte. Hilfen sie mir.'

The grip grew stronger and the voice grew louder until Sergeant Malone chimed in with a hoarse whisper that Joe shut the monger up or they were all dead. From somewhere a rifle muzzle stabbed cruelly into the temple of the wounded boy and he lay still, a puddle of dirty red swelling and then sinking into the muddy grass. A white-faced Ted jerked his head back towards the trench.

They had covered barely ten yards since the murder of the German boy when suddenly they were smothered in shadow as the aeroplane swooped low above them. They froze to the ground, comforted by the fact they were reasonably surrounded by corpses. But the aeroplane came back. There was no mistaking the fact they had been spotted. It turned tail and flew off over the rise towards the dead ground that concealed so many of the enemy.

'On your feet, laddies, we're rumbled!'

Malone was up and running fast. There was still at least a hundred yards to go and nothing for it but to try and get there before the alerted Germans could shoot them. They were up and running like the wind, jinking sideways, this way and that, as they had been taught so as to put off snipers.

Ted grimaced as he crunched through the exposed rib cage of a long-dead Frenchy. The coughing staccato of a machine gun opened up somewhere behind them, followed by bullets churning up the ground trying to tear them to shreds. They were running so fast the ground disappeared under their feet in a blur. The green of grass gave way to the pink-brown of mud. They could hear their own lads cheering them on and some were firing over their heads. Now bullets were whizzing in both directions as the alerted Germans sought to bring down the fleeing soldiers. Ted's leg hurt like Hell as he flew past Sergeant Malone and with a few feet to go gave a mighty leap, legs still pumping in mid-air. He landed with a thump against bodies and sandbags. He let go of his rifle as he rolled and everything went dark for a second. While he was still in a daze, there was another thump as the massive frame of Malone thudded in close by. Wincing in pain he managed to turn over and sit up, as hands seemed to come from everywhere to assist him. Shaking his head was a mistake.

Someone held a lighted tab to his lips and he took it gratefully with shaking hands. There was a massive roar as the sky went dark for a second but this time it was followed by another roaring shadow, and another. Everyone looked up at once to see the strange, bird-like shape of the German aeroplane disappear towards its own lines but this time pursued by two stubby green biplanes with their propellers at the back. They were harrying the enemy with their machine guns but the cheers of the lads died in their throats as the silver foil settled lightly around the trench once again.

Then Captain Bradford was there, looking at Ted with some concern before turning to an entirely composed Sergeant Malone from whom he extracted all the information about the massing of the enemy troops over the rise. Ted listened as carefully as his headache would allow and when the concise, clear report was at an end the captain turned to Ted and asked if he had anything to add. Ted felt his neck going red as he said no, Sergeant

Malone had done a grand job of passing along the facts. Then Captain Bradford was gone and Sergeant Malone was handing Ted his rifle.

'You lost this, Smith. That's a chargeable offence, you know.'

It was only when Malone reached out to gently pull the peak of Ted's cloth cap down over his eyes that he realised it was a joke.

Where was Joe? *Where the bloody Hell was Cockney Joe?* Suddenly every eye was cautiously peeping over the parados of bodies, bobbing up and down quickly so as not to become a target for a German bullet. Suddenly Tommy Dodd spotted him about thirty yards out, flat on his face and as still as a bucket. That was that then. Ted was at a loss for the thousandth time that awful day. Why does death always leave things unfinished? Sergeant Malone opened his mouth to organise the remaining lads when a sudden wild, whoop went up from no man's land. It was really hard not to stick heads up to see what was going on and only Fat Harry did, cautiously lifting the arm of a Canadian corpse with his rifle to peep through.

'It's Joe, it's bloody Joe! Give him some cover, man!'

The lads had hardly reacted when German rifle fire began to sound, but there was scarcely a second's hesitation as the ragged little crew brought their weapons to bear and began to return fire. Joe was running like the wind, his greatcoat flapping and billowing. His eyes were wild and he was laughing hysterically as he leaped and jinked his way to the trench. He was grinning from ear to ear as he bounded high into the air, bullets whipping all around him. Then the unmistakable brattle of the enemy machine gun was heard. It was just a short burst but Ted watched in horror as circles of red appeared, stitched in a diagonal line across Joe's chest.

Everything jolted into slow motion and silence as Joe glided overhead, trailing spindrifts of blood and still grinning like a Cheshire cat. He landed heavily on the blanket of bodies and lay still, face down, like a broken doll. They all looked on in dumb resignation as the blood pooled on the back of his greatcoat. No need even to turn him over. He was dead as a doornail.

Poor Joe, with his messed up mind and his messed up life. Everybody got dealt a shitty hand of cards now and again but few were as bad as Joe's, poor bugger. Well, he was out of it now.

The shooting had stopped. It seemed Fritz was content to have killed the lone Englishman. They were backing away, rifles at the ready.

Chapter 30

Boetleer's Farm, 1430 hours, Sunday 25th April 1915

Abruptly, a guttural shouting was heard from the ridge and the withdrawing huddle of Germans increased their speed without taking their eyes off the lads. The inhabitants of the trench watched as the enemy neared the crest turned tail to run back over the rise and disappear completely from view. A whistling scream came down out of the sky and the first 'plop' was heard as a shell buried itself in the mud. A split second later the carnage of saturation shelling was upon the helpless Durhams once more.

Ted did the same as everyone else, burrowing under the corpses like the rats he encountered as he did so. He was now hard up against the front trench wall and concealed under the dead. The ground moved and slid around him as explosion after explosion visited a terrible punishment upon the men. Once bright sunlight suddenly enveloped Ted as the bodies to one side of him were stripped away by a shell burst. He was momentarily fascinated by a whirling, headless torso, both arms flailing as it spun high in the air, trailing mists of red in great spirals. Then brutal darkness came again as he was suddenly thrust down and back through the fluid earth.

There was soil in his mouth and he felt as though he were being squeezed through a mangle when it came to him that he was being buried alive. He tried to scream and moved his arms in a sort of swimming motion, getting them above his head as he felt his legs being steadily compressed by the encroaching earth. Ted Smith had finished up his borrowed time and was now going to die the way he should have done, buried alive that day in June two years ago. No getting out of it this time.

Then the shelling stopped.

'Pull, you mongers, pull!'

Suddenly a great pain enveloped him. He was being hauled up by the wrists, first slowly, then ever more quickly until with an agonising wrench he was born back into the world of air and sunlight and blood. He was free to the waist and barely more than half conscious. Someone was dribbling water over his face and washing the mud out of his eyes and mouth. A knot of nausea started in his chest and rapidly rose to his throat and he vomited a mixture of phlegm and soil, feeling it stick behind the bridge of his nose. He tried to snort it away but it wouldn't move.

'Easy lad, easy Ted. We'll have you out in a jiff.'

The words were dulled by ears full of mud and a head full of pain as he tried to squint at his rescuers, but his eyes were stinging. He slid in and out of consciousness until finally he was free. Someone roughly held his eyes open whilst they were liberally deluged with dirty water and finally a bottle was held to his lips. He drank thankfully and greedily until the back of his throat caught fire as he realised it was rum. He coughed and retched a couple of times before sitting still on the newly excavated earth until his vision cleared a bit. Someone started feeling his legs, gently at first then more roughly. The hands transferred themselves to his body, then his arms. The man was looking closely at him, peering into his eyes. Ted knew him but could not place him.

'He'll do. Have to go now.'

The man was gone and someone – it was Fat Harry – thrust a rifle into his hands and patted him roughly on the shoulder.

'Welcome back, Teddy boy. Work to do, eh! Stand up when you're ready, bonny lad.'

He sat on the pile of earth and watched as things happened around him. It was raining again, that light, irritating rain the lads all hated so much. The shelling had stopped and the Huns weren't attacking. A little way along the trench Lieutenant Wilson and a party of men, including Sergeant Hanson, Corporal Huggins, Tom Dodds and young Willy Maddison were making ready to leave the trench. They looked fatigued and resigned to their fate. Tommy was trying to clean his spectacles on a wet rag when he caught Ted's eye and winked. There was no accompanying smile, though. Captain Bradford was suddenly there, shaking Wilson firmly by the hand and returning his salute.

Then they were gone – over the top. Everyone listened in silence for a while, but there were no gunshots, so they hadn't been spotted – yet.

A hand came down on Ted's shoulder and he looked up to see a serious John Merrigan who sat down beside him and offered him a tab. Ted still felt too sick and shook his aching head.

'You have to get on your feet, Teddy boy. They'll be here soon, and we have to make sure the bastards don't come round behind us again or we're done for. That's what Lieutenant Wilson and his little gang are up to.' He jerked his head to where the defensive party had exited the trench. 'You missed all the fun while you were buried in there, mate. That last salvo put paid to most of us all in one go.'

Sure enough, the horrors that decorated every inch of the fractured ground were testimony to the savage bombardment they had just endured. This part was no longer even a trench, just a big, wide 'V' shaped ditch full of every sort of remnants of humanity, floating in muddy red filth. And the rats. Only here and there stood a survivor and all were ashen-faced and silent. Ted's eyes were clearing up a bit now, but that only made him want to close them to the sights around him. Lieutenant Brass, wearing his cap but still without his tunic, appeared from somewhere with Sergeant Malone at his side, stumbling over the remains of the Durhams and rounding up a few of the men that remained to try to extend the line to the left in an attempt to fill the gap between the edge of the trench and the start of Lieutenant Wilson's defensive party.

This was crackers! It was open mustard fields without a stitch of cover. There was nothing to defend. The rain was increasing again as the party left the trench, although 'over the top' was no longer an accurate description because they simply walked to where the edge of the excavation had been, prior to the last artillery onslaught. They made their way up the now fairly gentle muddy slope until they neared the level of the field, and dropped down prone. The expected storm of bullets did not come.

There was no attempt at concealment now: just hard crawling on elbows and bellies through the field of the dead, until they were strung out in an exposed line right across the path the advancing Germans would attack through. John Merrigan had already gone whilst Fat Harry, Jacky Tait and Ted were nearly last out along with the two Canadian machine gunners.

'We should hold them up for about a minute – if we're lucky,' Fat Harry whispered to nobody in particular, and was silenced by a stare from Sergeant Malone.

They struggled, still lying face down, to release their entrenching tools from their belts to try to scratch up some sort of mound to stop bullets. The scraping of the tools, though muffled by the rain, still sounded loud enough to wake the dead, or at least the enemy.

Looking to his left Ted could see Lieutenant Wilson's lot behind a low wall next to a ruined farm building, well, more just a heap of rubble really, but better than the pathetic six-inch mound of mud that was all that stood between them and the enemy. You could lie as flat as you like here but from the top of that rise they could still shoot you in the arse. A little, grubby stream separated Lieutenant Brass' party from Lieutenant Wilson's.

Sergeant Malone tucked his watch back into his breast pocket. 'Nearly three o' clock, lads. If nowt happens until it's dark we'll nip back to the trench in shifts and grab a bite to eat, eh?'

The lads thought it was the worst bit of cheering-up they had ever heard. They all knew the chances of being alive when it got dark were shite.

Then a German aeroplane flew over them.

They were well aware of what would happen next and they were bloody right as well.

All eyes turned to the ridge and, sure enough one helmeted head popped up followed by another. They both disappeared again and shouts were heard, obviously orders being passed along. There was a muffled wave of derisory laughter too and that upset the lads more than anything. Were they really so few, so easy to beat?

A stick was thrust up into the air with a Tommy cap tied on the end. It was waved back and forth whilst some bloody comedian shouted something that made all his mates laugh again. This wasn't fair! The Durhams were new to the horrors of warfare but Ted thought that they had acquitted themselves pretty well considering. The Germans hadn't won the trench yet, had they? And they had paid dearly for trying, as well. His neck went red at the cavalier way they were being treated by the enemy and it made him harden his heart.

Another voice came from over the rise, this time firm and demanding, though nobody had a clue what the actual message was. A hearty 'Bollocks, Fritz' came from one of Lieutenant Wilson's party, which was followed by a little laughter and a sharp reprimand. All was silent now and remained so for at least five minutes. It was probably the longest five minutes the lads ever had to endure. They were no longer even sure if the Germans were going to attack any more. Mebbes they were just sheltering from the rain, smoking fags, and enjoying keeping the Durhams on their toes.

Then they came. All at bloody once! One second there was nothing and the next the air was thick with the cries of hundreds of German soldiers screaming and shouting and looking for all the world as if they would flatten the Durhams like a steamroller. Nobody waited for the order to fire, and the lads let rip into the massive wall of grey and blue. At first the firing was staccato but it didn't take them long to get into rhythm, ignoring the screaming and the bullets plucking at the earth around them and just concentrating on firing into the wall. Fat Harry wasn't the right shape for firing prone and as soon as it looked like the Germans were slowing down he attempted to kneel up to get a better shot.

One of the Canadians was shouting and lifted an arm to grab him but both men were cut down simultaneously to lie in a soggy red heap on the ground.

Ted stole a glance to his left to see how Wilson's lot were doing and his heart sank as he saw that the party was quite rightly defending from the attack in front and to the right; but they had not seen the Germans who were running up towards them from their left flank and using the low ruined walls of the farm buildings as cover.

They were surrounded on three sides.

Crash the bolt back!

Ted's party had troubles of their own, however, as the rush of screaming giants magically formed itself into ranks and fired through the rain into the Durhams like a colossal machine gun.

Crash the bolt forward!

It was absolutely bucketing bullets. It was almost as if the Germans were trying to overpower the English resistance by sheer numbers and a complete disregard for their own lives. They had no cover and had been halted some three hundred yards distant seemingly unable to gain any further ground because of the rapid and accurate fire of the lads. Ted was fascinated by the steam rising from the rifles, which were so hot the rain was evaporating from the barrels as fast as it hit them.

Grey uniforms were going down all over the place, but they would not withdraw. The Durhams on the other hand *could* not withdraw and had to keep up their extraordinary rate of fire in order to prevent the German advance. Ted thought it was like arm wrestling in the Blue Star. You were tired, you had had it and there wasn't an ounce of energy left in your aching muscles. You hadn't the strength to beat your opponent, but if you could just hang on until he packed in.

Just hang on.

They were breaking! The buggers were breaking. Some indefinable shift in the German body gave them away. One minute they were firing a storm of lead and the next they were turning tail and running back up the rise as fast as their legs would carry them. There was a stunned silence amongst the lads for a moment followed by a weak cheer and whoops of derision.

'Keep firing, you buggers. Who told you to stop? Shoot the bastards now!'

Sergeant Malone's voice boomed across no man's land and the firing recommenced. This time the shouting came from the Germans who were catcalling the cowardly English who shot retreating soldiers in the back. They continued to run until they disappeared over the crest of the rise.

'Cease fire lads, and hold your ground.'

Everyone looked to the left to see how the other party was doing and to their dismay the ruined buildings were now completely occupied by Germans, who were busily setting up robust defensive positions.

The only khaki uniforms to be seen were motionless on the ground.

No! There was Lieutenant Wilson and a bareheaded soldier, seated forlornly on a log with their hands on their heads and two big buggers of Germans covering them with their rifles. Wilson had a bloodstained bandage about his head but appeared to be holding steady. A machine gun was being dragged forward and placed behind the ruins of a low wall. In a few moments it would be firing right into the exposed line of lads.

Malone was looking around, trying to locate Lieutenant Brass. He spotted him off to the left – lying still.

'The company will withdraw back to the trench. Crawl backwards and don't take your eyes off the ridge or that bloody machine gun. Come on lads. Withdraw!'

They had no idea they could go backwards so fast, but the sight of a machine gun being rapidly assembled lent swiftness to tired bodies. The rain was making little pink rivers in the grass as it collected spilt blood and carried it back down the slope towards the trench.

They were praying, swearing, muttering or weeping as they clumsily squirmed their way back. Not in his wildest dreams had Ted thought he could take comfort in being in amongst so many of the dead, but the nearer he got to the trench the more sheltered his prone body became as he was slowly surrounded by more and more lifeless sacks of red-sodden khaki. Funny how the rats that had accompanied them on the way out were conspicuous by their absence on the way back.

Then the machine gun opened up.

It was well to Ted's right and he watched, numb with horror as the bullets arced slowly towards him, churning up chunks of grass and mud whilst dutifully gathering in the lives of the Durhams. He was amazed at how slowly the arc proceeded and how efficiently it snuffed out his comrades. Sergeant Malone was gone, not in a glorious charge, bayonet fixed and moustache bristling, but with a soft shudder of his recumbent body as he tried through sheer willpower to bury himself into the exposed mud of the field. Even after he became motionless, a fountain of crimson spurted at intervals from the back of his neck.

The chattering death came closer still, stealing the life of the last of the Canadian machine gunners as it headed towards Jacky Tait, who looked over at Ted, mouthed something through his tears and buried his face in the mud. Bullets thudded around him and moved smoothly on to Freddy Laidler who was thrown up into the air to land a lifeless rag doll. Ted's jaw dropped as he saw Jacky look up in amazement, apparently unhurt.

They didn't miss anyone else, though, killing and killing until they were a foot to Ted's right... when they stopped. A rapid conversation in German ensued as the crew cleared the blockage and Ted made peace with the Lord. He squinted against the rain, glancing up at the ridge to see loads of Germans sat watching the slaughter as if they were a crowd at a football match. They were holding coats and tarpaulin sheets over their heads to keep dry and were even smoking pipes! A rapid burst of German and the chattering death resumed... about a yard to the left of Ted. It harvested amongst others, a praying Tommy Vickers and a cursing Corporal Tremaine.

The gun stopped again. Daring a quick look Ted could see it was being dismantled. Obviously, having done its work here it was going somewhere else to wreak further havoc on the oppressed Allies. The soldiers on the rise were leaving as well.

This is it! Have to go now!

Ted was up like a startled hare and running back. He could see Jacky doing the same. They were surprisingly close and only a few bullets sang over their heads as they tumbled into the mud and gore and safety of the trench. Helping hands took them to their feet. Somehow John Merrigan was still there and so was George Moody. Everyone was looking out towards the railway in the distance where three trains were snaking their way towards the German lines.

The first one wheezed to a halt and all the wagon doors slid open at once. More Germans... hundreds of them... again! The lads were truly lost. A runner was sent to fetch Captain Bradford who looked haggard and worn out when he arrived.

His eyes were red-rimmed and he had clearly lost some of his resolve. He was left in respectful silence for a few moments as he looked helplessly as the vastly superior German numbers were swelled yet again by the arrival of the troop trains. There were only a handful of the lads left – not even fifty – and the one remaining machine gun was crewless and out of ammunition. The seconds ticked by and, at last, Captain Bradford seemed to have reached a decision. He still had his back to the lads and was staring out towards the German lines, but his shoulders rose and went back and his head lifted. When he turned it was more like the old captain. He looked at Lieutenant Wood of 'A' who had lately delivered a message and not yet been able to return to the east trench. Today, in the rain, his freckles made him look about twelve. The fact that the message was that reinforcements were on the way and they were to hang on 'at all costs' was little consolation to the weary troops.

Bradford breathed in deeply a couple of times and readied himself to address the pitiful remnants of what had once been a two hundred-strong company of men. There were to be no sonorous tones, no resounding rhetoric. There was only the tired voice of a man who had seen his beloved company thrashed to within an inch of extinction. He had evaluated the situation as professionally as he was able and realised that without the machine guns their already hopeless situation would become untenable.

There simply weren't enough Durhams left to win anything, nor would their sacrifice gain the Allied cause any strategic value. His duty was to the remainder of his company, which had fought vastly superior numbers of the enemy to a standstill time and again during that terrible rainy Sunday. For the majority, it was their first day of action and their last. Well, if he had his way, the survivors would continue to survive. If he had his way he would withdraw and save his brave lads for another day and a better fight. But orders were orders and reinforcements were on the way.

One more effort! Keep back the Hun until the reinforcements arrive and they can retire as heroes.

Just one more effort, boys.

His speech was cut short, however, as the roar of a Hun aeroplane drowned out everything for a moment and the metal foil that heralded violent, bloody death, fell like gentle snowflakes through the rain upon the huddled group of men in the mud below.

The awful shelling that followed the foil markers, ceased as suddenly as it had begun. Or rather it moved on to bomb shit out of the Gravenstafel Road where the remaining Durhams, along with the Canadians, Monmouths and the Middlesex suffered in turn. The survivors quickly began to burrow their way skyward out of the hastily thrown together redoubts formed from sods, sandbags and corpses. Ted was in the entrance to a dugout a few yards away from the machine gun emplacement. The dugout itself had collapsed long ago but the strongly reinforced tunnel ran back a couple of feet.

He crouched against the sandbags and rocked back and forth on his heels, and he was afraid. He was in the Valley of Death and his now shaken belief in the Lord left him fearful. He cursed himself for a coward and tearstains streaked his face to be washed away by the rain. There was no instruction given for an attendance parade but the survivors stumbled their way to the machine gun emplacement to find, miraculously, the weapon was still intact.

The pause had been too long. Usually at the ceasefire of a bombardment the Hun came running, screaming down upon the Durhams, but not this time. There was only the silence and the rain. No heads appeared over the ridge and none of the enemy occupying the ruined buildings off to the left behind them appeared to be taking any notice of the filthy rag-tag rabble that had once been the proud 'D' Company of the Eighth New Durhams.

'Sir!'

It was Lieutenant Wood, who was crouched on the remains of the fire step keeping an eye on the ridge. Captain Bradford turned to him and the eyes of the men followed. A single, flat crack rang out and Jimmy Barker fell back without a word to land at George Moody's feet, his bottom jaw shattered and blood pooling and spilling from his mouth in pulses, like a heartbeat. He blinked once or twice then lay still, staring into the rain whilst the screams of German soldiers rent the air for what seemed the thousandth time that day.

Captain Bradford opened his mouth to speak but he was cut short by the near-falsetto scream of Robin Blenkiron.

'Come on then youse bastards! Come on 'til I hit you fairly!'

Everyone turned in astonishment as Blenkiron cocked the machine gun and swung it round to face the oncoming enemy: he had retrieved a belt of ammunition from God alone knew where and loaded it into the weapon. With no further encouragement he let rip with the full belt directly into the charging mass. The lads didn't need a second hint – every rifle was firing into the wall of grey. They slowed down noticeably at the ferocity of the defence the lads were showing, particularly the Blenkiron boy manning the machine gun. His eyes were practically popping out of his head as he wept and screamed abuse at the oncoming Hun. It was as if the Germans couldn't believe their eyes. Where did this defence come from? There were only supposed to be a handful of them left.

Again, the Germans halted and the lads let out a weak cheer, but there was something different now, as though the rhythm had shifted. Something was wrong. Everyone ceased firing and looked around. The machine gun had stopped. Captain Bradford looked at Blenkiron who shrugged his shoulders. This time they really were out of ammunition. Then a sharp punch on his right thigh took the officer's attention and he looked down at the steadily increasing circle of red on his breeches.

The Germans had noticed the absence of machine gun fire too, and were regrouping ready for the charge that would finally crush all resistance in the trench. Corporal Lawrie shouted to commence firing but the volleys sounded weak and feeble without machine guns, the backbone that had supported their firepower throughout this terrible day. But the broadside had unsettled the Germans, who appeared indecisive and looked to be arguing amongst themselves. The Blenkiron lad was frantically opening every box the vicinity in the hope of finding more belts of ammo and with an exclamation suddenly held up two bottles of rum. Captain Bradford, who was busy tying his pistol lanyard around his thigh nodded.

'Well done, Blenkiron, pass it around quickly, lad.'

The light was beginning to go. Nobody took their eyes off the enemy as the bottles went from mouth to mouth. Bradford used the time to count his men. Thirty-three.

'Give 'em a volley lads, then another, then another. We've orders to hold this ground and hold it we bloody well will.'

This was slaughter and Bradford knew it. His mind raced as he fought to think of a way to save his boys. Then the decision was taken from him. Now it was Corporal Lawrie's turn.

'Right you mongers get lined up on those bastards and nobody fires until I give the order.' He didn't wait for any nods of assent as he paused for a heartbeat and then shouted, 'FIRE!'

Fire they did. They fired at will with the expertise engendered by hours of practice on the ranges at Morfa, Lumley Castle and at Gateshead. And once more the Germans, frustrated and angry, retreated.

The Durhams were by now almost completely surrounded. The enemy position to their left was now so far south that they were near enough in between the trench and the road behind Boetleer's Farm. They were at a position where they were firing on the trench from behind and to the left as well as in front and far to the right.

Behind their grisly defences the lads kept a sharp lookout until it was nearly dark. All the action sounded as if it was well behind them on the Gravenstafel Road but this was no time to take chances. Relax for one second and the buggers would be all over you. But there were no further frontal assaults, just a persistent level of sniping that was enough to keep them busy, affording no rest.

Where were the bloody reinforcements!

It was getting on to dusk now and the rain continued to pour down upon them. Some water was collected in whatever containers were available and the filthy rifles were sluiced clean of the mud that was starting to hamper their performance. It was dark enough now for the Hun to start sending up Verey lights – mostly over the farm buildings but some were purposefully over the trench. Evening wore on into night and the intermittent flares cast an eerie glow through the rain. In the darkness in between the lights, shuffling was heard in no man's land off to the left, until suddenly a machine gun opened up, practically enfilading the trench. That scared the lads. Taking cover where they could they hastily – and under withering fire – fabricated a redoubt across the trench out of sandbags and bodies. When the flares went out, the machine gun stopped until the next flare went up and there was nothing the Durhams could do but suffer this sporadic punishment, and pray.

It was after three the next morning and a thick, misty dawn was breaking over Boetleer's Farm. The rain had eased up a bit but the survivors in the forward trench were in a terrible plight. Thankfully, the German machine gun had been silent and there had been no Verey lights for some time. This did not of course mean that the Hun had been idle. Out there in the dark there was many a scuffling and a scraping to be heard, along with low, rasping voices whispering God knew what. Wherever such a sound was heard several 303 bullets were sent hurtling through the dark in that direction. But it meant no peace for the lads, who were now tired, few and increasingly desperate: but the orders were to hang on until the reinforcements came, and orders were orders. Every so often the men were instructed to number off loudly as if there were many more of them than there actually were, and they would pretend to change the guard at intervals even though the same weary men continued with the same weary duties. If the enemy got the faintest whiff that there were so few of them remaining they would be all over the trench like rats. The plan worked, however – either that, or the Germans couldn't be bothered. It was so quiet just then, that in the damp half-light, larks could be heard singing, and the melodious sound was almost magical.

Just for a moment there was no conflict. Just for a moment both sides listened, enraptured as the birds twittered their tuneful song. Then the peace was shattered by the drone of a German aeroplane low overhead and the lads' hearts sank as they waited for the silver foil to foretell their death. Not this time, though. The aeroplane went on towards the road beyond the farm where the main body of the men were positioned and a few minutes later the artillery opened up on them. 'D' had been spared.

There were several bombardments on the trench that day, mostly followed by a German push to infiltrate, but the Durhams fought like heroes. 'A' to the right and 'D' to the left took on the flower of Kaiser Wilhelm's army and fought them to a bloody halt. They were so pitifully few and becoming fewer by the hour.

Evening came again. It was shortly after 1700, and 'D' Company was still defending their scratch in the earth. It was now well behind the German lines on the west side and the pathetic handful of boys could not hold on forever. The promised reinforcements had not arrived and now that the enemy was slowly encircling the locality it was unlikely they would. There was no communication with the main body on the Gravenstafel Road so they were well and truly alone. The last bombardment had just lifted and sure enough a group of about fifty Germans came over the rise. They were reinforced by an enfilading machine gun that had mysteriously appeared during the night, off to their left, and was actually firing down the line of the trench making the damned thing practically indefensible.

Corporal Lawrie was doing a hero's job of bullying and encouraging the tired boys, exhorting them to yet another vicious salvo to try and prevent Fritz from getting into their trench, but they could not keep this up.

Chapter 31

Langley Park Colliery Village, Monday 26th April 1915

Bertha was pulling some tatie scones from the oven and trying to set the tray down on the hearth without upsetting them, which was an awkward job to say the least. It would have been easier if she had moved the scuttle first but she hadn't thought of that and was trying to shuffle it along with her foot to clear a space. Today had not gone well. Despite banking up the fire properly last night it had gone out and instead of just breaking it open this morning and putting the kettle on, the whole lot had to be dragged out onto the hearth and started from scratch. The handle was broken on the bleezer and she had burnt her hand taking it down from the fire. She was not in a good mood.

All this had put her miles behind and she didn't particularly want that. Harry Fairbairn was due any minute and either she would have been down the street doing her shopping or upstairs pretending to be out. Chances were that there would be no post for her anyway, although she positively ached to get a letter from Ted. It was just that she could no longer stand the attention she was receiving from this man.

She set her lips in a thin line and continued to cut the next set of scones from the pastry on the table when she heard the gate sneck go and looked up to see Harry coming up the yard. He didn't even walk properly, just somehow shuffled like a ferret or something. There was no escape. She was stuck at the table in full view with flour practically up to her elbows and he grinned at her as he sloped towards the back door. *Bugger!* She picked up a tea towel and wiped what she could from her hands.

This must be a letter from Ted. At last, her Ted had sent a letter. That, at least, would mean he was still safe. Only why did this man have to be the envoy? Why couldn't Langley Park have a decent postman? The knock came as she was walking towards the door and she braced herself for a second before she opened it. If her man had written to her she wanted the letter with all her heart but she could no longer bring herself to be in close proximity to this creature. He wouldn't just push it through the letterbox like he was supposed to. Oh, No! That way he couldn't cajole her into coming to the door and chatting. Once she had pointed at the letterbox through the window but he just grinned his weasel grin and waved.

She opened the door smartly and stood with her arms folded tightly across her chest. The pause in the proceedings was agonising until Fairbairn began.

'Them scones smell nice, they're always best fresh from the oven aren't they... specially with a nice cup of tea, like.'

All she could see was his runny nose and all she could smell was his leather postbag. She had no idea what the smell reminded her of but, regardless, it was repellent.

Where was the letter from her Ted? She finally steeled herself to speak. 'Can I have my letter, please, Mister Fairbairn?'

He looked momentarily surprised.

'Letter? There's no post for you this morning, pet, sorry, like. I was just walking up the street when I smelled your scones and wondered if you mebbes might have a spare one for a hard-working postman.'

Bertha's eyes nearly popped out of her head. The absolute bloody cheek of the man!

Fancy using a cruel ruse like that to get into a woman's house. She stuttered, her mouth dry.

'You... you shouldn't do that, Mr Fairbairn. Especially when my man's away, like.' Her voice faded away to nothing and she felt her cheeks going red.

'Aw, pet, you just need a bit company, man. Cup of tea won't hurt, will it?'

Her eyes were closed and she was praying to Almighty God to deliver her from this beast. She couldn't do it herself; she didn't know how.

Then the gate slammed with a crash.

Bertha jumped out of her skin as she and Fairbairn turned together to see the squat form of Freddy Wardle standing at the foot of the yard. This, however, was Freddy Wardle as Bertha had never seen him before. He was in his Sunday Best suit and his black boots. Draped across his chest was a row of medals that would have done a general proud, and in his hand he carried a wicked looking cudgel of shiny, dark brown wood.

He politely touched his cap to Bertha before addressing the postman.

'Sling your hook, Fairbairn, before I break both your bloody arms. Begging your pardon, like, Mrs Smith.'

Fairbairn turned his back on Bertha to stare hard at the diminutive but formidable figure of Freddy. He defiantly leaned his head to one side as he replied, 'You and whose army then... Mr Wardle?

But there was something strong in old Freddy this day, something indefinable. He stood stock still and calmly returned the insolent stare. It was this stillness, this confidence that eventually unnerved Fairbairn.

Freddy said nothing more, merely opened the gate and stepped aside, waving the cudgel ever so slightly. Fairbairn drew himself up to his full height and sauntered as casually as he could out of the yard, but he didn't look back at Bertha, nor did he look old Freddy in the eye. Then he was gone and Freddy shambled up to the back door and was surprised to see Bertha standing with the shovel in her hand, presumably ready to lamp Fairbairn with it if there was any kind of a physical confrontation.

Freddy's mouth was tight shut and his cheeks puffed out as he started to gag. Bertha practically pulled him into the scullery where he sank to his knees as she shut the door. He began a wracking spasm of coughing and couldn't get up off his hands and knees for quite a few minutes. Bertha gave him a hanky and had to turn away as he hawked copious amounts of black phlegm into it. Eventually, the attack subsided and he got up and tottered weakly to the proffered rocking chair by the fire. A mug of tea was placed gently in his grasp and he nodded his thanks. He frowned as he looked at the sodden handkerchief.

'I've got a hanky just the same as this one, fancy that.' He looked up at Bertha and gave a weak smile. 'I don't think our Mr Fairbairn will be bothering you again, pet, eh?'

Bertha looked down at Freddy. He had reverted to the weak old man with miners' lung and beat-hand, but the hard sparkle remained in his eyes.

'Mr Wardle, would you really have hit him?'

There was no pause before the reply. 'Why aye, pet. I'd have laid the bugger flat.'

He managed three tatie scones before he left.

Chapter 32

Boetleer's Farm, 1730 hours, Monday 26th April 1915

Captain Bradford took one look at his sorry little group and made his mind up. They had done all that had been asked of them. Now he must lead them to safety. He gazed through the rain at his men... no... boys. There was hardly one of them over twenty. He smiled at the wispy moustaches and the spots and the bum fluff on chins. The scared yet eager faces marbled with mud and tears that looked to him so unquestionably for guidance. Yes, they were just boys, but boys who had done a man's job of keeping a ferocious enemy at bay.

Well, no more.

They waited for the next assault which, thank the Lord, was not preceded by an artillery bombardment. This time the lads held their fire. They were ordered to crouch below the line of sight of the Germans so that no rifles were showing. It would do no good at all to let them see how few the Durhams were. Still closer they came until this time they were about forty yards from the lip.

Captain Bradford himself gave the order to fire. Thirty-odd widely spaced rifles swung up from nowhere, landed with wet thuds across bodies or sandbags and lined up on the oncoming troops.

The hail of bullets surprised the group of Germans and cost them dear in men. With a howl of dismay some turned to run whilst others, under the orders of an NCO who was at least as redoubtable as Corporal Lawrie tried to rally them into some sort of order: but the damage was done. The group was in disarray and was being cut to pieces by the curtain of lead being hurled at them through the rain. This advantage was short lived however as, with a guttural roar, at least fifty more of the enemy leaped over the crest and howled their way down towards their troubled comrades.

The ceasefire was bellowed out by Corporal Lawrie and without any further word the lads were off. Lieutenant Wood led the way with Captain Bradford bringing up the rear. He was limping from his wound but could still move fast enough to chivvy along the last of the men.

The Germans were in the trench, but a good way behind. A couple of pistol shots, courtesy of Captain Bradford, made sure they kept their distance. Ted was in the middle of the group but as he stumbled over the corpses his back felt dreadfully exposed. As they neared the communication trench his eyes widened in horror. He hadn't been here since he had occupied the trench and he could not believe it was the same channel.

Instead of wading through waist-deep water, there were so many dead that they filled it practically to the brim, forcing the retreating Durhams to expose their heads to the enemy. Suddenly it wasn't the pursuing Hun who was the danger, it was the buggers in the opposite trench that were picking them off now. Down went one hapless soul after another as all attempts to crouch as low as possible failed to hide them.

Ted was on the edge of the communication trench looking ahead to Lieutenant Wood, who had stopped dead for a second while he appeared to weigh something up. Then, bullets whipping around him, he skipped nimbly across the bodies as if they were stepping-stones. He was a true athlete as well, hopping and jinking with all the grace of a deer until a German bullet took him in the shoulder and spun him around like a top to fall onto the sodden carpet of dead. The men held their breath and watched. The young officer lay still for a second then grunted. He heaved himself painfully to his feet and, keeping low this time, continued to pick his way across the bodies. He was white as a sheet and his left arm dangled uselessly but he was up and moving.

Now it was Ted's turn, but the lads were starting to bunch which held everybody up and made them a much better target for the enemy to pick off. To his left he could plainly see the German trench and the helmets sticking up as the enemy aimed their rifles at the exposed soldiers trying to make their escape. He turned his attention back to his precarious footing, trying to ignore the zing of bullets punching the air around him. It was as if the whole world had donned uniform and been shoehorned into this place to die. He moved slowly, keeping low. The soldier in front of him sighed and fell flat on his face as a sniper's bullet passed clean through his head.

Ted had no choice but to gingerly stand on his back to step forward and was shocked to the core as the fallen man let out a piteous cry of distress as he did so.

He's not dead! Dear God, how can you have your head blown apart and not be dead? Ted shuddered in horror, stopping in his tracks.

'Get a fucking move on will you, man!'

He could feel the men behind him pressing so he closed his eyes as he put his foot between the fallen man's shoulder blades. There was nothing else he could do. His lips silently formed the word 'sorry' as the ensuing whimper reduced to a bubbling murmur when the man's face sank into the pink jelly that was his own brains. A rough hand grabbed Ted's collar and heaved him forward. Every footstep was on what had once been a living man.

A scream up ahead was someone slipping on a corpse and plunging down into the water beneath. It was Jacky Tait and only his head and arms were visible. If he hadn't had his arms outstretched for balance he would have disappeared for ever into the stinking pit of waterlogged bodies. Behind Ted, Sam Hurry let out a squeal like a girl and collapsed lifeless as another German bullet found its mark. They were being cut to bloody ribbons.

Then came the thunder.

* * * * *

The deafening noise was instantly recognisable as Allied fire by the deep boom of the guns and it came from up ahead. It was Captain Harvey and 'A' Company in the other trench giving the lads covering fire. Volley after volley crashed through the air towards the German lines and the ferocity of the attack caused the enemy to take cover for their lives. Ted was off the communication trench and treading across the comparative safety of bodies strewn thick upon fairly solid ground. He thanked the Good Lord and asked his forgiveness for ever doubting him. An instant later he thanked Him again when he received a slap on the shoulder from Jacky Tait, ashen white but smiling, saved from drowning in a sea of carcasses.

He also recognised the voice of Corporal Punshon of 'A' bellowing at them to keep moving along so as to let the remnants of 'D' Company get across to safety. Last across was Captain Bradford. He had lost his pistol and he was holding his right hand up to his chest with his left, blood was oozing between his fingers. He instructed Corporal Lawrie to ensure the defence of the communication trench in case the pursuing Germans should try to cross.

By the look of things 'A' Company had fared little better than 'D'. There were a few moments' conversation between the two officers and it appeared to be agreed that both companies would withdraw together and try to make it back to Boetleer's Farm or the lines along the Gravenstafel Road.

There were Germans to the front and away to the right in trenches and also to the left occupying the area vacated by the lads. There were Germans coming in by the trainload and holing up in the dead ground over the rise. In short, there were Germans everywhere and GHQ were more than likely unaware of just how many there were.

Abandon this locality to the enemy, that was the priority – it was no bloody use anyway, so far out in front of the proper line – and get word back about the massing of the enemy troops. They stood a better chance if they all went together, because that way somebody should get through and raise the alarm. The men of both companies were assembled and instructed to try to get back and pass on the information. It was up to them now.

There was a hasty amalgamation into one unit. It didn't take long as there were only about twenty of 'A' Company remaining and a few less in Ted's lot. They would leave the trench by the way they had entered only yesterday morning. They had been four hundred then, and they had reached the safety of the trench without a shot being fired. Now they weren't even forty and it was absolutely pelting with bullets.

This was the plan. Half the men under Captain Harvey would man the extreme right of the trench and throw heavy fire at the enemy to defend the evacuees by drawing the German guns. When the evacuees had left the trench and crossed the little stream they would form up and begin firing. That would draw the enemy fire towards them, giving 'A' Company a chance to join up. Hopefully, they could retreat in good order and make it back to the Boetleer's Farm or the road. Ted looked around as the lads prepared to leave the trench. Was it really only yesterday they had arrived with the petrol cans full of water which were so gratefully received by the beleaguered Winnipegs?

Corporal Lawrie barked out the order after a nod from Captain Bradford and they were off, scrambling out of the trench and over the dead whilst 'A' let off the biggest volley they could muster. The lads' hearts sank as they heard the familiar staccato brattle of machine gun fire but it took only a second to recognise it as their own. 'A' must still have one working! Now it was run like Hell through the rain until they made it as far as the little stream, and there turn and give the Germans the surprise of their lives by firing upon them for all they were worth.

This was the worst bit, running with your back to the enemy. The springy marsh grass under their feet seemed to give them a lift with every step. Only the odd bullet was whipping around them, good! The diversion was working... up to now.

They were across the stream in a single bound where the instruction was to turn and fire at will upon the enemy in order to allow the escape of 'A' Company. Ted, George Moody and the Blenkiron lad ended up on the extreme right as they dashed to the stream and now plunged down prone onto the soaking grass. Ted looked across the meagre line to see John Merrigan and Jacky on the other end in the cover of a few trees where most of the Canadian bodies seemed to be. There were only a few around Ted and some of them were little more than the disinterred skeletons of Frenchies, but there were a few freshly dead Winnipegs and Ted got behind one, resting his barrel in the small of the man's back as if it were a sandbag.

He awaited the order to fire and wished he had made it to the group of trees along with his mates. He could see John Merrigan and Jacky Tait near Captain Bradford, who was now sporting a rifle. They were all standing up and using the trees for cover in order to gain a bit of extra elevation. John looked across and caught Ted's eye. Then he flashed a grin and winked as if they had found each other across the bar at the Blue Star. This unfamiliar behaviour, in the rain and under fire, was so surprising that Ted automatically grinned back before turning his attention to the gunfire at the trench edge. Then the brattle of the machine gun abruptly stopped and the staccato thunder of the rifle volley ceased a couple of seconds later.

This is it.

All eyes turned to Captain Bradford on the edge of the little copse. He raised his rifle into the air and shouted, 'For the Eighth New Durhams, lads... FIRE!'

Bloody Hell, he was at least as good as Sergeant Malone! The lads began firing for all they were worth though they could hardly see the Germans, whose trench was up on a slight gradient, but they only had to pin them down to give 'A' the chance to evacuate. But there was no sign of them. What the Hell was going on? There was still very little in the way of fire coming towards Ted so they must still be firing at the lads in the trench. Ted and Jacky shot a glance at each other. It didn't take any conversation to realise their covering fire was useless, the Hun weren't being hit so they weren't taking any notice of the lads and continued to fire upon the trapped 'A' Company in the trench, probably reckoning they could wipe them out first then get after 'D'.

What the Hell use was that? The lads in the little copse were faring better than those in the open because they were standing up. There was some sign that the Germans were firing more into the trees but it was around seven o' clock and the light was beginning to fade, making the lads a harder target. Robin Blenkiron was first. Without a word he stood up, with absolutely no cover and took the stance, firing round after round into the enemy. George looked at Ted, his mouth a thin line of determination. Without taking their eyes off each other, they stood up too. 'A' Company were about to die trying to save 'D'. Well, not if the lads could help it. It didn't make that much difference but what difference it did make obviously mattered to the Germans, whose fire was suddenly drawn to the English lunatics who were standing up, bold as brass and without a scrap of cover, firing into their defences.

Crash the bolt back.

The Blenkiron lad went down first. His rifle hit the ground as he stretched his arms out wide and, almost in slow motion, fell silently to his knees and collapsed forward into an untidy heap to lie still for ever.

Crash the bolt forward.

Bullets were punching the air thick and fast now, and the lads in the trees had come out into the open as well. That made the Germans concentrate their fire on them all the more. They were so few and still they fell.

'A' were out, running like Hell towards the lads and turning now and again to let off a shot where they could. The Germans were out, too, sensing victory. They left their trench to present a target which, at last, the lads could properly see. 'A' were running like rabbits, avoiding bodies and leaping across the stream to bear down on the copse at lightning speed. A machine gun began firing and a couple of the 'A' boys went down.

Crash the bolt back.

With bullets singing all around them everybody was firing from the standing position, and now that they were all together a single order of command formed them into two ranks to began an orderly withdrawal. Suddenly there was a tremendous explosion from behind them.

Momentarily startled they looked around – and gave a weak cheer. The German advance had been stopped in its tracks by a mighty volley from a new source; 'B' Company had arrived and was less than three hundred yards behind them.

Everyone stared at the cocky figure of Major Ritson, ignoring rain and bullets alike, standing with his fists on his hips and dressing his men into good order. Although the recently occupied forward position was beyond sight of the farm or the Allied trenches, presumably someone had seen the lads after they had withdrawn as far as the copse and rightly surmised they would need help if they were not all to perish. Well, the reinforcement party was doing a grand job and for the umpteenth time that day the German advance came to a puzzled halt and wondered where the ferocity, never mind the numbers of the Allies came from.

Then the German machine gun sprang into action, spitting fire and death right through the middle of the Allies.

'Keep your heads down and run boys. We'll deal with the Hun.'

Major Ritson was as good as his word and the lads on the right, keeping low to avoid the savage Allied broadsides, beetled down to join them. Volley after volley they fired and then the machine gun stopped. The right flank of the lads, including Captain Bradford, was now part of the reinforcing unit.

The Captain was in line, firing his rifle to Major Ritson's orders like he was an enlisted man.

Slowly and deliberately they withdrew to the safety of the line, but the lads on the left had another path to tread. Where the machine gun had enfiladed the centre of the retreating men it had effectively split the unit into two.

Ted was isolated from the main group first by the machine gun fire and now by an advancing wedge of German infantry that was intent on their demise. He and George Moody were stuck out in the open without a cat in Hell's chance of making it back to the reinforcing party. They stood shoulder to shoulder in the dusk and fired into the Germans, whose attention was still being held by the tremendous firepower of Major Ritson's men. Ted wanted to say something with his last breath but he didn't know what.

'George?'

'Bollocks!'

They fired another couple of rounds together, keeping the Germans firmly focussed and the reinforcement party in the corner of their eyes. Suddenly the party changed. There was a flutter, a disturbance. Three men broke free and ran towards the pair of isolated Durhams. It was Corporal Lawrie, Jacky Tait and John Merrigan. Corporal Lawrie was crossing the undulating ground like a hare, head low and expertly avoiding the dead that were so thick on the ground. It didn't stop him taking a storm of bullets from the machine gun that had suddenly found new life. He was nearly cut in half across the middle when, spouting blood, he changed direction to head straight into the advancing German troops. He managed to let off a shot that sang high into the air as he began to stagger.

He was done for and must have known it because to the surprise of everyone – friend and foe alike – he drew himself up to a shuddering attention and stared directly at the enemy. He managed to hold himself up for two or three seconds before collapsing to join the throng of lifeless bodies that littered the ground so thickly.

Whilst the Germans were staring at the fallen body of the luckless Lawrie, Jacky and John ran on until they had reached Ted and George and continued past them, hell-for-leather.

'Howay, man!'

They followed suit at once through another thin copse and towards a low stone wall that marked the boundary of the yard at Boetleer's Farm. They vaulted the wall and used it as cover to fire at the enemy.

Regrettably, the machine gun had caught up with them as well. Ted and George were through the copse and no more than a few feet from the wall when Ted misjudged his footing and tripped over the remains of a corpse. He sprawled to the ground, his rifle doing slow-motion cartwheels in front of him as a burst from the machine gun studded the wall and ripped George Moody to bloody shreds. With a terrible cry he slammed to the ground, vomiting blood by the gallon. He tried to say something but it came out an obscene gargle. He was looking directly at Ted, his eyes popping and his mouth shedding his life's blood by the second.

Ted didn't want to look but it would have been unforgivable not to help his friend in his last seconds of life.

Then it dawned on him George was waiting for an answer. He had asked Ted something with his last terrible breath and he was waiting for an answer. The machine gun had moved on now but the rifles hadn't, and Jacky was urging Ted to get over the wall bloody sharpish. Every fibre of his being told Ted to do just that but he remained where he was and took George's outstretched hand in his own. He looked into those terrible bulging eyes and tried not to see the blood that was drowning his friend.

He smiled and nodded and prayed to the Lord God that he was doing the right thing. George's grip shuddered and relaxed and as his eyes went out he nodded, ever so faintly, and was still.

'Will you get over this fucking wall?'

'Now, you daft bugger, man. NOW!'

Abruptly, he was up and sprinting for his life. Bullets whistled past him and he wasn't sure if one hadn't plucked at his sleeve as he vaulted the wall to land in a heap behind a furiously firing Jacky and John... but without his rifle.

'On your feet, Teddy boy. Let's go.'

He was grabbed by both arms and half dragged, half carried, until the little group were behind what remained of the farmhouse. There was a wall about half a man's height running at right angles from the main building and the three squeezed into the corner near a pile of sandbags. The Germans were up to the wall now but a couple of rounds dampened their enthusiasm for trying to cross it.

Jacky spoke first. 'Round that corner's the dressing station. I saw it on the way in. If we can make it back to there we can use the buildings for cover to get back to the line, it's only across the road, man.'

Without a word John carefully stuck his head around the corner. There was the carcass of an outhouse about fifty feet away across a dirty yard from which they could follow a low stone wall and a couple of hedges practically all the way to the dressing station. There were no German troops in sight, but the unsettling thing was there were no English ones either. The Germans behind them seemed to have called off the chase for now, concentrating on Major Ritson's lot. There was a few seconds lull in the gunfire during which the moans of the wounded could clearly be heard in the dressing station.

They took this respite as a sign to get moving and quickly crossed the yard to the cover of the wall. Apart from terrorising the chickens they made it without incident, although all three were uneasy about the lack of soldiers – friend or foe – in the vicinity. Ted put his hand to his breast pocket and felt the hard lump of the tissue-wrapped locket which he was going to send to Bertha at the first opportunity. There was also the soaking mush that had been the collection of letters containing so much ill news from home.

No time!

Crouching, half crawling, the lads made their uneasy way across Boetleer's Farm towards the dressing station. They could see the gable end with a shored up opening that might once have been a door. They all froze at the sound of German voices somewhere behind them; the buggers were still there. Ted wanted his rifle, he felt naked and helpless without it but with any luck once they were in the dressing station he would be able to pinch a surplus one. They had reached the point where the wall formed part of the structure of the ruinous carcass of a lean-to netty. A long German rifle was leaning against it. Just as Ted was creeping past the door, it opened with a loud creak and he was suddenly face to face with a hard looking German sergeant who was fiddling with his trousers and had obviously just been for a piss. They stared at each other, mouths open, for a long second, the German soldier blinking against the rain, when a rifle butt flashed past Ted's ear and hit the man firmly between the eyes. He went down without a word and a rough shove in Ted's back got him moving again.

All the gunfire was relatively distant, up by the road somewhere, but the German voices behind them weren't, and what about this bugger here? He was the size of a bloody mountain! A quick glance around the wooden netty showed no sign of friend or foe. Obviously the farm had been abandoned – along with the dressing station – because of the overwhelming numbers of the enemy streaming in from every direction. This was the lot that had been brought in by train and there were hundreds of the buggers. The lads could see them coming down over the rise – the one on which they had been so close to death when they were in the forward trench with the Canadians.

'Half of bloody Germany must be coming over that hill.'

'Aye, and the other half's right behind us. Shall we get a move on, like?'

The consensus was that if they could get to the dressing station they could pass through it and it was only a short distance to the Allied trenches over the road. If they stayed where they were, the wall would protect them from the Hun who were chasing them but not from the buggers on this side who were coming up fast.

John spat in disgust. 'Stuffed!' and looked round in defeated hatred.

Ted disagreed. There was nobody in the little clearing between them and the gable end of the station so the time to make a dash for it was now. He swept up the rifle that belonged to the felled German sergeant. It was heavy and awkward in his hands, but a damn sight more comfortable than not having one at all.

'I'll go first and cover you if need be. We cannot stay here, man.'

They stared at each other for a couple of seconds.

Ted took a deep breath. The lads could hear gunfire both behind them and coming from the direction of the road now. This was it: move or die.

Ted loped across the muddy clearing; it was more craters than anything else. When he reached the shelter of the gable he closed his eyes for a second.

Up close, the shoring that protected the doorway looked a lot tougher than it had from back across the yard. A couple of timbers, supported at the bottom by a few sodden sandbags, held the planking in place. He heaved on the nearest one. It wouldn't bloody budge. Suddenly Jacky was beside him and between them they thumped and hammered and swore at the stubborn timberwork until with a creak it began to give.

Now they were tearing at the planks and the opening was getting bigger, but not before a guttural shout was followed by a couple of shots that took chunks out of the timber and showered Ted and Jacky with splinters. John began to fire from the wall as a diversion and the lads redoubled their efforts, scrabbling at the wet wood with bloody fingers and finally prising it away to reveal a damp interior that reeked of pain and death. Another bullet missed Jacky's shoulder by an inch, when suddenly a blood-curdling scream was heard from across the yard.

'Come on then, you buggers. Let's see what you're made of.'

Three shots went off in quick succession followed by a click and a curse. Then John was running directly at the stunned enemy, rifle in one hand and bayonet in the other, screaming at them for all he was worth. There were four of them with a larger group not far behind. He was running straight towards them out of the sodden darkness and hurled his rifle with such force that it struck the lead German across the shins and brought him down with a shriek of agony.

John was like a bloody maniac. He was on the group a second later and cut another down with a savage swipe of his bayonet. He was too close to shoot at, and the remaining pair had no stomach for hand-to-hand combat with this mad Englishman, so they turned to flee.

Ted and Jacky were in. They stood either side of the opening and began covering fire while screaming to John to come back. Ted was firing one round to Jacky's three, as he struggled with the unfamiliar weapon. John was now pelting hell-for-leather towards them through the rain while the mass of pursuing Germans fired a hail of bullets towards him. He was close. He was so bloody close, all mad eyes and swearing, when his throat opened up in a welter of red liquid and his legs began to give way. Still he came on, only now in slow motion as another bullet took his left knee out in a shower of bone and shiny gristle. He went down like a ton of coal and tumbled over and over through the dark to lie motionless in a filthy puddle of rain and mud and cow shit.

He did it for you.

Ted could see the silhouettes of the Germans as if they were in a photograph. Then he was spun round by Jacky who was shouting at him. What was he saying? 'Come on?'

The slap across his face brought him back and then they were running through the dressing station and past the wounded, some on beds and some lying on the wet floor, hurdling them where necessary to get to the other end of the building before the enemy reached the opening and fired in. The place was badly lit with a couple of oil lamps and a few candles. Shadows pounced and darted around them as they ran.

Jacky was well ahead, almost at the far end door when abruptly, inexplicably, four or five of the enemy appeared from nowhere in front of Ted. They were pointing their heavy rifles at him and all shouting at once. The buggers were pouring in through another doorway in the centre of the building as if they would never stop. One or two lifted their weapons and pointed them at the disappearing Jacky when Ted, taking a leaf from John Merrigan's book, screamed and threw his foreign rifle at them. They all looked round in complete surprise. He was fumbling in his breast pocket now, fishing out Bertha's silver locket, wrapped in the soggy mush that had once been the finest tissue wrapping paper.

'Leave him alone you bastards! Just you bloody well leave him alone! Jacky, catch, man.'

Ted slammed the locket in a perfect handball pitch over the heads of the Germans and watched it revolve, the silver chain unravelling as it alternately disappeared and reappeared in the motley light of the lamps. It was deftly caught by his friend the instant before he disappeared through the doorway and out into the darkness. A couple of the soldiers fired and made as if to follow but Ted was running towards them. He rapidly made up the distance until he was within the group. His fist downed one opponent and his elbow injured another who was trying to grab him from behind. He managed to get his hand up just in time to prevent a rifle butt from breaking his skull.

He was on his knees. Then he was flat on the floor, face down with half a dozen bayonets threatening to gut him from behind if he made another move. A succession of shots came in from the opening Jacky had disappeared through, and two or three Germans returned fire at once. With a complete disregard for the wounded, some of whom were kicked or shoved out of the way, they clattered through the building towards the door in order to better defend it. One of the Germans felt a pull on his tunic from a delirious patient and without even looking around hit him hard with his rifle butt. Shots were exchanged, several volleys being fired concurrently, proving there was more than just Jacky out there. Then there was a cry of pain as an Allied bullet hit one of the wounded.

A British medical officer seemed to materialise out of thin air. It was Lieutenant Stenhouse. He must've stayed on after the withdrawal from the farm. Completely ignoring the Germans he ran to the bed of the man who had just been wounded. His sudden appearance in the ghostly candlelight startled everyone and one of the troops at the door approached him, rifle at the ready. The M.O. was ripping a strip from some dirty sheet. When the shouting German waved his rifle at him he cuffed it away in annoyance and attempted to carry on but was shot in the midriff. His expression was one of complete surprise as he staggered back a few steps before going down.

'Sir!' Another British soldier, this time a lance corporal, appeared from behind a medical cabinet holding his hands high in the air. 'Don't shoot! Red Cross! See! I have to treat the wounded, see!' He pointed to the Red Cross on his arm as a shot rang out felling him with a wound to the head.

Ted saw the entire incident with one cheek pressed firmly to the floor and a bayonet at his neck. He dare not move in case he was next. He was in no doubt they would kill him without the slightest hesitation. He had no idea why they hadn't already.

More Germans were piling into the building and by now the only shots being fired sounded to be coming from up on the Gravenstafel Road. The bayonets were removed and Ted was roughly hauled to his feet and shoved up against the wall. Then the bayonets were back. A stout, lantern-jawed NCO looked closely at Ted. He said something to him but it made no sense so Ted shook his head and tried to shrug his shoulders. He received a savage punch in the belly in return. Muscular arms grabbed him to prevent his falling to the floor. He was jerked upright and the pain was awful.

The NCO said something else, which Ted thought best to ignore. The group opened to allow a giant sergeant with a massive cut and bruising to his forehead to come to the fore; it was the soldier John had felled at the ruined netty. Ted felt his neck going red and hot. Tears came but he set his lips and looked right back into the man's eyes. He was damned if he would let them see him cry.

He was a Durham.

I should be very glad if you would allow the Brigadier to inform the units and especially the Eighth Durham Light Infantry, how much I appreciated the good work they did and the gallantry displayed by all ranks.

Major General Sir W.F.L. Lindsay, KCB, DSO.
    Officer Commanding, Northumbrian Division.

The greatest possible credit is due to the Eighth Durham Light Infantry and the small detachments who, in spite of having their flanks turned and being enfiladed, remained in the Northern line, beating off all attacks and inflicting heavy loss on the enemy and thereby securing the flank for the Eighty-fifth Infantry Brigade.

General E.S.Bulfin, Officer Commanding, Twenty-eighth Division.

The attitude and bearing of the Durhams would have been splendid even if they had been seasoned troops, but considering that most of them were boys under fire for the very first time, it was a shame that they should have been expected to relieve part of this battalion.

Captain A. Northwood. Eighth Battalion, Second Canadian Infantry.

Chapter 33

Langley Park Colliery Village, Tuesday 11th May 1915

Bertha opened the official looking buff envelope.

With reference to Private Soldier Smith, Edward, 2505 of D Company, Eighth Durham Light Infantry. We deeply regret to inform you that the above Private Smith is missing, presumed captured on or about 2000 hours on Monday, April 26th 1915. Our informant tells us that he witnessed Private Smith's capture, that he belonged to the same section and that they were close together at the time. Private Smith appeared to be unhurt. We are not ourselves inclined to accept this evidence as final, but we thought it right to pass it on to you.
Please accept our deepest sympathy for your loss and our hopes that he might be returned to you in the fullness of time.
Lieutenant Colonel J. Turnbull, First Line Eighth Bn, The Durham Light Infantry.

It wasn't signed by him, instead the signature read 'Stevens, Adj' and it probably wasn't even written by him either. Never mind. She knew. That was that, then.

She already knew anyway. A couple of days ago she had stood defiantly looking out of her window with a level gaze at Harry Fairbairn as he sloped up the yard, not returning her stare, to shove an envelope through the letterbox and leave as quickly as he came. He always left her gate open, though. Petty-minded bugger.

It wasn't from Ted but from Jacky Tait. Half of it was crossed out in indelible ink by some intermediary who didn't want the world to know that the war wasn't going as well as expected, but there was enough information to let her know that her man was in the hands of the German monster for the duration of the conflict, however long that might be. God knew what they would do to him: her husband, her Ted.

The letter also contained a silver locket with a broken chain and in the locket was a photograph of her husband with a quite dashing pencil moustache. Bearing in mind she only had the wedding photo and one of him on crutches at the clinic door after he had broken his leg, this image of her debonair young man was, in his absence, a true Godsend. She put the locket to her forehead. Then she put it to her lips.

The tightness in her stomach was increasing and she held the locket there while she prayed for the safe return of her man, and for the new life within her. She promised the Lord God that she would serve him all her days if he would only deliver her Ted back to her. She never locked the back door again, just in case, like.

Postscript

The private soldier has never been made truly aware of the great, sweeping manoeuvres that constituted warfare. It has always been so.

For the private soldier, war consists of the smells and noises of the immediate surrounding area and instant obedience to the last order barked. Ted and his fellows were entirely unaware of the parts gallantly played around them by the Canadians, New Zealanders, the Suffolks, the Monmouths, the Middlesex, Northumberland Fusiliers and the host of Allied soldiers skimmed from all the dominions of the Great British Empire, whose gallantry, individually and collectively, led to the eventual defeat of the German forces in 1918.

Ted was never aware that he took part in the Second Battle for Ypres, or precisely what part the Durhams played in the action. Such was the confusion caused by lack of communication due to the unexpectedly heavy assault by the German forces that during the few hours that the Durhams were in the thick of the fighting; chaos was beginning to set in. The conflict was so intense and overwhelming that few messengers got through in either direction. Information did not get back to staff and orders did not make their way to the front.

In 1915, the command structure of the Allied forces was particularly rigid, whereas war itself was, and always will be, a fluid situation. Some orders, by the time they made it through to their recipients, were out of date, as the situation had moved on. This vagueness caused further confusion to the point where the officers on the ground were left with little choice but to interpret instructions as they saw fit.

Company commanders were beginning to act autonomously and it was down to them to carefully appraise any order they received and thence determine the best course of action.

The withdrawal of the Durhams from the forward trench had been valiant and performed in good order, as is witnessed in the war diaries of the day. Captain Bradford became separated from 'B' Company during the action but he made it back to the Allied line where he was picked up by a battalion of Northumberland Fusiliers. He had about ten men with him and fewer than twenty more returned to be counted. This was out of a total of the two hundred officers and men of 'D' Company. Jacky Tait was amongst those who made it back immediately. Ted was not.

* * * * *

The Germans did not break the Allied Northern Line, but Ted spent the next three years in prison camps in Germany, Holland and Lithuania where he was brutalised, tortured and used as slave labour.

He was repatriated in the December of 1918 when he went home to his wife and new daughter, Eileen Audrey – and back to his job as a hewer down the pit at Langley Park.

Due to ill health Ted retired early from mining in 1959 and died in November 1972 aged 78. Bertha was true to her word and was a deeply devout woman all of her life. They both served as officials in the British Legion for many years.

There were two further children born to the couple, Roland and Stanley, both of whom became miners at Langley Park Colliery. Bertha died after a long illness on Christmas Day, 1971 at the age of 79.